07-10-2010

THE TEMPEST'S ROAR

Also by R.A.R. Clouston from AuthorHouse

Where Freedom Reigns: A Great Thunder From The Mountain

Where Freedom Reigns: The Wrath Of God

THE TEMPEST'S ROAR

R.A.R. Clouston

authorHOUSE®

AuthorHouse™
1663 Liberty Drive, Suite 200
Bloomington, IN 47403
www.authorhouse.com
Phone: 1-800-839-8640

First published by AuthorHouse 5/21/2009

ISBN: 978-1-4389-6560-4 (sc)

Library of Congress Control Number: 2009902379

Printed in the United States of America
Bloomington, Indiana

This book is printed on acid-free paper.

Map © 2009 Matthew R. R. Clouston

To Zoe

CONTENTS

The Ten Commandments of the Ancients

1. Thou shalt have no other gods before me.

2. Thou shalt not take my name in vain.

3. Remember Godlight and keep it Holy.

4. Honor the Beings who gave thee life.

5. Thou shalt not kill another Being.

6. Thou shalt not take another Being's mate.

7. Thou shalt not steal another Being's food.

8. Thou shalt not bear false witness against another Being.

9. Thou shalt not kill a Human.

10. Thou shalt not speak with Humans.

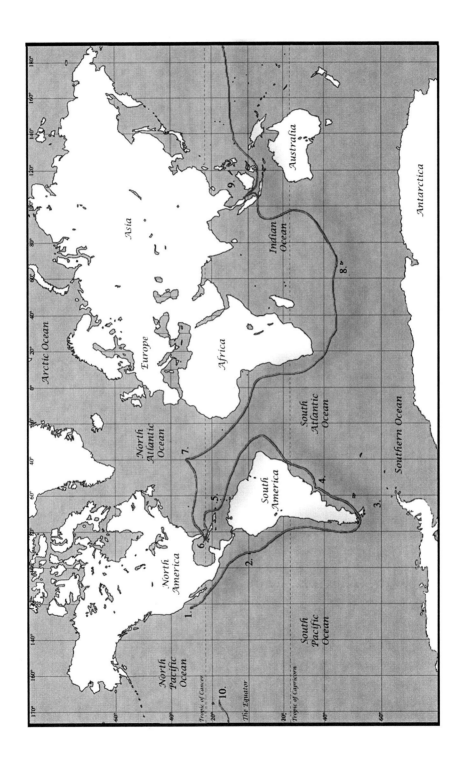

FORWARD

I shall begin my tale in the middle where it might have ended were it not for the grace of the one you call God, and I ask for his indulgence in its telling. For thousands of years my story has lived on in legend, as foretold by the Ancients and passed down through countless generations of the faithful. It was a promise unfulfilled until one night when a birth changed everything. No, it is not the story you think it is, but it is one that must be told lest you and your kind live on in ignorance of the world that lies beneath the Seven Seas and the whales and dolphins who rule over its dominions. This is the true tale of life, death, and renewal that takes place out beyond the thin blue line that divides your world from theirs: it is a world unlike anything that you have ever known and you ignore it at your peril.

The hero of my story is a white dolphin; a gentle wayfarer of the open waves driven by destiny through the Seven Seas. Hastened on by a purpose greater than his own, he rode rhythmic tides and relentless currents; slipping past jagged rocks and smooth sand beaches; across thrusting seamounts and bottomless chasms; free on the wind swell or locked in man's watery prisons. To the hopeful of whalekind he was the Chosen One, a warrior prince, a light shining in the darkness, but to the hopeless, he was a pretender and craven idol. To the humans who knew him, he was the link between their two worlds, but to himself he was just a child of God, no better or worse than any sentient being, striving to find his place in the universe, lost and alone on life's long journey to eternity. His odyssey was twenty years in the making, filled with equal measures of danger and delight, fear and fortitude, hope and desperation. Through it all, he fought against great odds and lived in constant jeopardy with few friends and countless foes; guided only by an inner voice that said to him, Go on. His was a crusade of cunning over strength, tenacity over temptation, and in the end, good over evil.

I shall call my hero, Apollo, but that is not his real name and the same holds true for all the players in my play. Whales and dolphins know of the taxonomy that scientists among your kind use to classify them into families, genera, and species of cetacea. But among their own kind they are known simply as beings. Since man first appeared in their world, beings have watched and listened to, learned from, and been persecuted by, the two-legged land mammals who call themselves human, but to the whales and dolphins there is very little humanity to be found in these untrustworthy and arrogant descendants of apes.

Fifty million years ago the ancestors of whales and dolphins left the land and entered deep blue water, never to return; ages before the first of your kind stood up straight and began to think of themselves as masters of the universe. Somewhere in the vast tableau of history, beings learned to understand your spoken languages, at least those of you who live near or travel on the seas; but long ago, they gave up any hope of establishing intelligent communication with your kind. It is ironic that man in his arrogance believes whales and dolphins will never understand human language, whereas beings know the opposite to be true.

The language that beings use to communicate with each other can be translated, with some accommodation, into human words as I have done in this story; however, the names by which they address each other do not lend themselves to such translation. But my characters cannot go nameless, so I have given them the names of Greek gods in honor of Aristotle, the first human to correctly call them mammals rather than fish, and in recognition of the fact that the word 'ocean' comes from Okeanos, the Greek god of sea and water.

If you are willing, I will take you into the world of Apollo. It is a world of three dimensions, a dense liquid sky through which beings fly with an easy grace, uninhibited by the force of gravity. His kingdom lies out beyond the restless blue horizon. It is filled with mystery and magic, mayhem and madness; a place of budding life and sudden death, where the light of the sun penetrates only the upper layers, leaving the rest of its vast dominions inked in eternal darkness. It is a world where man can leave no footprints, or find safe haven, or build structures upon its aprons that will outlast the endless ebb and flow of tides and time. And yet, as hostile and foreign as his world is to your kind, like Apollo, the blood that runs in your veins has exactly the same concentration of salt as every single drop of water in the ocean. In a very real sense then, the sea is part of you and you are part of it.

If you dare to come, you will find pleasure in clear, sunlit shallows above rippled sandy bottoms where tiny silver fish zoom and zip; and feel terror in deep, dark, cold waters where real monsters still dwell. I will take you beneath the waves to places where your heart has longed to go but your mind has been unwilling, and your body incapable of doing so. I will teach you things, which you otherwise would have never known and answer questions you cannot begin to ask. In return, I expect nothing from you save one thing; that you listen with your heart and not your head, and that when you are finished reading my tale you will join me in saving the planet we share before it is too late, for this is a tale of what was, is, and might yet be.

Who am I? For now, it matters not; all will be revealed in the end. Suffice to say that I am your guide, your interpreter and your teacher, but know this; I am not your friend. A more apt question might be, What am I? But enough of who and what, it is where and why that calls to us, and these questions must not be ignored. Time is of the essence and my story must be told to you, and all those like you, who stand upon the safe side of the shore. With your forbearance and by the grace of the Supreme Being who made us all, and in whose image you think you were made, I will now tell you my tale.

If you attend to the message carried upon my words, written in your language but translated from theirs, I promise that you will never again look upon the deep blue seas that surround you through the same eyes, or think about the whales and dolphins who dwell within them with the same mind; for it is they, not you, who rule the waves and you, not they, who is ignorant of the words and ways of the other. Whether you choose to believe it or not, you are not the only intelligent beings on this endangered blue marble drifting through space; this place of terrible beauty and untold potential that you call Earth but their kind knows as Planet Ocean. But if you turn a deaf ear to the moral of my play then all hope for tomorrow will be lost, and when we have all been dead ten thousand years, there will be nothing left to mark our passing except barren lands and empty seas; and in between on lonely shores, living stones will cry out in silence the three words that will serve as our collective epitaph; Arrogance, Intolerance and Stupidity.

And so let us begin, in the middle of my tale…

BOOK ONE

And it shall come to pass in the day that the Lord shall make his Light to shine upon the mighty waters under Heaven.
The spirit of the Lord shall come upon you, and he will drive darkness from the face of the deep, and deliver the great whales from evil.
God be praised.
God bring us the Light.

The Legend of the Light
Oral History of the Ancients

CHAPTER ONE

Kingdom Of The Ancients

"Never look down! Never look back," cried Pan to himself as his stout little body skipped along the surface of the temperate waters in the area of the North Atlantic Ocean known to man as the Sargasso Sea. His medium-size dorsal fin with its slightly curved shape set at mid-body, and dark gray cape on a light gray-flecked dorsal field with white underbelly, showed him to be what a marine biologist would call a Harbor Porpoise. At five feet in length and one hundred and thirty pounds, he was a poor match for the size and surge of the heavy ocean swells, and at twenty-five years of age, he had already lived longer than many of his species; but he plowed onward driven by a sense of purpose that forced his body and soul to do what his mind did not think possible.

"We must hurry. We dare not tarry," Pan chanted as he pressed on, performing the rapid roll with a little splash as he surfaced to breathe that is characteristic of his species, all the while trying not to think about the danger that lurked below—a danger he feared even more than man himself. High above, the summer sky was a perfect paleness of blue with a few wisps of white clouds that looked as if they had been painted with a dry brush, while twenty thousand feet below lay the world of eternal darkness known to your kind as the Hatteras Abyssal

Plain, but which beings call the deeps. Pan was a coastal being not used to the open ocean swells where his distant cousins, the pelagic whales and dolphins, were wont to roam. But now he found himself hurrying through the thin film of liquid silver that separates endless sky from bottomless sea, alone and terrified and yet determined to carry on.

"Never look down! Never look back," he said again. And he would not. He could not. He had to go on no matter how hard the going, for reasons known only to him; but soon all would know and when they did, he hoped he would finally find peace, one way or another.

Pan had left his home waters in the Gulf of Mexico a month earlier and except for the fitful hours of darkness when he hung in a half-sleep at the surface, with one eye open in the manner of all beings to avoid attack by the monsters that stalk the oceans of the night, he had kept moving, riding the northbound current of the Gulf Stream, steadily closing the distance between himself and his goal. (Beings know all the currents in the world's oceans and use them to their advantage; the greatest of these being the Gulf Stream). Alone and defenseless in the open seas, Pan had come far and had survived in the face of long odds where other beings, greater in size and strength might have failed. Now, exhausted and weak from hunger, he neared the object of his quest—a vast underwater plateau that formed the top of a steep-sided mountain jutting up from the deep ocean floor near the middle of the North Atlantic.

The seamount lay in less than two hundred feet of clear, blue-green water with well-defined edges that plunged into the abyss, twenty-four thousand feet below. Surrounded by a circular system of trans-oceanic currents known as the North Atlantic gyre and fed by the upwelling of nutrient-rich deep waters, the plateau supported the northernmost coral reefs in the Atlantic and teemed with sea life in all its myriad of shapes and sizes. With the exception of submariners in the navies of the global powers, modern man knew little and cared less about this rise from the sea floor. The ancient Greeks of your kind called it Atlantis, but beings know it by a different name—to them it is the Kingdom of the Ancients.

It is there that representatives of whalekind assemble once a year at the time of the Northern Hemisphere's summer solstice; the longest day of the year, known to beings as Godlight from the 'Good Light' as foretold in the Legend of the Ancients and proscribed in their Third Commandment. (Beings are guided by ten laws, or commandments, laid down by the Ancients, which are similar to your Ten Commandments, and while you would be right to think that this is more than a coincidence, you would be wrong in thinking that you were the source). The Gathering, as it is called, begins at mid-day on the solstice and lasts for seven days, during which beings convene a great assembly as they have done every year since the beginning of time. To understand this assembly, you must first understand the world of whalekind and how it is governed. Unlike your world where monarchism has all but disappeared, or been deemed inconsequential, in the world of beings this form of government remains as strong and true today as it was millennia ago. And for them, Planet Ocean is divided into Seven Seas, each of which is a separate and distinct kingdom ruled over by a king or queen.

To modern day beings these seas include the great bodies of water you know as the North and South Pacific Oceans, the North and South Atlantic Oceans, plus the Indian, Arctic and Southern Oceans. It has always been thus for whalekind but among your kind, the Seven Seas at one time referred to a different group of seas including; the Red Sea, the Mediterranean Sea and four others in that same region, plus the Indian Ocean, which is the only sea that has remained in your group of seven through the centuries.

The seven kingdoms are further divided into regions and territories, the number and nature of which varies by kingdom, with the North Atlantic and North Pacific having the greatest number, and the two polar oceans having the fewest. Within these territories dwell many tribes of beings, ruled over by chieftains, either male or female, who owe their appointment, and therefore their allegiance, to their monarch. In all cases, the governments of the seven kingdoms are what your political scientists would term elective monarchies, where the monarch is chosen by assemblies of the tribal chieftains within each kingdom. And among the many who desire such glory few are chosen. It is a source of disappointment for some, but rarely does it lead to trouble; unlike in your world where power and glory are the footservants of evil, and the pursuit of riches is paramount regardless of the consequences to people or planet alike—but I am getting ahead of myself.

Each year at Godlight, the monarchs from the Seven Seas travel to the Kingdom of the Ancients, along with a select group of senior members from their royal courts and tribal chieftains. They gather in a great assembly, which acts as the global governing body that rules over all the dominions of Planet Ocean. And presiding over the Gathering itself are the seven monarchs who form what is called the Sovereign Council. The duties of the general assembly, under the guidance and supervision of the Council, include preserving the oral history of whalekind; reaffirming the sanctity of the Ten Commandments of the Ancients; ensuring peace and tranquility within the Seven Seas; dispensing judgment over trespassers of these laws; resolving territorial or inter-species disputes; and most important of all, reaffirming their collective belief in a Supreme Ruler of heaven and ocean, the one you call God. The name by which beings refer to him cannot be easily translated into your language, but it comes closest to your words for father and mother all rolled together, so for the purposes of my tale the name God will suffice.

Unlike your kind, beings do not separate faith from governance, as they are united in the conviction that without a deep and abiding devotion to God, all is lost. To that end, each monarch legitimates the authority of his or her crown as being held by the grace of God, and as such each tends to assume a sacral aura. It is important that you understand this difference with your world, where democracy, either in the form of a presidential republic or a parliamentary constitutional monarchy, is held to be the best form of government. Viewing your world from beyond the thin blue line that separates it from theirs, with the religious hatred, crime, and poverty that characterize even your greatest democracies, beings would dispute this view.

Once the representatives of all whalekind are assembled at the Kingdom of the Ancients on Godlight, the Sovereign Council appoints one of their members to act as the leader of that year's Gathering. He or she is given the title of Moderator. At the time of my story, the Moderator was a Blue Whale whom I shall call Hera. She was the Queen of the North Atlantic Ocean and given that the Kingdom of the Ancients is located within her Kingdom, the Gathering that year had a special meaning for her. Hera was one of the largest animals ever to have lived on either land or sea, and along with her size and strength, her ten decades of life (middle age for a Blue Whale) had also given her wisdom far beyond that of the average being.

Pan had timed his journey to arrive at the Kingdom of the Ancients several days ahead of the summer solstice, in order to seek a private meeting with the Sovereign Council before they began their intensive seven days of governance. However, he had misjudged how long it would take him to traverse the open ocean, and as he approached the seamount, it was already late in the morning of the solstice. Sensing that his journey was near its end, and worrying that it might all be for nothing if he could not gain an audience with the Council, Pan let down his guard. And now, suddenly, he was no longer alone in the sea.

Ahead of him, on an opposite course and closing fast, three large shadows sliced through the waves. Their robust bodies were wide and smooth from head to flukes with tall, spike-like dorsal fins and the distinctive black and white color pattern characteristic of their species, known to your kind as Killer Whales, or Orcas, the largest members of the dolphin family. They were big males in their prime, each a perfect example of the ocean's most lethal killing machine, with fourteen pairs of large pointed teeth in both their upper and lower jaws; but on this day, maiming and mayhem were not on their minds—quite the contrary for their mission was one of mercy. The slow and steady movements of their flukes belied the urgency of their journey, and the restless silence of the sea was broken only by the soft whoosh of exhaled air as each animal broke the surface to breathe and then slipped beneath its seamless flow once again.

They moved in perfect harmony, narrowing the distance between themselves and Pan with each passing second. Their leader's name was Ares and with him were his brothers, Aegyptus and Danaus. All were similar in size and appearance; each one being approximately thirty feet long and weighing twelve thousand pounds, with identical black backs, flippers and sides, with white ventral zones that stretched from their lower jaw almost all the way down to their flukes. The sole visible difference between them was a slight variation in the grayish white saddle markings behind their six foot high dorsal fins but they all shared one thing in common, which was three identical sharp-edged cuts at the same spot near the base of their dorsal fins.

Even though they were too far away for Pan to see them with his eyes, he might have detected their approach with another of his senses. For you to understand this, a word about the sensory systems of beings is now in order. To begin with, beings perceive the world with their eyes as your kind does but there are some important differences. Given the positioning of their eyes on each side of their heads, beings still have some degree of binocular vision forward. However, this positioning provides them with excellent optical viewing beside, below, and even to some degree behind their bodies, which is crucial in a world where danger can come from any direction, at any moment. Beyond this, a more complex musculature and physical structure of their eyes and a greater number of photoreceptors when compared to the eyes of man, give them greater visual acuity both above and below the water. (In actuality, being's eyes are myopic in air but they learn to compensate for this without any difficulty.)

The second sensory system that beings share with humans is hearing. While they lack external ears, they possess the same basic parts of middle and inner ears, which allows them to hear sounds in the water. But beyond their eyes and their ears, beings possess another sense that allows them to perceive their world with far greater optical and acoustical acuity than man ever could. You refer to this as echolocation but I will call it their second vision or earsight. It involves the emission of bursts of high-intensity sound, which they use to bounce off objects in their surroundings, or the topography of the surroundings, and through this refined tool, a picture is created in their mind's eye more vivid, more detailed, and with greater precision than any that their eyes could provide. Moreover, they can share this image with each other through high-frequency sound such that a tribe of dolphins 'sees' the entire world about them at the same time: it is a shared experience that man will never know and you are the lesser for it.

Earsight is equivalent to what your military calls active sonar, and with varying degrees of intensity depending upon their size and species, beings can wield its power to many different purposes; from the broad scanning of underwater landscapes to the gentle probing of the bodies of other beings. They can also use it to emit powerful and potentially lethal bursts of sonic energy, the equivalent of a sonic boom, which can stun their prey or kill their enemies. In the great whales and large dolphins, earsight has a power and range far greater than that used in your ships of war, which beings call deathships, because sonar wreaks havoc with their delicate aural receptors and often causes them to beach themselves, where they die slow and painful deaths.

Using his earsight, Pan might have detected the approaching Orcas, but with his growing fatigue, he did not wield this power and thus was unaware of them. Of even greater concern, he did not sense another shadow that was closing on him from below. It was what you call a Great White Shark but the word that best matches the term that whalekind uses to describe these large sharks, and the other monsters that inhabit the deeps, including Giant Squid, is kraken. This kraken was twenty feet in length, swimming at twice that distance below Pan, and heading upwards with fearful jaws agape toward the unsuspecting porpoise in the ambush attack pattern typical of its species.

With larger prey such as elephant seals, sea lions and walruses, a Great White Shark aims to decapitate its victim, thereby preventing injury to itself. Its simple brain, which is not much more than a bulge at the tip of its spinal cord, is capable of discerning the size of its prey, and its head from its tail but little else. Without the ambush method of attack, the probability of a shark catching marine mammals would be greatly reduced. However, with a small seal or porpoise like Pan, a shark makes no such effort to aim for the head. Exactly where its teeth find purchase on the body of an undersized victim matters not, because with one bite the victim becomes a pile of fat and gristle slipping down the monster's maw.

But such would not be Pan's fate this day. At the last second, Pan caught a glimpse of the onrushing kraken, and powered by a sudden burst of adrenalin, he leapt high out of the water, twisting his body off to one side, and turning out of harm's way just as the shark reached him. The shark's momentum also carried it up out of the water and at the top of its flight; its jaws snapped shut sending paroxysms through the loose white flesh around its neck. For a moment, the giant beast seemed to hang there; suspended in air with its back arched, then it fell back into the sea with a titanic splash.

Undaunted by the missed attack, the shark launched itself toward the fleeing porpoise with a sweep of its enormous, hooked tail, quickly closing the distance between them, reopening its jaws and rolling its cold, black, pupil-less eye backwards into its head as it went. Somewhere in its tiny brain, the shark could already taste the porpoise's blood and flesh, and acid capable of turning bones into gelatin began flooding its stomach. But there would be no meal for the shark that day, or ever again.

At the last second before the shark caught Pan, it was hit from the side, just behind its pectoral fin, with such force that it caused massive damage to its internal organs, including its well-muscled two-chambered heart and its enormous liver. The blow had been delivered by Ares, who, like the other Orcas, had detected the kraken with his earsight long before it rose up from the depths. In this fight, the shark was hopelessly outmatched. At its best, it was little more than a life support system for its gruesome jaws, and it lacked the intelligence to know what had happened to it. But even in the simplest of living organisms, the instinct to survive is strong and the doomed kraken tried to escape, but to no avail. There was no rage in Ares' actions, just the cold and efficient termination of a mortal enemy. Ares struck the kraken again, with one more brutal blow, and then swam away, leaving the broken body of the dying shark to sink back into the depths from where it came.

While this was taking place beneath the waves, Aegyptus and Danaus reached Pan, who was hovering near the surface, and formed a protective wall on either side of him. Once there, Danaus, the youngest of the brothers, and by far the most free-spirited, looked down, and as he watched, the shark's body disappear into the deeps he muttered, "Food is a terrible thing to waste." Aegyptus ignored him and kept his attention focused on Pan.

Pan had no interest in looking at the kraken but the sight of the two Orcas did not exactly fill him with relief. "Frightens us. Frightens us," he whispered to himself.

Pan knew there are three types of Killer Whales that roam the seas; the first, are a noisy and sociable group who eat only fish. Man calls them Resident Orcas. The second type is reclusive and far more dangerous to other beings than sharks. This is because they eat only mammals, including other beings, in direct violation of the Fifth Commandment. These cannibals are called Transient Orcas and they are the pariahs of whalekind. Much is known among beings and man about both these types of Killer Whales. However, this is not the case with the third type of Orca, for they are a breed apart. They live far out in deep, bluewater and never interbreed with the other two types. And there is one major difference compared to the other kinds of Orcas, which is that although this third type occasionally kill and eat mammals like seals, walruses and sea lions, they never, ever eat other beings. In fact, their preferred prey are sharks. Man refers to this third kind as Offshore Orcas, and they are a fierce and noble breed best left alone by man.

"God—God be praised," stammered Pan as Ares rejoined his brothers. Pan spoke to them without opening his mouth in the way of all beings, by using a microburst of low frequency sound clicks and whistles. Beings use these to transmit an almost infinite amount of digitized bits of information in an extremely short period of time, far beyond the aural or mental capabilities of your kind. The only visible indication that Pan was communicating with the Killer Whales was the tiny stream of bubbles emanating from his blow hole. Pan's greeting was the traditional way one being greeted another. It was also used by beings on parting or during a normal conversation as a simple way of emphasizing a point.

"God bring us the Light," replied Ares, giving the proscribed rejoinder to Pan's opening remark, but there was no warmth in it, and it did little to calm Pan's fear. Ares was the oldest of the three brothers and the least sociable. Other than his brothers, he trusted every being equally, which was to say not at all. Without saying anything else, Ares moved closer to the terrified little being and probed him with his earsight, while Aegyptus and Danaus swam in protective formation on either side of Pan. Then Ares remarked with more condescension than cordiality in his voice, "So this is the little one about whom we have heard so much."

Pan, daring to interpret the comment in a favorable light, bubbled, "You have heard much about us?" He was always given to speak of himself in the plural. It was a simple affectation, which in his youth caused him problems with others his age who teased him mercilessly, but since he had no friends, as he grew older there was no one to tease him anymore.

"Us?" replied Ares with more than a hint of mockery.

Pan's exuberant tone, which was disproportionate to his diminutive size, coupled with the obvious feebleness of his physical condition, caused Aegyptus to intervene. "Ares, be gentle with our little cousin, for although his body is small his heart is big." Aegyptus was the most intelligent of the three brothers, and the most thoughtful.

"Indeed it must be to have made such a dangerous journey alone," added Danaus.

"A journey that but for our intervention would have ended up in the belly of the kraken," snorted Ares. But for all his posturing, even this mighty warrior of the seas, with his great strength, crushing bite and hunter's eyes, could not help but be impressed with the brave little Harbor Porpoise who had ventured so far from the safety of inshore waters on his personal quest. With his tough demeanor softening just a bit, Ares asked, "I assume that you are the one called Pan, is that correct, little one?"

"Yes, your Majesty," answered Pan, rising up on a passing ocean swell to gulp in a nervous breath of air and then sinking beneath the waves again to face the Orcas. They too, rose to breathe although not with the same frequency as Pan.

His reply caused the two younger brothers to laugh, in the fashion of their kind, which is to say that they gave forth a burst of sound and large bubbles that terrified a nearby school of anchovies and sent them spinning into a frenzied ball. "Your Majesty..." chortled Aegyptus, "That is a good one."

Ares gave Aegyptus a look that silenced him. The loving relationship between the brothers was the result of their shared blood, and fortified with the bonds that come with going into harm's way together. However, there was no mistaking who was the leader, and at that moment, Ares was in no mood for humor. He looked back to Pan. "Very well, come with us, and we will take you to meet with the Sovereign Council." He turned and with a powerful downward thrust of his flukes headed back in the direction they had come; his streamlined body melting into the spectral veil of blue and green that hung at the periphery of Pan's vision.

The other brothers, who were still hovering on either side of the porpoise, waited for Pan to follow. When he did not, Aegyptus said,

"We had best be off before the blood trail of the dead kraken brings others of his kind."

"Let them come," commented Danaus, directing a sweeping burst of earsight toward the shadowy world below. "I am hungry and was made all the more so by that missed opportunity for a feast moments ago."

Despite his primal fear of sharks, Pan hesitated. He wondered how Ares' knew of his name and his desire to meet with the Council. And despite Danaus' obvious disappointment at not being able to eat the kraken, Pan was still uncertain of which type of Orcas these three were. As far as Pan was concerned, to the one being eaten it made very little difference whether the one doing the eating was a whale or a fish. Summoning his courage, he asked, "Are you three—that is to say—you would not be—we mean…"

Danaus, the more intuitive of the three brothers smiled and replied, "We are Offshore Orcas and Guardians, Pan, if that is what you are wondering." Guardians were an elite group of beings, who served as protectors of their monarch. With the exception of Transients Orcas, any strong and able-bodied whale or dolphin could become a Guardian. However, Offshore Orcas most often served as Guardians and as Pan knew, they never, ever ate other beings.

"Oh, yes. We were wondering." Pan said with relief. *Goody, goody,* he said to himself.

Danaus put the matter to rest when he added, "Unlike those grotesque cousins of ours, the Transients, we do not eat our fellow beings. We consider that to be in very poor taste." Danaus chuckled at his pun, but Pan did not; Danaus took note and grew serious. Orcas necks are among the most flexible among whalekind (equal to Belugas who have almost human flexibility in theirs) and with his head, Danaus pointed toward the three sharp, short parallel scars near the base of Aegyptus' dorsal fin. "That is the mark of the Guardians. We get them when we are initiated."

Pan looked up at Aegyptus' fin and then surveyed the same marks on Danaus. "We see. Very impressive. Did they hurt?"

"No, little one. Not as much as that must have." He swam closer and with his flipper caressed the pale, crescent-shaped scar on Pan's flukes.

Pan sighed. "We do not remember the pain." He paused as a horrible memory flashed through his mind. "It was made by the kraken that killed our mother when we were very young."

"I am sorry, Pan." The Orcas' gentle tone calmed Pan, and were it not for the Guardian marks on his dorsal fin; Pan would not have thought Danaus to be a trained killer at all. In truth, Danaus had never taken to the harsher side of his role as a Guardian.

"How did you know we were coming to see the Sovereign Council?" asked Pan, now at ease with his huge and powerful companions.

"Such an audience was your intent, was it not?" asked Danaus, noticing the growing edginess of his brother who was now scanning the depths below them.

"Why, yes. Yes it was but we did not expect…"

"We can explain later. Now we must leave!" interrupted Aegyptus in the unmistakable tone of a command rather than a request. And they did just that. Together the three of them, two sleek, black and white, lethal killing machines flanking a stout little being with a heart ten times bigger than it had the right to be, headed off into the deep blue seas.

All his life, Pan had heard about the Kingdom of the Ancients. Like all beings, he had been told of its beauty and wonder by his mother when he was small, and as he reached adulthood, the glory and the greatness of the Kingdom had grown with each story from those who had been there. Few beings ever had this opportunity, which made its allure even more powerful. But nothing that Pan had ever heard prepared him for what he saw as he entered its realm in the company of the Guardians.

"Oh my," Pan gasped as they reached the edge of the seamount. "Oh my goodness," he exclaimed unable to control himself, which brought a smile to the face of Danaus. "We cannot believe we are here," he muttered. His head was moving so rapidly from side to side on his stout little neck that it appeared it might come unscrewed and drop into the luxuriant bed of coral that carpeted the broad, flat plain beneath them. Unlike the open ocean through which he had traveled so long and so hard, where other forms of life were almost non-existent, Pan now found himself surrounded by fish in all colors, shapes, and sizes, thousands upon thousands of them. The vast majority were what man calls bony fish, those possessing a skeleton, and while there were also numerous cartilaginous fish swimming about, including skates and rays, there were no sharks, not one. This emboldened Pan, who now began to swim ahead of his protective escort. They sped up to catch him.

"We have never seen such a quantum of fish before," Pan said to Danaus who was closest to him. While beings can count, and fully understand the principles of the science humans call mathematics, when they refer to very large numbers, such as thousands or millions, they use a term, which I translate as a quantum. To them this denotes an enormous quantity, regardless of its exact numbers, because the value of specificity beyond a certain limit is of little use in their world. A quantum of tiny fish meant a feast; a quantum of beings usually meant fun; a quantum of humans always meant trouble; and with any of these what did it matter if there were one thousand, or ten thousand, or more? Would the outcome be any different?

"We are so very hungry," Pan muttered to himself as some of the more tasty types of small fish swam nearby. "We think they look delicious," he added smacking his lips. He had not eaten in days and was tempted to snatch a few but he thought it might appear rude to his escorts, so he restrained himself. His thoughts of hunger were short-lived.

All at once, he heard a sound that was unlike any he had ever known, rhythmic and lilting, part chant, part hymn, part opus. It was a quantum of voices rising as one in a hauntingly beautiful chorus. You may be surprised to learn that beings can sing, but they can and do—of course, not as you know it—but in their own way they raise their voices in harmonic splendor. To other beings, the sound is beautiful and exhilarating, capable of filling their hearts with joy and stirring their souls with as much passion as a cathedral choir can do to yours. Whether it comes from one being or many, such harmonious sound is called whalesong, and only a few among your kind will ever hear it, which is a great pity.

Pan and the Guardians continued on, passing through the endless and ever-changing, diaphanous curtains of fish, whose sides flashed silver and gold in the muted shafts of sunlight streaming down from above. Then, in the filmy distance, Pan could see what appeared to be a wall of shadows, stretching almost from the floor of the plateau to the surface. For an instant he grew alarmed but he need not have feared, for as he and the Orcas drew near, he realized what it was. A tingling feeling ran down his spine, not out of fear but awe, for there before him, stacked in angled vertical rows, one upon the other, forming a vast spiral around a rise in the plateau's floor, was the Gathering. It was all that he had heard it to be and more, much more. He could now make out a quantum of beings, all swimming clockwise, in a gigantic, multi-tiered helix, tighter at the bottom and growing wider with each successive layer or tier, until it reached a width of three hundred yards at its top, like a giant living funnel of beings all moving as one, in perfect harmony of body, mind and voice.

Ares and his brothers halted at a point near the top of the funnel. Pan followed suit. Hovering there just beyond the outer edge of the spiral, with the majestic chorus filling his ears and stirring his soul, Pan saw that it was in fact two spirals, one inside the other, with the outer stream of beings all swimming upward, in ever-expanding circles until they reached the surface, where they each took a breath, then dove again to begin a downward journey on the inside spiral, doubling back upon their path, until they reached the bottom, and began all over again.

"Oh my, oh my. It is so beautiful," gasped Pan. He shot up to the surface to catch his breath then slipped back down beside the Orcas. From top to bottom, he could see that the entire living structure was two hundred feet deep. He could also see that inside the inner spiral, rising from the floor of the plateau, to a height halfway up it, was a rounded hump. It was once the top of an extinct volcano but was now covered with a splendid profusion with multi-colored coral. I shall call it Roundtop, and there, floating just above it, was Hera, the mighty Blue Whale, in all her enormous majesty.

"What are they singing?" Pan whispered to Danaus who floated gently in the clear, calm water beside him.

"It is the Hymn of the Ancients. The Gathering sings it together at the beginning of every day of Godlight," replied Danaus.

"Do you like it?" asked Ares.

"Oh yes. It is soothing to my soul," whispered Pan.

As they watched the slow upward procession, Pan saw beings representing almost all species of whalekind, some he had seen before but most he had only heard about. Among them were Minke Whales and Humpbacks; Gray Whales and Bowheads; Fin Whales and Right Whales, both Northern and Southern; Narwhales and Belugas, and too many other whales to name. And there were dolphins as well; hundreds upon hundreds of them in all shapes and sizes, from the prim and proper Striped White-sided, White-beaked and Hourglass Dolphins; to the congenial Spotted Dolphins, beings who looked like God could not make up his mind what color they should be; and the even more playful Spinner Dolphins. Also present were the larger and more sedate Rough-toothed Dolphins and perhaps the best known to your kind, Bottlenose Dolphins, whose intelligence and cunning was equaled only by their larger cousins, the Orcas. Pan also saw several types of Pilot Whales, who, like his three companions, were members of the dolphin family despite their names.

"Oh look. Look! Here come the little beings," Pan bubbled with excitement as he saw the smallest members of whalekind, the porpoises, who followed the dolphins in the vast procession. Among them were the common Dall Porpoises; and the much rarer Burmeister's and Spectacled Porpoises; and finally, several members of Pan's own species, Harbor Porpoises.

The entire scene, in all its majesty, with its sights and sounds, its pomp and circumstance, its solemn grandeur and resplendent glory, and its sense of timelessness, was almost more than the little Harbor Porpoise could take. He began to tremble and his heart skipped a few beats. "We are so blessed to be here at this moment," he said to the Guardians. "We have been given a glimpse of paradise." Then he added with a heartfelt sigh "We are not worthy." He was humbled beyond measure and although he did not know what the future had in store for him, at that moment Pan sensed that nothing would ever be the same again for him. He was right.

CHAPTER TWO

The White Dolphin

Several hours later, Ares escorted Pan into the presence of the Sovereign Council. They were meeting in a large circle, floating just below the surface of the glimmering, cerulean water, not far from the spot where the spiral had reached the surface earlier. The sun-dappled scene was as welcoming to the little Harbor Porpoise as it was nerve-wracking. These were the leaders of his world, upon whom all whalekind relied for guidance and direction. It was an honor just to be in their presence; one part of him was awed but true to the impetuous streak within him, another part was overflowing with undiplomatic excitement.

In addition to the Moderator, Hera, Queen of the North Atlantic, the Council was comprised of six other monarchs of the seas; Pluto, a Bowhead Whale, King of the Arctic Ocean; Dionysus, a Fin Whale, King of the South Atlantic Ocean; Poseidon, a Sperm Whale, King of the North Pacific Ocean; Eris, a Sei Whale, Queen of the South Pacific Ocean; Demeter, a Gray Whale, Queen of the Indian Ocean; and finally, Hermes, a Southern Right Whale, King of the Southern Ocean. All were great whales, which was how the Council had always been, because that was what the monarchs were; not that the members of the dolphin or porpoise families, who were much smaller in size, lacked leadership skills, but tradition was that only the largest of beings were ever chosen to be a king or queen. One reason was that the life span of the great whales commonly exceeded one hundred years, and sometimes approached twice that, which provided a depth of continuity of leadership unknown in the world of man. (Especially given your propensity to foolishly undervalue and ignore the elders of your kind.) But another reason was simply that no dolphin had ever asked to be king or queen. One day that would all change but that is an entire other story.

Hera, who was hovering at the opposite side of the circle from where Pan joined it, greeted him with a warm, "God be praised," but she was careful to modulate her greeting in recognition of Pan's small size. Had she not done so, the shock wave from her voice could have harmed the little being. Blue Whales are the biggest creatures that have ever lived, and Hera was a prime example of her species. At over one hundred feet in length and weighing two hundred tons, her huge body dwarfed Pan. She had a broad, flattened, U-shaped head with a large blow-hole splashguard that gave her an aloof appearance. Like all baleen whales, she had two distinct nostrils, which differed from the toothed whales who have only one. Despite her enormous size, she had a tiny, stubby dorsal fin set far back but her thick tail stock matched her body's bulk. Her mottled-blue-gray color appeared aquamarine underwater and there was something else about her that was most impressive; when she rose to the surface to breathe, her distinctive blow reached thirty feet into the air in a slender and spectacular column of spray that was the envy of all other great whales.

Pan froze at her greeting. Ares had instructed Pan not to speak until spoken to, but at that moment, he could not bring himself to reply, or do anything other than hover there in timid silence. What was worse, he found himself fighting off the terrible urge to pee, all of which made him open his blowhole while still floating several inches below the surface. This allowed water into his larynx, causing him to snort and sneeze, blowing a stream of water, impressive for his size, up into the air. Regaining his composure he said, "Oh, your Grace, we are so sorry." If beings could blush like humans, he would have been bright red at that moment. "We apologize but we always sneeze whenever we are nervous."

He bobbed his head once and muttered, "Of course it would help if we were at the surface before we breathed."

Some of the Council members laughed out loud while others only smiled, the degree to which varied by their species, as not all beings show emotion outwardly. The Moderator did not smile but there was no displeasure in her countenance, simply an expectation of proper manners. "Decorum, everyone. Decorum," she said in a firm tone with just a faint hint of amusement in her eyes. And what eyes they were: big, dark, and slightly 'pooched' outward in the way of all beings, but even more so given her enormous size.

Pan noticed that there was also a certain sadness about her. Although he did not know it, this was characteristic of all whales her age. It was a haunting loneliness that has its roots buried deep in a knowledge about the world and the ways of whales and man. It was, what I will call, The Look of Sadness, and once you have stared into a great whale's eyes and seen it, it will be etched upon your soul forever. (Only the most cruel and heartless of your kind, like the men and women from countries you call Japan, Iceland, and Norway, who make their living murdering whales, seem to be immune to it.)

Finally, in response to what Hera had said in her greeting, Pan replied, "God bring us the Light, your Grace."

Ares had already alerted Hera about the way that Pan spoke and she found it amusing, but her position of authority did not allow her to display it. "Now, Pan, what was so important that you requested an audience with the Council? And please, call me Madam Moderator."

"Thank you, your…that is, Madam Moderator. But before we answer may we ask you a question?"

"Of course. Go ahead."

"How did you know we were coming and that we wanted such an audience?"

She glanced at several of the other Council members and then looked back at the little being and replied in a slow, measured tone "Someone in your tribe, who knew of your intentions, told your chieftain…"

"Python," interrupted Pan with a steely look.

"Yes—Python." It was obvious the name did not sit well with her. She had heard disturbing things about him and his style of leadership and since his tribe was in her kingdom it was her responsibility to investigate, but due to the Gathering, she had not yet done so. She continued, "After the being in your tribe told Python that you were coming to see us, he sent some of his tribe after you, apparently with evil intent. Word of his actions spread among the other tribes in the Gulf of Mexico and out into the Atlantic. From there it did not take long for the message to reach us. Thus, we knew you were coming but we did not know why."

Pan had been living among a tribe of Bottlenose Dolphins in the Gulf for the past twenty years, ever since his mother died. For obvious reasons, given his species, Pan was not a bona fide member of the tribe but they tolerated his presence. But Python did not like having Pan around and were it not for the intervention of a female named Leto, who had adopted the orphaned Pan, he would have been banished long ago. Hera continued, "We knew at once that whatever it was you wanted to tell us must be important for Python to take such great exception to your plan."

Pan's expression clouded over. "Oh my." The implications of what Hera was saying sank in. In coming to the Gathering, he had unknowingly signed his own death warrant, but then again, he knew that he had had no choice.

Pan fell silent, until Hera prompted him, "Now please tell us, Pan, what you want from the Council."

With a sigh that sent a tiny little stream of bubbles up to the surface, he replied in a measured tone, "We did something in our past of which we are not proud—something we fear may have doomed all whalekind." The comment startled Hera but she said nothing. "We did not mean to, but we were young then, and foolish." He paused and bowed his little head and added, "And stupid. So very stupid."

"Go on," said Hera, her interest piqued. Due to her size, even though Pan was several feet below the surface, her back was above it. With a mighty blow, she took a deep breath and settled herself to hear Pan's story. The other Council members did the same thing and moved a little closer as they did not want to miss what Pan was about to say. To any human pilot flying overhead, it would have been a very strange sight; a circle of great whales gathered around a tiny porpoise with the Orca in close attendance. But there were no planes or prying human eyes, to spoil the moment.

Pan rose up and took another deep breath, then slipped back down to face the whales, closed his eyes and gathered his thoughts. From deep within the backwaters of his consciousness, where they had been held prisoners of his guilt, unpleasant memories from long ago and far away now came into the light of day. He opened his eyes and began to tell his tale, and as he did, his voice gathered strength and purpose.

"It happened this way. It was a soft summer evening, on the eve of Godlight, nearly twenty years ago when three shadows sliced through brackish water; swimming against the out-flowing tide in the place man calls the Florida Everglades. They stayed close to the center of the narrow channel of the estuary, as it wound its way through the salt marsh and mangrove trees. Their flukes drove them onward with a steady, determined rhythm, and the restless quiet of the summer night was broken only by the soft whoosh of exhaled air as each being broke the surface to breathe and then slipped beneath its seamless flow once again." There was an almost dreamlike quality to Pan's voice that drew in the giants gathered around him.

"They were adult Bottlenose Dolphins, one male and two females who were sisters. One of the females was much lighter in coloring, a pale gray, while the other two were the usual deeper gray, but under the pale glow of the moonlight, all three appeared as dark shadows moving as one, with a shared sense of purpose, joined together by an unspoken bond, and driven by the miracle and mystery of what was about to happen. Leading the way upriver was Leto, the one with the lighter coloring followed by her sister, Aurora.

"With the exception of their color, the sisters were almost identical twins, at ten feet long, with a weight of six hundred pounds, although at that moment, Leto carried the additional mass of an unborn baby within. The dolphin following close behind Leto and Aurora was a large male, twelve feet in length and weighing nine hundred pounds. His name was Helios. Unlike other tribes of dolphins in that part of your kingdom, Queen Hera, who live close inshore, these three were bluewater beings from a tribe that dwells on the edge of the deeps, at the outer edge of the Great Southern Plain. (Pan was referring to the plain that stretches westward, out into the Gulf of Mexico for over one hundred miles. You should note that all distances in my story are in nautical miles.)

There was a far away look in Pan's eyes as he added, "It is a place of great beauty where the crystal clear, azure waters turn to cerulean, then cobalt and finally midnight blue and black." He paused and for an instant Hera thought Pan was about to cry, but he did not. Instead, he steadied himself and continued, "Athena, the grandmother of Leto and Aurora had led her tribe from the Atlantic Ocean into the Gulf over fifty years earlier. Why the three bluewater dolphins were in that estuary, so far from their home was known only to them, but as they passed the raccoons and clapper rails feeding in the shallows, the muggy night air was heavy with a sense of impending danger; so palpable, so primal, that the lesser creatures took flight, or turned away from the waters edge, and sought safety elsewhere."

It was apparent to the Council that this little storyteller was possessed of a refined intelligence and a gift for the turn of phrase. His words carried a powerful imagery, and his tone and manner were engaging in a vaguely unsettling way. A few of the Council members murmured to each other as they began to anticipate where this story might be going, but their growing excitement was quieted by a stern glance from the Moderator.

"At last, in a wider section of the channel just beyond a sharp bend, where the bottom was more sand than mud, Leto stopped and turned to face her older sister and said, 'It is time. This will be the place where my child will be born. He will wait no longer.' Both she and her sister knew the baby was a male; the reason was more profound than that provided by their earsight." Pan paused and gathered himself because what he was about to say next would unlock a secret that would change everything for everyone, and not necessarily for the better.

"They knew the baby would be a boy because one year earlier Leto had had a dream in which an angel appeared to her. It was on a night when they were in their home waters, far out in the Gulf."

"An angel?" asked Hera.

Pan nodded.

"What did the angel look like?" asked a doubting King Dionysus

"After she had the dream, Leto told her sister that the angel came to her in a brilliant white light that filled the ocean around her, nearly blinding her with its radiance. She said that the angel looked like a Humpback Whale, but he was all white in color with huge flippers and a deep and soothing voice." Pan paused and looked at the Moderator for a reaction but he got none. "Oh, there was one more thing that we almost forgot. Leto told her sister that just before the angel appeared she heard the sound of whalesong."

"Whalesong! What whalesong?" asked Queen Hera.

Pan shook his head. "She did not know, but it filled her heart with great joy."

Hera exchanged a knowing look with the other sovereigns.

"The angel told Leto that she would have a male child whose skin color would be purest white, with a light in his eyes as bright and clear as that which occurs on the first day of Godlight; and that he would bear the mark of God upon his body." Pan paused again, rising up to the surface to grab a breath while the larger beings, who did not need to do so, waited impatiently for the words that they had already guessed were coming. Refreshed, Pan continued, "The angel told Leto that her baby would grow up to be a great warrior who would lead whalekind out of darkness, as foretold in the Legend of the Light. And the angel said that the child would be called, Apollo."

A burst of excitement swept through the Council. Hera sought clarification. "Excuse me, Pan. Did the angel say this child would be a warrior or a leader, who would save us all from evil?" Like many other beings, Hera was a pacifist who abhorred war under all its guises. She rejected the widely held interpretation of the Legend of the Light, that their salvation would involve killing.

Pan did not hesitate in his reply. "Both."

Hera nodded sadly and motioned with her flipper for him to continue but even though it was a gentle movement, the wave it sent through the water pushed Pan back several yards. With a look of mild annoyance, Pan swam back to his former position and began his story again, "As Leto looked around that spot in the channel, she said to her sister, 'The angel said my baby would be born in such a place.'"

"Aurora glanced nervously downriver and then looked back at her sister and replied, 'You must hurry, Leto. There is not much time.' Leto noticed that there seemed to be no joy in her sister's reply, only a dreary acceptance of what was to be, mixed with the faint hint of something else; a trace of bitterness mixed with anger. This was uncharacteristic of Aurora but the pain in her abdomen distracted Leto and she did not pursue the matter. Meanwhile, Aurora spoke with Helios, who hovered close by. When they were finished with their brief conversation, he swam ten yards back downriver, and stopped just past the bend. Only then did he begin to utter short bursts of high-intensity sound, directing his earsight along the watery path they had just traversed.

"Satisfied that Helios was positioned to serve as both look-out and guardian, and with her sister close by her side ready to act as midwife as was the custom of their species, Leto arched her back, then bore down with her powerful abdominal muscles, and within minutes her baby was born, flukes first. At four feet long and weighing forty pounds, he was a perfect replica of his mother in every way except one, and that made all the difference. As the angel had said, he was pure white, and on the left side of his head, just behind his eye, he bore a tiny birthmark—in the shape of a tiny, purple, five-pointed star."

There was murmuring again among the Council. Hera thought about what she had just heard and then added softly, as softly as a great a whale ever could, "As you know, Pan, the Legend of the Light said nothing about what the mark of God would look like."

Pan nodded and added, "But how perfect is a tiny star?"

Dionysus scoffed. "Why not a cross or a crescent? Or if a star, why not a six-pointed one? These are the marks that mankind use to symbolize their gods?"

Hera interjected. "You mean God, Dionysus. There is but one God and he is God of us all, man and whale."

Dionysus snorted. "You and I know that, Madam Moderator, but tell it to the humans as they slaughter each other on their battlefields, each following the sign of their *own* god into battle. Tell me, how can one god be on both sides?" Without waiting for her response he answered his own question. "The truth is that mankind is a godless force in the universe and a plague upon Planet Ocean, bent on self-destruction. And the greatest tragedy of all is that they will take us with them into hell."

Beings do not see heaven and hell in the same way as your kind does. The former is not some ethereal, fluffy cloud-filled realm above the sky, and the latter is not a bottomless pit filled with fire, because neither clouds nor fire have relevance in their world. Rather, beings believe that heaven and hell are absolute states of eternal bliss or torment respectfully, where the souls of the dead are sent based upon how they have lived their lives.

Hera ignored Dionysus' tirade but even as she did, she knew that a growing number of beings shared his views. "You must excuse King Dionysus, Pan. He does not believe that our God is the same one who watches over mankind."

Pan flashed a disdainful look at Dionysus, and then continued. "In addition to the star birthmark,"—he paused to see if the verbal storm had passed, which it had—"there was something about the baby's eyes."

"What about them?" asked Hera as her own eyes narrowed.

"There seemed to be a light behind them," said Pan.

"A light?"

"Yes. It was pure and clear and bright; a penetrating glow that made Aurora uncomfortable."

"Did the light trouble Leto?" Hera asked.

"No." Pan hesitated then continued, "As soon as the baby was born, Leto pushed him to the surface where he took his first breath of air. Then she whispered something to him and he responded to her."

It is the way of all beings that they understand their own language from the moment of birth; the unforgiving nature of their world dictates that it be so. Their knowledge of the languages of man is learned, but they do so with ease and the scope of this ability is limited only by their exposure to your kind; such that beings who live in the seas off Europe, or Africa, or Asia, understand many human languages, while those who spend their lives in the littoral waters of the United States, or Australia, only learn English.

Pan continued, "It was clear from Leto's behavior that she was not surprised by her baby's color. It was what the angel had said it would be. And even in the pale moonlight that hung like shimmering curtains in the otherwise gloomy waters, it was obvious that this baby was different from all those who had ever come before. Beyond his skin color, there was something about him that spoke to another time and place, an almost unworldly presence that reached out and touched your heart and captivated your soul." Pan stopped; his words and the image they created a powerful presence in the stillness of the ocean.

The Council was spellbound. Even Hera was now caught up in the magic of the moment. In the re-telling of the story of the birth of the white dolphin, Pan held the Council within his grasp. They hung on his every word. The fact that this small and otherwise insignificant being was having such an impact upon the mighty rulers of the Seven Seas was not lost upon Ares, who watched from just outside the circle. It was at that moment that the Guardian's feelings about the unassuming Harbor Porpoise began to change; somehow, he sensed that his fate and that of this little storyteller were now intertwined, for better or for worse, and forever.

Unaffected by the reactions of those about him, Pan pressed on with his story. "Sensing his mother's tenseness, but being too young and fragile to understand it, the baby ducked under water, nuzzled up against her and began to nurse. He closed his tiny eyes and gulped down the warm, rich milk, hovering close to her, nestled between her and his aunt.

Meanwhile, distracted from his guard duty by the birth, Helios swam up river to view the baby. It was a fateful mistake. His momentary lack of vigilance allowed another being to skirt out from within the shadows of the sea grass where he had been hiding and sneak one last, long peek at the newborn baby. His small size had allowed him to follow the dolphins undetected up the estuary and hide in the shallow water at the edge of the channel, there to await the birth. After seeing that the white dolphin had been born, the being headed downriver, carrying with him a message—a message that he thought would be welcome to those who had sent him on his mission—and one that he hoped would bring him stature in their tribe." Pan paused and momentarily his gaze drifted far away from Hera and the Council. No one said anything. Finally, Pan began again.

"The veil of night was loosening its grip upon the world and a pastel wash of pink and yellow was creeping over the horizon, as the being reached the mouth of the estuary. Using his earsight he located seven male Bottlenose Dolphins, similar in size to Helios but more sinister in appearance and manner. Their leader was the one called Python. He was larger than the others with very dark gray coloring, almost black. Hovering there in the shadowy waters, lit by the dim light of the coming dawn, the dolphins listened to the being as he swam in an excited circle, pinging, and clicking his news. When he was finished, they unexpectedly set upon the little being and beat him badly, stunning but not killing him. They told him if he ever said anything about what he had seen that night, or whom he had told it to, they would kill him. He knew they meant it.

"Satisfied that their spy had been dealt with, the leader and his gang turned and headed upriver. After they were gone, the broken and bruised body of the spy drifted out into the bay, carried by the tide until it reached other members of Python's tribe who had congregated at a safe distance from the mouth of the estuary, far from the spot where Python and his gang had been waiting. There had been a constant buzz of excitement among the group all during the night in anticipation of the birth, as foretold in Leto's dream, and which Python had been unable to keep from them.

"But now, as the beaten little being drifted by, silence swept across the group, beginning with the eldest among them, then the adults, followed by the younger members of their kind, until absolute quiet prevailed except for the muted clanging of a distant buoy and the waves lapping upon the nearby, muddy shore. Then, in a slow procession, they all turned and headed out into the Gulf leaving the spy to the sharks, and the white baby to his fate. While they had the numbers to intercede on behalf of Leto and her baby, they possessed neither the will nor the way to do so. They believed there was nothing more they could do for the white dolphin. And they were right. The little spy found out later that Helios and the white dolphin were dead. Python told them that Helios had murdered the baby and he, Python, had then killed Helios, but the spy never believed it. No one did. They all believed that Python had killed them both." Pan paused and then added despondently, "And with the death of the baby dolphin, would soon come the death of all whalekind."

As Pan neared the end of his tale, there was absolute silence. No one on the Council spoke or moved except for the slightest flick of their flippers to hold their positions in the gentle ocean swells. The seas around them that had been full of life filled with thousands of tiny fish when Pan began his story were now empty, devoid of color or movement. It was as if the great darkness, which the angel predicted, had now cast its shadow upon the sea. Pan was emotionally and physically drained. He hung in the water, barely unable to raise himself up to the surface to breathe. There was an air of vulnerability about him tinged in loneliness.

With every bit of strength he had left, Pan struggled to finish his story. He looked first around the circle and then at Hera and said, "By now you all must know that the spy was us. We are the one who killed the white dolphin—as certainly, as if we did the evil act by ourselves. We never told anyone, not even Leto that it was us that night who betrayed her. And now, we are asking the Council for our just punishment." Pan closed he eyes, lowered his head and flukes, and hung there in the water, like a small rainbow in several shades of gray, broken of spirit, with an empty soul and nothing left to live for. He waited for a moment then added, "We are prepared to die now." But nothing happened. Still with his eyes closed he said, "We are waiting…" But still nothing happened.

Finally, Hera moved her mighty bulk at a measured pace across the space separating them, and as she did the other members of the Council backed away. Pan could feel her coming, for even at a slow speed, the pressure wave in front of her was immense. He squeezed his eyes even tighter, waiting for the end. As she closed upon him, her enormous body towered over him and she could have dispatched him with one flick of her flipper, but she did not. Instead, the look in her eyes was one of tenderness. Then, in a deep and loving tone, she began to speak with power and authority. "First of all, Pan, we thank you for telling us this story and confirming what we have believed in our hearts for a long time."

His eyes snapped open. "You have heard it before?"

"Yes. But not is such great detail and up until now it was just a rumor spread by one of the beings who was also in the Gulf that night long ago. He saw you speaking with Python and he told what he saw to another being, who told someone else, and from there the story was passed across the Gulf, out into the Atlantic, and from there across all the oceans of the world, filling the hearts and minds of the faithful with a mixture of hope and despair: hope because the white dolphin had been born, and fear that he may have been killed."

Sound travels four times faster and carries much farther underwater than it does in air and the voices of the great whales can be heard by others of their kind over distances of up to a thousand miles. When combined with the fact that these leviathans travel along well-defined migration routes that crisscross the world's oceans, messages can be quickly transmitted from ocean to ocean, carried on the voices of these great whales that boom from the tops of sunken mountain peaks and echo through underwater canyons. I shall refer to this long distance communication as whalesound, which is not to be confused with whalesong, the latter being used to communicate more with the heart than the mind.

Hera continued, "However, up until this moment, we did not know the name of the Chosen One, or the firsthand details of his birth and the promise of his life as spoken to Leto by the angel. Now you have provided all this to us and all whalekind can rejoice in that knowledge."

Pan was perplexed, "But did you not hear us. We killed…"

She interrupted him, "No, Pan, you did not kill the white dolphin. No one did."

"Apollo lives?" Pan's head snapped up so quickly that he felt a twinge in his neck. At twenty-five, he was well past middle-age and his body was beginning to show it. But in that one moment, the years washed off him like waves on a steep beach. (Your scientists would say that Pan had already lived beyond the normal life expectancy for his species but they consistently underestimate the life span of beings because in your liquid prisons, they die long before their time).

Hera nodded her head. "Yes, little one. At least we have reason to believe he does."

"Goody. Goody!" shouted Pan. He exploded with excitement, rocketing away from Hera, then returned and did a giant barrel role around her enormous body as the other members of the Council watched in shock at the impetuosity of the little being. Finally, Pan calmed down and returned to his position in front of the Moderator, and with a mixture of joy and relief said to himself, *Thank-you God. Thank-you.*

"Are you quite through?" asked Hera trying to suppress a smile, which is a difficult thing for a great whale to do.

"Yes, Madam Moderator," replied Pan rather sheepishly. "We are."

"Very well." Hera continued, "For many years we believed, like you, that the white dolphin was dead. But then, five years ago, a Spinner Dolphin by the name of Janus, came to the Gathering and told us of a white Bottlenose Dolphin with whom he had been held captive at a place where human scientists study our kind located in California. Janus told us that the white dolphin possessed incredible intelligence and strange, mystical powers by which he held sway over all those about him, including the humans. Janus also told us that the white dolphin had a tiny birthmark on the left side of his head—in the shape of a star."

"A purple, five pointed star?"

Hera nodded.

"Oh my! Oh my—it must have been Apollo," muttered Pan. "Is he still there? In California?"

"No. Janus told us that two years earlier, he and Apollo, and some other dolphins were released by one of the scientists just before a typhoon hit the facility. They became separated into two groups and Janus lost contact with Apollo who disappeared near the Farallon Islands."

"Also known as the Devil's Teeth," added Dionysus with a perverse smile.

"It is a dark and evil place patrolled by kraken," added Hera with a sneer. (Adult Blue Whales have nothing to fear from Great White Sharks but their babies occasionally fall victim to them.)

"Do you mean that they allowed Apollo to slip away?" Pan exclaimed, trying hard to ignore the image of the kraken that swam though the backwaters of his recent memory.

"Yes. Janus never found Apollo. Even so, he thought the Sovereign Council needed to hear what had happened, and so he travelled around Cape Horn. However, the journey through the Southern Ocean was too much for him. He was very weak by the time he reached the Kingdom of the Ancients, and he died not long after telling us his story."

As a child, Pan, had heard frightening tales about the great Southern Ocean that forms the extreme southernmost portions of the Atlantic, Indian and Pacific Oceans, circling the bottom of the world. It is a vast unbroken sea where waves roll around the globe unhindered by land except for the three great capes that touch its northern edge; the Cape of Good Hope at the tip of South Africa, Cape Leeuwin in South Australia, and the most dangerous of all, Cape Horn, at the bottom of South America. Pan knew it to be an area of almost constant hurricane-force winds that can pile the waves into mountains of water over one hundred feet high, and where icebergs surf the thundering seas crushing everything in their path, and making any journey through it perilous for man or being.

Hera continued, "Then a year ago word came to the Council that there was a Bottlenose Dolphin being held captive on an island in the Bahamas archipelago called Sinclair Cay. It seems that when he was captured, this dolphin's skin was gray like others of his species but in captivity his skin had turned pure white. And what was more, the white dolphin was possessed of great powers of mind and body and spirit. The news came to us from another dolphin who heard it when he was captured in fishermen's nets. Before they threw him back into the ocean, they scraped his skin to see if underneath the outer color was a layer of white. Of course there was not and the fishermen were disappointed. As they talked among each other, the dolphin learned about the oceanarium and the white dolphin. After he was released, this dolphin told his chieftain who passed the news to us."

"So when do we go?" asked Pan with unrestrained excitement.

"Go where?"

"To Sinclair Cay, of course. We must go save the white dolphin right away."

"No, Pan. Rescuing him would be a near impossible task. He is a prisoner in one of man's water-filled prisons." She paused and then added with a heavy tone. "I am afraid that unless he can find a way to escape, Apollo may be lost to us forever."

"But that cannot be. That must not be. The legend said that he will save us in our hour of greatest need—and lead us out of darkness," pleaded Pan. "We must go. We *will* go. Whether you come or not."

Dionysus interjected, "You are a little fool. First, the oceanarium is built on land, which no water-borne force of beings, no matter how large or how strong could hope to overthrow. And second, we are far from being in a state of darkness. Our world is calm and peaceful, and except for a few minor territorial disputes, today's opening session of the Gathering was orderly. I do not expect the next six days to be anything different."

"But, how can you be so..." stammered Pan.

"You forget to whom you are speaking," snarled Dionysus cutting off the little being, and moving ominously toward him. As he did, Ares started toward the King, and it was clear from his expression who he was moving to protect.

"That's enough," said Hera, giving them both a stern look. Dionysus started to reply but then, seeing the Orca, thought better of it. Hera glanced at Ares, "I think we are done here, Guardian Ares."

Pan persisted, "But, your Grace. We must…"

"Pan," said Ares moving up just behind him. "It is time to go."

Impertinence, even when motivated by a noble cause, is frowned upon in the world of whalekind. But because Pan's mother had not been there to teach him, he was less fluent in the social graces.

Hera gave Ares an appreciative glance, not just for his help with Pan but also for intervening with Dionysus, then she looked back at the pushy but lovable little porpoise and said sympathetically, "Ares is right, Pan. You must leave us now. I want to thank-you for coming here and telling us about the night that Apollo was born. You are to be commended for your bravery and you are hereby forgiven for your sin, because you were young and knew not what you were doing."

"*My* sin!" retorted Pan. The excitement in his voice had been replaced by petulant discontent.

"Excuse me?" said the startled Moderator. She was unused to anyone taking such a tone with her, especially one so small. Muttering could be heard among the other Council. Ares closed the remaining distance between himself and Pan and laid his large paddle like flipper on Pan's flukes. Pan ignored him. He was not about to back away. The same drive and determination that had sustained him as he crossed a vast ocean to get there now would not permit him to back down from the Moderator.

"*My* sin occurred twenty years ago, and ever since then we have lived a pure life following the commandments of the Ancients. Whereas *your* sin of refusing to at least try to save Apollo will not be so easily forgiven by God on judgment day." (Beings believe, as an ever-diminishing number among your kind do, that at the end of life they will be called to task by God.)

There was an audible gasp from the Council. The sea grew silent. All eyes fell upon the diminutive Harbor Porpoise, and the immense Blue Whale, facing each other across a chasm of discordance. For a long while, Hera held her position ten yards in front of Pan, with her massive head cocked to one side, staring down at him through a big, cold eye. Even though she was troubled by his insolence, she could not help but marvel at his strength of purpose. In truth, she wished her Kingdom had more beings like him.

It was left to Ares to break the silence. "May I speak, Madam Moderator?" he asked with respect. She nodded. He looked around the circle, briefly making direct eye contact with each of the Council and then looked back at Queen Hera. "I can assure the Council that this little being means no disrespect. He is tired from his long journey..."

"We are *not* tired and we are *not* little," said Pan. "We are..." before Pan could finish, Ares slapped him with his flipper, not too hard, but with enough force to get his attention. Pan immediately stopped talking. His pride was hurt more than his body.

Ares began again, "I know Pan is grateful for the forgiveness he has received this day from *his* sin,"—Ares emphasized the word *his,* then continued—"and I would like to recommend that he be allowed to watch tomorrow's session of the Gathering to better understand the magnitude and complexity of the issues that this august body must deal with. Until then I propose to take him into my care. With your permission, we will retire now."

Hera quickly replied, "Very well, you may both be excused."

Pan hovered there before the mighty leviathan without saying anything. He glanced at Ares and then back at Hera, shook his head once and said, "God be praised," with more than just a little peevishness. Pan had a streak of this in him not uncommon to his species, which came from being so small in a world of giants.

"God bring us the Light," replied Hera with the strained patience of a mother toward her petulant child.

Before Pan could utter another sound, Ares gave him a firm shove that moved him back away from the circle. Then, in a rumbling voice that left no room for further discussion or debate, he said, "We are leaving. Now!" Pan nodded sheepishly and the two of them swam away. The roughness of Ares' actions, both verbal and physical, brought Pan to his senses. He swam meekly beside the Orca, who lectured his small companion, "You must learn, little one, that there are times to speak and times to listen and only the foolish do not know the difference."

"We understand," replied Pan struggling to keep up. "We do. But our mother taught us to speak our mind as long as we always told the truth. She said that because we are so small in a world so big, we have to speak up or not be heard."

"That is good advice, and I am sure that your mother was wise; however…"

"She was *very* wise…" interjected Pan, but his words were cut off as Ares came to an abrupt stop in the water, which caused a wave that spun Pan head over heels, carrying him ten feet further on. Pan turned around and swam back to Ares with a look of embarrassment in his eyes. "We apologize, Ares," he said with his head down. "Please go ahead. We promise we will listen."

With a stern look to add emphasis to the point he was making, Ares continued. "You are my elder, Pan, and I mean you no disrespect. But I have learned that sometimes what you do not say speaks far louder than what you do." Actually, in chronological years, Ares and Pan were the same age but given the differences in expected life span for the various species of beings, Pan was the more senior relatively speaking. Relative age is a rather complicated concept but beings have no difficulty dealing with it. It applies in your world as well but you do not realize it, as the year of your birth is a rather poor measure of your age.

Pan thought carefully about what Ares had said. "We understand. We are old but not so old, or so foolish, that we cannot learn. We will try harder to listen." He did understand; that part of his reply was sincere. But the second part lacked conviction, but not because he did not want it to be so. Throughout his life Pan had been an impatient listener, always in a hurry to speak. To him listening was simply the act of waiting to speak, especially when in the presence of those beings of lesser intelligence, who would have been better served by being quiet.

Physicians in your world might have diagnosed Pan's behavior as Attention Deficit Syndrome, and in the world of beings, there are also healers and caregivers, whales and dolphins who are skilled at curing the afflictions of their kind. Using earsight, they are able to detect both the physical and emotional maladies that often occur in beings. And many of these afflictions can be cured by the chemicals present in the flora and fauna of the sea bottom, which is an area of knowledge greatly lacking among your kind. However, there were no medicinal cures for the behavioral traits of this impatient and often short-tempered, little Harbor Porpoise.

For a long moment Ares did not say anything. He let the sound of silence create a vacuum in the space between them and waited to see if the little porpoise would seek to fill it. Pan did not. After satisfying himself that the lesson had been learned, Ares gave Pan a sideways glance and said, "Good. Now let us continue. We are almost there." They started swimming again through the blue-green waters and as they went, the slanted rays of sun grew pale, and the dancing fingers of light that penetrated the water grew shorter. Soon the dark waters below seemed to reach up toward them from the plateau, like ink seeping up a gossamer curtain that swayed in some unseen current.

They had gone a little farther when Pan said, "Guardian Ares?"

"Yes, Pan."

"Do you think we might get something to eat before we sleep?"

Ares chuckled, "Yes, Pan. I think that can be arranged."

Pan whispered, *"Oh goody, goody,"* and gave a quick snap of his flukes that propelled him into a tight barrel role. Then he fell back into formation beside Ares, and together, the mighty warrior of the waves, and the impetuous little loner who was trying so very hard to fit in, faded into the mounting shadows of evenfall.

CHAPTER THREE

A Call To War

In the half-sleep that is the way of all beings, Pan drifted on the dusky swells, rising and falling with each one as they passed silently beneath him on their journey toward the distant shore; driven by the wind and the unseen force of the moon whose gravity governed their world. Beings can feel the moon's pull deep within their bodies and, along with the gravitational and magnetic forces of Planet Ocean, it guides them with unerring precision on their open ocean journeys. They are also aided in their long distance navigation by sensing ocean currents and tasting the water through which they pass.

There are two reasons why God gave whalekind the ability to keep one half of their brains awake while the other half sleeps, and both pertain to survival. The first is that beings breathe voluntarily so they need to maintain a degree of consciousness or they will drown. The second is that no matter their size, beings are at their most vulnerable after the sun goes down, and as such, without this partial alertness they might soon fall victim to kraken or to the evil members of their own kind, Transient Orcas.

On the morning of the second day of Godlight, Pan awoke from what should have been a restful sleep. He had spent the night in the company of Ares and the other Guardians, above a pinnacle that rose up from the floor of the seamount. It was the place where the Guardians gathered when they were off-duty, and Pan had been thrilled to have been asked to join them. For the first time in his life, he had not been afraid as night approached, but despite this, he had not had a peaceful sleep. He had had a dream that troubled him and the memory of it was made worse by dawn's brooding sky and an angry sea, all of which purveyed a strange sense of foreboding.

Good morning, Pan," said Aegyptus. He and his brother Danaus had spent the night close beside the little one. "How was your night?"

"Not good, Aegyptus. "We had a dream. A disturbing dream."

"Was it a nightmare?" inquired Danaus with genuine concern.

Dreams play an important role in the lives of beings, far more so than they do among your kind. This is because whales and dolphins believe that dreams are pathways to the soul, carrying with them memories from their ancestors, glimpses of the future and, perhaps most important of all, messages from God. As I have already explained to you, only half of a being's brain is asleep at any one time, but they have the innate ability to continue the same dream when the half of their brain that was asleep wakes up, and the other half rests. What is more, beings know when they are dreaming and they can sometimes affect the outcome of their dreams, which is a skill that some among your kind possess as well.

It was not surprising that Pan's dream would draw Danaus' interest since he was the more sensitive of the brothers. Ares had warned Danaus many times not to allow his emotions to interfere with his duties, but the head is a poor master of the heart.

Pan thought about Danaus' question for a moment, forcing his mind to retrace its course through his dreamscape. "No, not exactly. We saw the white dolphin swimming through a sea of black, as black as the deeps…"

Aegyptus interrupted him, "Do you know what the deeps look like?" There was skepticism in his voice but it was tempered by a feeling that somehow Pan just might know what he was talking about. Beings often experience what human psychologists refer to as cognitive dissonance. This is because they rarely see just one side to any issue, or hold to a single viewpoint on any issue of significance. They believe that contradicting cognitions force their minds to embrace new beliefs and thereby reduce the dissonance. This is developed to a far greater extent in beings than in man and the best translation for the term they use for this is mindgap.

The source of Aegyptus' mindgap was the fact that the upper edge of the deeps began six hundred feet below the surface, far below the reach of most beings, and certainly below that of a Harbor Porpoise; but then again, Pan was not a typical porpoise. He had traversed two thousand miles of open ocean, alone and unprotected, and Aegyptus wondered whether he just might have been down there.

"There is no need to be rude," said Danaus.

"I am not being rude," retorted Aegyptus but he realized how it might have appeared that way and apologized to Pan. "I am sorry. It is just that the deeps are not a place where I could ever imagine you going. It is beyond the twentieth strata."

Beings understand man's method of measuring ocean depth in feet or fathoms, but they are far more adept at doing so with their earsight. Using this they are able to gauge ocean depths in the same way that they can determine the distance between themselves and another being or object. However, when communicating with other beings they prefer to use a method of describing the depth of the water based on its pressure. They can detect even the most subtle changes in water pressure and since this pressure increases in a linear manner at the equivalent of one atmosphere for each ten meters, or thirty three feet of depth, they often describe ocean depths in terms of the number of different pressure layers below the surface or strata. Therefore, twenty strata makes up the distance from the brightest, clearest crystal blue waters at the surface to the edge of utter blackness, where no sunlight ever reaches, six hundred feet below, and known to beings as the deeps.

"We understand," said Pan. "Your apology is appreciated. And no, we have not been to the deeps, but a Sperm Whale, who was a friend of my mother's, told us what it was like down there."

"Your mother had a friend who was a Sperm Whale?"

"Yes. She helped free him from a fishing net once. They became friends after that." He paused then asked, "Have *you* been down there, Aegyptus?"

The question and the image that it invoked in the Orcas' mind made him shudder, for even this unchallenged warrior of the sea did not like the deeps, and the evil that dwelt therein. "Yes. My brothers and I have all been there. It is a hostile and foreboding place."

All beings are warm blooded, with a normal body temperature the same as that of man and although they have no way to measure water temperature, they can tell whether the waters around them are warmer or colder than their body temperature. Beings tend to stay in waters that feel comfortable to them. While some beings, including Killer Whales, Belugas, and Narwhals can swim without discomfort in waters with a temperature near freezing, most beings prefer water temperature closer to that of their own bodies.

Danaus added, "There are kraken down there with long tentacles and razor sharp beaks that can tear out your heart." (He was referring to Giant Squid.)

"Yes, I know. Sperm Whales like my mother's friend hunt them for food," said Pan.

Aegyptus was impressed that Pan knew about the prey of Sperm Whales. "Did your mother's friend tell you about them?"

Pan nodded. "Yes and he had scars on his back from their suckers."

The pinnacle above which Pan and the Guardians were floating was not far from the edge of the cliff on the western side of the seamount. As Pan spoke, he kept glancing in that direction and he could feel a chill run through his body as he imagined the steep drop into the abyss just beyond it. He looked back at the brothers and said, "In our dream, the white dolphin was being pulled down into the deeps..."

"Pulled down!" exclaimed Danaus.

"By what?" asked Aegyptus.

"I do not know but suddenly he was surrounded by bright light."

"A bright light in the deeps? Then what happened?" queried Danaus, intrigued by the dream.

"The white dolphin swam toward it," said Pan.

"You mean he swam into the light?" asked Danaus.

"Yes. What do you think it means?"

"It means he died," said Ares who had joined them unnoticed.

The thought crushed Pan. "Oh, no! Please do not tell us that."

Ares shrugged. "All I know is that humans associate going into the light with dying."

Aegyptus interjected, "Perhaps, but it could also mean that God sent an angel to save the white dolphin from whatever was pulling him into the deeps."

"Yes. That would be a better meaning," said Pan.

"Yes. Much better," added Danaus.

"We like that meaning for our dream," added Pan.

"Enough of the dream," said Ares. "It is time for the second session of the Gathering to begin. Come, Pan. You should see this."

Pan sighed and tucked the dream into the back of his mind where it would lie quietly, almost forgotten, until another day. Then he joined Ares and Danaus and they swam toward the center of the seamount. Before Aegyptus followed them, he glanced toward the edge of the cliff and muttered to himself, "A hole in the deeps. What nonsense."

The Gathering had finished singing the Hymn of the Ancients by the time that the Guardians and their little charge reached the outermost edge of the spiral. This disappointed Pan but the sight of the river of beings moving in solemn procession to the surface and back again filled him with awe as it had the day before. As Pan took his position beside the three Orcas, close to the edge of the outer spiral and near enough to the surface for him to get his breaths without undue effort, he settled in to watch the proceedings.

At that moment, Dionysus, King of the South Atlantic Ocean, was finishing his opening address to the gathered throng. Like the others on the Sovereign Council, he filled a specific role in the global governance of whalekind. His responsibilities included what your government might call the Secretary of State, or Foreign Minister. He was hovering just above Roundtop beside Hera, while the other five monarchs who comprised the Sovereign Council swam in a slow circle just below them, inside the inner spiral. Like the representatives moving in the double spiral, the Council would occasionally rise to the surface to breathe but they did so in such an unobtrusive manner that it did not disrupt the orderly flow of business. This was the way that the governance of whalekind had been conducted since the time of the Ancients and the procedures rarely deviated from the norm.

Whenever a being addressed the general assembly, they did so from Roundtop. And when they spoke, a silence would fall upon the entire group, but even with that silence, the voice of a smaller being might not be heard at the top and bottom of the spiral. In that case, other beings stationed at strategic positions beside the spiral would relay their message. You might think that this would be confusing by creating an echo effect or a time delay, but beings have an innate ability to absorb a multitude of aural and visual stimuli simultaneously, and parcel these into different cognitive compartments, which their brains prioritize and process instantly.   However, given Dionysus' size, which at ninety feet was nearly equal to Hera, no one was having any difficulty hearing him. With a booming voice, he began his concluding remarks. "And so, it is the considered opinion of the Committee of the Environment that although the level of pollution in the oceans has increased since last year's Godlight, it has not yet reached dangerous levels. Therefore…"

"Therefore, you and your committee are either insane or stupid. Which is it?" asked a booming voice that echoed through the Gathering. It belonged to Poseidon, King of the North Pacific Ocean, and Minister of Defense. He rose up from the circle of the Council and took a position on Roundtop in front of Hera and Dionysus. Unlike Dionysus, whose gray and white body was long, smooth, and sleek, Poseidon's physique was quite the opposite; his purplish-black body was wrinkled and stubby, with a disproportionately large head and an underslung mouth with a narrow rod-like lower jaw filled with rows of conical teeth. At sixty feet in length and one hundred and twenty thousand pounds in weight, he was two-thirds the length of Dionysus and one-half his weight, but what Poseidon lacked in size he made up for in power and ferocity. Although no one at the Gathering would admit it, a fully-grown male Sperm Whale, like Poseidon, was a more ferocious fighter than Dionysus could ever hope to be. Poseidon's preferred prey were Giant Squid who were sixty-feet long with razor sharp beaks that dwelt in the deeps; while the prey of Fin Whales were smaller than raindrops upon the sea, and that made all the difference.

Poseidon's challenge to Dionysus evoked a collective gasp from within the spiral. It rippled though the living mass of beings, as if it were one giant organism upon whose body a stunning blow had been landed. It was followed by a prolonged and uncomfortable silence, made all the more so by the fact that the annual Gathering was known for its adherence to the rules of parliamentary procedure. Generally, it maintained an atmosphere of restraint and courtesy, although it had been less so in recent years, which some said was due to the lessons the younger generations had learned by watching humans. Poseidon's words and actions were so shocking in their intrusion upon this normal state of decorum, that for a moment no one on the Council, including Hera, knew what to say or do.

Regaining her composure, Hera moved forward, in front of Dionysus, who despite his size was a rather timid being, and as such was quite happy to relinquish his position. This brought Hera face to face with Poseidon. As the Moderator, Hera's power came not from her size, but from the respect that her office demanded. And so, as she drifted there above Roundtop, a giant shadow in the dappled sunlight of the cerulean waters, she eyed Poseidon with a coldness that sent a shiver throughout the assembly. After a pause, she replied, "What did you say?" The totality of her being was now focused upon the toothed leviathan floating in her path. But Poseidon did not back down, and for the first time in history, all could sense that the Moderator was about to lose control of the Gathering.

Before replying, Poseidon petulantly rose to the surface and took a deep breath that could last him for up to two hours if needed, which was longer than any other being. This ability traced to his species' hunting behavior that took them down to depths of over nine thousand feet, twenty times deeper than a baleen whale would normally go. This not only gave Poseidon a physical advantage but a psychological one as well over the Moderator. "I was speaking to Dionysus, not you, Queen Hera. Now stay out of this or…"

"Or what?" Hera's booming voice, now at full power, punched through the spiral and rumbled off into the distance toward the edges of the seamount, sending lesser denizens of its warm waters scurrying. She was putting up a good front but deep inside she realized that her position of power was at that moment beginning to erode. To the shock and amazement of the Gathering, a large group of beings broke ranks and swam toward Roundtop, forming a half-circle behind Poseidon. Once formed, they turned and faced the others with menacing solidarity and there was no doubt that what was occurring at that moment was a mutiny.

Poseidon stared at Hera and opened his jaw just wide enough to show his conical teeth. There was no mistaking his message. Out of the corner of her eye, Hera saw the Guardians begin to move toward Roundtop. This group of Killer Whales totaling thirty-six in number was divided into twelve teams of three, including the team of Aegyptus, Danaus, and Ares. It was the Guardians' responsibility to preserve the safety and security of the Gathering in general, and the Sovereign Council in particular, and it was apparent that they were about to challenge Poseidon. However, three teams, including one led by an Orca named Paris suddenly pulled away from the others and joined the beings behind Poseidon, making it clear where their allegiance was. This infuriated Ares and he made an aggressive move in Paris' direction.

Realizing that such a confrontation could only lead to bloodshed, and still believing that the matter could be resolved without acrimony, Hera signaled to Ares to stop. He did and gave the signal to the larger group of Guardians to do likewise, which they did with reluctance. All the while that this was taking place, Pan hovered where Ares had left him, transfixed by what he saw.

Seeing that trouble had been avoided at least for the moment, Hera softened her tone and manner. "It is apparent that something is bothering you, King Poseidon. What it is you want?"

Her attempt at diplomacy was rebuffed. "I want to address the Gathering," he replied harshly.

"Address them about what?" As she asked it, she wondered how many more among the Gathering were sympathetic to Poseidon. She prayed that none were.

"You will hear it with the rest of them," Poseidon snapped back.

Now, before I describe to you what Poseidon said to the Gathering on that fateful day, you must understand one important fact. While the brains of beings are similar to those of humans, they are larger in proportion to their body size and in most cases in their absolute size as well. Of even more significance, however, is that the brains of a whales and dolphins have more association cortex than humans, and it is in this area of the brain where thinking and reason occurs. And whereas the human brain must use a large part of its available processing capacity simply dealing with gravity and balance, whalekind lives in a buoyant world where gravity presents less of an issue. Having said all this, you should also know that the Sperm Whale has the largest brain and greatest processing capacity, of all living creatures, making it the most intelligent being on our entire planet, bar none. Beings are well aware of this and as such whenever a Sperm Whale spoke, they listened.

Before Hera could inquire further as to his intentions, Poseidon turned and in a voice powered by equal parts of anger and adrenalin, he began to speak. "My fellow beings, we are gathered here this week during our hallowed time of Godlight, for many purposes, not least among them is to preserve the legacy of the Ancients. It is those noble beings who laid the foundation for our great society, and to whom we owe everything, our laws, our culture, and indeed our very lives. It is they, in their infinite wisdom, who crafted the Ten Commandments that each of you learned as a child from the elders in your tribe, and which guide us in our daily lives. Like you, I have lived by those laws throughout my life.

"When I reached adulthood, I was proud and honored to have been chosen by my tribe to represent them; first, at our regional Council of the Eastern Mid-Pacific Rim; then at the Pan-Pacific Council; and finally when I became King of the North Pacific and served on this Sovereign Council. I do not have to tell you that the seven days we spend here each year are the most important in our lives. This has been true for beings ever since the beginning of time—and it has never been more so than it is at this moment."

Poseidon's edgy tone and manner troubled Ares. He did not know where Poseidon was going with this speech but he did not like it. He glanced at Hera but once again, she held him back by a subtle wave of her flipper. Despite this, he gave Aegyptus and Danaus a look that said to them, Be ready. It was the nature of the Offshore Killer Whales that the urge to attack their enemies was never very deep below the sleek and shiny surface of their skin, and they had not only the will but the way to do so. Even Poseidon, who was twice their size, would be no match for the swift killing abilities of a pack of Guardians.

Apparently oblivious to this threat or untroubled by it, Poseidon continued, "We now face a turning point in the history of our kind. We are the protectors of Planet Ocean, but it is not ours to do with as we please; rather it has been loaned to us by generations of beings yet unborn. And I say to you that our planet is now threatened with destruction by man, through his wanton disregard for the seas and all the creatures that live in them. He has already contaminated the land and now the evil tentacles of his destruction are reaching out to ruin the seas—by the dumping of toxic wastes that either kill us outright, or accumulate in mothers' milk to kill their first-borns; by over-fishing that robs us of our food supply and leads to death by starvation; by oil-spills that bring black death to our waters and the reckless drilling of the seabed to get even more oil; by noise-pollution, especially from their deathships that each year strands thousands of beings on beaches where they die a slow and painful death.

"And finally by global warming, which is heating our oceans and melting the polar icecaps, thereby increasing the ferocity and frequency of ocean-born storms, as well as further reducing fish stocks. All of these harmful acts, be they intentional or not, are upsetting the delicate balance of our environment and have brought the planet we share to the point of no return; once passed, all that awaits us are disease, desolation, and famine on both land and sea."

He paused to let that imagery sink in, then began again, gathering power and impact as he went. "Make no mistake, we are on the eve of destruction, and soon there will be no turning back. And so, I cry out to you to join with me, and those like me, who will not stand by and let this happen. To us has fallen the mantle of responsibility to put an end to the wanton carelessness of man. To us has fallen the destiny of saving Planet Ocean. To us has fallen the salvation of whalekind."

Poseidon paused once more to let their hearts and minds catch up with his words. Then he began again, slowly and with intensity in his words that rumbled through the water like the aftershocks of an undersea earthquake, "My fellow beings, listen…" The Gathering was already quiet, but many now held their breath a little longer instead of rising up to the surface, so as not to miss what he was about to say. "Listen…" he said once more, and absolute silence filled the seas about them. "Do you hear it?—It is the sound of the voices of the Ancients. They are calling to us from the past; down through all the generations of our kind, over millions and millions of years. They are saying, 'Rise Up! Rise up and take a stand against man the destroyer.' And if you do, as God is our witness, one hundred Gatherings from now, or one hundred times one hundred Gatherings from now, your descendants will look back and remember *this* day as the defining moment in the history of all whalekind: the day when each of you shook off your apathy and said, This *can* not be. This *must* not be. This *will* not be!"

Many among his audience were ready to express their support for him, to embrace his words and the thoughts behind them, but he would not let them—at least not yet. By the gestures of his flippers and expression on his face, he held back their response. He wanted them to experience an emotional upheaval, the likes of which they had never known: one that would cement their commitment to his cause and seal the fate of their common enemy, mankind. And the longer he held them back, the greater their response would be.

"Throughout our history, every being has had one sacred birthright that no other creature can take away from him or her. It is as fundamental to life as the food that provides sustenance to our bodies and the words of God that nourish our souls. It is the most noble of causes for which one being can lay down his life for another. It is simply, freedom! Freedom of the seas; freedom from persecution; freedom to go where we choose; and freedom to live in harmony with nature. We are on the verge of losing these freedoms, and once we let them go, they will be lost forever.

"My fellow beings, hear my warning. The evil that we face today does not swim among us. It is a clear and present danger but not from others of our own kind or the kraken. It is the devil on two legs who walks along the other side of the surf line, and looks out to sea with the seeds of our destruction in his hands. This is why I needed to speak with you this morning. From the bottom of my heart, I now ask you to join with me in demanding that the Sovereign Council issues a declaration of war upon mankind." There was an audible rumble through the entire Gathering. He waited until it quieted and then added, "May God have mercy on us all!"

For a long, lingering moment, a deathly silence fell upon the sea. The entire spiral appeared to be in a state of suspended animation, and those who needed to breathe did so with languid movements, their eyes revealing a stupor that had come over them. Even the quantum of little fish that usually darted through and around the spiral had disappeared. All was still, and somber, as silent as death.

Finally, Hera tried to regain control of the Gathering and respond to Poseidon's war cry. While her nature was not normally aggressive, on that day, at that moment, she broke with her character, and rose to the occasion. She swam over to where Poseidon hung in the shimmering blue light and drew within a few yards of him; face to face, two giants of the deep in hostile confrontation. Then in a deep voice that thundered down to the sea bottom and back to the surface, catching every being in its resonance, she said, "There—will—be—no—war!" Then tilting her head slightly to look him eye-to-eye, she added, "And for you to want a war with mankind, indicates that *you* are either insane or stupid."

Hera's challenge prompted another collective series of gasps and groans that echoed across the gathering and many beings now began to edge away from the spiral, in anticipation of the death match that must surely follow. But Poseidon remained calm. Instead of reacting in the way that might have been expected given his usually quick temper, he smiled at Hera, but it was an evil smile. "Madam Moderator, you know neither to be true. Moreover, I know that you share my views on the careless and wanton actions of man that I have given voice to this day."

His conciliatory demeanor caught her by surprise and she had to adjust her tone, which gave him the edge. "Yes, I do, Poseidon, but war with man is not the answer. It will only bring death and destruction upon us, and it will cast a great darkness upon the seas forever."

She had fallen into his trap. "Then, Madam Moderator, we are doomed either way." Turning back to the Gathering, he said, "My fellow beings, you have heard the Moderator admit that we are doomed. And I say let us not go meekly into that darkness. Let us go into battle with right on our side, and if we must die, let us do so bravely with one word upon our dying lips—Freedom, Freedom. Freedom!"

Hera could feel the rising tide of support for Poseidon. She knew she was losing the battle of words, just as surely as whalekind would lose the battle with man, and as a last resort, she offered something that caught even Poseidon by surprise. "What if we were to break the Tenth Commandment? What if we tried reason over rebellion?"

Poseidon snorted, sending a burst of air bubbles racing toward the surface that lay above them like blue lead. "Come now, Madam, do you really think that after all he has done to us and to our planet, man will now have a change of heart simply because we *speak* with him? Humans began speaking to each other one hundred thousand years ago and is their world any less hostile today than it was then? No, Madam. No. Humans are base and vile creatures who only respond to force, and we will show them a force far greater than they have ever know until all the seas run red with their blood."

"And ours," added Hera coldly.

Poseidon steeled himself. "Then so be it." He turned away from her and addressed the entire Gathering once more, shouting out two simple and yet formidable words, "To war!" Then without uttering another sound, he swam into the gathering shadows of the onrushing night, with his legion of followers, including Paris and his half-brother, Orion, both Guardians and their respective teams, following close behind.

Poseidon's call for war would soon echo around the world, sending fear into the hearts of every being, and plunging their souls into darkness. Within the weeks and months to come, it would create two global warring factions; those who chose to join with Poseidon and rise up against man, and those who saw it as an act of collective suicide. And although he did not realize it yet, drifting there, lost among the confusion and the chaos, a little Harbor Porpoise named Pan was about to become an unlikely hero in the battle to save whalekind. And what a battle it would be.

CHAPTER FOUR

The Gathering Darkness

"We do not understand," brooded Pan. "What did King Poseidon mean when he said he would wage *war* on mankind?" Pan was floating beside Ares near the surface on the crowding swells that gave hint to a coming squall. High overhead the sky had grown dark and threatening, and without the sun to light it, the waters around them were now a steel gray, making it difficult to see beyond the tight circle of Guardians congregating around them. It was a rather appropriate change in weather given what had happened hours earlier at the Gathering—a session that would come to be known in the grim days ahead as The Darkening.

"Just what he said," replied Ares.

With Pan and Ares were Aegyptus and Danaus. Behind them were the twenty-four other Orcas who had refused to join Poseidon's rebellion. Obvious by their absence, however, were the nine Orcas, including Paris, who had followed Poseidon when he stormed away from Roundtop. They, along with hundreds of other beings, had followed Poseidon out into the open ocean in a southeasterly direction and now these loyal Orcas, led by Ares, were all that Hera and the remaining members of the Sovereign Council had left to try to maintain some semblance of order over the beings who had refused to join the rebellion.

"But what does it mean?" said Pan who was more confused than frightened.

Ares did not answer. Instead he swam away to talk with the Council.

"What does what mean?" asked Danaus, frowning at his brother's rudeness.

With big eyes, Pan replied, "War."

Both Danaus and Aegyptus were startled. "Do you mean that you do not know what war is?" asked Aegyptus.

Pan shook his head. By the look on the faces of his two companions, he sensed that it was something that he should have known and a flush of embarrassment swept over him. Beings are quite susceptible to embarrassment. Unlike humans, there is no visible sign of it, but by using their earsight, beings can tell when one of their kind is in emotional distress.

"Do you mean that your mother never told you about war?" asked Aegyptus.

Unlike Guardians, it was not unusual for the average being like Pan to be unfamiliar with the term. While each kingdom had an army of marines, its primary purpose was to protect its subjects from the kraken that roamed the seas and lurked in its deeps. There had never been a regional, let alone global, war between beings in the history of whalekind. The disputes that arose were almost always dealt with within a given tribe, or between the chieftains of neighboring tribes and those which could not be so resolved were brought to the Gathering where the Council adjudicated the dispute. Their word was final and no one had ever challenged the Council's supreme authority—until now.

"No," said Pan wishing he had never asked the question.

Danaus, who was becoming a mentor to Pan, could sense the growing distress in him and replied in a sympathetic tone, "War is a great evil invented by man. It occurs when one group of humans wants to take something away from another, and they do so by force."

"You mean they fight with each other?"

"Yes. They fight and die in great numbers."

"By the thousands, sometimes millions," added Aegyptus.

Pan thought about it and then replied, "A quantum of dead children of God. That is very sad."

"Yes—it is," said Danaus. It did not surprise him that Pan was having difficulty absorbing the enormity of what had transpired earlier that day.

"Why does their faith in God not stop them?" probed Pan.

"Because most humans no longer believe in God," answered Danaus.

"And those who do, think he is on their side when they go to war," added Aegyptus with disgust. "It is quite revealing how a supposedly intelligent race does not want God in their schools, or public places, or government buildings, but they always seem to want him by their side when they march into battle. And as the bodies pile up, they keep on praying to him, asking for his protection and his help in winning the war, while their enemy does exactly the same thing. Such insanity is a reward unto itself."

"Is that why Poseidon believes that breaking the ancient code of silence between beings and man will not succeed—because mankind no longer believes in God?" It was clear that the idea troubled the little being, who up until that day thought that all intelligent beings on the planet believed in God."

"Either they do not believe in God," replied Aegyptus, "or if they do, they worship him through many different faiths, and disdain others who see him through different eyes. Some of the bloodiest and cruelest wars in their history have been what they call Holy Wars."

"Why does God not stop this?" pleaded Pan.

Danaus replied, "I do not know. Perhaps one day you can ask him."

For a long moment, Pan fell silent as the image of piles of dead human bodies weighed on his mind. His mother had taught him never to trust humans. She said they were a selfish and untrustworthy breed who often harmed beings, but in all her teachings, she had never once mentioned the concept of war. Then he asked, "How does Poseidon intend to fight with man?"

Danaus answered. "Ares thinks Poseidon intends to make the oceans unsafe for humans by killing them at the beaches when they swim, and by sinking the boats that venture out beyond the breakwaters of every seaside city and town."

Aegyptus, who was growing impatient with the conversation interjected, "I never liked Poseidon and it is clear that my distrust of him was well-founded. I think he is just crazy enough to send beings on suicide missions to foul the rudders of their deathships. He knows that no matter how big and powerful it is a ship without a rudder is useless."

"You mean like a society without God?" said Pan.

Danaus and Aegyptus nodded. Pan had put a period on the sentence of man's inhumanity to man, and the thought that Poseidon was now about to draw whalekind into that insanity was too horrible to envision.

"Pan," said Ares as he returned from his meeting with the Council and interrupted their discussion. "Queen Hera wants to meet with you."

"Me?" *Oh dear,* thought Pan. *She must think we have brought this trouble upon them.*

Ares looked at his brothers and commanded, "You two join us."

Together the three Guardians and the Harbor Porpoise swam over to where the Sovereign Council was gathered. Pan noticed that all the Council members were present except two: Poseidon, for obvious reasons, and Eris, which no one bothered to explain. He did not think it his place to ask. The lesson that Ares had taught him about not talking so much was having an effect, but Ares was too preoccupied to notice. The mood of the Council was somber, in keeping with the surrounding seas that had now grown cold and dark. Hera motioned for Pan to approach her, which he did. She could tell that Pan was frightened and she sought to put him at ease. "You need not be afraid little one."

Pan nodded and replied, "Thank you Madam."

With a deep sigh that could be heard and felt by the others including Pan, Hera began to speak. "Pan, as you can appreciate, the Council and I have much to do as we prepare for what lies ahead. As you have said, this growing darkness was foretold by the Legend of the Light, and echoed in the words that the angel said to Leto when he appeared in her dream."

"Yes, Madam," replied Pan with an obvious tremor in his voice.

The sight of the anxious but polite little being hovering before her in the growing shadows touched the mighty leviathan's heart and for a moment she wanted to reach out and comfort him, but this was neither the time nor the place to do so. "As you must have realized by now, Poseidon and his followers intend to kill humans in protest to their destruction of our planet. It will take him many months, perhaps even another Godlight cycle, before Poseidon is capable of forming an army large enough to embark on his war against man." She lowered her voice, "I pray to God that we will be able to stop him before then"—as she invoked God's name, the words of Aegyptus flashed through Pan's mind. He thought that Poseidon was probably calling on the support of God as well, and Pan could not help but wonder whose side God would be on, if either—"but in case we fail, the Council and I must prepare for the worst case where mankind unleashes their weapons upon us."

Pan nodded. "We understand, Madam Moderator." He was about to ask whether there was anything that he could do but he resisted the temptation as he felt that it would be a stupid thing to ask by someone so small and so unimportant in a world poised on the verge of intra- and inter-species warfare. He was wrong.

"Pan, there is something that we must ask of you."

Pan was stunned. "Yes, Madam. We would be honored to help but anything we can do would not amount to more than a grain of sand before the oncoming tide."

"We shall see, little one. We shall see," She stiffened. "What we are asking of you will be difficult and dangerous—and may be deadly."

Pan swallowed hard. *Oh my,* he thought. *Maybe this is my punishment for what I did twenty years ago.* "We understand and we are ready to give our all."

Hera smiled a sad smile. She was pleased that she had not underestimated this brave little being, and the thought had crossed her mind that in his safe passage across the open ocean he had been borne on the back of God. "Good. As soon as you have recovered from your long journey here, you will leave the Kingdom and head to the waters off Sinclair Cay." She glanced at the Guardians, "Ares, Aegyptus and Danaus will accompany you," then she looked back at Pan. "Once there, you will allow yourself to be captured by the men who collect beings for the oceanarium where Apollo is being held captive. It is called Oceania."

"A prison by any other name is still a prison," snarled Dionysus.

Hera silenced him with a look.

"How will we find these men?" asked Pan.

"You will let them find you. Their capture ship patrols the deep waters over the Tongue of the Ocean. Ares knows where it is. He has been there and seen this ship take beings prisoner, never to be seen again."

Pan gave Ares a nervous look. He was rewarded with a reassuring nod. Hera continued, "Once you are captured and taken to the oceanarium you must find the white dolphin and tell him what has happened here. If he is indeed the Chosen One, as we all hope and believe he is, he will find a way to escape, taking you with him." She paused, and then added in a somber tone, "But if he is not who we think he is, then you will stay there with him until you die."

A thousand questions flooded through the Harbor Porpoise's brain but one question took pre-eminence. It was the obvious one. "Why would these men want to catch us? We are but a simple being, possessed of no great beauty, skill or intellect. Surely, we are not a specimen that they would want? "

Hera smiled a gentle smile. She was growing to like this self-effacing, little being. "If you act as you normally would, simply skimming along the bow wave of their capture ship that is true. They will ignore you. But you must do more than that. You must do whatever it takes to attract the attention of these men, including ramming their boat if need be. Remember they are humans; they are susceptible to guile and effrontery."

Pan was about to debate this point but chose not to. If this was to be his destiny, then so be it.

"Will you do this, Pan?"

For the first time in his life since his act of betrayal that night in the estuary twenty long years ago, Pan now knew why God had put him on Planet Ocean. It was not to kill Apollo as he thought he had done; rather, it was to save him. All his fears and worries drained away. He knew what he had do to and he would do it, or die trying. Inspired by the nobility of this cause, he straightened his body, glanced at Ares and his brothers, then looked back at Hera and said, in a firm and steadfast voice, "Yes. We will."

Hera nodded her massive head in a slow and thoughtful acknowledgement of Pan's courage. There was also a sigh of relief from the other members of Council. As impressed as Hera was, she did not allow herself to believe that the mission she was sending Pan on had any more than a slim chance of succeeding. There were so many 'what ifs' associated with it; what if Pan did not make it to the Bahamas safely; what if he was not able to get captured; what if he was unable to make contact with the white dolphin; what if the white dolphin was not the Chosen One; what if they were unable to escape; and on and on…It was too much to think about. It would be what God wanted it to be. Nothing more, nothing less.

"We will leave in the morning," said Pan.

"No. That would not be wise," cautioned Hera. "I want you to stay here for the remainder of Godlight. You need to be strong and rested."—She glanced at his sides now grown lean by his journey—"And quite frankly, your body could use a little more fat."

"Yes Madam," said Pan. "We suppose we could use a little more rest and food." Even through the emotion of that moment, the thought of gaining weight did not bother him one bit.

"Good," answered Hera. She then motioned to Ares to approach her. It pleased Ares that the little one had been polite and had not interrupted the Moderator. This encouraged him that Pan would also listen to him on their long and dangerous journey. Once he joined Pan she said, "Ares, please see to it that Pan gets the food and rest he needs."

"Yes, Madam Moderator."

Then she bid them leave, and without further adieu, Pan and the Guardians left the Council and headed back toward the pinnacle for the night.

"How long will it take us to reach the Bahamas?" Pan asked with characteristic enthusiasm as he swam beside the Orcas.

"Three weeks maybe four," answered Ares. Ares knew that he and his brothers could have covered the sixteen hundred miles between the Kingdom of the Ancients and the Bahamas in half that time but he also knew that in the best of condition Pan could not keep up with such a pace. Even with five more days of rest, Pan would still be feeling the lingering effects of his long journey to the Gathering and despite the urgency about their mission, Ares knew he must not tire Pan unduly, since without him Hera's plan would not succeed. The reason was that unlike the smaller members of the dolphin family and porpoises, man had placed a moratorium upon the capture of Killer Whales, and as such, none of the Guardians could accomplish what Pan had been asked to do, even though any one of them would have gladly accepted the mission.

"That long? Well, we suppose we shall have to make allowance for how big and slow you fatboys are," said Pan with a mischievous grin.

In response to Pan's jibe, Ares gave the other two Orcas a knowing look and with a powerful down thrust of their broad flukes, they hurtled off into the growing shadows, leaving the cheeky little Harbor Porpoise alone. In an instant, he zoomed off after them, all the while hoping that what they said about kraken never venturing onto the seamount during the Gathering was true.

As Pan and the Guardians took their places above the pinnacle, night fell with an air of inevitability. The sun lingered in its journey across the sky; there were no shadows on the ocean to mark its movement or give measure to the passage of time. Near its journey's end, the sun hesitated for an instant on the horizon, as if reluctant to leave the seas unprotected by its comforting light, and then it dropped down below the waterline, and was gone. At the instant of the sun's disappearance, there was a pale green flash in the sky, which your kind calls St. Elmo's Fire, but beings know it as Angel's Breath, and after it had passed, the cold chill of darkness reclaimed the vast ocean wilderness once more.

In turn, the moon seemed slow to rise and weak in spirit that night, as if it knew the world of beings was about to change forever. After it gained its place among the stars and cast its glow upon shimmering ocean surface, two large bodies appeared, moving in unison, out beyond the edge of the seamount where the bottom dropped away into the deeps. One was King Dionysus, the Fin Whale, and with him, rubbing her lithe body against his, was the Sei Whale, Queen Eris.

Despite the fact that Dionysus was eighty feet long and Eris was fifteen feet shorter, the act that they were about to perform was one that was normally reserved for daylight when even in their aroused state they would have had a better chance of detecting the approach of kraken.

However, daylight lovemaking was not an option for them, as their liaison was an illicit one. Both had mates back in their home waters; his off the coast of New England and hers in the South Pacific off New Zealand, and what was worse, while Dionysus was smitten with the sleek and supple female moving beguilingly by his side, there was less of seduction and more of sedition in her heart.

"Tell me, Dionysus, what did Hera say this afternoon? Please," she whispered to him as her flipper brushed his abdomen.

"If you had been there you would have heard for yourself. And by the way where were you?" he asked not caring as his state of arousal neared a peak.

She ignored his question. "Please, I want to know," she said in a half moan that broke down whatever little resistance he had left.

"Oh, all right if you must know, Hera asked Pan to travel to the Bahamas. Now can we do this?" he begged.

But she arched her body away from him, which served to excite him more. "Why is she sending him there?"

Dionysus halted and hung there at the surface, a giant shadow with the tiny rays of moonlight dancing across his smooth gray back. He then told her about Pan's mission, leaving out no detail, and answered her remaining questions with a mixture of restrained excitement and mild annoyance. When she had learned all she needed to know she gave herself to him, and the waters roiled as they completed their nocturnal union. When they were done, she rubbed her head against his with a gentleness that belied her evil intentions, and then they parted, each returning to the safety of the seamount separately, to avoid giving away their secret. Eris told him that she would see him at the Gathering in the morning but it was a lie. He would never see her again.

The next morning was the third day of Godlight and despite the emotional turbulence of the previous day, all was as it should have been at the Gathering; or at least it seemed that way at first. As a result of the actions of Poseidon, Hera had asked all the representatives to remain at the seamount for another seven days beyond the end of Godlight to allow the Council to formulate their strategy before sending beings back to their home territories. All agreed with one exception, the Sei Whale named Eris, who was nowhere to be found.

"Has anyone seen Queen Eris?" asked Hera.

One by one, the Council members all replied that they had not seen her in two days. Dionysus said so as well, but of course, it was a lie. For one split second, Dionysus worried that Eris had not made it back to the safety of the seamount after their mating. *Maybe the kraken took her,* he thought. *Oh, God, I hope not. I should have escorted her back.*

But as he was wrestling with the mindgap that his act had engendered, there came a small voice from nearby. It was that of Pan who said, "We saw Queen Eris this morning."

"Where?" snapped Dionysus with almost enough concern to give him away.

Pan was taken aback by the intensity of Dionysus' question and wondered if he had seen something he was not supposed to. "We were gazing toward the edge of the cliff at the pinnacle when we saw her swim over the edge and disappear into the deeps."

"She left?" asked Hera and Dionysus at the same time.

"Yes," replied Pan.

"In what direction was she headed?" asked Hera.

"To the southwest," replied Pan.

"Not the southeast?" probed Hera, as that was the direction that Poseidon had taken.

Pan shook his head, "No. Southwest. Why may we ask?"

"Because when she did not show up for our Council session yesterday I surmised that she had already left to join Poseidon. And if so, she would have headed southeast, toward the tip of Africa."

"Why would she?" inquired Dionysus barely masking his guilt. "She does not share his views."

Hera eyed Dionysus with suspicion, "Whether she does or does not is irrelevant. She will follow him because they are lovers."

Dionysus was stunned. A flush of anger and embarrassment overtook him. "What! I mean, really?"

Ignoring Dionysus, Hera called the Council to order and as Pan swam away from them, he could not help but notice the angry stare that Dionysus gave him. Brushing it off, Pan joined Ares and his brothers at the edge of the gathering spiral. He promptly forgot about Eris but one day he would remember the look Dionysus gave him with perfect clarity.

Despite her doubts, Hera was wrong and Pan was right. Eris had headed off in a southwesterly direction. Sei Whales are among the fastest of all whales in the sea and with a four-day head start before Pan would leave for the Bahamas, Eris was racing toward a rendezvous in the Gulf of Mexico, on the orders of none other than her lover and co-conspirator, King Poseidon.

CHAPTER FIVE

Polaris

On the eve of the third day of Godlight, far to the south and west of the Kingdom of the Ancients, the white dolphin swam out of a large, sand-bottomed lagoon and entered a concrete canal at the oceanarium called Oceania. The huge complex was situated on picturesque Sinclair Cay, a small island in the Bahamas located just north of the Island of Andros. After the white dolphin left lagoon, a young, blond-haired woman standing on the edge of the waterway closed a gate behind him. The Cay was covered in palm trees and other lush tropical flora, and it was bordered by long stretches of fine, white sand beaches. To the west, the shallow, turquoise waters of the Great Bahamas Bank teemed with tiny fish of all colors and shapes, while on its eastern shore, the bottom dropped straight down ten thousand feet, into the foreboding deeps of the underwater canyon called the Tongue of the Ocean. It was in these waters, which were enriched with nutrients by upswelling currents from the ocean floor, where large pelagic game fish lurked, such as the Blue Marlin, a one-ton beast that drew anglers from all over the world. And, of course, there were kraken.

Judging by the number of your kind who traveled to Oceania each year, it was a veritable paradise, where the more affluent sought to get away from the tedium and worries of their humdrum existence. The oceanarium adjacent to the hotel complex was everything its owners intended it to be, providing their patrons with an opportunity to experience the beauty and mystery of the oceans without having to venture upon them, or in them, and face the dangers that lay therein.

Located at one end of Oceania's sprawling property were numerous lagoons filled with tropical fish, sharks, stingrays and other sea creatures. These were surrounded by overhanging boardwalks, and interlaced with acrylic underwater tunnels through which visitors could literally walk on the bottom of the sea floor. There were also five enormous swimming pools, some with man-made surf, or waterslides and waterfalls; a free-flowing river that meandered through the palm trees; and last but not least, a gigantic concrete tank surrounded on three sides by a high-walled stadium.

The open end of the stadium faced the ocean where the tank had a glass wall that had no seams or metal frames, giving the audience the illusion that it was part of the ocean itself. There were numerous other deep-water tanks and all were linked with the enormous sand-bottomed lagoon, which the white dolphin had just exited. Connecting the tanks and lagoon was a series of channels controlled by stainless steel gates through which the 'stars' of the oceanarium, its whales and dolphins, could be herded when it was time for them to perform.

In addition to being a giant sea world designed to entertain and educate its visitors, Oceania also had a marine research center at the other end of the island, where scientists from all over the world came to study marine life. All in all, even the most persnickety among you would say that the oceanarium was a clean, bright, modern, and well-run complex that served as a magnificent microcosm of the Seven Seas. And you would also most likely conclude that for all the creatures great and small, fish and mammal, swimming or crawling in its sparkling waters, it was a safe and comfortable, if confined existence. However, for the beings held captive there, it was a prison, where they lived tormented, cheerless lives, and died before their time, all the while longing for the freedom many once knew but never would again.

It is remarkable that your kind who value freedom above all else are so quick to deprive other sentient beings of theirs. Ponder this the next time you gawk at a Killer Whale or Bottlenose Dolphin begging for a handout of fish in such a demeaning water show. Ponder it and be ashamed.

The white dolphin swimming through the waterways of the oceanarium under the close supervision of the young blond woman, was different from the other beings held captive there, in more ways than just skin color. When he was captured in the waters of the Tongue of the Ocean five years earlier, he appeared to be a big and strong but otherwise ordinary Bottlenose Dolphin with the characteristic dark gray cape. However, it soon became apparent that he was no ordinary dolphin for two reasons; first, the other beings in the oceanarium acted strangely around him. It was as if they were in awe of him, even though he did nothing to court their favor; in fact, just the opposite for he tended to keep to himself. And second, after his arrival his skin began to turn white, which was unheard of for his species; and, even more remarkable, was a small, purple birthmark that became visible just behind his left eye. It was in the shape of a five-pointed star and upon seeing it; his human handlers gave him the name Polaris. It stuck with both the humans and beings alike. (What the humans could not know, of course, was that the new arrival had not given his real name to the other beings and with the exception of one Short-finned Pilot Whale, he barely even acknowledged their presence.)

"Polaris, how was your day with the children?" asked the Short-finned Pilot Whale as the white dolphin passed through the last of the gates and re-entered the large tank beside the stadium where the beings were kept when they were not performing. It contained millions of gallons of seawater, which was constantly replenished after it had been filtered to remove any dangerous chemicals, parasites, or bacteria. The walls of the sixty-foot deep tank were concrete that had been made to look like black volcanic rock, with a white sand bottom that was intended to give the appearance of a cove in a tropical sea.

For the first month after the then gray dolphin arrived his handlers tried in vain to get him to do the simple tasks and tricks that formed the foundation of their training regimen. He refused to respond to even their most basic techniques, and this seemed to have a negative effect upon the other beings who started to resist their training. It was as if they were trying to emulate him. As a result, the humans reassigned Polaris to the dolphin experience lagoon, or DEL, where people swam with the dolphins. When his skin turned completely white, the owners of the resort saw the potential of this transformation, and they once again tried to get him to perform in the show. He still refused to cooperate. Eventually they gave up and sent him back to the DEL, where they now could at least charge more money for anyone wanting to swim with a white dolphin.

For a while, Polaris spent the greater part of each day in the shallow waters of the DEL, where he seemed to have a special way with the children. This continued for many months until one day, when the parents of a little boy afflicted by what your doctors call autism, brought him to swim with Polaris. And from that point on, nothing was ever the same for Polaris or the oceanarium, because after one session with the white dolphin, the little boy showed dramatic improvement. Upon leaving the lagoon, the child hugged his mother for the first time ever, and soon thereafter began to talk in coherent sentences, stunning everyone.

Word of this spread and soon the resort had a waiting list several months long of parents wanting to bring their similarly afflicted children to swim with the white dolphin. And in every case, improvement was noted, more so in some than in others, but always enough that the parents left with their hearts overflowing with love for Polaris, and gratitude to the owners of Oceania. The owners too seemed to have been positively affected by the white dolphin for they now no longer charged anything for these sessions; however, they limited them strictly to mentally or physically challenged children. Polaris clearly loved these children and relished his days with them. In their own way, they were prisoners like him; locked behind the unyielding nature of their affliction, just as he was imprisoned behind the rigid walls of glass and concrete.

"My day was fine, Haemon" replied Polaris as he swam over to where the Pilot Whale was drifting with his bowhead pointing into in the strong current from one of the tank's large inlet valves.

"I just love the smell of the open ocean that comes through these pipes. Do you, Polaris? Do you love it?" asked Haemon with wistfulness in his voice.

"Yes," replied Polaris with a gentleness that showed he understood the longing in his friend's voice.

"Do you think that we will ever be free again to swim in bluewater?"

"Perhaps," replied Polaris.

Haemon moved slightly away from the pipe and murmured, "Yes, perhaps." Unlike Polaris, Haemon had been in the oceanarium almost all his life, after having been captured as a baby and taken away from his mother over thirty years earlier. "Of course, you get to swim every day in the large lagoon that must look and feel even more like the real ocean than does this tank."

"Neither is a good substitute for the real thing, Haemon."

"No. I suppose not." He paused but then his tone brightened when he asked, "Was Trainer Quinn there? And was she wearing that one-piece red bathing suit? I like that suit. It is pretty."

Haemon was referring to the young, blond-haired woman who had opened the gates for Polaris when he returned from the lagoon. She was in charge of the DEL. Even though Haemon knew her full name to be Caitlin Quinn, whenever beings refer to humans among themselves, they always attach a short descriptive title to the person's surname. And they never use their given name. As Haemon said her name, he closed his eyes and his mind locked on the image of her tanned, athletic figure moving in an undulating rhythm through the crystal clear waters, with her arms outstretched before, her lithe legs locked together and her long blond hair streaming back across her shoulders. For obvious reasons, there can never be any physical love between beings and humans, but that does not stop some beings from feeling strong emotional attachments to humans, or from appreciating their beauty.

"Yes, she was there," replied Polaris. "And she was wearing your favorite bathing suit."

Dr. Caitlin Quinn was a veterinarian by training, specializing in marine mammals, but she was a dolphin trainer by choice, and she was well liked among the beings. But to Polaris, there was something else about her; something beyond her physical beauty and gracefulness on land and in the water; and her charming ways with both beings and the children who swam with them—something special that he could sense and that he had only seen in one other human before. In some unfathomable way, she seemed to know that beings understood human language.

"You are so lucky to be able to spend your days with her and the children in the lagoon. At times it must feel like you are no longer a captive, does it not?" asked Haemon.

"Yes, it does, but remember, Haemon, it is a prison just the same," Polaris replied. As soon as he said it, he regretted it because it allowed another being to enter the conversation.

"Prison, hah!" snorted Erebus, a Long-finned Pilot Whale. "While you are out there in the warm, shallow waters of the lagoon letting the disgusting little brats fondle you, we are in the stadium tank performing stupid tricks that are humiliating and hurtful to our spirit." He paused then added, "I would kill them all if given the chance, the young ones included."

"Oh do shut up, Erebus," said Haemon. "We grow weary of your constant complaining."

During the five years leading up to this part of my story, Polaris had maintained a cordial but distant relationship with the other beings at Oceania. The one exception was Haemon with whom Polaris had become very close. While many of the other beings were bothered by Polaris' aloofness and his refusal to perform in the oceanarium, most left him alone. However, Erebus did not. He disliked Polaris intensely and made no pretense about it. Over the months leading up to the event, which I am about to describe, Erebus' hostility towards the white dolphin had increased to the point that it had now become apparent even to their human handlers, including Trainer Quinn.

"Who are you telling to shut up?" said Erebus arching his back in the threatening posture characteristic of his species.

At twenty-one feet and weighing five thousand pounds, Haemon was smaller and much older than his cousin with the long fins was, and by his nature, he was much gentler. Accordingly, he responded in his usual way to such a threat from his fellow Pilot Whale. "I apologize, Erebus. Please calm down." He spoke in a soothing tone and lowered his head in the manner that normally appeased the bully whale. But this time it did not.

"I am sick of you and your pathetic whining about bluewater. You disgust me. You are a disgrace to whalekind," replied Erebus. He began to swim toward Haemon, speaking in an aggressive manner. "You will never feel the embrace of the open ocean again, do you hear me!" As he closed on Haemon, it appeared that he was going to butt him with his large head. But before Erebus could make contact with Haemon, Polaris swam between them, which brought Erebus to an abrupt stop. "Get out of my way, Polaris," he growled.

Even though Polaris was a full-grown Bottlenose Dolphin, he was still only half the length and one fifth the mass of Erebus, and when he interjected himself between the two Pilot Whales, gasps could be heard from the other beings in the tank. The only beings who might have been a match for Erebus were Killer Whales, but there were currently none at Oceania. In recent years, there had been several incidents of Killer Whales at other oceanariums attacking their handlers, which had led to a moratorium on the capture of Killer Whales. Oceania's owners believed that it was only a matter of time until such a tragedy occurred at their facility, so they sold their three Orcas to an aquarium in the Netherlands; one of whom died in the transfer; a not uncommon occurrence.

"Let it go, Erebus," said Polaris with an air of calmness in his voice that belied the situation.

But Polaris' tone and manner had an inflammatory effect on Erebus. "You think you are so much better than us. Refusing to tell us your real name and going around with your beak in the air, answering to the name the humans gave you: Polaris, the high and mighty North Star. Hah! If you were as smart as they say you are, you would know that the Greeks called the pole star Cynosura, which means tail of the dog—that is what you are, nothing but a tail to the human dogs," he said it in such a booming voice that echoed off the walls of the tank. Then he lowered his voice and in a sinister tone added, "Move, Polaris—or die."

But the white dolphin did not move. Instead, he hung there, just below the surface, as night fell on Sinclair Cay, casting the tank into shadows. "I do not want to fight with you, Erebus," Polaris said quietly. There was a certain something in his voice that gave Erebus pause. It was the quiet strength mixed with a hint of danger lurking behind the calm facade that unnerved the larger being. For a moment, nothing happened as Erebus and Polaris' eyes were locked upon each other in a stare cold enough to freeze the tank. The tension built to a point where the witnesses to the stand-off were certain that blood would soon flow. Suddenly the underwater lights flicked on in the tank, and shafts of green light penetrated the gloom, casting an eerie glow around the white dolphin.

And then, to the astonishment of all, Erebus seemed to have a sudden change of heart. He began to tremble; a stream of bubbles gurgled out of his blowhole, and he defecated into the water, much to the disgust of the other beings who pulled away. Whales and dolphins always have to eliminate their wastes in the water of course, but decorum dictates that they do not do it in the presence of others. Polaris did not move or say anything more. Then abruptly, Erebus turned away and shimmy-swam to the far side of the tank, where he collapsed against the rocky sidewall. As he did, he kept muttering something to himself over and over again, "His eyes. Did you see his eyes?" But no one seemed to hear or care.

After it was over, Haemon swam up to Polaris and asked, "How did you do that?"

"Do what?"

"What you just did to Haemon."

"It was nothing," replied Polaris in a sober tone.

"Nothing? Like the way you cure the children? Is that nothing too?" demanded Haemon.

Polaris did not answer and for the moment Haemon let it go. But despite Polaris' protestations these things *were* something, something remarkable and noble, and yet, even in their goodness, they were somehow troubling to all those who witnessed them.

Several hours later, in the quiet of the night, when all the beings were resting in a half-sleep, a shadow moved in silence across the tank to the corner where Polaris always rested alone. In the dim half-light of the underwater lights set in the rock face of the walls, Polaris could see that it was Haemon who was approaching him.

"Polaris," whispered Haemon trying not to wake the others but there was no need for him to do so as the steady hum of the motors and filters in a pump house adjacent to the tank, and the sound of the water rushing through the inlet valves, masked any sound that Haemon made.

"Yes, my friend. What is it?"

Haemon swam up close beside the white dolphin and said in a whisper, "Erebus was right, was he not?"

"About what?"

"When he said that I would never swim in the ocean again."

Polaris looked at his friend with compassion. He thought about it for a long while then answered, "No, Haemon. He was not right. You will swim in the ocean again."

Haemon brightened. "I will! Are you certain?"

"Yes. I am certain. As certain as I am that I will return to my nostos."

Nostos is the name given by the ancient Greeks of your kind to the desire to return home to the place of one's birth. It is a life-force that all beings feel deeply in their soul. No matter how far they may roam throughout the seven seas, the imprint of nostos is always there, lingering just below the surface of their memory, drawing its strength from the psychic energy that flows between the unconscious and conscious mind. Regardless of whether they are born in deep bluewater far from shore in the birthing places of the great whales, or in the shallow waters of protected bays, or tucked away from the open sea in tidal estuaries like Polaris was, this inborn beckoning remains with them throughout their lives, and even though many beings never return home again, that does not lessen the influence of nostos upon their hearts and souls.

Polaris' words, spoken with such certitude, calmed Haemon. He sighed, "God be praised."

"God bring us the Light," added Polaris. Somehow, for reasons even he could not comprehend, he knew that the black whale would taste again the salt of the open sea, unfiltered and unfettered by man, but even as he said it, there was heaviness in his heart and a shadow on his soul: he did not know why.

Haemon hovered beside Polaris, as if trying to get up the will to ask him another question; one that appeared to trouble him even more than the first. Finally, he spoke. "Polaris, there is something that I need to know. Are you..." He caught himself, and started to turn away. "Never mind. I have no right to ask."

"Haemon, you have been a good friend to me during the years I have been here. You have earned the right to ask me anything you want," replied Polaris in a calm tone.

Haemon turned back toward the white dolphin. He felt a sudden rush of warmth come over him as he sensed that he was about to learn the one thing that he had hoped and prayed for, for so long. It was the same thing that the other beings at Oceania had wondered and, in some cases, feared, ever since Polaris' skin had turned from gray to white. Although Haemon had just risen to breathe moments earlier, he found himself short of breath and he rose up to the surface once more. This time he threw his entire head out of the water, which he had not done since he was a child. He sucked in the warm night air laced with the faint smell of jasmine, then settled down beside the white dolphin once more. He gathered himself and then asked a question, *the* question, "Polaris, are you the one of whom the Ancients spoke—the Chosen One who will save whalekind from evil?"

For a moment, Polaris did not say anything. He just stared across the tank, past the undulating forms of the sleeping beings, at the fake rock walls, far beyond which lay the open sea. Then he looked back at his friend and, with deep affection asked, "Why would you think I am?"

It was an evasive answer that did not deter Haemon. "For many reasons. First, because you are white—pure white."

Polaris stared intently at his companion as if trying to gauge the breadth and depth of his conviction. "Although I have not seen them, I have been told that there are other beings who are white." (He was referring to Narwhales and the several species of River Dolphins.)

Haemon shook his head. "That is different. You are a Bottlenose Dolphin and members of your kind are always gray; from pale gray to near black but always gray, never, *ever* white. And second, according to the Legend of the Ancients, the white dolphin would be born in a vast tidal wetland where heaven and earth meet the sea; a place such as that where you said you were born—the nostos that calls to you—the place that man calls the Florida Everglades."

"The place of my birth is similar to many such wetlands around the planet. There are beings in all the Seven Seas who have such a place of birth. These similarities are nothing more than coincidences with as little substance to them as the flimsy sides of a jellyfish. And just like the jellyfish, they slip away from us even as we try to grasp them."

"Perhaps," said Haemon, unable to hide the disappointment in his voice.

Polaris eyed his companion with compassion. He hesitated before saying anything more as the doubts he was creating in Haemon's mind were no less than those that he held in his own. Once, years earlier, Polaris had been told by a great whale, who had appeared to him under harrowing circumstances, that he was special; that he had been given a calling; and that his destiny and that of whalekind were intertwined, but that was many long years ago. And much had happened to him during those intervening years that made him doubt what the great whale had told him. With this angst and mental tumult swirling within him, like a maddening maelstrom, how could he be honest with anyone when he did not know the truth himself? Finally, he replied, "I will tell you this, Haemon. The only thing of which I can be certain is that Polaris is not my real name. The name which my mother gave me when I was born, before I was taken from her—is Apollo."

"Apollo?"

The white dolphin nodded, slowly, ponderingly, sadly.

Haemon thought about it then said, "It is a good name for a warrior prince."

"It is a good name for a simple being as well."

Haemon persevered. "I do not understand, Apollo, how can you doubt that you are the Chosen One? I saw the way you handled Erebus this afternoon. We all did. You did something to him; something that made him afraid. No one has ever done that before. Only the child of God could have done what you did to him."

"We are *all* children of God, Haemon. And whatever happened to Erebus today, he did to himself."

Haemon shook his head in frustration. "No. He may have brought it upon himself but he was not the creator of it. You did it to him. And besides, what about your birthmark, the star for which you were named by the humans, surely that is the mark of God?"

"Many beings bear marks from their birth and all such marks are put there by God. The fact that mine looks like a star from the heavens proves nothing."

Haemon was going to argue it further but his heart was no longer in it. If the white dolphin refused to admit his identity what good did it do for him to try to thrust it upon him?

Apollo moved closer to the Pilot Whale and stroked him with his flipper. "I have disappointed you, my friend."

Haemon shook his head. "No, Apollo. You could never do that. Despite what you may say, I am certain that you are the Prince of Light who has been sent to save us from darkness, and from this moment on, I pledge my life to you."

The white dolphin nodded and a tear rose in his eye. Like your kind, beings have tears although they are thicker, and as with the blood that flows in both your body and their bodies, the tears have the same percentage of salt as the ocean, because we are all born of the sea. "Whether I am who you say I am or not, I value your love and devotion. You are more precious to me than any treasure in the ocean."

And that was that. Neither being said anything more. Haemon was convinced that he was in the presence of the Chosen One—the warrior prince—and in his heart he sensed that he had been put in that place, at that time, to serve Apollo, and through him, to serve God. Something deep inside told him that he would be asked to give his all. And he would give it gladly.

CHAPTER SIX

The Seventh Gate

The fateful day that the white dolphin escaped from Oceania began like any other; sadly, it would not end that way. By nightfall, Haemon and Erebus would be dead; both as a consequence of Apollo's escape. Of even greater significance than these two deaths was the fact that Apollo would break the Tenth Law of the Ancients, the one forbidding communication with humans, and from that point forward, nothing would ever be the same again for either species. The inexorable chain of events that would lead to the salvation of whalekind, as foretold by the Legend of the Ancients, had now begun to unfold in the dominions of the Seven Seas.

"Please, Polaris, give me a sign that you can understand what I am saying to you," said Trainer Quinn, as she stood waist deep in the still waters of the lagoon. It was just after dawn and the children's swim with the dolphins program had not yet begun. Each day, before the program started, Quinn would open six gates, one at a time, to allow Apollo to swim from the residence tank to the large lagoon that lay close beside the ocean. She would close each gate behind him to prevent other beings from following but there was one gate, the seventh gate that she never opened for it was the final barrier that separated the lagoon from the ocean itself. Although there were other dolphins who swam with the children, Quinn reserved these early morning hours for time with the white dolphin alone. He had become her favorite, and among the other trainers, she made no effort to hide the fact that she cared for him; some said too much.

As usual at that time of the morning, they were alone in the lagoon and the white dolphin was floating close beside her, the way he often did when there were no others present. As she made her plea, she gently scratched his smooth white skin just behind his flipper, which he loved. It was not the first time that she had pleaded with him in this manner. More than any of the other beings with whom she worked, Quinn was convinced that the white dolphin could understand her words, not just the simple commands that the other dolphins learned, but everything she said to him. She was right, but he had never acknowledged it because the circumstances did not merit breaking so sacred a commandment. But that was about to change.

With concern in her voice, she said, "Tomorrow the owners of Oceania are going to send you far away from here, and I will never see you again." Tears began to roll across her smooth cheeks and fell as tiny droplets into the narrow band of water that separated them, as if seeking solace in its saline embrace. She lowered her head and rested her cheek on his back, grasping him in her embrace and pressing her body against him.

Her words stabbed Apollo in his heart as sharply as if they had been carried on the edge of a knife. His entire body tensed and his powerful back muscles strained against the arms encircling him. *Send him far away? To where? Why?* His mind began to race, skimming ahead of her words as if he was riding the bow wave of a speedboat. From her tone and manner, he sensed that his new home would be different from his confined but comfortable life in the oceanarium, and not in a good way.

She straightened up and stepped slowly through the warm water, taking a position directly in front of him and looked him in the eyes. Her next words confirmed his suspicions. "I *know* you can understand me and it is important that you listen carefully. I believe that the men who bought you intend to do you harm. They own an oceanarium in China but they also run a medical research company and I do not trust them." As she continued talking, it was clear that the future she described for him was worse than any he had ever known at the hands of man, but even with all that, he was still not prepared to break the Tenth Law. If by not doing so, his life was endangered than so be it. It must be God's will.

But then she said something else that shook his conviction. "I had a dream last night. I was swimming alone in the ocean; in deep, dark waters, and all about me were the bodies of many dolphins, and the seas ran red with their blood. Sharks were feeding on them and I tried to swim away but my arms and legs would not move: I knew that I was about to die. But at the last moment, you appeared and you saved me." She paused and tried to wipe away her tears, but her hand was wet and by that point, the tears were pouring down her cheeks. "Oh, Polaris I am so afraid. What if my dream comes true and you are not there to save me? What if...?" The recounting of the dream was too much. Her emotions overtook her and she could say no more. She lowered her head and began to sob. She was no longer the professional trainer; now she was a little girl again, alone and afraid.

As she described her dream to him, he could see it in his own mind. He could taste the blood of his brothers in the water. He could feel her fear. And it was at that moment he knew the time had come to break the law. He had come close to doing so once before with another human who cared about him, in another time and place. He had not done so then and had regretted it ever since. He would not let that happen again, ancient commandments aside. Then, he did it. Using his ultrasonic sound emitter, he unleashed a pulse of sound waves at a frequency beyond the range of human hearing that carried his thoughts directly into her brain, and even though she did not hear anything, in her mind's ear she heard his words more loudly and clearly than had a human shouted them. The message his thoughts carried through this mindlink were four simple words that would change everything forever: "Do not be afraid."

She snapped upright. Her mouth fell open. She had heard a voice in her head but no sound had passed through her ears. She stiffened and a look of astonishment spread across her face. Her eyebrows knitted and in a half whisper, she said, "What?"

Again, he directed his thoughts into her mind. This time addressing her by her name. "Caitlin Quinn, this is me speaking to you. I am the one you call Polaris. You are hearing my thoughts in your mind."

At that poignant, powerful, and pivotal moment in the history of Planet Ocean, Trainer Caitlin Quinn had become the first human ever to hear a dolphin speak, but for a few seconds more she still did not realize it. She began to hyperventilate, and struggled to control her breathing. Her knees grew weak and for a moment, she thought she might slip under the warm and gentle waves that caressed her like the loving touch of God. She stared at him for a long, questioning moment. Then, like sunlight suddenly appearing from behind a cloud to dance across the water, her expression changed from shock and surprise to joy. As she probed his eyes, her field of vision began to narrow and blur, until it was as if she was looking down a long dark tunnel that led directly into his soul.

"Can it be? Is this really happening?" she said out loud, with trembling voice. Her heart began to pound with such force that she was certain he could feel it, which, of course, he could.

He nodded slowly and said, "Yes. It is."

There. It was done. With these few telepathic words, the bridge between man and dolphin had been crossed and there was no turning back. All that had been between these two sentient species was gone and all that would ever be had now begun. And only God knew what the outcome would be.

Quinn stood there transfixed, overcome with ecstasy but at the same time terrified that this moment was a dream, that she would wake up at any second; but her fears vanished with his next words, "Do not worry, Caitlin, this is not a dream."

She let out a little gasp. "Oh my God. You can read my mind."

"I am not your God. I am but his humble servant as are you. And yes, I can read your thoughts."

She began to laugh, and shout for joy, and cry at the same time as tears of happiness flooded down her cheeks in wild abandon. Then she got control of her emotions and asked, "You know my name but what is yours?"

"The name my mother gave me was Apollo."

"Apollo!" She exclaimed. That is a good name. Oh thank you, Apollo, than you for confirming what I already knew, that your kind does understand our language. You have made my dream come true. You have made me the happiest woman on earth."

"I am glad," he said with a broad smile, the way dolphins can when they are happy. But then it faded and his tone and manner turned serious. "But you must promise me that you will not reveal this secret to anyone. At least not until the day comes when your kind are ready to deal with this reality."

She nodded. "I promise," she said and meant it. She knew she would be able to honor this request because no one would believe her anyway.

"And Caitlin, if your other dream should also come true, the one in which you are alone in blood-filled seas, know this, I will come to save you."

It was the release from fear that she needed. She threw herself onto him and hugged him so tightly that he thought they both would sink to the shallow sandy bottom. "Thank you, God," she cried out. "Thank you, Apollo." She closed her eyes and clung to him as if she would never to let him go.

With her clinging to his back, the white dolphin began to swim slowly around the lagoon. It was a touching sight; two sentient beings from different worlds, acting as one, locked together in love and a shared understanding of the greatest joy in the universe. And as they swam together in large, lazy circles, the sun took its time climbing up the eastern sky, as if it knew that something special had happened that morning and wanted to acknowledge the moment. Bathed in its golden glow, the palm fronds swayed to and fro in the gentle morning breezes off the ocean, and the tiny grains of sand on the beach sparkled like diamonds.

Out on the vast bay beyond Sinclair Cay, where the sweeping confluence of land and sky met the sea, the emerald and azure blue waters rippled in a gentle harmony of wind and waves and tides. And in the filmy distance at every point of the compass, the thin silhouettes of the other islands in the stream stood tone on tone against the bleached boundaries of vision. In the back of their minds, both dolphin and human sensed that this wonderful moment would be fleeting and might never come again, but that did not diminish its intensity. And for one brief shining moment, time seemed to stand still, as if the hand of God had reached down and stopped the spinning globe on its axis.

Several hours later, long after the morning swim with children program had ended, Apollo told Haemon what he had done. "You *spoke* with Trainer Quinn!" said the incredulous Haemon. It was dusk and he and Apollo were swimming together at the far side of the residence tank, well away from the other beings.

"Yes," replied Apollo without emotion.

Haemon looked across the tank towards the other beings, then back at his friend. "I suppose if there was any being who had the right to break the Tenth Commandment it was you." He drifted up to the surface to breathe then returned down beside his friend and asked, "What are you going to do now?"

"Leave here," was Apollo's simple yet loaded reply.

"Leave! How? When? Why?" the questions tumbled out of the whale's mouth like Sea Urchins rolling before the undertow.

Apollo told Haemon what she had said about him being sold. And how she had agreed to open the gates later that night.

"Good. I will go with you," said Haemon without hesitation.

"No. It will be too dangerous."

Haemon looked at the white dolphin with an intensity as great as his desire for freedom. "That is why you must not try this alone. You could be killed."

"If I am it is the will of God."

"Then let it be so for me too." There was no bravado in his voice, no air of self-importance, just a sense of purpose that could not be broken.

Finally, Apollo nodded his consent. "Very well." And that was that. The die was cast.

One hour before midnight, Dr. Caitlin Quinn walked softly along the metal walkway above the gate that divided the residence tank from the canal. She reached the latch and bent down to open it. Before doing so, she had turned off the underwater lights in the residence tank and in the entire series of waterways that connected the various tanks and lagoons of the oceanarium. As soon as the first gate swung open, Apollo swam through it staying near the surface so she could see him but at first Haemon did not follow.

"What is wrong?" Apollo said as he looked back at Haemon who was hovering just inside the gate. With his earsight, he could see that the black whale was trembling.

"I…I cannot do it. Go on without me."

Apollo swam back to the edge of the residence tank and whispered, "Yes, you can."

For a long moment Haemon did not move. Meanwhile, Quinn could see both the white dolphin and the black whale but she was not certain what was going on. The plan had been for Apollo alone to escape but now she could see that he seemed to want the Pilot Whale to follow him, so she walked ahead to the next gate. At long last, with Apollo's gentle encouragement, Haemon slipped through the first gate and swam beside Apollo toward the next one. The soft sounds of their exhaled breath blended with the cool night breezes and wafted away into the darkness.

The next gate was thirty feet away and because of the delay with Haemon, Quinn opened it before returning to close the first gate. Apollo and Haemon had already swum through the second gate as Quinn walked back to close the first one, so they did not see or hear another being who was following them, hugging the bottom of the canal, just out of the young woman's vision. In a similar fashion, Quinn's actions were repeated with each of the next five gates, all of which were spaced at a similar length along the waterway leading to the large lagoon by the sea.

By leaving the gate behind Apollo and Haemon open until she opened the next one, the other being was able to follow them undetected, slipping silently past the closed gates that led to side canals and the other tanks, timing his rise to the surface to breathe when Quinn was at her farthest from him, and then sinking again before she returned to close the trailing gate. It was not until Apollo and Haemon had swum through the sixth gate leading into the lagoon that the other being, Erebus, was discovered. Seeing that Quinn was staying beside the sixth gate as Apollo and Haemon passed through it, Erebus realized he had no choice but to hurry through it and risk being discovered by the other two beings, which he was.

"You!" exclaimed Haemon as he turned to face Erebus. "What are you doing here?"

"The same thing you are."

"What do you mean?" asked Haemon.

"Do not play dumb with me, my short-finned cousin. I know why you both are here."

"How do you know?" asked the angry and embarrassed Pilot Whale. He looked at Apollo, "I did not betray you, Apollo."

"Apollo!" exclaimed Erebus. "Your real name is Apollo?"

"Yes," said Haemon. "He is Apollo, the Prince of Light: the one the Ancients said would come to save us—and you had better back away or you will feel his wrath."

An evil smile spread around the underside of Erebus' bulbous head, forming a continuous line with the tapering gray streak behind his eyes, giving the impression that his melon had been glued onto the rest of his body. As he spoke to the white dolphin, he kept his gaze averted from Apollo's eyes. "I knew you were not who you said you were. But if you think I am afraid of some stupid legend perpetuated by weaklings like Haemon, you are mistaken."

All the while this conversation was taking place under the water, Quinn stood on the wall that bordered the side of the lagoon, halfway between the sixth and seventh gates. Seeing that there were now two Pilot Whales with Apollo, she became alarmed. This was not what they had planned but it was too late to turn back now. She assumed that Apollo knew what he was doing and she could hear but, of course, not understand what the whales were saying. To her it was just a series of high pitched clicks, squeaks and whistles punctuated by a frenzy of bubbles, but she could tell by their posture that there was trouble. She had closed the sixth gate and the last one, the seventh gate that stood between the whales and freedom, also remained closed. She was growing more concerned with each passing minute, not only about what was transpiring in the lagoon, but with the possibility of being discovered by the night watchmen; however, she decided to wait and take her signal from Apollo before doing anything. So she just stood there beside one of the light poles atop which were the floodlights that, like the underwater lights, were dark. Meanwhile in the water a confrontation was taking place.

"What do you want, Erebus?" asked Apollo in a calm tone.

"The same thing as you do, Apollo. My freedom." The white dolphin's name was not pleasant to Erebus as he said it. And still he did not look directly at Apollo. "If you are who Haemon says you are, then save us all."

At first, Apollo did not reply. The rising aggression in Erebus' voice was unmistakable but at least for the moment, there was no need to escalate the tension. At the speed of thought, (which is a step effect faster in beings than in your kind) Apollo considered the situation and the various courses of action available to him. He assessed a hundred iterations and permutations of his potential actions in a few nano-seconds, then he chose what he felt was the optimum solution, if not the most satisfactory. "Very well," replied Apollo. "You may join us."

"A wise decision," said Erebus with a smile but Haemon shook his head in disgust.

Apollo rose up to the surface and indicated to Quinn that he was ready. She nodded and went to the seventh gate and knelt down to unlock it but at that instant, the lights on the overhead poles surrounding the lagoon and the underwater lights all snapped on, flooding the entire area above and below the water in a harsh and angry glow. Simultaneously, three members of the security police appeared, flanking the lagoon. One of them rushed over to Quinn and grabbed her, turning her around and yanking her arms down behind her. Apollo lifted his head above the surface, or spyhopped as your kind calls it, and watched as she was led away, and just before she and the guard disappeared into the shadows beyond the wall of light, she glanced back at Apollo with tears in her eyes and mouthed the words, 'I'm sorry'. Then she was gone.

For a second, Apollo hovered there with his head above the surface until Haemon pushed him back down underwater, away from the danger represented by the guards. But there was danger beneath the surface as well.

"You stupid idiot," Erebus snarled at Haemon. "If you had not hesitated at the first gate we would all be safely in the ocean by now."

Haemon stared at his cousin and quipped, "Go to hell."

What happened next took place in mere seconds, faster than I can tell it here. Erebus circled away from Haemon, swimming to the far side of the lagoon, picking up speed as he did, then he turned and charged directly toward Haemon. As he had done the previous day, Apollo moved in front of Haemon but this time Erebus did not hesitate or stop. Apollo was not intimidated. Waiting until the last possible instant, Apollo deftly dodged Erebus' charge. Still accelerating, Erebus shot past the white dolphin and crashed headfirst into a steel beam on the side of the seventh gate. He hit it with such force that it broke his neck, killing him instantly. As his body slumped to the bottom of the lagoon, the two remaining security officers, thinking that the white dolphin had killed the Pilot Whale, pulled out their guns and began firing into the lagoon at Apollo.

Apollo dove to the bottom and the bullets sliced into the water like angry hornets, buzzing in downward arcs around Haemon and Apollo. With remarkable presence of mind, the once timid Pilot Whale stared at the closed gate that now stood as the last barrier between them and freedom. Then he looked back at Apollo and said, "Get ready to follow me."

Apollo knew at once what Haemon intended to do. "No!" he shouted. But before Apollo could stop him, Haemon charged the gate and slammed his head into it just below the water line, out of harm's way from the bullets. The gate shuddered but held fast and the collision momentarily stunned Haemon.

"Stop, Haemon. You will kill yourself," cried Apollo.

Haemon ignored him and as soon as the initial shock of the collision passed, he circled around and did it again. But this time he rose up and swam along the surface to be nearer to where the locking mechanism was situated. Like a mighty torpedo, Haemon's body sliced through the water, taking deadly aim at his target. This time he hit it much harder than before and the physical mass of the whale, powered by the force of his heart and soul, had the desired effect. The gate buckled in the middle and opened part way but not completely. The injured Pilot Whale rose up out of the water to survey the damage, and as he did, a bullet thudded into the blubber on his thick back. Undaunted, and powered by a force greater than his own, Haemon slipped below the surface and swam back away from the gate to ready himself for the final assault upon it.

Tormented by what he sensed was to come, Apollo swam up to the whale and pleaded for him to stop. Haemon looked at Apollo and smiled. There was a fire in his eyes that burned with a passion borne of twenty years in confinement and buttressed by the sense of destiny he now felt in his heart. He shook his head. "I cannot stop now, Master. I can taste the sea and there is no going back." Haemon gathered himself, summoning every ounce of strength, oblivious to the pain in his back and the blood that was now streaming out of him into the dark green water, and with all the might that his two and a half ton body could muster; he charged the gate one last time. This time it gave way and Haemon's momentum carried him out into the bay. Apollo followed close behind. They were free. At last. Free forever and after.

For a long while, the white dolphin and the black whale swam in silence, without stopping, moving as one, past the point of the land that marked the end of the bay, across the shallows and out over the edge of the Tongue of the Ocean. To a human eye, judging the way Haemon moved through the gentle swells, it might have appeared that he was not seriously injured. But Apollo knew otherwise. His earsight told him that Haemon was dying. Not from his collisions with the gate but from the guard's bullet that had pierced one lung and was lodged beside his brave but failing heart. It was not long before Haemon began to slow down. The movements of his broad flukes became weaker and slower until at last, ten miles out into bluewater, Haemon stopped swimming and could go no farther. He hung there in the glow of the moonlight with Apollo hovering close beside him. By now, Haemon's breaths were tinged with a fine spray of blood and he needed the assistance of Apollo to remain afloat.

He looked at the white dolphin and uttered with a pained smile, "We did it. We are free, Apollo. Free!"

Tears welled up in the white dolphin's eyes. "You did it, Haemon. I owe you my life."

Haemon coughed, hard, spewing dark red mucus out of his blowhole. "No. It is I who owe you; because of you I can now die where whales were born to die, out here in God's ocean not locked behind walls of concrete and steel. And I thank you for that, Apollo. I only regret that I will not be there with you when you fulfill your destiny." He coughed once more and began to slip beneath the surface.

Apollo struggled to keep Haemon afloat. It took all his strength to do so. "I will never forget you, Haemon," Apollo whispered. "You will always be with me, wherever my journey may lead."

The light behind Haemon's eyes flickered and grew weak. A profound peace came over him. Then, without self-pity or fear, the dying whale whispered, "It is time, Master. You must let me go." And with that, he pulled away from Apollo and sank slowly beneath the waves; his great body growing smaller, dimmer, sinking away from sight, down into the deeps, then at last gone, leaving nothing but a memory.

Apollo thrust his head above the waves and stared up into the night sky, where black clouds sailed like galleons before the silver moon. "No!" he shouted angrily. But only the whispering of the wind was there to greet him and he found no solace in its warm caress. He cried out again but this time his words were laden with pain and frustration. "If I am who they say I am, Lord, why could I not save him? What good is it to be the savior of all whalekind when I cannot save just one?"

There was no answer. Reason told him that there would be none but the force of faith had made him hope there might be. Alone in an empty sea, he hovered there, with a heart so heavy that it might have pulled him down into the deeps but for the will that said to him, Go on. He knew he must finish the journey that had begun so long ago and so far away. If he did not, his friend's death would have been in vain and he would never find the truth of who he was and why he had been born. And so, steeling himself against what had been, and what was yet to come, the white dolphin turned and headed due west, toward nostos, and wherever else destiny would lead.

CHAPTER SEVEN

Pilgrim In An Angry Sea

It took Apollo a week to travel from the waters off Sinclair Cay to Cape Sable on the southwestern coast of Florida. During that same period of time, the first hurricane of the season covered the nearly three thousand miles from its birthplace off the coast of Africa, reaching the Gulf of Mexico at the same time as Apollo. Beings are highly sensitive to changes in barometric pressure and Apollo had felt the hurricane coming long before it arrived. Normally a whale or dolphin sensing such a powerful atmospheric disturbance would have avoided being caught in its path, but Apollo was being driven by a different force, one far more powerful than wind and wave: it was an irresistible desire to return to the place of his birth. The location, in an estuary called the Shark River in the Everglades National Park, had been imprinted in his brain on the night he was born, and he was drawn to it with the uncanny navigational accuracy of his kind. But by the time the hurricane hit the waters of the Gulf, it was too late for Apollo to avoid the full fury of the storm and his return to his nostos would have to wait.

He would have made the journey in less time were it not for a detour that he took before heading to the waters off Florida. Guided by the stars and the magnetic pull of the earth, as well as the ocean currents, and using his earsight, which gave him a detailed mental picture of the ocean floor beneath him, he sliced across the azure waters of the Great Bahama Bank, pausing only now and then to feed on swarming schools of sardines. He was careful to avoid contact with other beings while his skin was white, but he had no intention of allowing it to remain so. He crossed the deep Santaren Channel, where the red clay bottom lay two thousand feet beneath him, hesitating briefly at the edge of the canyon. Only the great whales leap off the edge of the continental shelf without looking, because the deeps are home to the kraken, a threat that smaller beings ignore at their peril. He skirted past the Cay Sal Bank where he encountered a group of West Indian Manatees, then transited the Nicholas Channel, all the while probing the major sedimentary basin below him with his earsight until he found what he was seeking. There in the mineral-rich shelf sediments, off the northern coast of Cuba, he located the complex mixture of minerals; chromite, titanium, manganese, and gold that he needed to turn his skin gray. The only witnesses to his strange behavior were hundreds of Loggerhead Turtles, who watched in puzzled amazement as he raked the bottom with his head, sucking in the chalky ooze.

After finishing this unpleasant but necessary meal, he headed north across the Straits of Florida, staying one step ahead of the onrushing hurricane. By the time Apollo reached the western edge of the vast wilderness called the Everglades, the minerals had done what he hoped they would, which was to turn his skin gray, and to any human or whale, who might have observed his passage through the shallow waters, he was just another ordinary Bottlenose Dolphin.

Normally, the inshore waters of the coastal everglades would have been a welcoming place for the native son who had finally come home, but not on that day. The sea had been whipped into a turbulent cauldron of mocha-colored water flecked with foam, beneath seething clouds in countless shades of gray. As Apollo struggled to ride the crests of the surging waves, the incessant howling of the wind grew so loud and so intense that it overwhelmed his senses; depriving him of an accurate reading of the bottom beneath him. Despite his best efforts to stay in control, the raging sea tossed him around like flotsam and jetsam.

However, there was one benefit to the tumult that he was experiencing, which was that he need not worry about sharks for they were the first to flee from an angry sea. In vain, he searched for the mouth of the estuary where his instincts told him he had been born, but time soon ran out as the full force of the storm surge finally caught up with him. It roared shoreward with a vengeance, like a liquid avalanche, swallowing everything in its path. Apollo tried to escape its towering maw but it picked him up and slammed him down onto the beach of a small island, knocking him senseless. Then everything faded to black.

The dream began as it always had. He was lying in shallow water, only half covered by it, stuck in a soft wet substance that oozed up around his stomach. To one side, there were tall strands of green and yellow grasses, swaying and dancing, as if moved by an unseen force. On the other, there was flat, dark water where his senses told him danger still lurked. The same danger that had chased him into the shallows where he had become stranded. Alone. Abandoned. Afraid. Overwhelmed by the sudden, strange reality of his new existence, he whimpered. In the distance, he could hear the cries of another of his kind. 'Apollo' she cried. 'Where are you? This is your mother. Come to me, little one.' He answered but she did not hear. He tried again, but to no avail. Her voice faded and then ceased altogether. He trembled with fear and ached with a strange, gnawing feeling in his stomach.

All at once, he glimpsed a shadow in the channel beside him, its black dorsal fin slicing through the brackish water. It was another being, the same one who had chased him. The being drew near, moving in silence, with a purpose that instinctively he knew was evil. It stopped and for a moment it lingered there, seemingly uncertain of what to do next. Then, it turned and swam out into the channel, moving in a big circle and headed back directly toward him. Closer, it came. Faster. Stronger. But at the last second, it stopped, right at the edge of the riverbank, and then it turned and disappeared into the dark water and was gone. From the other side, in the tall grasses, three strange, upright forms appeared out of the milky haze. They towered above him. He knew at once they were not his kind. Garbled sounds emanated from their mouths. One of them reached down and caressed his skin, sending a chill through his little body. He tried to flee but he could not move. Then one of the three creatures picked him up and carried him away. Away from his mother. Away from nostos.

When Apollo awoke from the dream, the storm had passed but his troubles were not over. He was lying in the soft sand on the beach of one of the tiny, nameless islands that form the western boundary of the Everglades. Bruised but not broken, he had lain there all night. Alone. Vulnerable. The waters of a channel carved out by the storm surge flowed by him only yards away; so near and yet so far. Through the night, he had kept the hungry crabs at bay with the flick of his flukes and flippers, and the damp night air had provided a degree of soothing comfort, but now as the sun rose overhead, his skin began to dry. As his muscles tired, the bulk of his body weight pressed down on his lungs making breathing difficult. Without help, he knew the end was near. He closed his eyes once more.

"Do you think he is dead, Python?" said the strange voice breaking the silence that had enveloped him. Apollo's eyes snapped open and he saw two large Bottlenose Dolphins hovering nearby in the clear waters of the channel. One was a normal shade of gray but the other had skin so dark that it appeared black, and at first Apollo thought him to be the shadow of the other.

"No," replied the one called Python. "He is alive but barely."

The first dolphin spoke again. "God be praised."

Python did not give the prescribed reply of 'God bring us the Light'. Instead he snorted, "Come, Tisiphone. Let us be off. They are not here."

"And leave him here to die?"

"He is not our problem."

Changing tactics, Tisiphone replied, "This stranger is big and strong. He would make a fine addition to our tribe."

Python spyhopped and surveyed Apollo with his eyes. Then he gave a terse, "All right."

"How shall we get him back into the water?"

"Watch," Python replied. He swam out away from the steep beach, then turned and rushed back toward it, stopping at the last moment and twisting his body so that his powerful flukes could add an extra push to the wave that he had created. It surged across the few yards of sand that separated Apollo from safety and flooded the beach around him. It was not enough. Python looked at the first being and said, "Do it with me."

Together, the two beings repeated the same act, working in unison and leveraging their combined mass of over half a ton, this time pushing a much bigger wave onto the shore. For a second Apollo gained some buoyancy but quickly lost it again. However, on the next try, with an even greater rush by the other beings, it worked. Apollo was able to wriggle free and return to the safe haven of the channel. As soon as he reached it, he zoomed out into the middle of the channel and back again, rolling once and slapping his flukes hard upon the surface, which panicked a school of young Weakfish. Then he swam over and came face-to-face with the other two dolphins.

"God be praised," he exclaimed.

Tisiphone flashed a nervous look at Python, then replied, "God bring us the Light."

The gray dolphin's nervous demeanor did not go unnoticed by Apollo. "Thank you. You saved my life and I shall not forget that. Permit me to introduce myself. My name is Polaris." He had already decided not to reveal his true identity to these strangers. It was a wise decision.

"I am Tisiphone, and this is Python. He is the chieftain of our tribe."

"It is an honor to meet you both," Apollo replied tipping his head twice in the manner of a male dolphin when greeting an unthreatening stranger. Tisiphone did the same but Python did not.

"Polaris!" snorted Python. "That is a human word." Python's threatening tone and manner were not new to Apollo. It was the same kind of reaction that he had experienced many times in his life, including most recently in his final encounter with Erebus. This not only happened to him during the times his skin was its natural white color, when perhaps he could understand it, but also when he was wearing the gray coat of masquerade, as he was at that moment. For some reason, some beings saw something in his eyes that provoked animosity, or worse.

Apollo eyed Python carefully. "You are right, Chieftain Python. It is the name my human captors gave me. I have spent most of my life in their prisons and I do not know my real name," he lied. His respectful address did little to soften Python's tone.

"Where were you born?" asked Tisiphone. "Your dialect is similar to ours but there is a certain strangeness to it."

"I do not know." It was another lie and it made his conscience flinch.

"Where are you coming from and what brought you here?" probed Python. It was obvious that he did not like what he was hearing.

At first, Apollo did not answer. Instead he stared deeply into the black dolphin's eyes the way that he had done with Erebus. Then he replied softly but firmly, "I am a simple wayfarer of the open seas stranded by the storm. Where I have come from matters not and what brought me here matters less. I mean you no harm and that should be all that matters."

Python seemed confused, conflicted. His expression tightened. "My senses tell me that there is nothing simple about you, stranger."

Apollo did not comment. Instead, he continued to stare into Python's eyes. For just an instant, he thought he saw something there, a hint of recognition, a fleeting memory, but then it passed.

Finally, Python nodded and said, "Very well."

Surprised but pleased by the unusual behavior of his chieftain, Tisiphone brightened and said, "Well, now that that is settled, I think we are done here. Shall we go, Python?"

But Python was not ready to leave. His gaze remained fixed on the stranger. "For a wayfarer of the open seas these inshore waters are a strange place in which to have been traveling."

"I might say the same of you. I can tell that you are the chieftain of a bluewater tribe, are you not?" He had correctly deduced that Python and Tisiphone were pelagic dolphins not given to swim in littoral waters.

A sly smile slipped across the black dolphin's face. "Yes. We are." He stared at Apollo long and hard, then added, "I like you, Polaris. Come with us."

Apollo shook his head. "I appreciate your kind offer, but I must respectfully decline. I have somewhere else that I need to go."

Python's smile vanished. "I insist."

"No. But thank you anyway."

Python turned and gave a short shrill call downstream toward the open waters of the Gulf. Within seconds, five large gray forms materialized out of the deeper water. They quickly formed a semi-circle behind Python, facing Apollo. Once they were in place, Python looked back at Apollo with the matter-of-fact haughtiness of someone who could back up his words. "Shall we go?" There was no mistaking the implied threat behind his invitation.

A tense moment followed. Apollo was not afraid. He had been in worse situations. Under normal conditions, he might have been willing to fight Python and his gang. But the hurricane had taken a lot out of him and, for a reason that he could not fully understand, he chose not to force the matter. "Very well."

"Good choice," said Python. With that he turned and was gone.

With a sheepish shrug, Tisiphone said, "I am sorry for my chieftain's manner."

"It is all right." Then together, he and Tisiphone swam down the channel that had been cut into the beach by the storm surge and headed away from the island with the other five beings following close behind. As they departed, Apollo asked, "Who was Python referring to when he said they are not here?"

Tisiphone tensed. "Two females of our tribe, sisters by the names of Leto and Aurora."

The names meant nothing to Apollo. "Why would they be here?"

Tisiphone shook his head. "It is better that you do not ask."

And he did not. Instead, he followed Python and the other beings through the maze of islands toward the Gulf. Along the way, they passed an island that man calls Shark River Island, situated just off the mouth of its namesake estuary. As they did, Apollo felt a quickening in his heartbeat. A strange feeling came over him and he knew at once it was the river where he had been heading before the storm caught him—the river that led to the place of his birth—his nostos; so close and yet so far. For a second, he was tempted to break away from the others and head up the river. But he did not. Fate is a powerful master and Apollo sensed that his fate was about to lead him on an odyssey that would circle the globe before bringing him back home again; that is, if it ever did at all.

Unlike the Bottlenose Dolphins who lived in the inshore waters along the western edges of the Everglades National Park, whose home ranges were rarely more than one hundred square miles in size, Python was the chieftain of a tribe of offshore dolphins that roamed over an enormous crescent-shaped territory. It ran along the edge of the Florida escarpment, roughly paralleling the coastline from the Keys all the way around the Panhandle, almost to the city of New Orleans. Python was a restless traveler who never wanted to stay in one place very long: some in his tribe said it was because he was searching *for* something while others speculated that he was running *from* something. Whichever it was, he ruled his tribe with an iron will, and any being who rebelled against his authority soon disappeared, never to be seen again.

At the time of my story, which was in early summer, the tribe was preparing to head to the waters off Louisiana for the brown shrimp season. As soon as the trawlers began to fish again, Python and his tribe would be right there behind the boats, gorging themselves on the disoriented and disabled shrimp that had escaped the trawl nets. But for the past month they had been living closer inshore than normal, at a place just beyond what the nautical charts of man refer to as the ten fathom line, approximately fifty miles due west of Shark River Island. A heavy population of Dusky Anchovy had kept them there for the better part of June; right up until the hurricane arrived, and spoiled their hunting. Now the fish were gone and it was time to head north.

It took Apollo and the others several hours to reach the place where Python had left the other members of the tribe, but when they arrived, they were all gone, except for one.

"She has arrived," said the being without explaining further.

Python was pleased. He turned and ordered his gang to follow him and swam away, heading west, further out into the Gulf.

Tisiphone turned to Apollo and said, "Come, Polaris. We must hurry!"

"What is it?"

"You will see" Tisiphone answered with unbridled excitement.

They were off once more, skimming across the surface, while below them, the sloping plain spread out like a vast, partially open fan of rippled sand, dotted here and there with the refuse and wreckage of mankind. They were heading toward the distant cliff called the Florida Escarpment, and the dangerous deeps beyond. They swam at top speed for the rest of the morning, and well into the afternoon until finally, Tisiphone slowed, and then stopped. Apollo found himself drifting just below the surface of the crystal clear waters of the Gulf, one hundred miles west northwest of Shark River Island. One thousand feet below him, the sea floor slipped away into darkness, continuing its downward slide until it reached its final depth of twelve thousand feet only a few miles west of where they were. On the underside of the sea's surface, the reflection of the afternoon sun painted the undulating ceiling in an ever-changing pattern of liquid silver, while all around Apollo, shafts of golden sunlight streamed downward, probing the waters of indigo with slender fingers until finally fading into the nothingness.

But the physical beauty of the waters that surrounded Apollo was nothing compared to what he found in them; for there, hovering before him in a giant semi-circle, one thousand feet across and several hundred feet deep, was a quantum of beings of all sizes and shapes, including large whales such as Minke, Fin and Humpbacks; smaller whales like Beaked and Finned Whales as well as False Killer Whales; and most numerous of all, dolphins; including Common and Striped, Spinner and Spotted, Rough-toothed; and last but not least, Bottlenose Dolphins.

During the final twenty minutes of their journey, Apollo had detected this gathering with his earsight but it was not until they came upon it that he witnessed the full magnitude of it. And what was especially unnerving was that the group, as large and diverse as it was, was absolutely silent. Apollo had learned long ago that silence in the sea was often a precursor to danger, but the scene before him did not seem threatening. Quite the contrary. In the few short years that he had lived in the wild, he had never seen an assemblage of beings as large as this, and at first, he wondered if it was *the* Gathering, which he had heard about in his youth. He would soon discover it was not.

"Wait here," said Tisiphone.

"What is all this?" asked Apollo.

"You will see," Tisiphone replied and swam off to find the other beings from his tribe.

Apollo turned his attention to the sweeping blue panorama that lay in silent stillness before him. Despite the stark beauty of it all, Apollo could not help but feel a sense of impending doom. Lessons learned in the ocean are hard to forget and those who do usually do not live long enough to regret it.

Soon Tisiphone returned and with a terse, "Follow me," he led Apollo toward the semi-circle of Python's tribe. Tisiphone motioned for Apollo to take a place at the edge of the tribe. Off to his far right Apollo could see Python. Beside him were two females, one of whom was a paler shade of gray that made her stand out from all the others. They were looking at him and talking in an animated fashion with Python, but he could not hear what they were saying. One of the females in particular was staring at him and there was something about her manner that gave him pause. Then, to his surprise, the two females left Python's side and swam toward him. When they reached him, the paler one did not say anything while the other female asked in a harsh tone, "Who are you?"

"My name is Polaris—but I am sure Python already told you that."

She did not reply. Apollo could feel the tenseness within her. After an awkward pause, the other female said, "Hello, Polaris. My name is Leto, and this is my sister, Aurora." Leto flashed a stern look at her sister, who gave Apollo a perfunctory nod. Leto looked back at Apollo and their eyes locked. A chill ran through Apollo's body but it was not one of fear. Quite the opposite; it was akin to that which your kind feels when you meet a familiar stranger and you instantly feel a connection, as if you have known them all your life. Apollo could tell that Leto felt it too and for a long, awkward moment that was in a strange way comforting to both of them, neither said anything. Aurora saw what was happening between her sister and the stranger and she did not like it one bit.

"Come, Leto," barked Aurora and then she swam back toward Python.

"You will have to excuse my sister. She does not take kindly to strangers," said Leto who clearly did not want to leave. She hesitated and then finally said. "I must go."

"Perhaps we can talk later," said Apollo. She nodded then swam away. As she did, he felt a twinge deep inside but he did not understand what or why. Eventually, he forced his attention back to the scene before him. He probed the depths with his earsight, which at first only revealed a small school of Anchovies that had blundered into the circle of beings, and was now darting this way and that in synchronized terror. Hovering in the flickering afternoon light, Apollo drifted slowly up to the surface

94

to breathe, as did others all around the semi-circle, each making their move as seamlessly as they could so as not to disturb the seriousness of the moment. Time, which beings measure simply by the movement of the sun, moon and stars, ticked slowly by and Apollo wondered how long he would have to wait to discover their purpose in being there. Then it happened; one moment there was nothing before them and the next minute, the sleek, sixty-foot long body of a Sei Whale materialized out of the depths; like a goddess of the night come to minister to her worshippers. Although Apollo could not know it, the Sei Whale was Eris; seductress of Dionysus and mistress of Poseidon, come to do her part in the impending war against mankind.

Eris' spoke only briefly to the gathered throng of beings: it does not take long to say the word war nor to tell where, when, and how it would commence. After she finished her impassioned plea, she urged all the beings gathered there that afternoon to do Poseidon's bidding. And with regard to the timing, she told them that the war would begin on the next Godlight, exactly one year from when Poseidon had stormed out of the Gathering.

When questioned by one being as to why that date, Eris said there were two reasons; first, it would take that long for the call to war to be heard across the Seven Seas and for the armies of freedom to be recruited. To that end, Eris said she was only one of many beings who had been chosen by Poseidon to spread the message around the world, just as she was doing with them in the Gulf. And second, she reminded them that Godlight was the start of summer in the Northern Hemisphere, which was where ninety percent of the world's human population lived, and as such, it was the start of the three-month period when the greatest number of humans would be in or on the ocean.

This would give Poseidon's forces an ideal opportunity to disrupt the world of man and destroy as many of them as they could, in every way they could; from attacking them when they swam, to sinking their small boats, and the most ambitious of all, by rendering larger ships inoperative by fouling their rudders, even if it meant dying in the process. Their overriding objective was to make the oceans of the world a hostile and unforgiving place for all mankind. And then, when chaos reigned supreme upon the bluewater, and whales ruled the seas,

Poseidon would establish communications with their leaders, to reset the world order and stop the destruction of the oceans.

In addition, Eris told them that after their meeting was over she would leave the Gulf of Mexico and head south along the coast of South America, spreading the message as she went. Then after rounding Cape Horn, she would gather her army in her Kingdom of the South Pacific, and lead them north to rejoin Poseidon at his base of operations near Johnston Atoll, seven hundred miles southwest of Hawaii. When she was finished her story, she asked to speak with Python in private and the gathering broke up.

Later, after his private session with Eris had concluded, Python returned to his tribe. He had a sly smile on his face. First, he spoke privately with Aurora and told her to take Leto and the other females and return to their home waters. He said he had been given a mission and that he would see her when he returned. She objected but he refused to discuss the matter. Reluctantly, she left and took the other females and young ones with her. As they departed, Leto gave one last longing glance at Apollo; then they were gone. Python then spoke with his gang and Apollo. He said Eris told them what she had discovered from Dionysus; namely that Pan, the little Harbor Porpoise whom they all knew, had been sent by the Sovereign Council to Sinclair Cay to attempt to free a white dolphin; a dolphin who was supposedly the Chosen One.

When he heard this, Apollo tensed and his eyes narrowed but he tried hard not to let his emotions show. Python said that Pan was traveling in the company of three Guardians, Offshore Killer Whales, and they would likely arrive in the Bahamas ten days hence. He further stated that Eris' instructions had been for him to gather a large group of beings and move swiftly to the waters off Sinclair Cay, where they would lie in wait to ambush Pan and his bodyguards when they arrived. Their mission was to kill Pan and prevent him from finding the white dolphin.

It was obvious to Apollo that Python had not needed extra convincing to accept this mission, but Apollo did not know why. He was unaware of Python's actions on the night he was born twenty years earlier, and he knew nothing about the little Harbor Porpoise named Pan, who had played a pivotal role that night, other than what Python had just told them. For now, all that Apollo could determine was that the situation was tense and about to get even more so.

By his tone and manner it was apparent that Python was thrilled. Now his nemesis would come to him, and what was even more pleasing, he could kill Pan on the orders of Eris; what could be better? Instead of worrying about being punished for his actions long ago, or for killing Pan, now he could do it with the full blessing of King Poseidon. And by doing so, he would eliminate the threat Pan posed, because other than his gang, Pan was the only one who knew the true story from the night the white dolphin was born.

After briefing his gang on what Eris had said to him, he told them that they would leave the next day. He ordered them to circulate among the other tribes at the gathering and put together a war party numbering at least forty beings. "Get some Roughies," he shouted to the gang as they headed off to recruit the others. "But no Spinners." By Roughies, he meant Rough-toothed dolphins, a reclusive breed with short tempers and sharp teeth, while Spinners were exactly what the name implied. They spent half their time leaping up out of the water and twisting their bodies through the air. They were the clowns of the dolphin world, reluctant fighters at best, and certainly not killers. Python then swam over to Apollo and said, "Polaris, you will come with us."

"I am not a fighter," replied Apollo watching Python closely to gauge his reaction.

Python's expression darkened and for a moment, he did not reply, as if weighing the situation. Then he said with a sly smile, "Something tells me that you are. And a good one." He stared at Apollo, as if mesmerized by something he saw there. "You know, Polaris, I have a feeling that we have met before but …"

"What?" It was at that moment that Apollo sensed that he and Python had met somewhere before, long ago but the memory of it, if it was there to be had at all, danced alluringly in the deep waters of his memory, never quite coming close enough to the shores of his consciousness to be fully grasped.

"Never mind, replied Python. "Fighter or not, it will not matter, I do not expect much of a fight. And you, my mysterious friend, are coming with us whether you want to or not. We leave at first light."

And that was that. Apollo, the white dolphin now in disguise, would join in the ambush of a Harbor Porpoise, named Pan, who had been sent by the Sovereign Council to save the white dolphin. Apollo could not help but be affected by the irony of the situation, but whatever the eventual outcome, he knew one thing; he would take no part in any killing. Or so he thought.

CHAPTER EIGHT

The Tongue Of The Ocean

The Tiger Shark was big for its kind, measuring sixteen feet from its rounded, shovelnose to its scimitar-like tail. It weighed eleven hundred pounds, excluding the eighty-pound Yellowfin Tuna that it had swallowed whole earlier that night, and was now being turned into milky pulp, bones and all, by the shark's caustic stomach acid. The acid had had little effect, however, upon the Florida license plate or the gold and diamond Rolex wristwatch that shared the stomach with the hapless tuna. Had the shark possessed a brain the size and complexity of a being it might have had an interesting tale to tell about the inedible contents of its stomach; but as it was, its brain had only the most rudimentary of cognitive abilities; all of which were, at that moment, tightly focused upon the group of dolphins resting near the surface on that warm, humid night at the edge of the Gulf Stream, near Islamorada in the Florida Keys.

Over the preceding three days, the group led by Python, including Apollo had covered over half the distance between their starting point in the waters of the Gulf of Mexico and their destination at the Tongue of the Ocean on the east coast of Andros Island in the Bahamas. They had averaged over one hundred miles a day. It was an exhausting pace and some in the group had threatened to quit unless they rested. Python finally acquiesced and said they would get a late start on the fourth day, knowing that they had less than one hundred and fifty miles to go before they reached their final destination across the Straits of Florida.

That evening the dolphins had feasted heartily on the vast schools of Black Mullet that populate the coastal shallows of the Keys. To the untrained human eye, it might have appeared that the torpedo-shaped fish were playing a game with the dolphins, as they raced through the turquoise waters and leapt high into the air, landing in and among the dolphins. However, the rapidly diminishing numbers of the fish soon gave measure to the one-sidedness of the game. And when the scales of the last of the mullets settled slowly to the floury sand, the full-bellied dolphins separated into three groups to begin what they thought would be a long, leisurely night of rest, oblivious to the danger lurking below

Whenever possible whales and dolphins, even in such a large group, prefer not to sleep in deep water, where they are more vulnerable to sneak attack from kraken, and this night was no exception. Accordingly, the three groups chose to float in the welcoming shallows. However, with the deeper waters of the Gulf Stream flowing so close by, just beyond the edge of the coral reef, Python had assigned several members of his gang to keep watch. Throughout the night, they would all take turns doing this but when it was Tisiphone's turn, he was so tired from the journey that he fell asleep. It was the last mistake he would ever make.

The night was nearly over when the long shadow of the shark slipped silently over the edge of the reef and snaked upwards, toward the nearest group of beings. There were two dolphins directly in the kraken's line of sight; one was Tisiphone and the other was Apollo, who was the closer of the two to the oncoming jaws of death. But as sometimes happens in your world, there are times when one person dies and another lives even though both were in equal jeopardy. This is often passed off as simply the luck of the draw, but in the world of beings, no outcome is ever attributed simply to chance. To the contrary, beings believe that who lives and who dies is part of some mysterious and unknowable plan and they attribute the timing and circumstances of death to the will of God, regardless of whether it seems either just or unkind.

And so it was at that moment, the kraken bypassed Apollo and struck Tisiphone, dealing him a mortal blow. The startled cry of the doomed being brought Apollo and the others to full alertness, and within a matter of seconds Python and the other gang members set upon the shark, bombarding it with deadly sound waves to confuse it, and then pummeling with their beaks until its body was turned into a quivering mass. In the process, the kraken's stomach ruptured and its contents spilled out, including the gold and diamond watch, which was still running, and the license plate that flipped and fluttered on its way down, landing face up on the rippled bottom.

While the kraken was being terminated with extreme prejudice, Apollo attended to the dying Tisiphone, shepherding him to the surface and speaking with him in comforting tones as his life force drained slowly into the sea. By the time Python joined them, Tisiphone was dead. Together, Python and Apollo pushed his body out over the deeper water of the Gulf Stream and let it go. Slowly it sank into the depths and was gone.

"What did Tisiphone ask you?" asked Python as he and Apollo swam back to join the rest of the dolphins, who were now eager to resume their journey, having no desire to remain in the bloody waters where other krakens were sure to come.

"He wanted to know if I believed in God," replied Apollo. He was deeply saddened for the death of all beings, pure of heart or otherwise, mattered to him, and beyond that, Tisiphone had saved his life; a debt that could now never be repaid.

Python scrutinized Apollo and asked, "Well. Do you?"

"Yes. Do you?"

Python scoffed, "Why should I? What has God ever done for me?"

"He might ask the same of you," replied Apollo with a penetrating stare.

Python was taken aback by Apollo's reply. After a long pause he changed the subject, "Who are you—really?"

Apollo remained calm. "I told you, I am Polaris."

The answer did not satisfy Python. "No. I do not think so—Aurora believes you are the white dolphin."

How did she know? Apollo wondered but he maintained his composure and did not look away as some beings (and humans) do when they are lying or simply withholding the truth, which amounts to the same thing. In Apollo's case it was the latter. "Obviously I am not. My skin is gray."

Python was unconvinced. "Aurora said that you probably used magic to change your skin color. She said the white dolphin has mysterious powers and can even change himself into a kraken if he chooses."

"Does it matter what she thinks or says?" Apollo asked, playing to Python's weakness, which he had correctly sensed was a difficulty in dealing with females. Apollo had even begun to wonder if there was more to it than that. Perhaps Aurora was the real chieftain of the tribe, in effect if not in fact.

There is a reason that being societies are usually matrilineal, and it is not because females are larger than males, although in most cases, such as the great whales, they are; and it is not because they are more designing, even though that is often true. The real reason is quite simple; females are smarter than males. Period. Even though they sometimes do not choose to let that fact be known, depending upon the circumstances. (This is also true among your kind although half of you would probably deny it.)

Python soured at the question. "Of course not," he snarled and swam off to join his gang without pursuing it further.

Apollo knew that the matter was not settled but at least for the moment the challenge had passed. Within a few minutes, the large group of dolphins, less one, headed due east, out into the Gulf Stream and across the Straits of Florida. Apollo, the lonely outsider, followed but as he swam through the warm seas in the dawning light of day, he began to wonder if he ever would belong anywhere. It was a heavy burden to bear because loneliness is a more sinister hunter than any made of flesh and blood, on land or in the sea, for it is the one hunter that its prey cannot escape.

There are few places in all the Seven Seas with as dramatic and intimidating an underwater topography as the Tongue of the Ocean. From the sky, it appears to be a lazy, backward J, painted in midnight blue against a shimmering azure background but in reality, it is a deep, oceanic trench separating the islands of Andros and New Providence. What makes it so mesmerizing and menacing is that the waters of the Grand Bahama Bank that border it on three sides are less than ten feet deep, while only a few yards away, on the other side of the fringing barrier reef, perpendicular rock walls drop straight down to a depth of six thousand feet at the southeast end of the blind canyon, and over ten thousand feet deep at its northwest limit where it joins the Providence Channel. And it was in this place of stark geological grandeur that Python and his band of killers now gathered, in the shallow waters surrounding Sinclair Cay; the island upon which the resort called Oceania was located.

"Is that the edge of the deeps?" asked one of the Roughies as they approached the reef that marked the edge of the trench. The line of demarcation was sharp and unmistakable; two vast stretches of water, one azure, the other indigo, lying side by side in stark contrast; one side warm and welcoming, the other dark and threatening, separated by a thin ridge of coral that served as a threshold between safety and the unknown.

"Yes," responded Apollo.

"Have you been here before, Polaris?" asked Python. He was now certain that this charismatic stranger was not who he claimed to be. The incident with the kraken had elevated this thought to a new level but he was still not ready to accept that Polaris was the white dolphin. Perhaps it was because he did not really want to know.

"Yes. Why do you ask?" asked Apollo in a tone that startled the Roughie who was not used to beings questioning a chieftain.

"No reason," replied Python. He swam over to the edge of the cliff and peered down into its depths.

Apollo and the Roughie followed. So did the others. The water was so clear that they could have seen an object one hundred and fifty feet down, but beyond that point all definition was lost and their earsight, with its range of one thousand feet was useless beyond that depth. For a moment none of them said anything as each was lost in the terrifying beauty of what lay below.

"Is it as dangerous as they say it is?" asked the Roughie. His species had large eyes set well back on a narrow head, which gave them a vaguely reptilian appearance and at that moment his eyes were huge with fear and wonder.

"No more or less so than the open ocean," said Apollo. "The threat lies in the suddenness of the transition from the safe haven of the shallows to the darkness of the deeps. It is like day turning into night with no dusk in between, and foolish indeed is the being who does not approach this divide with caution for such dark waters are the kraken's domain"

"The kraken's domain. What blather," chortled Python. "I am not afraid. Watch this." He circled back across the shallow sand flats, his shadow skimming effortlessly through the crystal clear water. Then he turned and headed at high speed toward the brink. When he reached the reef, he burst up out of the water and leapt high into the air in a sweeping arc that brought him out over the edge of the canyon, where he plunged back into the sea and sank like a rock into the abyss.

After plummeting ninety feet diagonally down and away from the cliff face, something made him come to an abrupt stop; something deep inside—a cry from the shadows of his soul that sent a chill running down his spine, washing away the exuberance of his foolish actions. Whereas a moment ago he had been drifting over powdery white sand in sun-sparkled shallows, surrounded by three dozen beings, now he suddenly found himself all alone in the deep blue sea, as if he had been transported to the farthest reaches of the open ocean, with all its dangers and abject isolation. His heart began to pound. His eyes grew large. He glanced nervously around at his surroundings. In front of him was a panoramic view of the carbonate wall that dropped straight away until it disappeared into the gloom, while to the sides and behind him there was nothing except a vast blue emptiness—an emptiness that reached out now to swallow him.

Sensing danger, he scanned the depths with his earsight but no echoes returned to paint a mental picture of what lay below. *Behind you!* a voice cried out in his brain. He spun in place, his pulse rising now to the point of panic. Before he could direct his earsight in that direction, he saw it with his eyes: a dark shadow at the periphery of vision, closing on him at high speed. *What have I done?* flashed through his mind: he knew it was too late to call for help from those above the cliff. *Please God do not let me die here* he prayed. Atheism and imminent death are mutually exclusive even in a being like Python.

He braced himself for the pain of the kraken's bite. In seconds, the shadow took shape. It was not a kraken but a Black Marlin, and it was still coming at high speed. But when the giant fish saw that Python was not a school of Mackerel, it lunged up and away, becoming a silhouette against the shimmering ceiling above. Then, before reaching the surface, the marlin turned away from the cliff face and with several thrusts of it mighty tail disappeared into the blue void. Python did not wait to see if there were any other large pelagics in the vicinity. He rocketed back up the cliff face and punched over the reef with such velocity that he nearly bowled over the amused dolphins who had observed his encounter with the giant fish. They could barely contain their guffaws.

"Is something funny?" he asked angrily.

No one answered. Their smiles vanished.

"Good. Now let us get back to why we are here," said Python pretending nothing untoward had happened, but it had. The truth was that he had been frightened, really frightened, and that fact frightened him even more. It is the way of bullies, in their world and in yours that their aggression is a façade. He shook it off. "I expect that Pan and the Guardians will reach these waters tomorrow or the next day."

Beings are very good at estimating the time it takes for ocean transit, which varies directly with the size and speed of the smallest member of the traveling party. In this case, they knew when Pan and his escorts left the Kingdom of the Ancients—right after the last day of Godlight—according to Eris. They also knew how long it had taken Eris to reach Sinclair Cay, which she had made a point of passing on her way to the Gulf of Mexico. She claimed it was just curiosity that drew her there but the real reason was that the lure of the white dolphin was a magnet to her even though she knew she would not be able to see him. Knowing these two things, they were able to estimate with some degree of precision when Pan and the Guardians would reach Sinclair Cay.

Python continued, "We must prepare our plan of attack. Just as Eris did, they will likely approach from the northeast, moving down the Providence Channel, continuing across the north end of the Tongue of the Ocean until they reach the shallows surrounding this island. We will…"

"No. They will not come here," interjected Apollo with more certainty than he perhaps should have, given who he really was.

"Why?" asked a puzzled Python

"Because according to what Eris told you, Pan intends to be taken by Oceania's capture boat, and it usually patrols the waters further south, nearer the canyon's end. That is where Pan and the others will head, not here."

"How would they know all that?" asked Python.

"How did they know about the white dolphin's presence in the first place?" retorted Apollo. His way of answering Python's questions with a question never failed to lead the chieftain exactly where Apollo wanted him to go.

"Of course. You are right," said Python, still not quite sure what to make of Apollo's thorough grasp of this matter. "Do you know what this capture boat looks like, Polaris?"

Apollo nodded as the image of the dreaded vessel powered through his mind. How could he ever forget it? It was the cause of his five years of imprisonment. "It is a large white boat with blue and gold trim, and the name *El Sargento* on its stern."

"The sergeant," muttered one of Python's gang who had been raised on the Mexican side of the Gulf of Mexico and understood Spanish. "That is a strange name for…"

"Shut up," said Python as he eyed Apollo with a mixture of suspicion and curiosity. His detailed description of the capture boat resurrected Python's belief that Polaris was really the one they called Apollo, the one who had been taken by this boat five years earlier. *But how could he be?* he wondered since the white dolphin was supposedly still trapped in the oceanarium. From the start of their brief but intense relationship, the words and ways of this stranger had created a mindgap in the belligerent bully. One part of him distrusted the dolphin whom Aurora was convinced was Apollo, the now full grown and somehow disguised white dolphin who Python had tried to murder twenty years earlier. That part of his psyche told him to kill Polaris now and be done with it. But there was another part of his brain that held him back. In some perplexing way, he was filled with a sense of wonder and awe. He felt an unspoken attraction to the stranger; one that drew him closer, like a doomed fish to a shiny lure. And try as he might, he could not shake that feeling. After an awkward pause, Python asked, "How do you know all this?"

Without making any effort to explain or construct a lie, Apollo replied, "I just do." As he said it, he turned his head and locked a cold eye upon Python. And the more intense that Apollo's stare became the less forceful Python became.

Much to the surprise of the others, that ended the discussion. "I see," said Python. The confrontation was over. Their leader had backed down once more from the stranger, once too often for most of them, but no one chose to challenge Python for they knew to do so would bring swift retribution. Python looked at the others and said, "We will swim south. Now!"

Apollo interjected, "Actually, southeast would be better. On the far side of the canyon there is a bend in the wall where we can remain hidden from the earsight of the oncoming Harbor Porpoise and Orcas." Apollo's knowledgeable comment pleased Python and seemed to mollify the gang for the moment. But Apollo knew that the time was fast approaching when he would have to declare his allegiance to one side or the other, and there was little doubt in his mind whose side he would take.

The boat, El Sargento, was a new generation of near-shore research vessels, sixty-five feet in length, with an eighteen foot beam, drawing six feet of water with its modern, high-speed hull design. Its fantail provided ample space for research and/or capture-related activity with an easily accessible dive platform. It towed a twenty-four foot Zodiac inflatable boat with twin, one hundred and fifty horsepower outboard engines. To your kind it might appear innocent enough, even somewhat appealing in its sleekness, but to Apollo it was a devilship, capable of running down even the fastest beings and ensnaring them in its capture net. Apollo would also tell you that despite the best efforts of the crew, many of the beings trapped by its net did not survive capture. Apollo had been one of the lucky ones, that is if being placed in a glass and concrete prison for the rest of your life can be considered lucky.

The captain of El Sargento, who was piloting his boat through the choppy waters of the Tongue of the Ocean, suddenly realized that something was happening that appeared to be quite a fortuitous coincidence. His sonar revealed two different groups of dolphins converging upon each other, and while he could not understand why, he intended to capitalize upon it. His sonar revealed that the first group approaching from the north was made up of what he thought were three medium size whales and a small dolphin or porpoise, he could not tell which. The second and much larger group, made up of smaller whales or dolphins, was approaching his boat from the east.

The first group was, of course, Pan and the Guardians. They were heading toward the capture boat intent on fulfilling their mission, when their earsight alerted them to the other group of beings. It had not taken Pan and the Orcas long to realize that their mission would have to be aborted due to the appearance of this second group, whose intentions they could tell were not friendly. They knew this because the fast approaching dolphins had refused to reply to their greeting calls and among beings, this was a clear sign of trouble.

Soon the two groups of beings converged and Python and his band of killers formed a large circle around Pan and the Orcas. As they did, Python noticed that the one he knew as Polaris had disappeared. He scanned the seas for the missing dolphin, but he was nowhere to be seen, so Python turned his attention back to the attack. Meanwhile, Ares and his brothers, Aegyptus and Danaus, had positioned themselves as three spokes of a wheel, with their broad flukes toward Pan in the center and their heads with their lethal rows of conical teeth, facing outward toward the encircling dolphins.

At that same moment, the captain, ignoring the shouts of a young blond woman in a half wet suit on the fantail, headed the boat toward the circle of beings. "Stop!" she shouted at him repeatedly, fearing that they would hit the dolphins. Finally, the captain slowed the boat before reaching the circle. As it coasted to a stop, he ordered two crewmen to launch the Zodiac and set the net. The significance of what was taking place beneath the water was lost upon the captain but not to the young woman. All he saw was an opportunity to capture a large group of dolphins. However, she sensed that there was something terribly wrong about the entire situation.

First, the presence of the three Orcas troubled her, not just because of the regulations against capturing or harassing them, but because it was highly unusual for them to be seen in those waters, and for them to associate with their smaller cousins. And second, she could tell by the circling behavior of the larger group of dolphins that a fight was about to take place. She yelled at the captain to abort the capture but he ignored her. The Zodiac's twin outboards roared to life and the two crewmen steered it away from the mother boat at high speed. Oblivious to the capture boat and Zodiac, Python sent in the first wave of attackers.

"Get ready," said Ares as Python's dolphins closed on them.

"God be praised," added Aegyptus, thinking that his younger brother would add, 'God bring us the Light' since that was how they always began a fight with their mortal enemies, the kraken. But Danaus did not reply because at that exact moment, the Zodiac passed over him and the blades of one of the outboard engines pierced his skull, killing him instantly. Ares and Aegyptus turned just in time to see their brother's lifeless body beginning its long slide into the abyss. But there was nothing they could do about it because by then the first wave of attackers had plowed into them, and soon they were locked in a brutal battle for their own lives.

Aegyptus grabbed one of the Roughies by the throat, ripping it open and flooding the crystal clear waters with a bloom of crimson. He did the same to two more, while Ares slew three others with equal ferocity. (The full force of a Killer Whale's attack is a frightful thing to see and your kind should consider yourselves lucky that these warriors of the waves never, ever attack humans. But many of Python's gang were not so fortunate on that terrible morning in the Tongue of the Ocean.)

"Oh no" moaned Pan as he saw Danaus die. Ignoring his own safety, the little porpoise swam down under Danaus' body and tried to buoy him up. It was a valiant but futile gesture and it nearly cost him his life. As the dead Orca sank, the suction created by his huge body prevented Pan from getting out from under him. "Oh no," cried Pan again, but this time it was his own death that loomed before his eyes as he sank slowly into the depths.

Meanwhile, high above, the battle raged on as the first wave of Python's killers pulled back to reconnoiter, leaving seven of their comrades dead in the blood-soaked waters. The two remaining Orcas were, as yet, unharmed. "Where is Pan?" shouted Ares as he surveyed the scene and readied himself for the next wave of attackers.

Aegyptus looked around. "I do not know."

Suddenly, he reappeared and he was not alone. Rising from the depths, the exhausted little Harbor Porpoise was being carried toward the surface by a Bottlenose Dolphin. At first the Guardians misinterpreted what was happening and Ares was about to attack the dolphin until he saw that he was helping, not hurting, the little one.

After helping Pan get a breath, Apollo brought him back to the Orcas. "I am on your side," he said as he assumed the position that Danaus had held.

"Who are you?" asked Ares, still not letting down his guard. Apollo did not answer as the next wave of killers was upon them. Leading the charge this time was Python and when he saw that Apollo had taken the side of the others, fury overtook him.

By now, the Zodiac had closed the circle of the huge net and had tied back up to the capture boat. All that the crew had to do now was to cinch the enormous purse seine and all the dolphins, dead or living would be trapped. Seeing this, the blond woman jumped into the Zodiac and cast it off from the capture boat. She put it in gear and started to pull away, going slowly so as to not hit any dolphins. This allowed one of the crewmen to jump back into the Zodiac and grab her. In the struggle, the throttle lever was bumped all the way forward and the Zodiac leapt across the water. As it did, the woman lost her balance and was thrown overboard into the sea, which was now a seething mass of bodies and blood.

At the instant the woman fell into the water, Apollo recognized her. It was Caitlin Quinn. He was overcome with angst, as his instinct was to rush to her and protect her from the melee, while his sense of duty dictated that he stay beside the Guardians. Even as he wrestled with this mindgap, he knew that the tide of battle was turning against them. Python had been a cunning adversary, never fully committing all the dolphins at once, but sending them in waves, while holding some in reserve.

There was a momentary lull as the attackers pulled back for what Apollo knew would likely be the final assault. Taking advantage of the moment, Apollo told Ares he would be right back, then he swam away to help Quinn. She was struggling amidst the mayhem. What was worse, the blood had attracted a school of Blue Sharks and they were now milling about on the outside of the net. It kept them at bay but it was only a matter of time before the kraken would discover that the bottom of the net was open and attack from below.

Apollo reached Quinn's side and brushed up against her. She was startled at first but realized that the dolphin was trying to help her. As a dolphin trainer and veterinarian specializing in marine mammals, she was well aware of the numerous instances of dolphins in the wild acting to save humans and she clung to him as he gently pushed her toward the Zodiac. The crewman, whose anger had now turned to concern, headed the Zodiac in her direction. Then something happened that sent a jolt through Quinn's body. The color of the skin on the dolphin's cape was light gray, almost pale but just behind his left eye she saw it, barely visible but it was there nonetheless—the star birthmark. During the trip to the Tongue of the Ocean with Python and his gang, Apollo had been unable to find the minerals on the sea floor that would keep his skin gray. The effect was wearing off and Apollo knew sooner or later someone would notice it, which is exactly what Quinn now did. "Oh my!" she gasped. "Apollo, is it you?"

Using the same method by which he had spoken with her that night in the lagoon, he answered, "Yes. I told you I would be here to protect you if your dream came true."

"Thank God," she sighed, laid her head on his back, and held onto him tightly. The Zodiac reached them and the crewman reached down to her. She tried to avoid him but Apollo said, "Go with him. I will be back." Then he pulled away from her, slipped beneath the waves, and disappeared. "No!" she cried but it was too late. With a sudden jerk, she found herself back in the Zodiac.

Apollo reached Ares and Aegyptus just before the next wave of attack began. Ares glanced appreciatively at Apollo and said, "Your help is most welcome stranger."

Apollo acknowledged him with a grim smile.

"Here they come," shouted Aegyptus, as the next charge of Python's gang took shape.

Recovered now from his near drowning but still not certain of who the strange dolphin was, Pan tucked himself behind the brothers and whispered, "We do not want to die."

And they would not for at that moment, rising up from the deeps came the haunting sound of whalesong. Apollo recognized it at once and he knew that all would be well.

"What is that sound?" asked Ares.

"That," replied Apollo "is the sound of our salvation."

The whalesong continued for a few moments longer and was then followed by another sound, this one more visceral. It was a high-pitched keening sound made by a school of giant Blue Marlin, twenty-four of them, each approximately fifteen feet in length and weighing over two thousand pounds, with wicked sword-like bills three feet long. Their enormous bodies pushed a shock wave of water before them as they drove upward out of the deeps, aiming their attack directly at Python and his gang. To Apollo's great relief, he saw that the billfish were accompanied by a Humpback Whale. "Zeus!" Apollo cried out. "You came!"

Over fifty feet in length and an equal number of tons in weight, Zeus' stocky body, jet black above and pure white below, moved effortlessly through the water, powered by broad flukes with serrated trailing edges that were all black with a unique white criss-cross pattern on their underside. His exceptionally long flippers, one-third of his body length, were pure white on both top and bottom, and they were spread apart at a downward angle, looking like angel wings to Apollo and his companions who watched his arrival in awe. Zeus had a large rounded projection at the tip of his lower jaw that was also pure white and there was an air of authority about him wrapped in nobility and grandeur. While the Blue Marlin launched their attack on Python and his gang, Zeus swam over to Apollo and said, "Did you doubt that I would?"

But Zeus did not wait for a reply. "Time for this later." With that, Zeus joined the school of Blue Marlin in their attack upon Python's gang. The fight did not last long as the Humpback's huge flukes crushed the heads of attackers, while the deadly swords of the billfish stabbed and slashed the bodies of others. The few killers who survived the initial assault, mostly the larger Roughies, tried to escape but Ares and Aegyptus made short work of them. When it was over all the attackers were dead except Python whom the Guardians brought before Apollo.

Finished with the fight, the Blue Marlin gathered in formation in front of Zeus, who looked at them and nodded. Then, without further adieu, the giant billfish disappeared into the deeps.

Pan's heart was all in a flutter and he cowered before the leviathan. "Scares us. Scares us," he muttered to himself.

Apollo smiled at Pan and replied, "Do not be afraid. Zeus is my friend—our friend." Then he turned his attention to the Guardians and Python.

"Here is their leader," said Aegyptus proudly.

"Yes. I know. His name is Python," said Apollo.

"Shall we kill him," said Ares without emotion.

"Yes. Kill him," said Pan, peeking out from behind the others.

"Shut up you little traitor," snapped Python. "You always were a coward."

"We will show you who is a coward," said Pan forgetting himself. He moved toward Python, arching his little body as if to fight the black dolphin but Aegyptus intercepted him and nudged him back.

"No. Let him go," said Apollo.

"What!" said Ares. He was grateful for the stranger's help in fighting the killers and for saving Pan but he was not going to take orders from him.

"Why?" asked Aegyptus.

"He saved my life once. I owe him this," replied Apollo.

As much as Ares would like to have killed Python, he backed down. He understood and accepted Apollo's reason.

Python eyed Apollo carefully, not believing what he was hearing but Apollo dispelled any doubts the black dolphin had. "Go. Now!"

Python sneered at him, "I would not do the same for you."

"You already did." Apollo said softly, "We are even."

"No," snarled Python. "We are not done yet, Polaris, you and I." Then he turned and swam away. Apollo watched him go and as he did, he sensed that Python was right. But he shook off the feeling and glanced at Zeus who nodded slowly as if to say that he had done the right thing.

"You should have let me kill him," said Ares in a measured tone. To him the only good enemy was a dead enemy.

"No. There has been enough killing for one day," said Apollo. Then remembering Caitlin Quinn, he said, "I have something I must finish. Wait for me here." He left the others and shot up to the surface. Quinn was standing on the fantail of the boat and he headed toward it. She saw him coming, dove into the water, and swam to him. They met and she clung to him like she had done that morning in the lagoon many weeks earlier. Then with her holding on tight, Apollo slowly swam in a large circle around the boat while the captain and crew stared in disbelieving silence. "Thank you, Apollo, for saving my life," she murmured.

"Just like in your dream,' he answered; his thoughts intermingling with hers inside her head.

"Yes," she said with a shadowed smile. Her voice trembled. "I do not want you to go but I know you cannot stay."

He did not answer. What could he say? She was right. The chasm separating their two worlds was even greater than that which lay below them. Finally he said, "I must leave you now."

"Will I ever see you again?" she asked pressing her head against his.

"I do not know."

She nodded sadly. They reached the boat where she climbed back onto the dive platform and turned to look at him. They shared a last, lingering look then he slipped beneath the water and was gone.

With tears streaming down her pretty cheeks, she climbed back up onto the fantail where the captain was waiting for her. Still in awe from what he had seen, he asked her what she would like him to do. "Take me home," she said struggling to maintain her composure.

He nodded sympathetically. By that time, they had already collected the capture net and secured the Zodiac, and soon the boat was headed away from the bloody circle of death, with Caitlin Quinn standing on the fantail, gazing forlornly at the churning wake. Despite her sadness, somewhere deep inside, a tiny voice cried out in joy for in that moment when the white dolphin saved her life, two sentient beings had shared a moment of pure love, unfettered by the complexities of ego and id; a love that she was certain would last forever.

When Apollo returned to the others, Pan and the two Guardians were waiting in eager anticipation. Their eyes were locked upon him in a strange and probing way, while Zeus hovered nearby. Apollo could tell by their expressions that Zeus had not revealed his secret. For a moment no one spoke. Finally Pan swam forward and asked, "We were wondering…that is we were…"

Ares interrupted Pan. "We want to know who you *really* are."

"The black dolphin called you Polaris, but we do not believe that is your true name," said Aegyptus. "Tell us, please. Who you really are." There was an undercurrent of excitement and expectation in the Orca's voice, and the expressions on the faces of the others showed they shared the feeling.

"There is something else," added Ares, motioning with his flipper toward the left side of Apollo's head. "There on the side of you head. A mark, in the shape of a star. We did not see it before in the heat of battle. But now it is clearly visible."

Pan's eyes grew wide and he uttered a little cry. He swam closer to Apollo and looked at the birthmark and suddenly he was overcome with emotion. There it was. The same mark he had seen twenty years earlier on the baby white dolphin. "Oh my," he muttered. "Oh my. It *is* you."

Apollo glanced at Zeus who gave him a subtle nod. A vast stillness fell upon the waters of the Tongue of the Ocean. At the surface, the waves became calm, as calm as the deeps below, while high above the sun hung in a pale and empty sky, its liquid light cascading into the cerulean water, encircling the small gathering of beings in sparkles of white and gold. And in the center of the circle of light, alone among the others, the wayfarer of the open waves, who had spent his entire life in and out of the watery prisons of man, hung there in solitary silence; freed now of the encumbrances of man but not those of his own kind. In his newfound freedom he was about to take on a burden greater than any imposed upon him by man, for he was now being asked to carry the hopes of all whalekind upon his shoulders. It would be a heavy and unforgiving load.

Finally, Apollo nodded. "You are right. I am not who Python thought I was." He paused. Neither Pan nor the Guardians moved. No one dared to surface to catch a breath lest they miss the words that were about to be spoken. Words that would resonate across the Seven Seas. Apollo's earsight told him that the hearts of the three beings who had come to these waters to save him were beating in unison, their minds hanging on his reply, and their souls joined as one in a collective prayer. He knew what they wanted to hear; what they needed to hear, and at that moment he realized that in the grand plan of the universe, what *he* wanted or needed was no longer of any consequence. Who he had been was past. Who he was now and would ever more be was all that mattered. Gathering himself, Apollo glanced at Zeus once more and then looked at the others and declared, "My name is Apollo. And even though you cannot tell it at this moment my skin is white—pure white."

Ares and his brother gasped while Pan became so excited he was afraid he would pee right there and then.

"The white dolphin of whom the Legend of the Ancients spoke?" asked Ares with controlled emotion.

Apollo stared at the Killer Whale for a long moment, but before he could answer, Zeus did for him, "Yes. He is the Chosen One."

"Our Master has come," said Pan in spellbound adulation.

Apollo let out a soft sigh and said, "I am *not* your master. I am your servant. I am all that you want me to be and all that God will allow me to be. Now and always."

"We knew it!" exclaimed Pan. "Goody, goody." Then with bounding joy, he shot up to the surface and threw himself into a high leaping, twisting flip, in a move that mere months ago he would not have been able to do.

"God be praised," whispered the awe-struck Aegyptus.

"God bring us the light!" said Ares softly.

It was a turning point in all their lives. It was not the end of darkness—a darkness that was encircling Planet Ocean—it was not even the beginning of the end, but it was certainly the end of the beginning. The Ancients' prophesy had been fulfilled. The Chosen One had come. While none of the beings gathered there, save perhaps Zeus, could know it, that moment marked a sea change in the history of whalekind; between all that was and is, and would ever be.

For a few moments more, they hovered there in silence, bathed in the glow of an emotional sunrise that flooded the waters of their souls with warmth and light, and most of all, hope. Then, slowly, inexorably, thoughts of what lay ahead cast a shadow upon their joy, and brought them back to the present. It was left to Apollo to refocus them upon the task at hand. First, he led them in a prayer for their fallen brother. It was a thoughtful gesture that only served to reinforce all that he had become. And then, with the courage and conviction of the warrior prince they so desperately wanted him to be, Apollo gave the command to leave. Together with Pan, the Guardians, and Zeus, they turned and headed toward the Kingdom of the Ancients to seek whatever fate had in store for them and for all whalekind.

CHAPTER NINE

The Last Best Hope

Twenty-one days after leaving the Tongue of the Ocean, Apollo and his companions reached the Kingdom of the Ancients. The late summer sun had lost its luster and gray clouds ruled the fading skies. To that point, they had been spared the hurricanes that sweep across that part of the Atlantic Ocean at that time of year, but as they neared their destination, storm clouds waited for them in more ways than one. Their journey had been uneventful. Long days and restless nights, with their minds filled with fading memories of the bad times they had left behind, and their hearts filled with sadness for the brother whom Ares and Aegyptus would never see again. Danaus' absence was more noticeable than his presence had been on the journey south, and each Guardian bitterly regretted that they had not had a chance to say good-bye. But even as the brothers struggled to deal with this, Zeus had been a source of comfort to them. His kind words and reassurance that one day they would all be reunited made the loss bearable.

Their journey had carried them through the surface layers of the vast blue ocean that lay over the Hatteras and Nares Abyssal Plains, skirting south of the Bermuda Rise and pressing on toward the Atlantis Fracture Zone. They had made good time as Pan, the smallest of the group, seemed to have gained strength since the outbound journey.

Ares noted this and had commented upon it, saying he believed it was due to the exercise that Pan had received during his extensive open-ocean travels over the past three months. Aegyptus agreed. Pan politely acknowledged their views but deep inside he knew it was something different. He could feel it; a growing sense of well being and a return to the vitality of his youth, which he attributed to the presence of Apollo. And nothing anyone could say to the contrary would change his mind.

However, Pan's burgeoning spirit was soon deflated as they approached the Roundtop at the center of the vast plateau, for it was not what it had been two months earlier. There was no sound of voices raised in a heavenly chorus; no stately procession of kings and their courtiers filled with pride and a common sense of purpose; no bright rays from a summer solstice sun to blanch waters resplendent with marine life: there were none of these things. Where once there had been sound, warmth, and light, now there was only silence and emptiness, and a sense of foreboding as deep and dark as the abyssal plain that lay just beyond the edges of the Kingdom.

When the group reached the rise at the center of the plateau, Hera, the beleaguered Moderator of the failed Gathering, and two other members of the Sovereign Council; Dionysus and Pluto, kings of the South Atlantic and Arctic Oceans respectively, were waiting for them in the naked waters turned hostile by an autumn storm come early. The somber looks upon their faces cast a pall over what should have been a jubilant homecoming; complete with the return of the brave little Harbor Porpoise with the white dolphin—the last best hope of whalekind.

The first thing that Hera did was to speak to Ares and Aegyptus with compassion in her voice. "I am sorry for your loss." Word of the battle at the Tongue of the Ocean had already traveled far and wide across the Seven Seas to both friend and foe alike.

Ares spoke for both of them. "Thank you, Madam Moderator."

Hera continued, "Danaus died in a worthy cause. One for which I fear many more will give their lives, but no loss will be more keenly felt than that of your brother."

Aegyptus acknowledged her kind words with a sad smile and then swam off to be alone. As he disappeared into the gray waters, Ares said, "Do not worry, your Grace. He will be ready when duty calls."

Hera continued, "It calls to us now, Ares. And soon we must answer." She paused and then gave a warm smile to Pan and his companions. "Welcome back, Pan. You have done well. Word of your courage has spread throughout the Seven Seas."

"Thank-you, Madame Moderator," replied Pan with shy smile. "May we present to you our honored guests? First, Zeus. He is…"

Hera interrupted Pan. "Hello, Zeus. It is good to see you again."

"And you, your Grace," Zeus answered warmly.

"You two have met before?" said the startled Pan.

"Yes. A long time ago. When I was young and Zeus was still old," Hera said teasingly.

"You still look young to me," said Zeus.

"Thank you, but I do not feel young."

Without waiting for Pan to get to him, Pluto said, "Hello Zeus, you old sealord you."

"Pluto, my good friend," said Zeus warmly. Then in a bittersweet tone he added, "I was sorry to learn of your father's death. He was a good and wise king."

Pluto's warm expression chilled. "Thank you. For one hundred and seventy years my father avoided murderous whaling ships only to be killed by primitive humans in an outboard with hand-held harpoons."

Zeus nodded. "We shall miss your father very much."

The greeting between Zeus and Dionysus followed. Its nature revealed that they also knew each other but there was no warmth on either being's part.

Pan and the Guardians were surprised by this interchange between the Council and Zeus and it only served to add to the air of mystery that surrounded the Humpback Whale. Throughout the journey back to the Kingdom, Zeus had said very little, and often it appeared that his mind was elsewhere. Pan was certain that there was more to this black and white giant than met the eye but he could not quite figure out what it was. Apollo on the other hand was not surprised. Awed by the mystery of it all, Pan presented Apollo to Hera and with graciousness that befit her position she said, "Please forgive me, Apollo, for not welcoming you with greater hospitality than this sad moment permits. Your presence honors us at this dark time."

"The honor is mine, Queen Hera," said Apollo. His greeting made the Queen smile.

Finally, Pan introduced Apollo to Pluto and Dionysus. Both seemed uncomfortable, as if the legend was bigger than the reality. This is often the way of legends, but it would not be so in this case, as they would soon discover. Pluto's initial shyness soon melted away and he welcomed Apollo with a heartfelt greeting, edging over to the smaller being and rubbing noses with him, in the way of all beings from the northern seas. Apollo reciprocated the gesture.

However, there was no refinement or warmth in Dionysus' response. "I thought you would be pure white," he snapped.

The effect of the minerals that Apollo had eaten on his way to the Gulf of Mexico had not yet fully worn off, giving his body a ghostly, pale gray tinge. Before Apollo could reply, Hera admonished her colleague, "As usual, Dionysus, you have spoken before you know the facts."

Dionysus started to protest but Apollo interjected with grace and poise. He explained what had turned his skin gray and advised that it would soon be pure white again. Dionysus was not satisfied, but a glare from Hera backed him off at least for the moment.

With the greetings done, Hera turned to the situation at hand. "You must be weary from your journey and I suggest that we reconvene after you get some rest and food. Then, I will brief you on the growing difficulties in our world, and share with you my thoughts on what must be done to avoid the coming war."

"You are most thoughtful, Madam Moderator," replied Apollo. "I *am* tired, as I am sure are my companions but our enemies are growing stronger by the hour. So please tell us now. "

"Very well," replied Hera. "The news from the far corners of our domain is not good. There have already been skirmishes between our forces and those of Poseidon. And what is worse, we have learned of several fatal attacks by his followers upon humans."

"Oh my. They have killed humans!" exclaimed Pan. He turned to Apollo and gasped, "Poseidon has broken the Ninth Law."

Dionysus snapped, "Excuse me, Queen Hera, but before we presume to trust this pale gray ghost, or his little sycophant, with an update of the current situation and details of our battle plans, I think we deserve to know more about him."

"Who are you calling a sycophant?" Pan asked with a wave of anger rippling across his stout little body. Then he looked at Apollo and whispered, "What is a sycophant?"

Ares answered for Apollo as he moved closer to Pan. "Never mind, Pan, for you are not one." He did it in part to comfort Pan and in part to let Dionysus know that Pan had powerful friends.

"What do you want to know, Dionysus?" demanded Hera.

"To begin with, I want to know who he is and where he came from," retorted Dionysus.

With barely restrained annoyance Hera replied, "We already know *who* he is."

Dionysus weighed in deeper. "We know who he says he is. Before I bow down before one who may be a false idol, as you seem so willing to do, I need to hear more."

An icy silence fell upon the group of beings hovering above Roundtop. Hera was angered by the stridency of her South Atlantic counterpart and for the second time in an equal number of months she secretly wished that the mantle of Moderator had not fallen upon her. For a tension-filled moment, no one spoke. Finally, Apollo broke the silence. Casting a knowing look at Zeus, he turned back to the doubting king and asked, "Very well, King Dionysus, what would you have me tell you?"

Dionysus said simply, "Everything."

Hera was quick to reply. "You are a fool, Dionysus. You have always been so. These are times when we least can suffer fools."

Dionysus stiffened and started to drift toward the queen; a not unintentional drift. There was no mistaking his intent, which prompted Ares to move to intercept him. He was joined by Aegyptus who reappeared from the shadows. Before any contact occurred, Hera's voice boomed out, "Hold!" which they all did. She stared at Dionysus and said in so deep a rumbling voice that Pan could feel it in his rib cage, "Dionysus, your quick anger and sharp tongue will one day cost you dearly, but fortunately for you, that day is not yet here. Now move back to your place and be quiet." Dionysus was taken aback by the stridency of her command and he did as he was told. Hera motioned for the Guardians to back down and all were impressed by the confident manner with which Hera had dealt with the situation.

With calm restored, Zeus turned to Apollo and said, "Go ahead, Apollo. It is time."

Apollo, who had remained calm throughout the confrontation, nodded knowingly at the mighty Zeus. He paused to gather his thoughts and as he did, everything grew still and quiet in their surroundings. Then he began to speak, in a rhythmic and almost hypnotic manner.

"I do not remember the night I was born, save what has come to me in my dreams—actually one dream, the same dream that has haunted me over all the years since. I was stranded in shallow water, stuck in a soft wet mud and sand beside a deep channel. I could hear the cries of another of my kind. There was comfort in her voice. 'Apollo,' she cried. 'Where are you? Apollo. This is your mother. Come to me, my little one.' I tried to answer but my head was out of the water and I could not make her hear me. Her voice faded and finally ceased altogether. I was alone."

Apollo paused again as emotion overtook him. The beings listening to him felt it too, even Dionysus, although he tried not to show it; for the moment of birth is the first and perhaps greatest joy that a being will ever know, and to be separated from his mother in that moment was a pain unimaginable. Apollo composed himself. It would be the last time he would ever talk about that night to anyone, but it would not be the last time that he showed signs of deep emotion, for there would be many opportunities to feel the pain of loss in the dark days ahead.

He began again. "Suddenly, there in the water beside me I saw a presence. Long and black. It drew near, moving in silence, with a purpose that I sensed was evil. It stopped, for a moment it lingered, and then, certain of its purpose, it circled and began to swim toward me. But at the last second, it turned and disappeared into the dark waters of the channel. From the other side of me, three forms appeared out of the haze. They were humans, but of course, I did not know that then. One of them reached down and caressed my skin, sending a chill through my body. I tried to escape but I could not move. Then one human picked me up and carried me away."

"Where did they take you, Apollo?" asked Pan with wide eyes.

"Patience, little one," interjected Zeus. "All will become clear."

Apollo smiled at Pan. During their journey to the Kingdom, Pan had confessed to Apollo what he had done that night and asked for his forgiveness, which Apollo had unhesitatingly granted. And what was even more important, Pan had confirmed for Apollo what he had already suspected after his recent experience in the Gulf of Mexico, that the pale gray dolphin called Leto was his mother. However, Pan did not know, and therefore could not tell Apollo, who his father was. Still, it had been crucial revelation to Apollo. During those first weeks together, Apollo had grown quite fond of Pan, and he sensed that their lives would be intertwined as long as they both lived.

Apollo continued, "They took me to a cabin beside a river and they made a pen in the shallows into which they placed me. They tried to feed me little fish but I was not ready for solid food. I hungered for my mother's milk. The next day a group of other humans came and took me away; to a place they called Ocean World"

"Ocean World," said Pan. "Is that like Oceania where…"

"Where beings are held prisoner and put on display along with pathetic pinnipeds who clap their flippers and balance balls on their noses for food," snorted Dionysus.

Apollo paused for a moment, which had the effect of isolating Dionysus, and quieting him. But ever the diplomat, Apollo did not want to embarrass the Fin Whale. "Dionysus is right: beings are held captive in these glass and concrete liquid prisons but candidly, at that point in my life, were it not for my human captors I would not have survived. It was the first of three times in my life when humans have saved my life."

"The third time being when Trainer Quinn freed you?" asked Pan who by then knew the story of Apollo's escape from Oceania.

Apollo nodded. For a moment he seemed lost as the mention of Quinn's name washed a wave of sadness over him.

Pan looked at Hera and the two kings and said, in the smug but lovable little way of his, "We saw Trainer Quinn during the battle. She was very pretty." Getting no reaction from the three monarchs other than a patient smile from Hera, he looked back at Apollo and asked, "What was the second time?" Out of the corner of his eye, Pan saw Zeus give him a look. He fell silent. "Sorry. We promise we will be quiet."

Apollo began again. "I spent the first seven years of my life at Ocean World but it seemed longer. The color of my skin made me stand out from the rest of the beings. Although there were many different kinds of beings held there, the humans kept me with other Bottlenose Dolphins most of the time. And for most of the time, I felt very lonely even among my own kind. They were uncomfortable around me, because I refused to perform the tricks that the trainers tried to teach me, and I would not react to the simplistic intelligence tests that they tried to give me. This frustrated the trainers, and they took it out on all of us. It was during those long, lonely days that I came to know the dark side of man, his arrogance, his stupidity, and his cruelty. I saw the tragic effect this had upon my fellow beings, many of whom went mad. Very few ever lived to their full life expectancy. And in perhaps the greatest irony of it all, the humans justified our imprisonment in the name of saving our kind. They told themselves that by increasing man's exposure to those few of us in their water-filled cages, they were helping to save all whalekind, when the greatest salvation would have been to leave us alone in the oceans in the first place. The call of the wild ran deeply even in the few beings born in captivity, and they longed for the day that they might know the freedom that God had intended for them. Of course, none ever would.

"The days turned into months, and the months into years, and all the while I kept to myself. Then one day, I did something that changed everything. One of the beings, a Spotted Dolphin, was sick and one night I overheard the trainers saying that he was going to be 'put down' in the morning, which I had come to know is a euphemism for murder. The humans who are trained in the healing arts, or veterinarians as they are called, use a different word, which is to euthanize. It sounds more professional and vaguely peaceful, but the end result is the same. The veterinarians could not tell what was wrong with the dolphin but of course, the rest of us knew. He was not physically ill but morbidly depressed. He wanted to die and the humans, although out of ignorance not compassion, were all too willing to grant his wish.

"I could not allow this to happen so I spent all that night with him, talking to him about how precious life was, regardless of how bad the circumstances. I spoke of love and hope, and how God did not want him, or any of us, to die. The next morning when they came for him I remained by his side and would not allow the trainers to single him out. Whenever a human came near him, I pushed them away, sometimes in a threatening manner, and then returned to my sick friend's side. This went on for a quite a while, during which I would not allow anyone to get close enough to administer the deadly needle. When the Spotted Dolphin saw that I was willing to risk my own life for his, he shook off the darkness that had overtaken his soul and became animated and alert.

In celebration, together we performed several complicated jumps, which I had described to him during the night to take his mind off dying; jumps that the trainers had never seen before. This startled the humans and they did not know what to make of it. One of the veterinarians, who had seen me hovering nearby to them the night before, as they discussed their plan, said to the others that the only way I could have done what I did, was if I understood what their intentions were. He was convinced that I understood their language, which, of course, I did. He and the other veterinarians wanted to keep me there, but when the owners of Ocean World heard this, they decided I was worth much more as a research subject than a performer.

"The next day, that same veterinarian came and told me what they were planning to do because by then he was certain that I could understand him. He said that I had been sold to the National Marine Mammal Research Institute, run by the United States Navy in Point Reyes, California. I neither let on that I understood him nor did I fight them when they came to take me. Actually, I rather liked the trip, especially the part in the aircraft, even though I was wrapped in wet blanket in a metal box. It was like being a Flying Fish that could stay up forever—well almost.

"And so began my five years at the Institute. After my experiences at Ocean World, where I suffered long days of boredom, my new life was anything but. Of course, it was not as exhilarating, or threatening, as I now know the open seas to be, but at that point in my life captivity was the only world I knew. Unlike the work being done with lesser marine mammals, such as the seals and sea lions, the Navy recognized that the captive dolphins and small whales possessed a higher level of mental function, and they treated us as such. It was an exhilarating time for me as I was exposed to humans who possessed a far higher degree of intelligence than those at Ocean World. While this did not approach our level of cognitive abilities, at least they were humans that I could respect and admire.

One in particular, a Captain named Jackson, who was a neuropsychiatrist, took a particular liking to me and me to him. It was the beginning of a strong friendship that ultimately led to his saving my life; the second human to do so,"—he glanced at Pan—"but more on that later. Captain Jackson had spoken at length to the veterinarians at Ocean World, and as a result, his hypothesis was that I could understand human language. At first, I did not behave in a way to confirm that belief, especially not in the presence of others.

"But, after a while, all that changed. Captain Jackson was so charismatic, so conscientious, and so compassionate, that I could not help but like him. And so, not long after I arrived there, I began to cooperate with him and his team. Now it is important that you understand that I did not break the Tenth Commandment, but I did respond to his experiments. Although these were based upon what Captain Jackson and his colleagues believed to be leading edge theory in the world of cetacean neuroscience, they were still rather simplistic with respect to the reality of our world.

"I acted in a way that gave him hope for what might one day be a breakthrough in communication between man and dolphins and, more importantly, I made him look good to his peers and superiors. Unfortunately, it became apparent to me that the intentions of this latter group were less pure than those of Captain Jackson. I suppose I should have known they would be, since the institute was owned and operated by the Navy, whose primary mission is, after all, to make war not peace—a fact that is even more threatening to us today as we face the danger of a war with mankind.

"The research that Captain Jackson and his team were conducting was focused upon using software that ran on a new, and highly secret, quantum computer that the Navy had developed. The program was called Qubitware and Captain Jackson was convinced that the algorithms it utilized would be capable of deciphering whale and dolphin communication and translating it into English, and vice-versa. Even though the theory was flawed and its applications were quite clumsy, I acted in such a way to lead Captain Jackson to believe that it was working, at least at a rudimentary level.

"During that time, I became close friends with two other beings in our section; a Spinner Dolphin by the name of Janus, and a Bottlenose Dolphin named Morpheus. Under my guidance and control, the other beings working with us also cooperated with the humans, at least to the degree that I directed. Soon our group of thirty beings was the largest and most successful of all groups at the Institute. It was comprised mostly of Bottlenose and Spinner Dolphins, but with a few Striped Dolphins as well. Captain Jackson and his team had become the heroes of the Institute and we were his prize students. They were heady days for both humans and dolphins alike—but, sadly, they were not to last.

"The beginning of the end came because the Rear Admiral to whom Captain Jackson reported had become jealous of his subordinate's success and the fame that went with it. He went out of his way to denigrate and undermine Captain Jackson's work. It was the first time in my life that I witnessed the jealousy that many humans fall prey to. The admiral had his own theories on how the research should be conducted, which my fellow dolphins and I intentionally sabotaged because we had taken a disliking to him. This was a mistake.

"Soon, Captain Jackson was reassigned to another part of the Institute, where they were studying the use of dolphins in the war on terror. Since the Navy scientists were aware of our earsight, which they call active sonar, beings were being trained to locate and kill, or terminate with extreme prejudice to use their terminology, rogue human swimmers who might try to plant bombs on the hulls of Navy vessels. Meanwhile Janus, Morpheus and I, and our fellow former subjects from the Qubitware work were placed in a series of interconnected pens located in Drakes Bay, and we were left there to do nothing. We were joined by another group of dolphins who had been part of another project that the admiral had also cancelled. We were, in effect, rejects, which depressed everyone, including me.

"Often at night Doctor Jackson would come down to the dock and sit with his feet dangling into my pen, and he would talk to me at length, about his dreams and disappointments. I felt responsible for his reassignment because of my treatment of the admiral, so I would hover there in the glowing light of sunset and listen intently to him. I never gave him any sign that I understood what he was saying, but he sensed it anyway, of that, I was certain. Then one stormy autumn night, when the weather was as unpleasant as the message he came to give me, I learned that he was being transferred to another Navy research base in Hawaii. But the hardest part of what he was saying was that I would not be going with him. It was a sad time for both of us.

"My days with Captain Jackson were indeed over but not the way I thought as nature now took a hand in determining my fate. All during that day, a typhoon had been gathering power off the California coast, and late in the day it had taken a sudden and unexpected turn toward land, and the center of its landfall was Drakes Bay. By the time darkness fell, the seas were running high and we were being tossed about inside the pen. Its high steel mesh walls to seaward were specially designed to prevent us from jumping over them and all we could hope for was that the mesh itself would break before our bodies did, but as the full fury of the storm hit the coast; our chances of survival were looking very slim.

"And then, just when all hope seemed lost, Captain Jackson appeared and placing himself at great risk, he opened the gates between the pens and the bay. As the other beings headed out into open water, I was only able to get a few seconds with him. It was then that I almost allowed my emotions to overtake reason. As he knelt on the dock, holding onto a cleat to keep from being blown away, I came close to performing a mindlink, but I did not. Thinking back on it now, I am sorry that I did not. Instead I turned and struggled away through the towering swells, toward the open ocean where the other beings were waiting for me. I did not look back to see if he was still there, watching me but somehow I knew he was."

Apollo eyes glazed over and his voice trailed away. By now, it was growing dark and Zeus suggested that they had had enough for one day. Hera agreed. She and the two kings went to rejoin their royal attendants, leaving Apollo and the others to spend the night above Roundtop. Pan was the first to drift off to sleep but as Apollo followed him into the half-world of dreams, a strange thing happened. He had a dream in which he felt like he was being dragged by something down into the deeps. He tried to pull away but he could not. Deeper and deeper he went, until his lungs were bursting and his heart pounding, and then, as abruptly as it began, it was over. He awoke with a start. He was floating on the surface with Pan asleep on one side of him and Aegyptus on the other, while Ares, ever on guard, swam in a slow circle just below them. Zeus was nowhere to be seen, which did not surprise Apollo. In the all the times during his life when he and Zeus had been together, Apollo had never seen Zeus sleep. Apollo did not know why but he chose not to ask, as some things were better left unknown.

CHAPTER TEN

The Devil's Teeth

Apollo slept very little that night, and given that beings sleep only in half-measures to begin with, he had very little sleep at all. By morning, the three monarchs had gathered around him again along with Pan, the two Guardians, and Zeus; the great whale having reappeared with the dawn. There was a chill in the air and the ocean's surface was choppy with tiny wisps of white dancing across the tops of the gray-blue swells. Despite the stinging wind and gloomy skies, everyone's spirits were upbeat and they seemed eager to hear Apollo's story continue. And so Apollo wasted no time picking up where he had left off the night before.

"The years I spent at the Naval Institute had been the best years of my life. I did not know it at the time, but the challenges I had known up to that point were nothing compared to those that lay ahead. However, by the morning after my escape from the Navy's pens, my attention was not focused upon the future because the present was almost more than I could handle. The fierce winds and furious seas had driven me and the other beings thirty miles to the west of Point Reyes, to a place that human sailors know today as the Farallon Islands, but ancient mariners called the Devil's Teeth.

"As I recount this part of my story, you must remember that I had never been in bluewater before, and in keeping with the ancient name for the islands in whose proximity I now found myself, those black and greasy seas were about to give me an indoctrination straight from hell. To make matters worse, sometime during the night, Morpheus and I had become separated from Janus and the other members of our research group, and as dawn broke we found ourselves in the company of eleven dolphins we did not know.

"Mercifully ignorant to what we were about to encounter, we swam through the turbulent waters on the eastern side of the largest of the islands. As we drew nearer to the rocky shore, I spyhopped and surveyed the ramparts of jagged black rock thrusting skyward. Hovering there, my ears were filled with the raucous sounds of seabirds that were swooping and soaring above the waves or perched on the ragged cliffs, where their droppings had sullied its granite walls with streaks of pink and brown and white. One thing that I remember in particular was the coppery hue to the surface of the water. I wondered what could be the source of this strange tinge. I would soon find out.

"In the years that have transpired since those first faltering hours of freedom, I have come to know and feel at home in two kinds of seas; first, in the inshore waters where land and sea meet in gentle union, where rippled bottoms of sand underlie sparkling blue waters too shallow for kraken to prosecute their attacks; and second, in the open ocean where heavy swells roll like mighty titans, toward a distant landfall. In those clear upper layers that overlay the deeps, both first and second vision give ample warning to danger below and there is nothing to impede escape in any direction. In either case, shallow seas or open ocean, I feel that I am the master of my fate, ready for whatever may come my way.

"However, in those dark and ominous waters surrounding the Devil's Teeth, I encountered the steeps for the first time; that is, the abrupt interface of land and sea where vertical walls of rock rise high above the waves and also slip down beneath them with sinister ease toward the deeps, disappearing into inky darkness. On that day, in those black waters, I discovered that the steeps are an evil and foreboding place, where the margin between life and death is as slim and slippery as the towering cliffs and plunging rock face itself.

"Thinking back upon it now, I suppose the stillness of the seas through which we swam should have given me cause for alarm and signaled what was to come, but it did not. In marked contrast to the raucous seabird cries overhead, the dark waters were silent, as silent as death itself. I have long since learned that a complete lack of noise is not your friend in the ocean, for it is this silence that precedes the appearance of the kraken as they stalk their prey, and the absence of sound usually indicates the presence of danger. Such was the case that menacing morning when the first among our group was to die.

"The kraken, or Great White Shark as man knows it, that rose up from out the depths was bigger than any creature I had known before. It was a female, twenty-one feet long, seven feet wide, and six feet tall not counting her dorsal fin. Her body was nothing more than a gigantic life-support system for a mouth. Devoid of all but the most primitive of intelligence, she moved through the water with speed and dexterity as the warm blood in her veins, which is unique among all sharks, gave strength to her muscles and powered her enormous tail. The Spinner Dolphin beside me never saw the kraken coming and if there can be any mercy in such a death, it was in the swift decapitation that attended the collision of being and beast.

"The force of the attack drove the kraken's body half-way out of the water with the headless dolphin hanging from her tightly clenched jaws. Then in a thunderous crash of foam and blood, the kraken folded upon herself back into the water and disappeared into the depths, swallowing the body of the dolphin as she went. She was trailed downward by the severed head of the dolphin, which sank slowly away from us, its sightless eyes fixed in a stare, until it blended into the blackness below.

"Shaking off the initial shock of the attack, I called out to the others to close ranks and head for open water; I had realized too late that there was no safety to be found up against the steeps. Although I had never seen a kraken before then, I had heard tales of them from beings who had been born in the wild, but this beast was more horrible than any in the tales they told. And yet, even though I could not bring myself to admit it, the truth was that deep inside, tucked away in the recesses of my mind, where fear moves in lockstep with obsession, I felt drawn to her sinister beauty and horrible singleness of purpose; she was truly a ghastly and yet faultless union of form and function. That feeling still haunts me to this day.

"Falling into a tight formation, we started to swim away from the island but we had not gotten far when the second kraken took another being. This time it was my friend, Morpheus, swimming at the back of our group. To swim last in line was the most dangerous position, but someone had to be last, and Morpheus insisted that it be him. It was characteristic of his selfless nature and it cost him his life. Like the first kraken, this one was also a Great White Shark, but slightly smaller in size. As the kraken rose from the depths, it targeted Morpheus, who, at the last second, avoided being decapitated but still suffered a mortal wound to his belly. As his blood gushed into the water, turning it a coppery black, I could sense his terror and feel his pain. We both knew what had to be done. And in that knowledge, my heart sank to the sea floor.

"Morpheus and I had become close friends over the years we spent together at the institute. He had been born and grown up in the wild and his free spirit and boundless energy were undimmed by the glass and concrete walls that imprisoned us. He and I spent many nights alone together cruising around the holding tank. We talked of life and death and renewal, for he believed strongly that our existence on Planet Ocean does not represent the totality of what God had intended for us. He spoke with a passion that was contagious and as much as he loved life, he was unafraid of death—and he made me promise him that should he ever be faced with a slow and painful death in my presence, that I would give him a GoodDeath.

"I knew it to be a duty proscribed to each of us by the Ancients when faced with such a hopeless situation, but of course I had never seen it performed much less having done it myself. But I could not let him die in slow agony so with a hard charge and swift thrust of my beak into his temple I administered a GoodDeath to my brave friend, Morpheus. Seconds later the kraken returned and took his now lifeless body in his mouth and disappeared into the darkness below. As the kraken departed, I could see from the two claspers on its underside that it was a male. It made no difference to the danger the rest of us still faced but I remember wondering what gender the next one would be. It is strange how your mind fixes on such irrelevant thoughts when death is so near.

"It did not take long for my question to be answered, for no sooner had the second kraken vanished, than six other sharks materialized out of the darkness. These I could see were all females like the first. I called to my fellow beings and told them to gather around me in a tight knot, and my mind raced to find an escape from the living hell that surrounded us. Morpheus had taught me that Great White Sharks are stalkers who ambush their prey and I resolved that if these beasts were to kill us, we would make them do so in an open fight. So I charged one of the kraken, the biggest one.

"It startled her and she swerved to avoid me. It was a grand and foolish gesture, but as it turned out, it was unnecessary because she did not attack. Instead, the six sisters of evil just kept circling us, eyeing us through black orbs as empty and uncaring as the deeps. So I attacked another and this time I succeeded in ramming her side, which made her swim a few yards away, but she soon came back. Seeing that my attacks neither harmed nor frightened them, I gave up. My actions had only delayed the inevitable. In that moment of desperation and hopelessness I closed my eyes and for the first time in my life I said a prayer. It was one that Morpheus had taught me. It goes like this:

> *Heavenly Father, we are so small and*
> *thy oceans are so mighty, please protect*
> *us through the long and perilous night.*
> *And if it be your will that we do not live*
> *to see the dawn, I pray that you will take*
> *us into thy Good Light.*

"As I said this prayer, I felt something come over me, a strange feeling of peace. When I finished praying, I opened my eyes, expecting to see the kraken's conical head and gaping jaws looming before me. But I did not. The sisters were still swimming near us but we were no longer the object of their attention. Something had distracted them. Then I heard it too. From out of the deeps of the devil waters, there came the glorious sound of whalesong: it was the same hymn Pan and the Guardians heard at the Tongue of the Ocean, being sung by the same voice as deep, pure, and beautiful as if God himself were singing it. I will never forget the words or melody and at that moment, they were etched forever in my soul."

Apollo began to sing softly but with a power that came from the soul. As he did, Pan and the Guardians hummed along.

I lift mine eyes unto the skies
from whence my God shall save me.

He feels my pain and once again
he calms the seas around me.

I will not fear the Tempest's Roar
or the kraken's ragged bite.

For I know he will comfort me
through the long and darkening night.

And with the dawn will come the sun
to drive away the darkness.

Mine enemies shall all be dead
my victory will be ageless.

And when at last my days are done,
freed from the ocean's soft embrace.

I will lift mine eyes unto the skies
and dwell with God in paradise.

Apollo stopped singing and began recounting the story once more. "The singing grew louder and louder until it saturated our senses and lifted us up on its hauntingly beautiful refrain. Suddenly the seas about us were empty. The kraken were gone. It was then that a Humpback Whale materialized out the vast nothingness. It was Zeus,"—Apollo glanced at Zeus who smiled at him—"the same great whale who saved us mere days ago. Of course, I did not know it then, but he was to

135

become my protector, my mentor, and my friend. Back then he looked as mighty and majestic as he does here with us today, with a robust body, black as night on top, and a belly and flippers as white—well, as white as—me ."

A murmur rolled through the group but they soon quieted.

"Despite his imposing size, his presence was immediately calming to us. He told us to follow him. We did not need to be asked twice. Soon we were all skimming across the waves far to the west of the Devil's Teeth, riding his wake, and leaving behind the bodies but not the memories of our two lost friends. Not that the death of the first being, whom I had only barely gotten to know, was any less important, but as we placed countless miles between us and that horrific place, I could not get Morpheus out of my mind. I still cannot to this day.

"Many hours later, once we were safely out to sea, I was able to thank Zeus and ask him questions about who he was and how he came to save us. Given the juxtaposition of my prayer with our salvation, it occurred to me that Zeus had been sent by God. I took him to be an archangel on great white wings with a voice to soothe our souls and a body to save us from the kraken's bite. Zeus will deny that he is an angel but I will tell you in front of him, that if Zeus is not an angel, then angels do not exist."

Apollo paused and glanced at Zeus again who neither admitted nor denied the accusation. Hera seemed pleased with the idea but Dionysus did not. Zeus acknowledged Hera's gentle smile but when his eyes met those of Dionysus, there was no warmth on either part: the tension in the water was palpable.

At Zeus' urging, Apollo began again. "Regardless of whether Zeus is or is not what I believe him to be, I will tell you this, he is a powerful and perplexing being with an aura of mystery and magic about him that makes him unique among whalekind, at least to the extent that I know such things. He knows more than he says and he says less than I would like. Pan and the Guardians saw evidence of this in our battle at the Tongue of the Ocean, where he commanded a legion of Blue Marlin to attack our enemies."

This statement brought another murmur to the lips of Hera and Pluto and seemed to add to the discomfort of Dionysus. Pan noticed this for he was an observant and intuitive little being and he made a mental note to steer clear of the Fin Whale.

"Given what lies ahead of us now as we face the possibility of war, I am thankful that Zeus is on our side, just as I was on that morning in the far off Farallones. After escaping the kraken, we kept swimming out to sea until we finally stopped at a place where Zeus said we would be safe, and while the other beings, now ten in number went off to feed, I decided to talk to him about another being—one whose past, present and future troubled me more than any other—me. I told him about my life up to that point, its highs, which were few, and its lows, which were many. I told him about my long years of captivity and my few days of freedom. I told him about the loss of one friend and the death of another—a GoodDeath that I had administered. All the while, he listened patiently to my self-pitying diatribe.

"And then I asked him a flurry of questions, including; who were my parents and where was my nostos? Why was I white and why did I find it so hard to fit in with others of our kind? Why did some beings take an immediate disliking to me without provocation? Why could I not bring myself to do the bidding of humans like other beings do? And finally, I asked him two fundamental questions—who was I and why had I been born?

"Zeus listened patiently and then told me not what I wanted to hear, but rather what I needed to hear. He said that I was not alone in not knowing who my parents were but that one day I would. He said the pathway back to nostos is contained deep within each of us and that I would find it by following my heart. He also said that nostos is not necessarily the place where you were born, but it is rather the place where your heart dwells. He told me my skin was white because that was what God wanted me to be, and that it was because of my white color that some beings found it hard to accept me: that they judged me by the way I looked rather than by the way I acted.

"He pointed out that while I had refused to do the things that humans wanted me to do that were wrong, such as the demeaning animal tricks at oceanariums, I had no difficulty in doing those things that I knew instinctively were right, such as helping handicapped human children, or helping the scientists at the institute who were trying to find ways to communicate with our kind; an outcome that might ultimately eliminate their persecution of us. And finally, he told me that the answers to my last two questions would be found not in my past but in my future, and in the way I chose to live my life from that point onward.

"One could interpret everything Zeus had said to me as guidelines for all beings to live by each day that God gives us but then he told me something else—something that pertained only to me; something that would change everything from that moment forward. He told me—he told me..." Apollo tried again to continue but he could not.

Up until that point in Apollo's narrative, the memories of his early life had flowed freely but now he seemed uncertain, hesitant, and afraid. A great weariness came over him. He seemed lost and alone among the group of beings gathered around him above Roundtop in the center of the Kingdom of the Ancients. Deep emotion stirred in the hearts and minds of the others, cracking even the harsh façade that Dionysus endeavored to maintain. A distant stare filled Apollo's eyes; as the images in his mind's eye shifted from what had been to what was to come, and with that shift came the burden of greatness that few beings will ever know and fewer still will understand. With a deep sigh, Apollo said, "I am tired. Please give me pause."

For a long moment no one said anything. All were caught between wanting to let Apollo rest and needing to hear what Zeus had told Apollo on that day they first met—a day they sensed had been an auspicious one not only for the white dolphin but also for all whalekind.

Finally, Zeus broke the charged silence. "I will tell to you what I told Apollo on that day. And in this telling I will place upon you a burden unlike any you have ever known, or ever will again in your lives: it is a burden of knowledge, and responsibility, and duty as wide and deep as the sea itself. It will place upon you an obligation that once accepted can never be shirked. And if you accept it, it will lead to only one of two endings for your lives; either glory or death; the chances of the former being slight and the latter all but certain."

Zeus paused and looked with great import around the group, including Pan, the two Guardians, and the three monarchs, stopping for a moment when his eyes fell upon Dionysus; then continuing until he had made direct eye contact with them all. "If you are not prepared to share this burden, which Apollo has already taken upon himself, then you must leave this place now and never return." He stopped speaking to allow them a moment to ponder the matter. No one moved. No one spoke. All were frozen in time and place as each wrestled with the magnitude and implications of Zeus' words.

It was left to the smallest being among them to speak first. "We are staying here," said Pan, "at Apollo's side until glory or death overtakes us."

One by one, the others, including Dionysus, made no move to leave. Each affirmed in words and manner their commitment to the cause. Seeing this, Zeus smiled and nodded. He looked at Apollo and saw the shadow of weariness lift like sunrise on a summer sea. And he saw that it was good. Then with presence and purpose, Zeus began to speak again.

"On that day seven years ago, I told Apollo that the time would come when a great evil would fall upon the Seven Seas; when beings would turn upon each other with a hatred that we had never known; akin to that which man has inflicted upon himself since time began. I said that this darkness would lead to killing; killing of each other, and killing of and by man; such that the seas would run red with the blood of whales and man alike. And that this season of killing, if unchecked would lead to an eternity of darkness.

"I told him, that just as the Ancients had prophesied, one day there would come a being who would rise up to lead whalekind out of darkness. I said that day had come, and that he, Apollo, was that being." Zeus paused as all eyes fell upon Apollo. Pan and the Guardians had already heard this revelation three weeks earlier at the Tongue of the Ocean but that did not lessen its impact. For the three monarchs, it was an affirmation of what they had believed when they sent Pan to Oceania but they reacted to it differently. Although each maintained the poise that accompanies the wearing of a crown—metaphorically speaking—each displayed different emotions, but the differences were noted only by Zeus.

Zeus began again, "I explained to Apollo that this undertaking would lead him on an odyssey around the globe, during which he would face many obstacles and live in constant danger, and that success was not pre-ordained. I warned him that if he should fail, whalekind would fail with him. But I also told him that he possessed certain skills and abilities not given to every being—abilities that would serve him well in the tasks that lay ahead."

There was a murmur among the beings gathered around Zeus. It was apparent that Apollo was uncomfortable with what Zeus was about to say but the great whale said it anyway, for there is no half-telling a full truth. "Apollo possesses the same ability to communicate with other beings as do you, but he can also project his thoughts directly into the minds of other creatures, including those of equal intelligence such as yourselves, as well as those of lesser intelligence, such as fish, marine mammals and not least, humans. In so doing Apollo can control the minds and actions of others, great and small. He can touch their hearts where they are touchable and reach into their souls where they exist."

Pan's eyes grew wide. "We believe that you, mighty Zeus, also possess this ability for we saw with our own eyes what you did with the Blue Marlin."

Zeus acknowledged this to be true. By the looks of Hera, Pluto and Dionysus, they were impressed but not surprised for such abilities had been the subject of much rumor in the world of whalekind, but none of them had ever known any being who had the skill.

"Can he read our minds as well?" asked Dionysus.

Zeus stared at the king and replied, "No." It was a lie.

"How does one go about acquiring such a skill," bubbled Pan excitedly.

Zeus smiled a half smile. "One cannot, my little friend. It is God-given."

"Pity," said Pan. He turned to Apollo and with an impish grin said, "Make us do something, Apollo."

"Pan," said Hera sharply. Her powerful voice startled the little porpoise. Seeing this, her tone softened and she added, "Please, let Zeus finish."

"Sorry, your Grace." Even though he did not let on, Pan suspected there was more to Apollo's powers than that.

Zeus began again, "This was an onerous message to share with a being as young and naïve as Apollo was then. At first, he did not believe me. Then he grew angry and asked what if he was to refuse to accept the mission. I told him he had no choice. Finally, he asked how I came to know all this. I told him then, as I tell you now, that I just do. You will have to accept that fact for there are things in life that one must accept on faith…"

"Because without faith all is lost," interjected Pan.

Hera frowned at Pan but Zeus smiled. "Yes, Pan. That is right." Zeus looked at the others and added, "For now, all you need to know is that I am the messenger, and Apollo has been chosen to shine my Message of the Light in the darkness."

"The messenger," whispered Pluto who had remained silent up until that point, which is characteristic of beings from the northern seas. They are a solitary society of beings, spending much of their lives under and around blue ice. The King of the Arctic Ocean had had doubts about the Loyalist cause, but this most impactful of revelations sealed his support.

"We are ready," said Pan. "Just tell us what we are to do."

"Not yet, little one," cautioned Zeus. "But soon." Zeus asked Apollo if he felt he could go on with his story.

Buoyed by the collective energy around him, Apollo said that he could and began again. "I accepted the challenge that Zeus laid before me and I am heartened that you have now done the same." As he said it, he looked at each of the beings hovering before him in those cold, gray waters of the North Atlantic. "Zeus was not surprised at my decision. He told me that he would always be there for me when I needed him but not always when I wanted him. And then he added that the ultimate success or failure of my mission would depend on me not him.

"Zeus then advised me that the odyssey on which I was about to embark would be divided into three parts; the first of which would take me down the west coast of South America around Cape Horn and up the east coast to the Caribbean, where it would end with another long period of captivity by man. It would be the last of such imprisonments that I would have to endure and one from which I would escape again with the help of a human as I had done at the Institute, but this time it would be a female, which you now know proved to be true.

"The second part of my journey would begin after my escape from Oceania and bring me here to the Kingdom of the Ancients, which it has now done, and the third and final leg would be the longest and most dangerous of all: it would take me the rest of the way around Planet Ocean, passing through all but one of the Seven Seas, until I returned finally to nostos—assuming I survived that is. He also said that for the first two legs of my journey I needed to eat some minerals that I would find on the sea floor that would turn my skin gray, as we have already discussed.

"However, for the final leg he said I would be among friends and a disguise would no longer be necessary." Apollo glanced at Pan and the two brothers and smiled. "Friends in whose company I now feel secure." Pan and the Guardians nodded with deep admiration for their leader.

"Zeus added that during the first leg, I would face four challenges that would test me to make certain I was worthy of the role for which I had been chosen, and that failure in any one of these challenges would end my mission and possibly my life. He said that these challenges would measure me on four personality traits, courage, cunning, commitment, and character, the first of which I had already demonstrated at the Devil's Teeth.

"With that my conversation with Zeus about the future ended. I was overwhelmed by what he had told me, and by what he was asking of me, but I knew in my heart that I had no choice. It was late in the evening of that first day of freedom when Zeus and I finished talking and he suggested that I get some rest. And so it was, after we rejoined the other beings, whose future was now in my control, we retired for the night. As I drifted into a half-sleep that night, my thoughts traveled to the islands man calls Hawaii and Captain Jackson. I wondered if I would ever see him again. I still do."

Apollo's thoughts drifted away from his story and Zeus suggested they take a break for a few hours to feed and rest. Reluctantly they agreed.

CHAPTER ELEVEN

On The Wings Of Eagles

Several hours later, after all were refreshed, Apollo began his tale again. "The next morning dawned clear and bright. The seas were calm and there was no sign of kraken; however, my heart sank when I saw that Zeus was gone, and for an instant, I feared that our encounter with the kraken and our rescue by Zeus had all been a dream. But when I counted the other beings and found only ten it soon became evident that it had not. Two were gone, including my friend Morpheus, and the unsettled looks upon the faces of the others served to reaffirm that the experiences of the previous day had been all too real.

"Then I heard the far off sound of a being singing. The source was to the west of our position and receding. I knew it had to be Zeus. I spyhopped and there in the distance, I saw our mysterious visitor as he arched his back and began to dive. His broad flukes rose up in the air, and I could see the sunlight reflecting off its smooth wet surface and water cascading off its serrated trailing edge. He hovered there, for a lingering moment, and then disappeared. A wave of sadness washed over me, but then I heard Zeus' sonorous voice calling to me. It boomed out across the waters. He called my name, and then I heard him say one word, just one, Believe. That was all, just Believe. Nothing more. Nothing less. And then he was gone.

"The rest of that day was hard. They would get a lot harder. After watching Zeus disappear I told the other beings that I was headed south, around Cape Horn and into the Atlantic Ocean and I invited them to join me. Since all but one of them had been born in captivity, they had no nostos and the prospect of venturing out on their own in the open ocean was intimidating. I neither magnified the danger we would face nor did I downplay it but knowing now what was to come, I regret that I did not err on the side of the former. All chose to accompany me.

"Our journey took us southward paralleling the coast of California, staying to seaward to avoid the roving tribes of Transient Orcas who hunt Gray Whales on their migration routes south to their winter range in the Gulf of California. We did this on the advice of one of the beings in our group, a Striped Dolphin with a loud and infectious laugh, named Ganymede. Like Morpheus he had once been wild and free and he knew about the Transient Orcas who prey upon marine mammals and other beings. I did not know Ganymede while we were both at the Institute but in those first few days after our escape, I came to respect and trust him.

"Our deepwater transit southward was interrupted only once by my search for the minerals Zeus had told me about. I found them lying on the seabed in coastal waters and within a few days after eating them my skin began to turn gray, such that by the time we reached the southern tip of the Baja Peninsula, I was no longer white. It was a strange experience, rather like living inside the body of another being, disturbing and yet in some ways liberating. From that point forward, anyone with whom I came in contact would treat me for who I was, not what I looked like.

"It took us over four weeks to travel the thirteen hundred miles from the Farallones to the mouth of the Gulf of California, staying well out to sea to avoid the polluted waters in the places man calls Monterey Bay and the Channel Islands, both of which are sites where he has dumped radioactive waste. Ganymede warned me that these sites, and ten others just like them on the Pacific Coast of California, were vast dead zones where the sea floor, and the poisons it contained, was as deadly as any kraken, perhaps even more so, because it had the potential to kill us all.

"Along our way south, we began to transition from the California Current to the North Equatorial Current. I was not happy with our progress and while my search for the minerals had added to the transit time, the truth was that after our years in captivity our bodies were in poor condition. At the pleading of the least fit of our group, we decided to rest when we passed Cape San Lucus and reached the Gulf of California. There in the milky, jade-colored waters we spent the next two weeks, feeding, resting, and growing stronger due to an exercise regimen that I instituted based it on what Trainer Quinn had taught me. Most complained but all complied. The gulf was filled with a bounty of feeder fish and Ganymede made a game out of chasing them into a large ball, which helped keep everyone's spirits high. The warm and shallow seas were not to the liking of kraken and the days we spent there were pleasant ones free from fear of attack.

"Shortly after the Winter Solstice, the Gray Whales gathered there began calving. Up until then they had tolerated our presence but once the calves were born, the mothers became very protective making the situation tense. Adding to our discomfort was the fact that the Gray Whale is one of the most unpleasant of all the great whales, in both personality and appearance. It did not take long for me to sense a nastiness about them that lurks just beneath their pitted and mottled skin. Ganymede said humans call them 'devil fish' and that their bad temper traces to the fact that they make the longest annual migration of any being, traveling five thousand miles from their northern summer feeding grounds off Alaska to their winter calving areas in the Gulf of California, being preyed upon by Orcas every step of the way. In addition to their wearisome annual migration, they are bottom feeders whose prey consists primarily of amphipods for which they forage in the mud at the bottom. This heavily encrusts their skin with barnacles and sea lice, making them the ugliest of all beings.

"Regardless of the cause, their bad behavior convinced me it was time to leave. Zeus had also warned me to get around Cape Horn before the start of winter in the Southern Ocean, so I got us moving again. And so, with six months to go and nearly six thousand miles between us and the Cape, my little band of dolphins, three Spinners, two Striped, and the rest Bottlenose set off once more.

"For the next five weeks we made better progress due to our improved conditioning. The warm California Current that we rode southward toward the equator, paralleling the coast of Central America, also helped. We stayed well out over the deeps that fill the Middle America Trench, until we reached the Galapagos Islands, nineteen hundred miles south of the Gulf of California. There we crossed the equator although, unlike human mariners, the event meant little more to us than simply a transition from the Northern to the Southern Hemisphere.

"We soon met a tribe of Strap-Toothed Whales, who were most hospitable. Their wave-like markings of white, yellow-gray and black were striking, and the adult males of the tribe had the most unusual feature in that two of their bottom teeth protruded out of their mouths and curled upward and backward over the top of their upper jaw, making it difficult for them to open their mouths. I wondered how they ate but I did not ask for fear of appearing rude, but based on their robust bodies it apparently was not a problem for them. By the grin on Ganymede's face, I could tell that he also found their appearance amusing but like the rest of us, he received them in courteous silence. It was not until after we left the Galapagos that he had a good belly laugh, and try as I might to not do so, I joined him, as did the others, and for a while at least, we forgot our troubles. Our mirth did not last long.

"The going soon got more difficult when we encountered the Humboldt Current flowing northward against us. There was an offsetting benefit in the strong upwelling of colder, nutrient-rich water from a depth of eighteen strata that provided us with an abundant supply of anchovies upon which we grazed for days on end as we headed south along the coast of Ecuador and Peru. Were it not for the exercise we were getting, our bellies might have grown fat from this rich diet. Each night when we rested, we took turns on watch, and I encountered no resistance from the group, as the memory of the Devil's Teeth was still fresh in all of our minds. The journey had been uneventful since leaving those deadly seas and I was worried that the ease with which we were traveling would lull us into a false sense of security. In addition, thoughts of the three more challenges Zeus had predicted were ever present in my mind. My concerns proved to be justified when we reached the waters off some volcanic islands two thousand miles south of the Galapagos Islands. A passing Southern Right Whale, one of few beings, other than the Strap-Toothed Whales, we had encountered to that point, told us humans call the islands Islas Juan Fernandez.

"By then we had been traveling almost continuously for four months, which meant that it was now near the end of February. As we approached the largest island, called Robinson Crusoe, we encountered our first storm since leaving California. It was mild compared to the typhoon we had experienced at Point Reyes, but we were tired and as the island loomed before us, we decided to seek shelter in a deep and narrow bay at the southwest side of the island.

"I remember having reservations about entering it. However, as we hovered near the mouth of the bay we encountered a large school of Spotted Eagle Rays—the name of which was provided to me by Ganymede. He said they were a formidable creature with powerful jaws, grinding teeth, and whip like tail with two deadly stingers at its base. But he also knew them to be harmless unless provoked, and as such, they were no threat to us. They were strikingly beautiful with upper bodies of brown with smudges of white, and graceful wings over nine feet across.

"Seemingly unbothered by our presence, they began passing by us, singing softly as they went. There was a sad and wistful quality to their voices and their confident passage into the steep-sided channel that led into the lagoon reassured us. Like the others, I did not relish the thought of spending a night in open water during a storm so together we joined with the rays, and swam through the channel. Once in the lagoon, all seemed secure but at my insistence we still mounted a guard. I took first watch along with Ganymede, and after completing my watch I soon lapsed into a fitful half-sleep.

"Ganymede woke me at first light. By his agitated state I knew something bad had happened. He said that two dolphins were missing and another was dead. He took me to the mouth of the channel that led to the sea, and I saw what had gone unseen the night before. The walls were pitted with caves and lurking in the mouths of each, I could see the heads of huge eels. Ganymede told me they were Wolfish. While we were watching, one of the creatures swam out of its cave to attack another smaller member of its kind. Both were light brown with black markings. The larger of the two eels was over seven feet long with a thick, powerful body and a long dorsal fin with large pectoral fins. Its powerful teeth made short work of the other eel. Ganymede said when he and another being had come looking for the two missing beings, they tried to swim past the Wolfish and were attacked. He narrowly avoided being torn to shreds but his companion was not so lucky. Ganymede surmised that the two missing beings had met a similar fate.

"It was a disheartening and desperate situation. We retreated to the lagoon to consider our options and then I noticed that the Eagle Rays were gone. Ganymede said they had left at first light, singing again as they departed. By now, the rest of our group was awake and they clustered about me, asking more questions than I had answers. Finally I asked for some time alone and Ganymede took them to the far side of the lagoon while I returned to the mouth of the channel. *How did we enter unharmed last night* I wondered. *Could it have something to do with the Eagle Rays* Then it hit me. I rejoined Ganymede and asked him whether he and the other being had swum into the channel with the rays that morning or after they had left. He said it was the latter, which confirmed my theory. The Wolfish were afraid of the Eagle Rays, which had served to protect us the night before. But once the rays were past, the Wolfish were free to attack. Ganymede agreed with my analysis and we knew what we had to do.

"I called the others over and explained our plan, which would depend of course upon the rays. Thankfully, the rays returned that night and when they left the lagoon the next morning, singing as they went, the eight of us were clustered tightly among them. When we reached the open seas, we hovered there watching the rays go, pale brown ghosts gliding on hypnotic wings through the early morning light, their hauntingly beautiful melody still lingers in my memory. After we were safely at sea again, I realized that I had demonstrated the second trait of which Zeus had spoken that of cunning. I was pleased that the eight of us had survived but I was saddened by the loss of three more beings and I wondered how many more would die before my journey was through. I was right to be concerned, as you will hear." Apollo stopped talking and his mind drifted away again.

The afternoon sun was beginning its downward slide and at Hera's urging, they took another break but she said it should be a short one because they were all eager to hear the end of Apollo's tale. As eager as he was to finish it.

CHAPTER TWELVE

To The Horn And Beyond

An hour later, Apollo began his story again. He would not stop now until he was done. "It was a weary group of seven beings who followed me southeast from Isla Juan Fernandez to Tierra del Fuego. The days were growing shorter and the water colder. The ocean had lost all traces of the bright colors of azure blue and cerulean that we had known farther north: it was now midnight blue, darkening our spirits along with it. I think all but Ganymede regretted their decision to follow me south but none abandoned the group. In hindsight, it might have been better for them if they had.

"We should have covered the seventeen hundred miles to Cape Horn in three weeks; instead it took us over four and autumn arrived a week before we did, bringing with it stormy skies and heavy seas. In part, this was because we had to fight the Humboldt Current that flowed north along the coast of Chile, comprising the eastern boundary of the South Pacific Gyre, a vast trans-oceanic circle of currents that I had heard about and now experienced for myself. But in truth, it was more than that: the emotional and physical trauma we had faced during the past four months was a far greater impediment to our progress than any river in the sea could ever be. The fact that we were now approaching the tempestuous Southern Ocean, and faced a passage through the most dangerous strait on the planet did little to strengthen our spirits. Our low emotional state presented a daunting challenge to my ability to lead my companions through whatever lay ahead, and to compound the tough tenor of the moment, I sensed that I would face my third challenge in the perilous waters at the tip of South America.

"Before I describe what transpired in our passage from the South Pacific Ocean into the South Atlantic Ocean, I must take you back several days and several hundred miles from Cape Horn. Three and a half weeks after leaving Robinson Crusoe Island, we encountered a group of over one hundred Peale's Dolphins made up of several tribes who had gathered together before the onset of autumn in the Southern Ocean. These energetic beings with robust, black and gray striped bodies had a pleasing manner about them that, at least momentarily, distracted us from what lay ahead. They knew the waters at the ends of the earth and we found a mix of both foreboding and fortitude in what they told us; albeit more of the first than the second. The fear pertained to their tales of mountainous seas in the Drake Passage, which they said was a vast confluence of heavy water that exists in a state of constant turmoil between Cape Horn and the South Shetland Islands, five hundred miles farther to the south, near Antarctica; the land of eternal ice. (At the time of Apollo's journey, it could be called that; but even now, as I recount his tale, the ice at both ends of the earth is melting.)

"They told us that Cape Horn is actually a towering cliff, on the tip of an island that rises fourteen hundred feet above the spot where three mighty oceans meet: the South Atlantic, South Pacific, and Southern. They explained that the reason for its deadly reputation is that the prevailing winds are westerly, and they race around the bottom of the world unimpeded, passing to the south of the Andes Mountains, which forces them through the strait between the Cape and the Shetlands. This relentless force of wind creates a current of water flowing eastward at fifty miles a day, far greater than any we had experienced in our journey thus far. The flow of water rages across rocky shelves on the sea bottom creating waves sometimes ninety feet high, which would mean certain death for us were we to try to pass through them. Based on what they were telling us, it was clear that such an endeavor was beyond our reach. This was the fearful part of what they told us. But it was not the whole story.

"In contrast, the encouraging part of the message the Peale's Dolphins gave us was that there was another way to get to the Atlantic, which was through the Straits of Magellan, a natural passage between the Atlantic and Pacific Oceans, separating mainland Chile and Tierra del Fuego. As soon as they said it, I recalled hearing Captain Jackson discussing this subject with his colleagues. He remarked how even the Navy's mightiest ships, the nuclear aircraft carriers, avoided Cape Horn in their transit from the South Atlantic to the South Pacific, by sailing through the Straits of Magellan rather than risking a journey around the Cape itself. If the most powerful deathships ever built by man were endangered by the Horn, how could we expect our fragile bodies to survive it? The decision was easy.

"The Peale's Dolphins were not of a mind to lead us through the Straits, but they gave us directions and wished us well. They advised us that while the eastern opening to the Straits is a wide bay, the entrance to it on the western side, which we were now approaching, was made up of a number of access points; and they cautioned us the safest one was the one hundred mile long stretch of water from the Queen Adelaide Archipelago through to the main part of the Straits itself. Unfortunately, in our eagerness, we missed that access point and instead entered a much narrower and more turbulent channel at the southern end of what is aptly named, Desolation Island; and that made all the difference—between life and death.

"It was late in the day as we began our long swim through this narrow passage. You might question my decision to enter this passage after our experience at Isla Juan Fernandez and you would be right in doing so. But I allowed emotion to overtake reason, and in my anxiousness to reach the South Atlantic Ocean, I ignored the tiny voice that dwells within all of us, a voice, which at that moment cried out to me: Go back! Go back!"

Apollo paused, his audience drew a little closer to him, eager, and yet hesitant to hear what was to come. With a sad sigh, he began again, "What happened next was more unspeakable, more terrible than anything that befell us at the Devil's Teeth. Before I describe it, I must explain something that you may find hard to accept: for all their gruesomeness, at least Great White Sharks possess a certain stark beauty, a sleekness of form and a suppleness of function. Despite the fact that they are capable of killing our kind in a most gruesome manner, they are magnificent in their malevolence. However, no such grudging compliment can be paid to the kind of kraken we were about to encounter. It was a beast among beasts; grotesque in its ugliness, reviling in its ill-formed shape and more wicked in intent and actions than anything that has ever lived below the waterline. Indeed, if there can be any creature on land or sea that most embodies the devil himself; it is what man calls the Giant Pacific Octopus.

"The encounter with this kraken began when we came upon a further narrowing in what was already the narrow channel; bordered on either side by high rock walls, and there in the flow of water, left of center, was a huge whirlpool that threatened to swallow us, one and all. We heard it long before we felt the first faint tugs of its angry vortex. We stopped above it and reconnoitered. Had we come upon the whirlpool nearer to the Pacific we might have turned back but as it was we had traveled over fifty miles and were too tired to retrace our path. So, after probing the swirling dark waters, which lay before us, we decided that we would risk it rather than turn back. I chose to go first and I instructed the others to wait until I made it safely beyond the maelstrom before following me. And so it was that the third of the challenges, which Zeus had foretold, now began to unfold."

Apollo paused again and thick tears welled up in his eyes. Then with a contriteness in his voice that made his listeners want to reach out and comfort him, he began again. "It grieves me to report to you that in this instance, unlike the other challenges we faced, I alone survived—and in that survival, a part of me died. Were foresight as clear as hindsight, I could have, and should have, stopped what was to come. But it is not, and I did not, and the others paid the ultimate price for my mistake.

"I made a large circle in the stream to gather speed, and then I headed toward the narrowing in the channel, keeping as close to the steeps on the right side as possible. The maelstrom had created a churning and seething wave that pushed against the easterly flow of the current and gave the effect of a great ship plowing through a boiling sea. But, of course, there was no ship behind the wave and as I dove into the heart of it, I half-expected to be sucked into its gaping, gulping maw. It did not happen. Instead I found myself on the far side of the whirlpool, in the violent but manageable eddies downstream, slightly winded and choking a little on the fine spray that swirled above the water, coating the rock walls with a slimy sheen.

"But my passage had not been without incident, for in the fraction of a second that transpired as I passed by the center of the whirlpool, to my right and below me in the darkness, out of the corner of my eye, I spotted what appeared to be a cave, and in its mouth I thought I saw something; something odd; something vaguely sinister; but exactly what, my eyes could not discern and my brain could not interpret. It took but a moment to gather my wits and catch my breath, and turn to face upstream with the intent of calling out a warning to the others to be careful, but of what I was not sure. It mattered not for as soon as they saw me emerge alive on the far side of the narrowing, the seven dolphins, the last of our brave little band of beings from Point Reyes, plunged headlong into the wave, one right after the other, and followed me, oblivious to my warning.

"I do not know how many of the beings in all were caught by the monstrous kraken whose arms stretched thirty feet from tip to tip, and whose body must have weighed at least six hundred pounds, but I saw three of them so entwined as the monster rose up from its dark hiding place to grab them, and pull them into its maw, where they were torn to pieces by its savage beak. Only part of its enormous head rose up above the surge of the current, enough to show me one wicked, red eye, and at the peak of its upward thrust, it stared downstream at me, as if to thank me for bringing it such a grisly feast. Then it sank beneath the blood-flecked foam and was gone.

"In the horror of that moment there was no time for me to rush back upstream to their aid; no time to try to impose a mindlink with this hideous monster, even if such a thing was possible; and no time to call for help from Zeus, had he even been anywhere near." As Apollo said this, Pan glanced at Zeus but got no reaction. "There was only time to watch the innocents die because of me. I did not see what happened to the other four members of my group, including Ganymede. Perhaps the kraken got them too; or perhaps, in trying to avoid the beast, they were sucked into the whirlpool and drowned. I suppose I shall never know—but their memories weigh heavily upon my soul."

Apollo broke off his narrative. The light behind his eyes faded with the approaching night in those waters over Roundtop. The other beings remained quiet as their minds absorbed the full tragedy of Apollo's journey down the west coast of South America during which he had suffered the loss of all his companions. Zeus said nothing; however, the others suspected that he knew what was yet to come in Apollo's journey. And in that realization, they wondered why Zeus did not come to Apollo's rescue at the maelstrom? Why did he save them at the Devil's Teeth but not at Isla Juan Fernandez or Tierra del Fuego? If he really was an angel, why did he let some die while Apollo lived? And more to the point, what did it say about God that Apollo would be sent on a divine mission but left alone in his hour of need? These were crucial questions but since none dared ask them of the great whale, no answers were offered.

Finally, Pan broke the stillness. He swam slowly over to Apollo and caressed him with his flipper. And when Pan spoke, he did not try to excuse what had happened by saying something trite like *It was not your fault* or *You tried your best,* because Pan sensed that these were not the words that Apollo wanted or needed to hear. Only Apollo knew whether it was his fault, or if he had tried his best, and nothing anyone else said would make it any better, only worse. Instead, Pan simply said, "We are so very sorry for your loss."

Apollo acknowledged the little one with a sad nod of his head but said nothing. An awkward silence fell upon them until Hera asked, "Shall we continue with this tomorrow, Apollo?"

Apollo did not answer at first. Instead, he looked to Zeus who nodded solemnly that he should. Gathering himself, Apollo turned back to Hera and replied, "No. I think it best if I finish the rest of the story now." Hera acceded to his request for she could tell the need for rest was overpowered by the need for the expiation of his grief…and guilt.

Apollo began again. "I spent a week—it might have been two, I'm not sure—lingering downstream from the whirlpool, hoping against hope that Ganymede or one of the others would appear, but they never did. One morning I thought I heard Ganymede's carefree laugh and I spyhopped to look upstream, but it turned out only to be the cry of a seabird. Other than the first few hours of my life, I had never been alone, ever; and the loneliness I felt in my heart during those dark and dreary days, as the westerly winds of the onrushing winter, stirred the waters of the Straits into a cold froth, was greater than I had ever known, or care to again. If loneliness were droplets of water, mine could have filled the seas.

"I fell into a deep depression. I did not eat, I did not swim. I did not even want to live. I forgot everything that Zeus had told me and I cared little about my destiny. Several times during that period, I headed back upstream and hovered on the edge of the maelstrom debating whether I should end it all. Whether I should sacrifice myself to the kraken as retribution for my failings. And I must confess that I nearly did. But then one night, I had a dream. A dream in which I saw the faces of all whalekind looking to me for leadership, and when I awoke, I stopped feeling sorry for myself. It was at that moment that I remembered the third trait, which was commitment. I had lost my faith and found it again. And that was that. I left the whirlpool behind me and never looked back.

"I swam the rest of the way through the Straits of Magellan and headed out into the South Atlantic Ocean. As I swam north and east following the coastline of Argentina, I was helped by the strong northerly flow of the Falklands Current. At the time, I did not know these to be the names of the land to my west and the current upon which I rode, but it did not matter. I was possessed with the overwhelming desire to put as much distance between me and Cape Horn as possible.

"Unlike the west coast of South America, I soon found that along its eastern shore, the Continental Shelf was much wider, stretching farther out into the open ocean than I was disposed to go. This broad plateau was not altogether unwelcome to me since the depth below, at between ten and fifteen strata, was less intimidating than the deeps over which my companions and I had traveled on our journey southward. While the reality did not support the perception, I felt safer sleeping unguarded in those relatively shallow seas, where my earsight could probe the sea floor below me and scan the waters around me.

"For the next three weeks, I traveled steadily northward leaving the Southern Ocean far behind me. It was late autumn and the days were growing shorter, but I made good time until I reached the broad delta of a river, twelve hundred miles northeast of Cape Horn. It was there that my life took yet another dramatic turn, because there I met Aphrodite, a Bottlenose Dolphin, like me. She was the chieftain of a large tribe of beings who made their home along the seaward edge of the mouth of the river called Rio de la Plata, or the River of Silver, which I discovered was a rather inappropriate descriptor for the vast, silt-choked marginal sea that stretched one hundred and eighty miles inland from the ocean to where the Paraná and Uruguay Rivers meet. Our initial encounter did not go well and could be characterized as one of marked contrast: I immediately was enthralled by her while she took little notice of me."

Apollo's eyes lost their focus and his gaze slipped away from the beings before him. "I shall never forget the moment we met. It was a clear and cold morning in mid-May, and I was swimming through the dense seawater of the salt wedge, where the fresh water of the Rio de la Plata estuary floods into the South Atlantic Ocean. I encountered a large school of sardines who had been driven into a frenzied ball by Blue Sharks and Yellow Fin Tuna, neither of which represented any threat to me. Their flashing silver sides and rapidly synchronous movements, penetrated now and again by savage thrusts of the predators from below, and diving seabirds from above, mesmerized me; to the point that I did not see the Bottlenose Dolphins approaching from landward. I had only made one pass through the swirling mass of feeder fish when, suddenly, the fish disappeared and I found myself the hunted not the hunter.

"The beings formed a tight circle around me and for a moment we all froze in place; hovering there in the murky waters now devoid of fish, as a shower of tiny silver scales cascaded down around us and disappeared into the shadows below. I felt the dolphins probe me with their earsight, and I was thankful that my skin was gray not white. I did not know what their intentions were, but they had not given me any reason to be afraid. Before I could say anything, the circle parted and a female appeared. She was more beautiful than any being I had ever known; long, lithe, and lovely, with an easy grace about her. Her skin was mostly gray with strong countershading, dark dorsally and light ventrally, without sharp lines of demarcation in between. And her firm belly had a delicate pinkish hue that I had never seen before on any being. At nine feet in length, she was two feet shorter than me and only two-thirds my weight.

"She said nothing during her approach, or when she swam slowly around me, never once making direct eye contact. I assumed by her manner and by the way the others reacted to her, that she was the chieftain of the tribe. I expected that she would introduce herself to me, and I found myself growing energized by that prospect, but she did not. Instead, without saying anything, she turned and swam away.

"'Wait!' I called out but she either did not hear me or did not care. She was soon followed by all but one of the tribe, a young male who stayed behind only long enough to tell me that I was not welcome there, and that if I knew what was good for me, I should continue on my way. 'Who are you?' I asked.

"'We are the East Rio de la Plata tribe,' he replied.

"'What is your leader's name?' I asked.

"'Her name is Aphrodite…' He was about to say more but he was interrupted by another being, who swam back to where we were and ordered him to leave. 'Yes, Narcissus,' he replied to the other being.

"Narcissus, who was bigger than me and more robust in body, turned to me and snapped, 'Leave here, stranger, or die.'

"'No, I replied, which startled him, but only momentarily.

"'Then you will die,' he said. He started toward me when I heard a female voice ring out, strong and clear and powerful, and yet with an allure that her position of command had not dulled.

"It was the voice of Aphrodite and soon she reappeared followed by other members of her tribe, including several older females who, I assumed, were her attendants. Unlike our first encounter, this time she looked at me. For a moment we hung there, locked in each other's gaze, neither saying anything, and for just the briefest of an instant, I thought I felt a connection with her but if there had been any it soon vanished; the magnetism of the moment, real or imagined broken by the indifference of her tone when she inquired, 'What is your name?'

"I had difficulty finding my voice. 'Ap-Ap-Apollo,' I stammered and felt myself trembling in her presence. I grew angry. *What is wrong with me?* I wondered. I had never acted that way before even in the face of danger. But I was younger then, and foolish, and I had yet to learn that this was danger of a different kind—for danger of the heart is far greater than any of the mind and body.

"'Ap-Ap-Apollo' snickered Narcissus. 'Gr-gr-great name.'

"Aphrodite flashed a look at Narcissus then turned back to me. I scanned her face for a hint of compassion but found none. 'What do you want, Apollo?' she asked.

"I answered without thinking, speaking directly from the heart. 'To not be alone.'

"My answer gave her pause. She eyed me warily and asked, 'Is death more desirable than loneliness?'

"Without hesitation, I replied, 'If you must ask, then you have never been alone.'

"At first she did not answer. She just stared at me, perhaps evaluating the message behind my words. Finally, after a long silence, she answered, 'Very well. You may stay with us for the night and we will see in the morning if you prove worthy to remain.' With that, she turned and swam away followed closely by Narcissus and the others save the young male.

"After she was gone, I asked him what proof she was referring to. He smiled and said, 'You will compete in the Contest.' Then he told me to follow him, which I did, feeling quite the fool but resolved to put an end to my foolishness the next morning, in whatever contest lay before me.

"The entire tribe was gathered together at first light the next morning. We were fifty miles out into the ocean, beyond the outward edge of the river delta where it began its lengthy, downward slide toward the distant deeps: out where the bluewater was free of the silt from the river. For the moment, I was alone with the young male who explained that the Contest would consist of three events; the Jump, the Race; and the Dive. He said that Narcissus, who was the captain of Aphrodite's Guardians, had chosen three dolphins, each of whom was the most skilled at that particular event whereas I would have to compete in all three. To win the Contest, I would have to win all three events outright, and if I won, I would be invited to join their tribe. However, a loss in one or two of the events would lead to my being banished from their tribe. I asked him what would happen if I lost all three events. He hesitated and then replied that their code of honor would require that I be executed. As the crowd gathered around us, I sensed that most of his fellow tribe members had come hoping to see me lose all three events.

"To assist me, he said I would have someone appointed as my second who would coach me through the events, although I doubted that it would be a sincere effort. Finally, the young male told me that Narcissus would judge the Contest, a clear conflict of interest but what choice did

I have, other than to flee, which I was not prepared to do. Narcissus arrived and asked me if I understood and accepted the rules.

"I said that I did and he turned and looked at the tribe members and asked, 'Who will be the second for the stranger?' It was obvious that he did not expect an answer.

"No one spoke up. But then Aphrodite appeared and to the shock of everyone, including me, she replied, 'I will be his second.' Narcissus was stunned and angered by her reply and he started to question her but a sharp look from her silenced him. He laughed it off and stated that there was no way I would win even one event and that he looked forward to killing me. It was an unsettling way to begin the Contest but at least I knew his intentions, and I secretly promised myself that I would take him with me if I was to die.

"However, there was no need for any such bravado, for things did not go as Narcissus expected. Much to his chagrin, I easily won the first event, jumping one full body length farther than the impressive but losing leap of the first of Narcissus' Guardians. He had been the best jumper in the tribe and had never been bested until that day.

"It was hard for me to read Aphrodite's reaction to the outcome, but if anything she seemed mildly pleased. In the next event, the Race, which entailed me and my opponent swimming over a three mile, triangular course, marked at each corner by a member of the tribe, my margin of victory was significant; so much so that Narcissus demanded that the three beings who had been stationed at the corners confirm that they had seen me pass by, which they all did—reluctantly.

"The final event involved me and my next opponent diving down to the bottom, which lay ten strata beneath us, picking up as many mollusk shells as our ability to hold our breath would allow, and bringing them back to the surface. It was not a speed event; rather it was one of endurance and strength. By now it was obvious by their expressions that some of the members of the tribe were beginning to root for me, so Narcissus cancelled the proscribed rest period between events and quickly started the third and final event. At his count of, 'Three, two, go!' we were off, pointing our heads down and disappearing into the deep blue liquid haze below.

"According to the young male who recounted the events later, after six minutes Narcissus' dolphin returned to the surface and spit out six mollusk shells in front of Narcissus and the dolphins crowded around him. It was an impressive number, apparently two more than what might normally be expected in such an event, and there was a loud cheer from most, but not all among the tribe. They knew it would be a difficult number to beat. All eyes and heads turned downward and a collective burst of earsight probed the depths, but to no avail. They could not locate me.

"Two more minutes passed and the tension built, and when it appeared that something bad had befallen me, Aphrodite swam away from the crowd, which is what I had hoped she would do. I surfaced beside her and as much as she tried to hide it, I could see that she was pleased. I asked her how many shells my opponent had brought up from the bottom and she told me six. 'Good,' I replied and spit out three shells. At first she did not understand but without questioning me she followed me back to where the others were waiting. Upon seeing me re-appear, there was a cheer from many in the crowd, which angered Narcissus. After quieting them, Narcissus asked me how many shells had I retrieved. I answered the question by spitting out five shells one after another. There was a collective groan as all saw that even with my longer time below, I had fallen one shell short of winning the third event, and thereby the Contest.

"Of course, I had returned to the surface with eight shells, which only Aphrodite knew. To her it was a truly remarkable feat, but the truth was that I had had help when I was at the bottom, for as I dove and began my search I was suddenly joined by a group of Cownose Rays, who presented me with the eight shells, all in one neat pile so that I had no trouble gathering them. I did not understand how they knew what I was doing but I was not about to reject their help. It was the second time that rays had assisted me and I was grateful for it.

"Narcissus was of course relieved to see that his team had won, which served to add more prestige to his position within the tribe. He then ordered me to leave the tribe at once and never return. But to his and everyone else's surprise, Aphrodite overruled him. Invoking her authority as chieftain, she said that my performance had proven me worthy of joining them. There was a loud murmur of support for her decision from everyone except Narcissus of course. He gave me a grudging nod and swam away.

"After the crowd broke up Aphrodite looked at me and said, 'That was gracious of you not to embarrass Narcissus, even though it meant that you could not join the tribe.'

"'I saw little to be gained by embarrassing him,' was my reply.

"She studied me for a long moment and shook her head in admiration. 'I like you.'

"'I like you too.' I said. For a moment we remained there, alone. It was an exquisitely uncomfortable moment. Finally, she asked me to come with her and we swam off together to join the others. Over the next few weeks and months I became a useful member of the tribe, and I was even able to build a bond of mutual respect, if not friendship, with Narcissus. It was the happiest time in my life but somehow I knew it would not last.

"In retrospect, had Aphrodite and I remained just friends, and I her loyal subject, I might still be there to this day. But even though a tiny voice called to me from the depths of my being, telling me that I should not stay, each day that I spent with Aphrodite became like a tonic to my soul: her presence filling me with ecstasy and dulling my wits. I forgot about the twelve beings with whom I had faced the jaws of hell at the Devil's Teeth, all of whom were now swimming in an eternal sea; I grew deaf to the call of nostos and I kept telling myself that my destiny could wait. Autumn turned to winter, and winter to spring, and by the time summer arrived in those fertile waters off Argentina, I had become blinded by my obsession with the river goddess called Aphrodite.

"Those months with the tribe were not only good for me, but with my help the tribe grew larger and stronger. At my urging, we joined forces with other tribes from other parts of Rio de la Plata; including Bottlenose, Striped and Dusky Dolphins, and even one small tribe of Franciscana Dolphins, whose ghostly gray coloring reminded me of my true color, which I made sure remained hidden by eating minerals I found in the silted delta of the river. I had become a key member of Aphrodite's governing council and even though I tried to hide them, my feelings for her had become obvious to all; so much so that one day; Narcissus took me aside and warned me to be careful. He said she was as conniving as she was beautiful; that males were only a means to an end for her, nothing more. I dismissed his warning, taking it to be the jealous ramblings of a rejected suitor. How foolish I was, how stubborn, how much in love. If anything, his warning made me want her even more but then he said something that would come back to haunt me; he said that while she might give me her body, she would never give me her heart—because she had no heart to give. I laughed it off but he would have the last laugh.

"Then it happened. One moonlit mid-summer's night, when the seas were calm, and all seemed right in the world, Aphrodite and I became lovers, and although I did not know it at the time, that was when the tide turned in my sojourn at Rio de la Plata."

At this point Apollo fell silent. His mind drifted back to that exquisite moment but he was obviously not comfortable sharing with his audience the details of the actual physical act of mating. What he remembered but did not tell them was that Aphrodite asked him to accompany her on a night swim into the warm shallows of the estuary. There, tucked behind a low-lying island, in the gentle eddies; she initiated the act, beginning with mouthing him and rubbing her tongue over his face. Even though he had never made love before, he knew what her actions meant, but still, out of his naivety, he asked her what she was doing. She laughed in the gentle little way that he had seen her do with other males in the tribe, and continued licking him. He felt a quickening in his lower body. Then she began rubbing her body against his and stroking him with her flippers. He was uncertain at first of how to act but soon instinct took over and when she presented herself to him, he rolled on his back and, then as they swam together in a wide, lazy circle, nose to nose, and belly to belly, they consummated the act.

"Apollo," said Hera. "Are you all right?"

Hera's question brought Apollo back to the present. "Yes. Sorry." Then he continued, "Afterwards, we fell into a blissful half-sleep, although in those shallows, tucked tightly up against the tree-lined banks, we had little to fear from anything or anyone, except perhaps ourselves. When the first probing rays of dawn streaked the silver surface of the waters with red and gold, Aphrodite woke up and nuzzled against me. Caught up in the wonder of the moment, and forgetting the warning he had received from Narcissus, I blurted out, 'I love you, Aphrodite.'

She gazed at me with a gentle, half-smile, nuzzled me and said, 'Thank you'. It was hardly the reply I expected, and it was in that moment everything became clear; who she was and what I was to her.

I was crushed but I was determined not to show it. The truth is that even though her body and not her heart was all I would ever possess, in my stupidity, I convinced myself that it was enough. Over the course of the next three months, as summer faded into autumn, I became her constant companion, confidant and lover.

"It was a heady time for me made even more so when one day in early autumn, one year after I had been accepted by the tribe, and eighteen months after I escaped from Point Reyes, Aphrodite announced to the tribe that she was appointing me to replace Narcissus as head of her Guardians. She had given me no warning in advance of her announcement, and it caught me quite by surprise as it did the others, most notably Narcissus. But he was gracious in his congratulations despite his embarrassment. It should have been a warning sign but by then my head was too big for my body. I was king to her queen, moon to her sun, wind to her waves, or so I thought. Then, one fateful night, she asked me to kill Narcissus, and in an instant, my goddess became a witch.

"Aphrodite accused Narcissus of conspiring to overthrow her with the elders of the vast tribe over which she now ruled. I did not believe her but she was adamant and demanded that I kill him right away. She added that if I did not do this for her, she would assume that I was part of the conspiracy and would have me executed as well. I was stunned. I told her that I had to sleep on it. I left her and swam out into the ocean far from shore and spent a fitful night, wondering what to do. If I murdered Narcissus I knew it might only be a matter of time before her next lover did the same to me. But one part of me refused to believe that and as I swam through those dark seas I am ashamed to admit that I began to plan Narcissus' execution. Looking back upon it now, I cannot believe those evil thoughts actually crossed my mind but they did. I was obsessed with my love for Aphrodite.

"I did not sleep at all that night. With the dawn came a return to my senses. I would not be a murderer even if it meant forsaking the only happiness I had ever known. So without saying good bye to Aphrodite, I turned my back on Rio de la Plata and headed north, up the coast, and as what I will call the river blindness drained out of my body, I realized that I had passed the fourth and final challenge that Zeus had described; my character had been tested and not found wanting. And it was at that moment, somewhere far out at sea, I thought I heard whalesong. I wondered if it was Zeus and I so desperately wanted it to be. How I longed to see his face and hear his voice. But I remembered what he had said to me on that day so long before; that he would be there for me when I needed him, not when I wanted him. The line between need and want is a fine one, often steeped in disappointment and despair, and I sensed that I had not yet crossed it. To this day, I still sometimes wonder what happened to Aphrodite and Narcissus after I left, but in my heart, I do not care to know.

"I spent the next two months swimming up the coast of South America, following the route of Southern Right, Fin and Humpback Whales' northward migration. At one point, I passed some of these behemoths but I spoke with none and they sought no discourse with me. It was as if I had become a pariah among whalekind; a self-imposed one perhaps, but a pariah nevertheless. With only the occasional Green or Leatherback turtles for company, I followed the edge of the deeps around the bulge of the continent staying close to the coast to avoid having to fight the southbound Brazil and South Equatorial Currents. Eventually, I crossed the equator for the second time, at the Cone of the Amazon River, leaving the winds of winter and the bitter memories they carried far behind. I picked up the North Equatorial and Guiana Currents and rode these until I reached the archipelago man calls the Windward Islands.

"There I turned north and swam on, past the Leeward Islands and Hispaniola, moving north and west, heading toward nostos, the call of which grew stronger in me with each passing mile. But when I crossed the Tongue of the Ocean, I was captured by the men from Oceania— you know the rest of my story and I see no purpose in repeating it."

Apollo's tale was finished. It had taken a lot out of him and his demeanor was as dark as the seas that surrounded them. Silence fell upon the seven beings drifting together in the heavy swells rolling across Roundtop. Finally, Hera spoke, "You have done well, Apollo. You have been subjected to menace and misfortune, and you have prevailed over both those fickle masters. You have proven that you possess the four traits of which Zeus spoke; courage, cunning, commitment and character. And it is clear that in the first two legs of your odyssey, God has been your constant companion—which says to me that you are indeed the one we believe you to be; the Light of which the Legend spoke; a warrior prince who will lead us out of darkness. We thank you, we honor you, and the voices of all whalekind will soon cry out your name—Apollo, Apollo, Apollo."

If there could be but a single moment in time when the tides of the Seven Seas turned in unison at the beckoning of the moon, when all the planets were in perfect alignment around the sun, and when all the energy of the universe was focused upon one solitary being, it was then and there: every one of them felt it, not least of all, Apollo himself. It was a heavy burden for him to carry but such is the way of life, when few are called upon to save the many, and fewer still rise to meet the call, regardless of the cost to mind, body and soul. Pan had found Apollo; Apollo had found himself, and whalekind had found their hero. It remained now to be seen whether together they would find salvation from the evil that loomed just over the horizon. An evil for which Poseidon was but the servant and man was the unknowing master.

BOOK TWO

*The Lord shall come with his strong hand to stay
the Kraken's ragged bite, and his mighty voice shall
be heard above the Tempest's Roar.
Fear not when your enemies rise up before you, for
his Light will shine upon the restless sea, and you
shall know victory in his name.
God be praised.
God bring us the Light.*

The Legend of the Light
Oral History of the Ancients

CHAPTER THIRTEEN

Over The Edge

The next day dawned bright, clear, and cold, in stark contrast to the gloom of the previous evening. The sapphire seas were calm and quiet, deceptive in their temporary innocence. Driven by the steady Northeast Trade Winds, languid swells rolled in a stately procession across the Kingdom of the Ancients, bound for distant landfall on the coast of America, oblivious to the tempest's roar that would soon thunder through the Seven Seas. It was September 21st, the beginning of spring in the Southern Hemisphere, which is where Apollo and his new company, the Company of the Light, would soon be headed. Three months had passed since Pan had first arrived at the Kingdom of the Ancients, and nine months now lay ahead to the start of the war on mankind, according to the timetable set by Poseidon; a timetable that had to be stopped, no matter the cost.

As the sun slithered up over the eastern horizon, Hera called the beings to a meeting above Roundtop. With her were Kings Dionysus and Pluto; Guardians Ares and Aegyptus; Pan and Apollo; and the ever-mysterious Zeus. With the exception of the latter being, they all looked weary and careworn, which was not surprising given the present circumstances. Apart from the weather, there was one other thing that differed from the night before; the waters around them were once again full of life, as a quantum of tiny silver-sided fish darted here and there and everywhere, somehow sensing that the beings' minds were preoccupied with thoughts other than hunger.

Down below, the luxuriant coral forest that covered Roundtop was in full bloom, in bold defiance of the North Atlantic winter that hovered at the margins of the calendar. It was a strange juxtaposition of gloom and bloom, as the sky above and seabed below formed bright boundaries to the shadows of emotion born on the faces of the beings floating on the liquid layer in between. And this ominous dichotomy was not lost upon Pan who found it unsettling.

After Hera welcomed everyone to the meeting, she looked at Apollo and his companions and said, "Before we discuss the status of our war planning, I must share with you some troubling news of recent attacks on humans. They…"

"They have begun already?" interrupted Pan, always the first to speak but never the first to listen.

"Yes," she replied gravely, giving the little Harbour Porpoise a stern look. "I am afraid they have not been limited to the Pacific Ocean. Some have occurred within my kingdom."

"Here? In the North Atlantic Ocean," asked Ares, with the cold cunning of a warrior who was ready for war and sensed that it was ready for him. While he held no malice toward humans and was sorry that they had been attacked, the fact that they had now sealed Poseidon's fate did not displease Ares at all.

Hera nodded grimly. She knew exactly what was behind Ares' question and it saddened her. The reality that a war was now inevitable was devastating.

Ares continued his questioning. "What about in the South Atlantic?" As he asked it, his stare sliced through the water toward Dionysus. It was no secret that the Guardians did not trust the Fin Whale, and although Ares could not prove it, he believed that Eris had learned about their mission to Sinclair Cay from Dionysus. Had there been proof, Ares would have killed Dionysus already but as time would tell that would not be necessary. Someone else would do it for him.

"No," replied Hera. "At least not that I am aware of." Her answer only served to deepen Ares' suspicion.

Dionysus quickly added, "Apart from attacks in the North and South Pacific Oceans, there has only been one incident, which was here in the *North* Atlantic, off the New England coastline." His emphasis on the word north was layered with defensiveness.

"That is correct," said Hera. "Sadly I must tell you that it was a horrible attack, one that will surely attract the attention of the U.S. Coast Guard." Beings do not fear the sleek white ships with bright red bow stripes for they know the humans who sail in them are their friends. But Hera knew that would soon change if these attacks on man continued.

"Tell us about it, your Grace," said Apollo with deep empathy for the monarch's troubled soul.

Hera paused for a moment as the distaste for the story rose up in her gorge. Then she began, speaking in slow and measured tones. "It was three weeks ago, on the weekend that the Americans mark as Labor Day."

"Americans," growled Dionysus. "They are an odious people." Then catching an angry stare from Hera, he added insincerely, "but they do not deserve to be killed even as they kill us."

"King Dionysus, you know that Americans no longer hunt us like the cruel and uncaring peoples of Japan, Norway and Iceland still do," she admonished.

Dionysus retorted, "Is death from pollution any less permanent than that from a harpoon? Some might argue that at least the harpoon kills quickly." He turned to Zeus and asked, "What do you think?"

Zeus was not one to speak first and think later, as his questioner was. After giving the question due consideration, he replied, "It is a matter of intent, King Dionysus. If I were to kill you intentionally, without justification, I would be guilty of a crime. But if I were to kill you purely by accident, then I would be innocent. The latter would be an unfortunate circumstance from which I would learn so as not to do it again"

"Either way I would still be dead," Dionysus snapped.

Zeus' eyes narrowed and there was a knowing smile on his face. "Yes, indeed. As you would be if I discovered that you had committed a capital crime, such as treason for example."

Zeus' comment stabbed through the water like a shard of ice, and sent a tiny shudder through Dionysus' body that went unnoticed by everyone except Zeus. But it had the effect of quieting the contentious King.

"Please continue, Queen Hera," said Apollo.

She began again. "There was a tour boat out of Provincetown on Cape Cod. It was filled with families who had gone on what humans call a whale-watching cruise." (Such cruises are generally well tolerated by beings, some of whom even use the occasion to show off for the gawking crowd.) "When they approached a tribe of Pilot Whales, approximately forty in number, the whales attacked the boat, staving in its hull and sinking it before the crew could launch life rafts, or radio for help." (Beings can detect radio transmissions with their earsight). "Many humans went down with the boat and the rest floundered in the choppy seas. Then the whales"—her words caught in her throat—"grabbed the survivors in their mouths and pulled them under the water, drowning them all."

"Oh my," whispered Pan. "Oh my."

"It was several hours later before the little bits and pieces of wreckage of the overdue sightseeing boat were found by the Coast Guard, so the humans will never know that the Pilot Whales were to blame," interjected Dionysus. It was a heartless thing to say but it was true. The incident would not give a warning to mankind that a force of evil had been unleashed upon the seas. It would take a more concerted effort to do that, one which Poseidon and his followers were all too eager to initiate.

"The whales killed the children too?" asked Aegyptus, who loved human offspring and often watched them from afar as they played in the surf on summertime beaches."

"Yes," said Hera with a heavy nod of her massive head that sent a little wave around the gathered circle of beings, rocking them, especially Pan.

"What kind of Pilot Whales were they?" asked Apollo coldly.

"Long-finned," she replied with an inquisitive look. "From a tribe whose home waters were over the Grand Banks off Newfoundland."

"Very strange," said Pluto, the normally reticent Arctic Ocean King who, up until that point, had been studiously quiet. "Beings from

Canadian waters are usually quite peaceable." Among members of the Sovereign Council, it was generally considered improper to make a comment about beings in another monarch's kingdom and the Grand Banks were part of Queen Hera's domain, but she did not mind.

"They were probably starving because of the over-fishing by humans," interjected Dionysus. "Humans have destroyed the North Atlantic codfish stocks through their greed and stupidity."

"Hunger does not justify murder," snapped Hera. "And I might point out that in over-fishing the humans have also hurt themselves." (The Queen was referring to the devastating economic blight that had befallen the Newfoundland fishing community where the fleets now sat idle.) She looked back at Apollo and asked, "Why do you ask?"

Apollo's eyes were fixed in a stare into his own past. "No reason, your Grace." It was a lie but an innocent one, as he did not wish to bring up the unpleasant subject of Erebus.

"Where are the Pilot Whales now?" asked Ares with restrained fury in his voice.

"We do not know. After their horrible deed they vanished," replied the Queen.

Apollo probed deeper. "How did you learn this?"

"Some Harbor Porpoises—perhaps relatives of yours, Pan—witnessed the killing and recounted the story to a passing Fin Whale, who then told us." Even in the few minutes it had taken to recount the event, Pan thought he saw another wrinkle appear on her tired face.

"Were the other events of which you spoke in the North and South Pacific Oceans, similar in nature?" asked Apollo.

"Not exactly. Most entailed whales sinking small, private yachts and drowning their adult crews. However, there was one incident where a large, overcrowded ferry boat was sunk in the China Sea; again the work of whales according to our spies in those waters. Of the four hundred humans packed onto a boat designed for half that number, fewer than fifty were left alive when rescue boats arrived."

"Do you think humans know the cause?" asked Apollo.

"I do not know," Hera answered. "Perhaps."

"Whether they do or do not, it is only a matter of time until they feel the full fury of Poseidon's evil intent and react," interjected Zeus who had been listening with a pained expression on his normally serene face.

Apollo looked at Hera and said, "Queen Hera, please tell us how you plan to deal with this."

"Yes. I suppose we must get to that. Well, as we speak, word has gone out to all the chieftains of the tribes in our three kingdoms to mobilize their forces." It was obvious by her tone and manner that she gave this war cry with great reluctance. She added, "I shall refer to these armies as the Loyalist forces from this point forward."

"What does Poseidon call his side?" asked Apollo.

"He and Eris have formed what they call the Federation of the Free," replied Hera.

"Federation of the Doomed," is more like it growled Ares.

"I would prefer Federation of the Misguided," said Hera, who was still struggling with the idea of killing her fellow beings regardless of their intent. "However, the truth is that even with all the marines from all the tribes of my kingdom, and those of Kings Pluto and Dionysus, we will be no match for the Federation's forces. They outnumber us by over three to one."

"What of the other kingdoms in the Southern and Indian Oceans?" asked Apollo.

"King Hermes wants no part of the coming war. He said that few humans ever come to the Southern Ocean and he sees no reason to become involved in a war that will take place in distant seas. And Queen Demeter says her religion prevents her from taking part in the killing of either whales or humans. She has ordered her subjects throughout the Indian Ocean to remain neutral."

"Neutrality in time of war is another word for cowardice," snarled Ares.

Dionysus chortled, "We will see how long her prayers protect her and her subjects from the lethal arsenal on the deathships when man realizes beings are intentionally killing his kind."

Zeus looked at Ares with compassion. "Ares, my warrior friend, sometimes it takes more courage to remain neutral than to heed the battle cry of war." Then he turned to Dionysus and said sharply, "He who belittles faith has none. And life without faith is worse than no life at all."

There was an awkward pause. Dionysus was uncertain of whether or not he had just been insulted or threatened again. But being the bully that he was, he chose not to trade barbs with the steely-eyed Humpback.

Hera, ever the politician, broke the silence. "Despite our inferiority in number, we still must prepare for the possibility of an all-out war between our forces and those of the Federation."

"How many marines do you have?" asked Apollo.

"I have asked King Pluto to serve as our Minister of War, and I will let him answer."

Pluto cleared his throat and began, "The combined strength of the forces that we will be able to muster from within our three kingdoms is nearly twenty thousand marines, comprised of many different species, with the split between whales and dolphins approximately two to one. In addition, we have one hundred Guardians, most of whom are Offshore Orcas like our two brave friends here with us today." He acknowledged Ares and Aegyptus with an appreciative nod of his large head.

Apollo asked the obvious next question. "How big is Poseidon's army?"

"We cannot be sure, but we estimate that he may have over three times as many marines as we do, with several hundred Guardians, including both Offshore and Transient Orcas. This latter group is surprising and we do not know what Poseidon offered them to repress their cannibalistic tendencies."

"He probably told them they could eat the losers," snickered Dionysus.

"The Transients will not pose a problem," said Ares with a disgusted growl. It was no secret that the only beings Transient Killer Whales feared were their Offshore cousins. And with good reason.

Pluto continued, "With such an imbalance in numbers, I believe that our best defense is to go on the offense and I have recommended to Queen Hera that I lead our combined Loyalist forces to the Pacific to attack Poseidon's home base at once."

"Without the Southern and Indian Ocean armies it would be a suicide mission," said Ares coldly.

Pluto was undaunted. "That may be, Guardian Ares, but it is a risk that I am prepared to take. We must stop King Poseidon before it is too late."

Ares nodded his head in agreement and frustration because there was no easy solution. For a moment, everyone fell silent. Hovering there above Roundtop, the entire group rose and fell on the ocean rollers as they passed slowly by on their inexorable journey toward land. Were it not for the harsh reality of what was happening on the far side of the world, all might have been lulled into a false sense of security by the ocean's passive caress.

Seizing the moment, Pan interjected, "We agree with King Pluto. We should attack Poseidon's home base at once." Then he added almost as an afterthought, "Where is Poseidon's home base?"

"It is near Johnston Island, in the middle of the North Pacific Ocean, at the eastern end of the Mid-Pacific Mountain range," replied Pluto. "Half way around Planet Ocean."

"We could make it," replied Pan with his usual resolve.

Hera smiled at the tough little ocean wanderer who was obviously eager to charge off into the fray, as he had done to Sinclair Cay. As small as Pan was, there was no denying what the tenacious little Harbor Porpoise had accomplished so far. "I am sure you could, Pan."

"Oh, please," snorted Dionysus. "Can we get back to the issue here?"

Pan gave the King a dirty look with a scrunch of his mouth. No one noticed except Zeus who winked at Pan, which emboldened him further but before he could say anything else, Hera glanced around the group and said, "I am concerned that Ares may be right and I have told King Pluto that I am not yet prepared to launch a frontal assault on the Federation's forces." She looked at Apollo and said, "Which brings me to what I must ask of you, Apollo." She paused then continued with a noticeable heaviness in her voice and a far away look in her eyes. "I do not know what the Ancients knew, or what meaning lay behind their words in the Legend of the Light; none of us can know these things. But it is my belief that the best way you can serve the forces of good against evil, is to travel to the Southern and Indian Oceans and ask King Hermes and Queen Demeter to align their forces with ours in this just cause.

"If anyone can change their minds and get them to join the forces of good it is you. Even with their help we will still be outnumbered but our chances will be greatly improved." She paused again. Then with a sigh she added, "But even as I ask this of you, my heart is troubled for it will be a journey fraught with great danger: the seas between here and there are filled with roving Federation war parties eager to kill any beings loyal to our cause. And what is more, the current state of disharmony in the oceans has given rise to free-roving bands of pirates, made up of wicked beings who have aligned themselves with neither cause, and who see this as an opportunity to indulge themselves in the misfortune of others."

Apollo did not have to think long or hard about what the Queen had laid out before him. Like her, he had no idea what the Ancients had intended for him, but Hera's proposal seemed as worthy an effort as any. "I accept," he said with a forthrightness that gave everyone gathered there cause for hope.

"We will go too," said Pan with a power beyond his size.

"As will we," said Ares speaking for himself and his brother.

Apollo looked questioningly at Zeus but even as he did, he seemed to know the answer. "I will join you when I can," said Zeus. "But first there are other matters that I must attend to."

"Matters more important than this?" asked Dionysus.

Zeus shared a knowing look with Queen Hera and answered solemnly, "Yes."

"Your help will be most welcome whenever it comes, Zeus," said Apollo. Then he turned back to Queen Hera and said, "My Company and I will leave as soon as we have rested from our journey here."

Pan liked the thought. "Yes, we *are* a company. Apollo's Company of the Light."

"It is a good name," said Hera. "And a wise decision. You must eat heartily for you will need all the strength you can muster on such a long and dangerous journey to the bottom of the world and back."

"Yes, the Company must eat heartily," echoed Pan.

Aegyptus joined the discussion. "Apollo, I think you also should eat more of the minerals that color your skin, for I can already see that your disguise is wearing off."

"Thank you for your concern, Aegyptus, but from this point on in my life, I will show my true color." It was a noble gesture, characteristic of Apollo's newfound sense of duty. Fearing for his safety, the answer troubled Aegyptus and his brother but they did not argue. Zeus also said nothing.

"Well, at least one thing will be on your side," said Hera. "It is spring in the Southern Ocean, and by the time you reach the Cape of Good Hope, five thousand miles south southeast of here,"—she glanced at Pan, mentally calculating how many miles a day they would be able to cover,—"it will be summer and your journey from the Cape through the Southern Ocean to King Hermes' kingdom will be tolerable, if not comfortable."

"We will do it in less time," mumbled Pan, not liking the implication behind her words.

Apollo smiled at his little friend. Then he looked at the Guardians and said, "We will leave one week from tomorrow. And may God bless us as we go over the edge."

"Amen," said Zeus.

"Amen," added Pan with a nervous glance around the group.

"Over the edge," said Ares with a clear sense of purpose.

"Yes. Over the edge!" echoed Pan loudly. Then he looked at Apollo and asked, "What edge?"

Apollo chuckled. "The edge of the Kingdom, my little friend." He pointed with his flipper in the direction of the perimeter of the plateau upon which sat the Kingdom of the Ancients.

"Oh, *that* edge," said Pan nervously.

And so it would be. In seven days time, they would leave the Kingdom of the Ancients for what all knew in their hearts might well be the last time. And then, Apollo and his Company of the Light would head out across the vast abyssal plain made up of seven great ocean basins that lay between them and the Cape of Good Hope. Given their noble mission, the Cape was aptly named but in the weeks and months ahead, the words 'Over the edge' would come to mean much, much more.

CHAPTER FOURTEEN

Thunder In The Sea

"Did you ever stop to think about the paradox of mountains?" asked Pan as the group of four beings passed to the east of the Sierra Leone Rise, two hundred miles off the west coast of Africa, eighteen hundred miles southeast of the Kingdom of the Ancients. It had been nearly four weeks since they went over the edge and, with the exception of Sundays, when they rested, they had swum steadily for ten to twelve hours each day, averaging ninety miles by nightfall. It was the afternoon of the twenty-eighth day since starting their journey and they were making good time as they rode the Guinea Current toward the equator, which lay four hundred miles further south. The seas had been kind but they all knew it would not last.

"What do you mean?" queried Apollo, who was now pure white, as white as he had been on the night of his birth. Their conversation was taking place as they slipped seamlessly through the rolling swells of the West African seas. Aegyptus swam slightly ahead of them while Ares was somewhere below and behind. Zeus was noticeable by his absence.

"Well, for humans a mountain is something that towers over them, making them seem small and insignificant. For them to see the view from its peak they must climb its sides; a journey that is arduous and often fatal. Whereas for beings, we spend our lives above the mountains, like those over which we are passing at this moment. From our vantage point, we can see the majesty of a mountaintop; while the bottom of a mountain holds no appeal for us, because it is rooted firmly in the deeps, where we prefer not to go."

"I had not given much thought to mountains, either above or below the waves," replied Apollo. "But your point is well-taken."

"Do you suppose that is why the soul of man is cloaked in darkness while that of beings is filled with light; because man spends his entire life looking up at mountains and wishing he was on top, while we spend our lives looking down on them, thankful we are not at the bottom?"

Apollo did a barrel role around the porpoise, fell back in line beside him, and said, "Pan, you truly are a remarkable little being."

Pan grinned and shot up to the surface where he performed a forward roll that would have made his dorsal fin appear like it was on a revolving wheel to humans had there been any to see it. But of course there were not. When he returned to Apollo's side he said, "Yes, we are remarkable. Very remarkable indeed. And we appreciate your recognition of that fact. However, we would hasten to point out that we are not little. We are quite big for our size." He said it with the cheeky giggle that Apollo had come to love.

Apollo nudged him with his flipper and said, "Come, Pan. Let us fly." They quickened their pace and together the two of them zipped along through the blue-green water at the surface of the vast open ocean, high above Pan's paradoxical mountains, seemingly oblivious to what lay ahead or below.

It was late in the day and the sun had begun its long slide into the western Atlantic when Ares caught up with them and ordered them to stop. Apollo could see that not all was well. "What is it?" he asked the Guardian.

"We are being followed." Ares' response was delivered without emotion but even so, the words sent a chill through Apollo's body, and brought a wide-eyed look to Pan's face.

"By who?" queried Apollo.

"They are Pilot Whales. About forty of them." Ominously, he added, "Long-finned."

"Oh my! Are they the child-killers?" asked Pan.

"I think so," replied Ares. "They fit the description Queen Hera gave us. For several days now, I have had a feeling that we were being followed, so this morning I held back and allowed the three of you to get well ahead. I moved off at a right angle to our course and waited. It did not take long for them to pass me by. They were swimming in a tight formation, in complete silence; but even at a distance, I could tell who they were and count their number. They have stopped for the night, seven miles behind us, and they sent out two scouts to make sure we were doing the same."

"Where are the scouts now?" asked Pan glancing into the shadows behind Ares.

Ares answered coldly, "Dead."

His answer hit Pan like a breaking wave, and he fell silent.

"How long before the others miss them?" asked Apollo.

"The scouts would be expected to watch us during the night and report back tomorrow at dawn. The others will have no reason to believe that something is amiss until then."

The Company grew quiet as the thought of so many killers so near sank in. Finally, Apollo said, "They are coming after me." He expressed what the Guardians were thinking.

"Yes," said Ares. He and his brother exchanged a knowing look.

The thought troubled Pan. "Maybe they are just pirates."

Ares shook his head with a look of grim inevitability.

"What do we do?" asked Apollo.

"Well, we cannot stay here," said Aegyptus.

"No. We must keep moving," added Ares.

"You mean swim at night?" exclaimed Pan. He had grown up sleeping in the relative safety of shallow water, preferably heavily weeded, or even better, within tangled mangrove forests, and the thought of swimming at night, when the kraken prowled the open seas, terrified him.

"Yes. We will head northeast. The Pilot Whales will not expect that and tomorrow when they discover that we are gone, they will continue southward, which will put us on their tails."

His brother nodded his agreement. "Following an enemy is better than being followed."

Apollo agreed.

"Good," said Ares. "We will rest until moonrise, and then we will head northeast as fast, and for as long, as the little one here can manage."

"We can manage quite nicely, thank-you," said Pan, muttering *the little one* under his breath.

"By tomorrow afternoon," continued Ares, "we will reach the coast of Africa, where we can rest in safety. Then after a day or so, we will continue south, except that we will follow the coast where we can seek shelter should the child-killers find us again."

"Very well," said Apollo.

Four hours later, as the moon rose over the Atlantic, the Company headed northeast as fast as they could, and leaving luminescent wakes behind them as they plowed through the night seas. Pan was determined to show them that he was capable, and throughout the long night and arduous day that followed he did just that; such that by the time they stopped twenty hours later, he was as euphoric with his accomplishment as he was exhausted. When they reached the warm, shallow waters surrounding the place man calls the Bijagós Archipelago, which is an area of immense biological diversity off the coast of Guinea-Bissau, Ares took first watch while the others slept. Later Aegyptus switched with him.

Apollo and his Company of the Light stayed in the protected waters of the archipelago for four days. They fed on pilchard, hake and cuttlefish, a particular delicacy that was introduced to Apollo and Pan by Aegyptus, who was more of an adventurous gourmet than others of his kind were. The Guardian taught them to snap the creature's internal shell, or cuttlebone, by pinning it against the bottom, then lift it and beat it with their heads to drain the toxic black ink that cuttlefish use as a defense mechanism. Then take it back to the sea floor and scrape it along the sand to separate bone from flesh, and eat the latter. Apollo took a liking to the slippery meal with eight arms and two tentacles. But Pan did not. He mistakenly grabbed one by an arm rather than crushing it, which allowed the creature to wrap its tentacles around his head and release its ink. This sent Pan into a blind panic during which he rammed into the side of Ares, who did not find it amusing. After he was saved by Aegyptus who pulled the cuttlefish off Pan's head, Pan vowed to stick to food with tails. (I should point out that another reason Apollo liked killing and eating this creature was that it was related to the octopus that still haunted his memory.)

Once the Company had regained their strength, they headed back out into the open sea where they caught the Guinea Current again. Heading first south and then east, under the bulge of Africa, they rode the current for ten days, covering nine hundred miles. When they reached the Guinea Rise, they turned and headed south once more, following the migration routes of Fin and Humpback Whales, passing the lands of Cameroon, the Congo and Angola on their way. Soon they came up against the South Equatorial Current that flows in a counter clockwise motion around the vast South Atlantic gyre. Apollo had fought this same current on the other side of the ocean when he journeyed up the coast of South America, and as they turned into it, and felt its force against them, Pan remarked how nice it would be if all the rivers in the seas flowed in the direction they were traveling. None of the others chose to point out the inherent problem with this concept: instead they plowed forward, determined to get to the Cape of Good Hope before the Long-fins found them again.

For the next three weeks, their trip was uneventful until they crossed the Walvis Ridge, fourteen hundred miles south of the Guinea Rise. It would have taken less time were it not for the headcurrent. At the ridge, the sea floor rose nearly twenty thousand feet from the Angola Abyssal Plain up to within a few hundred feet of the surface, and it was there that trouble reared its ugly head again, or actually, their ugly heads, all forty of them. Ares' earsight detected the Pilot Whales long before his eyes did. Ever since their close call at the Sierra Leone Rise, Ares had taken the lead while Aegyptus followed up in the rear. As soon as he detected the approaching whales, he turned and got Apollo, Pan, and Aegyptus into a tight formation. His mind raced over how best to meet the onrushing assassins; there were not many options.

"You two stay between Aegyptus and me," he commanded Apollo and Pan. The latter needed no convincing but Apollo refused and insisted that he be one prong of a three pointed star with heads out, tails in and Pan at its center. Ares agreed as there was no time to argue and his last words to all of them as they waited for the killers to materialize out of the seamless wall of blue, were, "Take as many of them with you as you can."

For a second Pan wondered where he was supposed to take them, then it struck him with the force of a tsunami that Ares meant kill them—and he wondered if he would be able to kill even one of them before they killed him. He peered out from between the two Orcas, directing his earsight toward the unseen killers as they bore down on them, one thousand yards away, now nine hundred, and then eight. He felt his heart pounding so hard he wondered if he might die of a heart attack before their teeth tore into him, and the thought made him angry. "We do not like dying," he muttered. "We do not like it at all."

As the four of them hovered there in the steel blue waters off the coast of Namibia, waiting for the inevitable, Apollo closed his eyes and said the word, *Believe,* three times to himself.

"What is that?" Pan cried out.

Apollo's eyes snapped open. "What?"

"That!" said Pan. "Listen. We hear thunder."

Apollo and the two Guardians listened intently. Ares' looked up at the liquid mirror overhead, and the filmy blue canopy beyond it, and said, "It cannot be thunder. The skies over the sea are clear." But then he heard it too. It was a heavy, rumbling sound; repetitive, rhythmic, and growing louder by the minute.

"I hear it," said Apollo, "Pan is right. It is like thunder rolling through the sea."

"Frightens us. Frightens us," whispered Pan.

By this point the sound was too intense to miss: they could feel it in their bones. And then two things happened almost simultaneously. First, the outswimmers of the tribe of Long-finned Pilot Whales appeared, with their expressions marked by evil intent they were now fully visible to the eyes of Apollo and the others. But at that moment, the sound of thunder in the sea began again and grew so loud that it got the attention of the Long-fins as well.

"Look!" exclaimed Pan. Off to their right and closing fast was an enormous shadow. It appeared black at first, and then it flashed silver and back to black again. It was larger than the biggest whale that had ever lived, and far more frightening, because there was no definition to it, no way to determine its form or intent. And it was bearing down upon the Long-fins.

"A gigantic kraken!" yelped Pan.

"No. It is much too big to be a kraken," said Apollo as he and the others watched in awe.

By this time, the main group of the Pilot Whales arrived on the scene and like their outswimmers; they came to an abrupt stop in the water. The whale who appeared to be their leader glanced in the direction of Apollo, and then his eyes were drawn back to the onrushing shadow. As it closed on them, his eyes grew wide and he shouted something at the others. In unison, they turned and with frantic thrusts of their tails, they disappeared into the blue gloom from where they had come.

One danger was now gone but the other grew closer. Apollo, Pan and the two Orcas hung there in silence, watching this unfold. Uncertain as to what would happen next, they kept their eyes focused upon the enormous shadow, which by that point had stopped swimming and was floating there, a gigantic writhing, flashing mass of death and destruction.—Or was it?

All at once, Apollo saw it for what it really was. "I do not believe it!" he whispered with a grin.

"What?" asked Pan. "What do we not believe?"

Ares saw it too. "Remarkable!" he said, backing down from fight mode.

"It is a miracle," added Aegyptus, who also now realized what it was and also relaxed.

Pan still did not understand. "What is a miracle? Would someone please…" he did not finish his sentence.

Before their eyes, the giant shadow beast dematerialized, and revealed itself to be a swarming mass of sardines, millions upon millions of them, or a quantum's quantum in whalespeak. The molten mass of silver and black bodies morphed through several other fluid shapes, some of which were nebulous, while others were more discernible, like a tumbling oval and a swirling cone. Finally, after a mesmerizing moment, the tiny fish formed an enormous ball, as big around as a great whale is long, and slowly rolled away into the blueness of the sea, until at last it was gone. But after it departed, the sea was not empty, for there, appearing from behind the ball was a huge, boxy black shape that hung at the edge of nothingness, like a rock wall that had broken away from its mountain.

Pan was the first to recognize what it was. "It is a Sperm Whale." He had seen such a great whale before and remembered well the nature of its shape.

Ares was impressed. "You are right."

"Is it Poseidon?" asked Apollo more out of curiosity than concern.

"No," said Ares. There was no fear in his voice but some caution. Of all the beings in the sea, a full-grown Sperm Whale is the only one who is a match for Orcas, even when the latter hold an advantage in number.

The great toothed whale moved effortlessly through the sea toward them and stopped. At first, he did not speak. Instead, he hung there in the blueness of the sea and eyed them carefully.

"We are not afraid of Sperm Whales," muttered Pan. From the experiences in his youth, he knew that Sperm Whales did not eat beings. "We like them. But this one is not making a very good impression on us. We think he is very rude."

"Excuse me?" asked the Sperm Whale with a bemused smile. His powerful voice boomed through the water.

Pan was startled. He had not meant his last comment to be heard. He had forgotten that Sperm Whales have the best hearing of all beings. Apollo and the two Guardians could sense that the stranger meant them no harm and they were amused by Pan's predicament.

Emboldened by the whale's friendly demeanor, Pan scolded, "We think you might want to introduce yourself now that you have impressed us with your magic."

The Sperm Whale chuckled. "I performed no magic, little one."

Pan retorted, "We are not little, we are…"

Ares cut him off. "I am Ares, Guardian of Queen Hera, ruler of the North Atlantic and Moderator of this year's Gathering." By his no-nonsense tone and manner, Ares made it clear that the issue of who did what could wait until they knew the identity of the stranger and his intentions. Ares also made a point of not introducing his companions until this had been determined.

The levity in the Sperm Whale's voice disappeared but he was not offended by the Guardian's cautious demeanor. He knew that was the way of Guardians and would have expected no less. "With apologies, Guardian Ares. Permit me to introduce myself. My name is Triton, and I would like to welcome you to my home waters." The Sperm Whale had a huge squarish head typical of his species and thick body covered in wrinkles. At sixty feet, he was twice as long as Ares and Aegyptus but nearly ten times as heavy, and there was one more thing about him that grabbed the other beings' attention. He had several ugly round scars on his body.

"You say these are your home waters?" asked Ares.

"Yes. I was once a Ranger here," Triton answered. Rangers were beings loyal to a particular king or queen who were assigned as protectors of the kingdom, similar in role and responsibility to Guardians. However, unlike Guardians, whose primary roles were to protect the monarch, Rangers patrolled the outer reaches of a kingdom, protecting common beings from danger, including kraken or other creatures who would do them harm.

Satisfied by Triton's reply, Ares started to introduce his traveling companions. "This is Aegyptus. He is…"

"Your brother," interrupted Triton but with obvious respect. Turning to the other two beings, Triton continued. "And you are Pan, and I can see that you are indeed big in spirit," he added with a smile. Before Pan could react, Triton looked at Apollo, and said, "And you are Apollo. I am honored to be in your presence." The whale tipped his huge head in a sign of respect.

Apollo was surprised and flattered. "How do you know us?"

"Word of your mission has spread throughout the Seven Seas, to both friend and foe alike."

"As we have just seen," replied Apollo. "Thankfully, the Long-fins were deterred in their attack by that school of sardines."

"The Long-fins will be back," said Ares glancing around their little gathering.

Triton smiled and replied, "No. I think not."

"I do not understand," said Apollo.

"Let me explain. First, I am sorry to inform you that King Dionysus ordered the Rangers and Guardians in our Kingdom, to find the four of you—and kill you." Ares and Aegyptus tensed but Triton quickly added, "Let me assure you that I am a Loyalist and you have nothing to fear now in these waters."

Ares probed, "How can that be since you said that…"

Triton cut him off. "Be patient my friend." He turned and issued a deep, booming call into the royal blue nothingness that surrounded them. And then that sound began again. BOOM, boom, boom. BOOM, boom, boom. BOOM, boom, boom. It was the same thundering sound they had heard before, but this time it was deeper, more resonant, and close enough that they could now tell it was the rhythmic chanting of a group of great whales. Ares and the others quickly scanned the seas with their earsight and realized that Triton had not come alone. Then their eyesight confirmed what their earsight told them, as out of the blue haze a group of Sperm Whales appeared, sixty in all, giant black beings swimming in perfect formation, sleek, strong, and unafraid. On they came. BOOM, boom, boom. BOOM, boom, boom. Until at last they surrounded the Company of the Light on all sides.

Ares' heart sank. Thinking that Triton had been lying about being a friend, he shook his head in anger and frustration. "I am sorry, Apollo for I have failed you."

"No, Ares," said Apollo with a deliberate smile. "You have not failed me." He peered down into the deeps with eager anticipation. "I know who was behind the magic."

"Who is it? Who is it?" asked Pan excitedly swimming in a tight circle but staying close to the Guardians, just in case.

"It is me," said the booming voice from below. All eyes flashed toward the sound of the voice and there, rising from out of the depths, was none other than the mighty Zeus.

"Zeus! You old devil you," said Apollo with a broad smile.

With a wry look Zeus replied, "Well you are half-right, my friend. I am indeed old."

"Zeus!" exclaimed Pan. He zipped over and rubbed his tiny body up against the Humpback. "We knew it was you who made the fish appear like a giant monster to chase away the Long-fins."

"Oh did you now?" inquired a bemused Zeus.

By now, the Sperm Whales had formed a protective circle around them and one of them approached Triton and said, "It is done, your

Majesty." Triton nodded solemnly then looked at Apollo, "The Long-fins will trouble you no more."

Apollo nodded. The meaning of Triton's words was clear.

"Did he just say your Majesty?" asked Ares.

"Yes. I apologize for keeping my true identity from you. I wanted to wait until Zeus appeared. I am King Triton. Ruler of the South Atlantic Ocean."

Ares eyes narrowed. "What happened to King Dionysus?"

Zeus answered for Triton. "King Dionysus is dead and with him died his treachery. That is why I could not join you when you left the Kingdom of the Ancients. Queen Hera suspected that Dionysus was a traitor and she asked me to investigate it. I uncovered his evil deeds and dealt with him." There was finality in his words that left no doubt what he meant.

"He conspired with Eris did he not?" asked Ares, as his earlier suspicions were now confirmed.

"Yes," said Zeus. "Honor and duty are sometimes slaves to love."

"Only among fools," replied Ares.

Apollo tipped his head to the King. "I am honored to be in your presence, King Triton."

"Thank-you, Apollo. But it is I who should bow before you." Then Triton looked at Zeus and said, "My army and I must be off for we have more forces to gather in the far western corners of my Kingdom before we round Cape Horn and enter the Pacific."

At the mention of Cape Horn, Apollo tensed as the memories of the kraken and his lost companions flashed through his mind.

Zeus nodded. "Very well, King Triton. May God speed you on your journey. We will meet you again on the far side of the world."

"Yes. At Johnston Island, six months hence," replied Triton. Without further adieu, Triton and his marines departed, making the same chanting sound as they went but this time it was welcome to the ears of the Company of the Light.

It had been a splendid meeting in the waters of the West African Sea, imbued with magic and majesty. For a few more minutes they all hung there, riding up and down in the gentle open ocean swells, then Zeus looked at Apollo and said, "It is time that we left this place."

"Are you joining us this time?" asked Apollo with trepidation.

"Yes. For now," Zeus replied. It was a qualified reply but Apollo chose not to pursue it. For now was better than not at all.

"Goody, goody!" exclaimed Pan.

"Then, let us go," said Apollo. And with that, one by one the Company of the Light headed south, bound for the tip of Africa, and beyond; filled with faith, hope, and an iron will. In the days to come, they would need all three.

CHAPTER FIFTEEN

Under The Southern Cross

Darkness fell slowly on the first day of summer at the bottom of the world. The sun lingered in the western sky, as if reluctant to take the plunge into the Southern Ocean, that vast expanse of circumpolar water from which it had not yet fully driven out the chill of the long Antarctic winter. Despite the burning orb's best efforts to melt them, small icebergs called growlers still patrolled the waters, as they would throughout the summer months, oblivious to the season's softer calling. They were a constant reminder of what had been and what would soon be again, for summer here was little more than a blink of the eye on the frozen face of winter.

It had been three months since Apollo and his Company of the Light left the Kingdom of the Ancients, and on that first summer night, the weary Company found themselves in unusually calm waters off Marion Island, the larger of the two Prince Edward Islands, nine hundred miles southeast of Port Elizabeth, South Africa. The islands lay approximately four degrees below the line of latitude man calls the fortieth parallel, well inside the danger zone known to your mariners as the Roaring Forties. The Company had fought the Benguela Current most of the journey down the coast from the Walvis Ridge, and then stayed far out to sea as they rounded the Cape of Good Hope to avoid the Great White Sharks who frequent those waters. Neither the Guardians nor Zeus had any fear of these sharks—but to confront them unnecessarily would distract Apollo from his mission and they chose to stay well clear.

After they rounded the Cape and entered the sub-antarctic Indian Ocean, they felt the full force of the powerful Agulhas Current, which flows southward along the East African continental shelf at over one hundred miles a day, creating enormous swell-waves that regularly vented their wrath upon ships and the humans who sailed in them. However, on that warm December night, as the Company settled down to sleep, the sea was calm and flat, like a giant black mirror reflecting the light of a billion stars back into space. From their current position to their planned rendezvous with King Hermes at the Kerguélen Archipelago, fourteen hundred miles to the east, they would benefit from the current as it slowly meandered along the southern edge of the Indian Ocean. They would need all the help they could get because the tranquility of that clear, starry night belied the danger that lay ahead.

Zeus had armed them with the knowledge of what they were about to face. He, like others of his species, had traversed the path through these frigid waters many times before. The Company would head out again at dawn but at that moment, as Pan and Apollo floated effortlessly on the seamless margin between sea and sky, Pan's mind was not focused on their journey but rather on the stars overhead, which seemed as unreachable as the God who made them. Melancholy had overtaken the little Harbor Porpoise with the big heart who was far, far from home and uncertain of whether he would ever see it again.

"What is that?" whispered Pan so as not to wake Aegyptus and Ares. Zeus had insisted upon handling guard duty that night so that the brothers could get a good night's rest. Like Apollo, Pan was aware of the fact that Zeus never slept. It was just one more puzzling aspect of this enigmatic whale's nature, but on that night, the Orcas were grateful for it.

"What?" said Apollo.

"There, in the sky."

Apollo followed Pan's eye line upward and saw it, four bright stars and one lesser one in the shape of a cross. He studied it for a moment then answered, "I believe it is what man calls the Southern Cross. I remember Captain Jackson saying that ancient mariners used it as a navigation guide through the southern seas."

Pan continued to stare up at it. "We like it. It is very beautiful." There was a hint of sadness in his voice but Apollo did not notice.

"To many humans a cross is a symbol of God."

"Why?" asked Pan.

"Because of a man called Jesus Christ, who died upon a cross. Many believe he was the son of God."

"Humans think God's son was a man?"

"Yes. Some do."

"Do they think God is a man also?"

"Yes, at least those who believe in him."

"Beings do not think God is a man,—do we?"

"No."

Pan nodded slowly trying to grasp it all. "How did this man called Jesus die on that cross?"

"Other men hung him there and left him to die."

"Why?"

"Because they were afraid of him."

With his eyes still fixed upon the Southern Cross, Pan whispered, "That is very sad."

Oblivious to Pan's mood, Apollo added, "Captain Jackson said mariners have an expression that beyond forty degrees south there is no law; beyond fifty degrees, there is no God." Apollo thought the expression was amusing. Pan did not and Apollo finally realized that his companion was in no joking mood. Over the past several weeks, Apollo had noticed a change in Pan's attitude as self-doubt and anxiety passed like wraiths through the light behind Pan's once-sparkling eyes, and Apollo was now angry at himself for not being more perceptive of Pan's demeanor at that particular moment. With tenderness, he asked, "Are you all right, Pan?"

For a long moment, Pan did not answer and when he finally did, it was with a question, "Do you believe in God, Apollo?"

"Yes. I do. Why do you ask?"

Pan sighed. "Because we are afraid that we are going to die soon. And we hope that God will be there to take us."

It was not the first time that Apollo had had someone close to him say such a thing. Haemon had done so on the night they escaped from Oceania and the memory of his dead friend flooded back into Apollo's mind. On that night, in what seemed a lifetime ago, Apollo had lied when he told Haemon that death was not imminent. It had been a well-intentioned lie but Haemon had seen right through it and Apollo vowed never to do it again. But this was different. Somehow Apollo knew that Pan was not about to die. He moved closer to his little friend, caressed him with his flipper, and replied, "We are all going to die, Pan, but your time has not yet come. This I know to be true as surely as I know that one day you will see your nostos again." He said it with conviction that rose up from deep within, from the place where truth dwells.

Pan's eyes brightened a little. "How did you know that we were thinking of our nostos?"

"The same way I know that you will see it again after we are through with this mission."

Pan accepted Apollo's answer without question. "Will you be there too?"

Apollo hesitated before answering. Floating there in the silent sea, with his smooth skin glowing in the soft starlight, he searched for a way out of the moral dilemma that loomed before him. Finally he said, "Yes, Pan. We will go there together." Unlike his first two responses, Apollo was uncertain that this was true. The little inner voice that neither whale nor human can twist into an untruth, cried out to Apollo, telling him that when Pan returned to the place of his birth, Apollo would not be with him. But as much as he had promised himself he would never tell another lie, in this case he could not bring himself to extinguish the tiny spark of hope that now flickered inside the little porpoise's heart, the light of which was now visible in Pan's wide, innocent eyes.

Pan relaxed and the anxiety that had had him in its grip lessened. He smiled a hopeful little smile. "God bless you, Apollo, and thank you—for everything. We think we shall sleep now."

Apollo said goodnight to Pan but he would find no rest himself during the remainder of that night. Pan's words had created a storm of cognitive dissonance that rolled across the ocean of his mind. In part, Apollo felt deep satisfaction in the nobility of their mission and the faith that his followers, Pan and the Guardians, had in him; but at the same time he felt great sadness and he worried that neither solace nor great achievement lay ahead for them, only pain, and loss, and failure, and that fear weighed heavily upon him. *Believe*, Zeus had said to him. *Believe,* he said to himself, but even as he said it, he wondered if he did, or if he ever would. With this mental tempest raging within him, and the sound of his own doubts roaring in his ears, he looked back up at the sky but the Southern Cross was nowhere to be seen. Dark clouds had appeared obliterating Apollo's view of the heavens.

By dawn the next morning, the Company's brief reprieve from the winds that give the Roaring Forties their name was over. They left the relative calm of the lee shore of Marion Island and headed out across the windswept sea, traveling eastward above the line of underwater cliffs that formed the edge of the Crozet Plateau. The seafloor on their left was less than six hundred feet below them while off to their right the bottom dropped straight down to a depth of sixteen thousand feet. They soon passed the Crozet Islands, where Zeus had forewarned them that Transient Killer Whales hunted the islands' huge breeding seal population. When the Company came abreast of the islands, several Transients swam out to investigate the passing travelers. As was their nature, the killers made no sound as they approached the Company, but when they saw Zeus and the two Guardians, they quickly returned to their in-shore waters. Pan was frightened by the incident but to Apollo it was just an annoying distraction. Once safely past the islands, the Company headed out over the abyssal plain with Zeus in the lead, plowing through foam-flecked rollers in a slate gray sea, eastward toward the Kerguélen Archipelago where they were to meet King Hermes.

Over the next two weeks, they made good time and covered nearly eleven hundred miles, or three quarters of the distance to Kerguélen, without incident until one cold and gray morning when their temporary respite from danger was shattered. It began with the appearance of a group of Hourglass Dolphins who approached the Company in a highly agitated state, seemingly out of place in the cold waters, thick and sluggish like liquid glass. After a hurried exchange of greetings, the chieftain of the dolphins, a stocky female with the distinctive hourglass-shaped white markings along her black flank, warned them they should change their course. She said that a fleet of whaling ships lay directly in their path, and that the whalers had killed a female Fin Whale, with whom the dolphins had been traveling, and were now trying to murder the Fin Whale's baby. Upon hearing this, Zeus became furious and told the Guardians to take Apollo and Pan North while he went to see if he could help the baby Fin Whale. Apollo was adamant that they should all go together, which is what they did.

When they arrived at the scene, they found a factory ship flying the Japanese flag, with the word RESEARCH painted in big white letters on its black hull, moving slowly through the blood-soaked sea. As your kind measures it, the ship had a displacement of 7,500 tons but while beings can gauge the amount of water displaced by a ship's hull by using their earsight, they do not describe ships in those terms. Instead, they classify them according to the level of danger they represent, from harmless pleasure craft, to fishing boats with potentially hazardous nets, to ships of war with their sometimes-murderous sonar, to ocean-going tankers that spread black liquid death upon the waters. However, Zeus knew it was not this factory ship that represented the greatest danger to beings of all of man's vessels, but the others in its fleet called catcher ships. For they existed for one purpose only, which was to slaughter innocent beings.

As the Company drew closer, they were shocked and saddened by the grisly scene before them. The stern of the factory ship was divided into two wing-like doors that were spread open wide, through which its crew was hauling the bleeding carcass of the mother Fin Whale, flukes first up a steep steel ramp. Meanwhile the frantic baby was swimming beside its mother's body, rubbing its head against hers, trying to throw itself onto the ramp as she was being pulled into the gaping jaws of the ship.

"What is that?" asked Apollo.

"It is the factory ship of the fleet," said Zeus. "And despite the word RESEARCH written on its side, these humans are here for no such thing. Their sole purpose is to murder our kind under the guise of research. When they get the body of the mother Fin Whale on the deck, men with long knives will butcher her into pieces that are then taken below decks where they will be processed into food and oil."

"You mean the people on that ship murdered her in order to eat her?" exclaimed Pan.

"Not the crew but humans back in their home country; it is a place called Japan. The Japanese and two other nations, Norway and Iceland, still permit the hunting and butchering of our kind."

"Maybe we can get Transient Orcas to acquire a taste for the Japanese," growled Ares.

Pan laughed but Apollo did not. "You sound like Poseidon, Ares." It was not a compliment.

Ares grumbled. "You are right. I am sorry."

Pan stared at the stern of the ship and cried, "Are they going to kill the baby too?"

As they watched, the question was answered for them. When the head of the mother disappeared into the ship, the stern doors swung closed and the ship's engine roared to life, sucking the baby whale down into the giant propellers where it was chopped to pieces.

"Oh no! No," exclaimed Pan. While he and the others stared at the tragedy before them, Zeus scanned the surrounding seas.

Apollo noticed and asked, "What are you looking for?"

"Their hunter-killer boats," replied Zeus.

"Which they euphemistically call catcher ships," added Ares.

"What does euphemistically mean?" asked Pan.

"It means it is a lie," explained Apollo. "It is the way humans lie to themselves."

"Ares is right," added Zeus. "The factory ship always travels with smaller, faster vessels called catcher ships. But there is a big difference between catching and killing. They are equipped with guns that fire projectiles called harpoons with tips that explode after they pierce the skin of the being."

"Killing them instantly?" asked Pan with wide and pained eyes.

"Not always. Often the whale drowns in his own blood," added Ares angrily.

It did not take the Company of the Light long to find the hunter-killer ships, or vice-versa. As they scanned the seas, their earsight revealed a ship one thousand yards away to the south and closing fast. At seven hundred and fifty tons it was one tenth the size of the factory ship, but far more lethal. It was bearing down on them and a human was getting the harpoon gun ready on its upswept bow.

Zeus looked at the Guardians and said, "Take Apollo and Pan, dive deep and swim north until mid-day before you turn east again. I will join you when I can."

Apollo started to protest. "But…"

Zeus gave Apollo a stern look that left no room for debate. "You *must* go. It is not your destiny to die at the hands of these barbarians. I will deal with them."

"Very well." Apollo tasted a bitter irony in his throat for he had been charged by Hera to stop Poseidon from attacking humans, even now, as they were being attacked. Out of the north there came the fast-throbbing engine sounds of another catcher ship also heading their way; and then another in the east; and one more in the west.

"They are coming to kill us," cried Pan.

"Not us," said Ares without emotion. "It is Zeus whom they are after."

Pan flashed a fearful look at Zeus, hoping Ares was wrong. But a solemn nod from Zeus told him he was not. "You and Apollo are too small to bother with, and they are not interested in the Guardians as food. They might still kill them out of anger because they believe all Orcas are competitors in the hunting of great whales. But right now they seek only to kill me."

"We cannot leave you, Zeus," said Ares. "My brother and I will each attack one catcher ship, you take the other two."

"No!" replied Zeus and by his tone, it was clear that he meant it. "I need you to protect Pan and Apollo. Apollo's journey *must* continue. As soon as I draw the first catcher ship away, the others will follow me. You must leave. Now!"

Reluctantly Ares agreed. With that, Zeus headed off in the direction of the large factory ship. After he left, Apollo and the Guardians spyhopped. Pan tried but he was too small. The others could see the captain as he stood on the walkway beside the bridge. At first, the man did not move, but as Zeus gathered speed and continued on a collision course with his ship, he disappeared inside the bridge. The ship began to turn away from the onrushing leviathan. But it was too late.

"What is Zeus doing?" asked Pan frantically. "Please tell us."

"He is going to ram the ship," answered Aegyptus grimly.

"But the hull is made of steel," said Apollo.

"Frightens us. Frightens us," muttered Pan.

With a cold and knowing smile Ares said, "He is aiming for the rudder."

And that is exactly what Zeus did. Just before he reached the ship, he slipped beneath the surface and then with a sickening thud that echoed throughout the surroundings water, the mighty whale rammed the rudder at full speed. The collision shook the ship and caused loud alarms to go off.

Ignoring what Zeus had told them to do; Apollo looked at the Guardians and said, "You must help him." They nodded and sped off toward the factory ship.

"Come on," said Apollo to Pan. "We are going too."

"But Zeus told us to leave here," said Pan. During their journey, the Harbor Porpoise had grown fond of the Humpback Whale and vice-versa. To watch them swimming together was quite a remarkable sight; the little gray bundle of nervous energy and the staid and mighty, black and white leviathan, moving in harmony through the seas. Pan did not want to disobey Zeus' orders but he could not bear the thought that his giant friend was hurt, or worse. He did not know what to do.

Apollo decided for him, "Come little one. Zeus needs us."

Pan nodded. His fear turned to anger, and his anger to determination. "You are right. Let us go help Zeus sink the ship and kill its crew. Every single one of them."

With Pan by his side, Apollo swam toward the factory ship. By the time they caught up with the Guardians, the ship with its bent rudder jammed tightly against the hull, was steaming in a tight circle. Zeus was nowhere to be seen. Hurriedly they scanned the depths but found no sign of Zeus there either.

"Where is he?" shouted Pan. "We must find him!" Pan swam in a tight circle aiming his earsight in every direction at once. The others were more disciplined in their search.

"Look! There he goes," shouted Ares, pointing with his head in the direction of the nearest catcher ship. Ares dove and headed in that direction followed by the others. When they surfaced, they saw the catcher ship in the distance but it was coming directly at them, with its high bow, almost elegant in design were it not for its dreadful purpose, smashing through the surging, silver-green seas. A man was standing on the bow holding onto the back of the cannon that was pointed directly at Zeus, who was swimming on the surface halfway between the Company and the ship.

Struggling to keep up with the others, Pan skipped like a tossed stone from wave-top to wave-top, ten yards behind Apollo and the Guardians, who, in turn were several hundred yards behind Zeus. Then, just as Zeus got within a hundred yards of the catcher ship, he came to a sudden stop in the water. The ship also slowed and the gunner took careful aim in what he must have thought would be an easy kill. He was wrong.

"What is Zeus doing?" asked Pan frantically, as he and the others stopped to observe what was about to happen.

"I do not know," replied Apollo who was just as confused as Pan.

Ares was neither confused nor frantic. "He is going to let them shoot him," he said with a mixture of admiration and sorrow in his voice.

"Let them shoot him! Why?" asked Pan.

Ares looked at Pan and said, "I think Zeus is going to drag the catcher ship into the mother ship and sink them both."

Aegyptus agreed. "Yes. That is exactly what he is about to do, just like in the legend of another great whale sinking a whaling ship long ago."

"Oh no!" exclaimed Pan.

"Oh yes," said Apollo. He resigned himself to the fact that Zeus was now about to sacrifice his life to protect theirs. Even if the explosive head of the harpoon did not kill Zeus outright, it was unlikely that he would be able to tow the catcher ship into its mother ship with enough force to sink them. Either way Zeus was doomed.

Ares spyhopped again and saw that the three other catcher ships were also closing on the Humpback Whale. Seeing this he slipped back beneath the waves and said, "It is time to go. There is nothing more we can do here. Zeus' sacrifice will be wasted if we die here with him."

Oily tears welled up in Pan's eyes and he hung his little head and sobbed. Apollo and Aegyptus nodded in a sad and lonely silence. Together they all turned and headed away from the convergence of cold-blooded murderers and the selfless being in that cold and hostile sub-arctic sea.

Once they were a safe distance away, they stopped and directed their earsight back toward the scene, for as painful as it was to watch the death of their hero, they could not bear to turn their backs on him in his final moments. Just as the Guardians had correctly surmised, within seconds of stopping, they heard the firing of the harpoon gun and the heavy thwack as it hit Zeus' body. For an agonizing moment, they tensed, waiting for the sound of the secondary explosion. But it never came.

"The harpoon head did not explode!" exclaimed Apollo. He looked at Ares for affirmation.

"You are right," replied Ares. "Let us go back and see." It was a foolhardy thing to do but they all followed Ares without hesitation, such was the bond that had developed between the Company of the Light, that even death could not sever it.

As they approached the killing zone, they scanned the water beneath the waves with their earsight and stopped every few yards to spyhop. What they saw stunned them, for there, not more than a hundred yards away, was Zeus plowing through the waves, his powerful body straining against the steel cable that tethered him to the catcher ship. Before their eyes and those of the disbelieving crews on the other ships, all of whom had slowed to a stop, the bloodied but unbowed whale was dragging the catcher ship through the waves at high speed; so fast that the sweeping bow of the ship was throwing off an enormous wave. To an uniformed observer it might have appeared that the catcher ship was chasing the whale. But of course, in this case it was the ship, not the whale who was the prey.

"What is happening?" asked Pan popping up and down. Too small to see well in a spyhop, he dropped down under the waves and focused his earsight in the direction of the deathly tug of war. Finding that insufficient he shot back up again. "Tell us. Tell us."

"It is the most incredible thing that I have ever seen," uttered Ares.

Apollo did not say anything. Instead, he closed his eyes and began praying to himself. Pan also prayed but he did so out loud.

"Heavenly Father, we are so small and
our enemies are so mighty, please protect

> *us through this dangerous fight.*
> *And if it be your will that the mighty Zeus*
> *is to die, we pray that you will take*
> *him into thy Good Light."*

Hearing Pan, Apollo opened his eyes and when Pan finished he whispered, "God be praised."

To which Pan added, "God bring us the Light."

As they finished their prayers, Zeus reached the mother ship. He was still driving hard against the weight of the catcher ship, and at the last second, he dove under the hull of the crippled mother ship, which by now had given up its fruitless effort to break out of its circular course and was sitting dead in the water. For a few seconds the ocean was filled with a loud screeching noise of steel on steel, as the cable rubbed across the factory ship's keel. Then, all at once, there was a deafening, crunching thud followed by a groaning, grinding sound.

Apollo and the others spyhopped once more and saw that the high, pointed bow of the catcher ship had sliced into the side of the factory ship right in the middle of the word RESEARCH. For a few seconds nothing happened as the heavy swells rocked the T-shaped wreckage violently, ramming the catcher into the other ship ever more deeply. Finally, the sea broke the ships apart and the catcher ship was wrenched out of the gaping wound. It drifted back a few yards and its crew scrambled across the deck trying to launch a life raft. Then with the sea pouring into its torn bow, the ship pitched forward, turned stern up and with a loud whoosh of air, began its plunge to the bottom of the ocean. For a instant, the Company was thrilled but their emotions soon turned to terror, as they saw that the sinking ship was pulling the cable with it, the other end of which held the harpoon that was still buried in Zeus' back.

"Oh, God. Please no!" gasped Apollo.

Pan drew close beside Apollo. Time stood still as the brave and mighty Zeus, readied himself for what was to come. Bleeding heavily from the wound in his back, he looked in their direction and yelled, "Be off with you!" Then, the rapidly disappearing cable reached its end. First, Zeus' head and upper body were pulled under the water, then his lower body and finally, his enormous flukes rose up, silhouetted against the sky in the last act in the ballet of death, and then, he was gone.

Pan began to shake uncontrollably, which brought Aegyptus over to his side. The Guardian tried to comfort the distraught porpoise, while Apollo just hung there, staring into the depths, unmoving except for the rise and fall of the heavy swells. Ever vigilant, Ares turned away from the scene and raised his head up out of the water expecting to see the other catcher ships bearing down on their position. Instead they were now clustered around the mother ship, which he could see was listing far over on its side. Its crew was abandoning ship and the smaller ships were doing their best to save them but the seas, which had grown more violent during the battle, made rescue difficult. Apollo joined Ares as they watched the mother ship roll completely over, and then with a groan and a loud burst of air, it slipped stern first beneath the waves and was gone, dragging down all but a few members of its crew with it.

Apollo and Ares hung there, tails down, rising and falling on the swells, watching the survivors flailing in the water as they waited to be picked up by the remaining catcher ships.

"Should we go kill them?" asked Ares with cold eyes and a colder heart. He had never killed a human before, the Ninth Law of the Ancients having prevented any such thoughts from entering his mind, but now he could have done so without any burden of conscience.

At first Apollo did not answer. The cruel and brutal actions of these humans were foreign to him when compared with the good deeds of Trainer Quinn and Captain Jackson but as easily as Ares could have killed the humans, Apollo could not. He simply shook his head, no.

Ares did not argue, "Let us leave this Godforsaken place."

Apollo nodded. *Believe,* Zeus had said to him. *Believe,* he had once said to himself. But Zeus was gone and Apollo could not bring himself to say it now. He doubted he ever would again. With that, they slipped beneath the waves, rejoined Pan and Aegyptus and headed east.

CHAPTER SIXTEEN

Awash In Blood And Tears

The home waters of King Hermes, Ruler of the Southern Ocean, were located at the Banzare Seamount at the bottom end of the Kerguélen Ridge at sixty degrees south latitude, which happens to be the unmarked boundary, set by man between the Indian and Southern Oceans. However, the King had sent word to the Company of the Light via whalesound that he would meet them six hundred miles further north at Grande Terre, the main island in the Kerguélen Archipelago. It was a gracious gesture given that the weather and ocean conditions they would face at Grand Terre were likely to be less stressful than those further south. However, as Apollo and his three companions rounded the north end of Grande Terre Island late on a gray and rainy Antarctic summer afternoon, their stress level was as high as their spirits were low.

It had been one week since Zeus disappeared beneath the waves and the protected waters on the lee shore of the island were a welcome respite from the open ocean. One of the King's Rangers, a Southern Beaked Whale named Chiron, met them in a wide bay at the mouth of a fjord. He was nearly the same length as Ares and Aegyptus but thinner with a long, gray, tubular body covered in linear scars, and a small dorsal fin set far back. He had a bulbous melon head and a long beak, and his lower jaw extended past his upper one with two triangular teeth protruding at its end, which gave him a slightly silly, yet vaguely intimidating, look.

After a courteous but restrained greeting, Chiron escorted them across the bay toward the fjord. The Company followed him through choppy blue-gray waves topped with flecks of white toward distant sea cliffs. Apollo could tell that Pan was troubled by the Ranger's aloof manner, but it did not bother or surprise Apollo. Given the pitiless nature of their domain, Hermes' subjects were a tough and hardy group of beings, comprised of Southern Right Whales like the King, along with several other kinds of greater and lesser whales; including Fin, Sei, Minke and Humpback Whales among the former group; as well as Beaked and Long-Finned Pilot Whales in the latter. There were also several species of dolphins in the kingdom, with the largest group being Hourglass Dolphins, a boisterous breed who often traveled in the company of Fin Wales, as the Company had already discovered.

What made Hermes' monarchy stand out from the other kingdoms in the Seven Seas was that he had a particularly fierce group of Guardians, made up entirely of a special group of Offshore Killer Whales, who were renowned for their strength, and cunning, and courage. Ares and Aegyptus had descended from these Southern Ocean Guardians, and their father, three times removed, had been a member of this group. (Beings do not have a word for grandfather or great grandfather. Instead, they use a multiple of their word for father to denote prior generations and the same method applies to their mothers. In this way all their antecedents are considered their mothers and their fathers, which makes their bond with the past stronger than among your kind, where you rarely know or care about anyone beyond two generations back.). As such, Apollo's two Guardians were returning to their ancestral waters, and both grew excited at the prospect, at least as excited as an Offshore Orca ever gets.

After they neared the mouth of the fjord, the waters grew calmer, gradually changing from the blue-gray of the ocean, to the blue-green of the bay, and finally to jade green. It was not a color that Apollo had seen before and the narrowing channel had a vaguely unsettling quality about it. For a second he felt an urge to turn back as the memories of another narrow channel rose up in the dark waters of his memory.

But he did not. They continued past a small island on which sat the abandoned ruins of a human settlement with rotting wooden docks and rusted tin-roofed buildings. Its long-since departed human occupants had given the place its name, Desolation Island, in recognition of the desolate and foreboding landscape on either side of the fjord, with its steep-shouldered shorelines and barren, brown hills beyond. As they travelled up the fjord, Pan kept scanning the milky waters beneath them but he found nothing there, no fish, no seals, no seaweed, just a sloping staircase of stone descending into darkness. It was very unsettling and it made him draw nearer to the Guardians.

The trip up the fjord seemed to take forever due to the slow pace of Chiron, and Apollo grew restless, but eventually they entered a wide bay where the sun broke through the clouds, warming the backs of the weary wayfarers. The bay was surrounded by steep cliffs and in the background, the snow-covered peak of Mount Ross emerged from behind the cloudbank to serve as a silent sentinel to the stark setting. King Hermes was waiting for them in the bay, flanked on either side by several of his royal retinue. There was another being with the King who caught Apollo's attention. It was a female Southern Right Whale, the same species as the King.

"Welcome, Apollo," said King Hermes, "we are honored to have you and your Company in our domain. You have already met, Chiron, but allow me to introduce the rest of my court." As the King spoke, his eyes flashed beyond the group of four seeking their fifth member. Apollo noticed but allowed the King to continue with the introductions.

The first introduction was that of Lady Selene, the King's mate. Despite her large head and dark, rotund body, she displayed a quiet self-assurance and an easy grace that captivated the Company. (In the world of beings, unlike in yours, thinness in females is not a prerequisite for beauty). The second introduction was that of his Chief Guardian, an Offshore Killer Whale named Boreus, who hit it off instantly with Ares and Aegyptus, his blood cousins many generations removed. And the final introduction was to Hector, a Pygmy Sperm Whale, who was another of the King's Rangers. At twelve feet long, Hector had a robust but wrinkled, steel-gray body and tiny, falcate dorsal fin. His squarish head with a tiny, underslung lower jaw had a mark behind his eyes that looked like a gill and gave him a superficial resemblance to a shark. Pan was taken aback at first by Hector's shark-like appearance but the warm and friendly greeting that he gave to Pan softened the awkwardness of the situation.

"Where is our good friend Zeus?" asked the King.

Apollo stiffened. "It is with a heavy heart that I must tell you, your Majesty, that Zeus is dead."

For a second the King was stunned and could not speak. Lady Selene asked, "How?"

With a mixture of anger and pain in his eyes, Apollo replied, "He was killed by Japanese whalers seven days west of here. He died saving us from this abomination of mankind." An awkward silence fell upon the gathering.

"But he took many of these revolting humans with him into the deeps," Ares added with grim pleasure.

"Oh the tragedy of it all. It pains my heart greatly," said the King. After a brief pause during which he gathered his composure, he told Apollo that the island had several abandoned whaling stations upon it, one of which they had passed at the mouth of the fjord. He added, "During the time of my father, such ships were the scourge of these southern seas, but now there are only a few nations who still send their ships here to inflict their barbarity upon our kind. If only the rest of mankind could realize the magnitude of the tragedy that whaling has inflicted upon the world's oceans. Here in the Southern Ocean alone the number of great whales has fallen from the millions to the thousands in just four generations. Where once two hundred and fifty thousand Blue Whales roamed, now there are only five hundred; Sei and Minke whales have fallen to a similar extent; and there are not enough Sperm Whales left in my Kingdom to count. As for Humpback Whales like Zeus, and Southern Right Whales like Lady Selene and me, we once numbered over one hundred thousand each in these Antarctic waters, but now there are only a few thousand of us left." He caught himself and then with a quiver in his voice he added, "A few thousand less one."

"When will it stop?" asked Pan.

"When there are none of us left to kill," replied the King.

Lady Selene added with a sigh, "Or when the Japanese, Norwegian, and Icelandic children grow up and put an end to the bloodlust and brutality of their parents."

"I fear we will not live to see that day," said Apollo.

For a few minutes the waters of the bay grew silent once again until, at last, Lady Selene said, "Apollo, you and your Company must be tired. It is time that you rested and ate. Some of our Rangers are keeping a large ball of herring trapped in a nearby bay. I trust that you and your darling little companion, Pan, will find these to your satisfaction." Pan's face flushed with embarrassment and he gave the Lady a broad smile, but said nothing about her reference to his diminutive size, which from any other being would have brought a strong rebuke.

Then Lady Selene turned to Ares and Aegyptus, and with a penetrating stare that was both alluring and unsettling, she said, "And for you, brave Ares and Aegyptus, Guardian Boreus will take you back down the fjord to the ocean and show you where you will find some Six-gilled Sharks, whose flesh will satisfy your hunger." Six-gills were a deep-water species of shark who were the bottom-feeding scavengers of the polar seas.

"Thank-you, my Lady," replied Ares eager to taste shark flesh again. Throughout their journey, he and his brother had fed mostly on fish, rays, and cuttlefish, not having the time to go hunting for their favorite prey. Now with Apollo and Pan in the safe company of Hermes, they were free to indulge themselves on shark flesh and indulge they would.

"Come, my cousins," said Boreus, "we have much to discuss about our common ancestors whose warrior blood runs in our veins. Let us go make these seas safer by killing some kraken."

"Kill a few extra for us," shouted Pan after them but they did not hear him. However, Lady Selene did and in a motherly fashion she asked, "Have you encountered Six-gilled Sharks, Pan?"

"Oh no, Lady Selene. But we have come close to being eaten by other members of their kind and we think that Planet Ocean would be a better place if a few more sharks were eliminated."

"Do not be so sure," she answered with a gentle smile. "All God's creatures serve a purpose, Pan, even those for whom this purpose may be unclear to us."

"With all due respect, your Grace, we think that being killed and eaten serves an excellent purpose for sharks." As soon as he said it, he saw the look of mild rebuke on Apollo's face and he wished that he could learn to keep his little mouth shut.

Lady Selene was not offended. Instead, she said softly, "Perhaps you are right little one." It served to break the tension and Pan took the opportunity to rise up to the surface and take a deep breath before sinking back down and resolving to stay silent. It would not last but at least he was trying.

"I hate sharks too, Pan," said Hector. "I have killed many in my time. Not adult Six-gilled or Great Whites, of course, but those my size or smaller including their young. All members of my species are quite adept at doing this because we look like them, as you may have noticed, which allows us to get close before we rip open their bellies and spread their entrails into the sea," His coarse comments displeased Lady Selene but she said nothing. She had learned never to admonish any of her husband's Guardians or Rangers for they served a vital purpose in the kingdom.

In contrast, Hector's words endeared him to Pan and it was apparent that they were going to be best buddies, even though Hector was twice Pan's size and lacking Pan's wicked wit and wily ways. Emboldened by Hector's tone and manner, and casting a furtive glance in Apollo's direction, Pan asked, "Tell me, Hector, have you ever killed any Japanese whalers?" *Oops. We just did it again. My bad. When will we learn?* Pan muttered to himself.

King Hermes interrupted the discussion, "Enough talk of our enemies, be they above or below the waves. Come now, my good and gentle guests, we will dine and then you must rest. Tomorrow we will talk of your mission and how I can help you."

And with that the gathering ended. Tomorrow would be another day when there would be time to reflect upon the past and contemplate the future. For now, all that mattered was food, rest, and good fellowship, all of which would be provided in abundance during the coming days in the protected waters of that remote fjord at the bottom of the world.

On the following day, and on each day thereafter, King Hermes and Apollo took advantage of an unusually mild spell of sub-antarctic summer weather and spent the time swimming together through the clear, cold waters around the smaller islands of the Archipelago. It was a welcome break for Apollo and for his three companions as they enjoyed the company of their new friends, during this brief timeout in their long-distance journey. Ares and Aegyptus forged the bonds of brotherhood broken long ago when their ancestors left the Southern Ocean and headed north. Meanwhile, Pan and Hector became close friends, as the Pygmy Sperm Whale seemed, at least in part, to fill a void in Pan's heart left by the death of Zeus. Together they chased Crabeater Seals along the shoreline, and dashed in mad circles around windswept islets, or floated lazily on the surface of the fjord under the warm summer sun.

But as wonderful a time as it was for Apollo and his Company they knew it could not last. Apollo would eventually have to broach the subject he had avoided throughout his stay; that of asking King Hermes to join forces with the Loyalists against the Federation. It was a difficult question to ask the King who had previously declared his neutrality. It was made more difficult by the fact that Hermes and Poseidon had been close friends, just as Zeus and Poseidon once were. Zeus told Apollo that his friendship with Poseidon ended when the King declared war on mankind, but Apollo was uncertain of whether Hermes felt the same.

Finally, after two weeks in the company of King Hermes, late on a beautiful summer afternoon, as the setting sun cast its rays across the dusty highlands and flat-topped peaks of Grande Terre Island, Apollo summoned his courage and dealt with the issue at hand. He and the King were swimming together at the farthest inland point of the fjord that had been their home away from home, when Apollo looked at the monarch and said "Your Majesty, the time draws near for my Company to take leave of this place and continue on our journey. You and Lady Selene have been most kind to us, and through your hospitality we have regained our strength and learned to accept the loss of our teacher and mentor, Zeus."

The King smiled knowingly and said, "Apollo, this planet is a giant ball of bluewater interrupted occasionally by lumps of dirt, and on that dirt there dwells an insignificant and self-serving race of bipeds who do us and the planet great harm. Our beloved brother Zeus was the victim of their evil ways and his loss is a heavy burden for you to bear, but you must carry on. Zeus would have wanted it so and were you to quit now, his sacrifice would be made meaningless."

Apollo nodded. "You are right. The truth is that on that horrible day when Zeus died, I came close to giving up on everything, my mission, my Company of the Light, and even my life. I was overcome with grief and self-pity, but I know now that I must carry on without him." Apollo paused, gathering his courage to ask the pivotal question.

He did not get the chance. The King smiled and said, "My son, I know what you are going to ask me, and the answer is yes. From this day forward, I will direct my kingdom and its military forces, such as they are, to join with your cause. We are a small kingdom, smaller than all the others except the Arctic Ocean, with few subjects and even fewer warriors. At first I did not think it right to commit my subjects to the war that looms before us. Poseidon was once my friend and it grieves me to think that so many beings will die in the months ahead because of his ill-advised and selfish act.

"But I now realize that staying out of this war will not make it go away, or keep us safe from evil; for if we allow the Federation's forces to kill humans, then we are all doomed. The whaling fleet that murdered Zeus will pale in comparison to the global fleet of deathships that will unleash hell upon us in such great numbers, and with such terrible force, that I fear our kind will disappear from the face of the planet.—So yes, my brave young friend, as you leave this place to seek the same commitment from Queen Demeter, know that when you face Poseidon in the far off Pacific Ocean, my army and I will be there with you."

"Thank you, King Hermes." A wave of relief washed over Apollo but he did not get a chance to dwell in its sweet embrace.

"Before you continue with your journey I must ask you a question. Are you certain that Pan and the two brothers truly share your desire to carry on with this mission?"

Apollo started to say yes but then he caught himself. "I had not thought to ask them. But I will."

"Do you think they will give you any other answer but that which you seek?"

Apollo thought about it. It was a good question and Apollo realized that he had perhaps taken their commitment for granted. "You are right, your Majesty. Perhaps it would be better if I did not ask the question. Will you?"

The King shook his head. "No. I am afraid that they will not say anything different to me than they would to you. I propose that we leave it to Lady Selene, for she has a softer touch that can reach beyond their minds and into their hearts. She also possesses powers of foresight that allow her to see visions of what might be. Although she cannot tell the future with certainty, she can see beyond the veil that separates now from then, and she may be able to guide you in your journey."

Apollo was not sure he wanted to know the future even if he could. But he nodded and said, "I accept your offer. Please ask Lady Selene to speak on my behalf on this matter. You are a wise leader, King Hermes and I am forever in your debt for the counsel that you have given me. You remind me of…" the words caught in his throat. "You remind me of Zeus."

It was the kindest thing that Apollo could have said to the King; kinder and more flattering than all the words of praise Hermes had heard in all his days, both from those who meant them and those who did not. A broad smile slipped across the whale's mouth. "Thank you, Apollo. Thank you very much. Now come, we must return to the others. Tonight we will feast and sing the praises of the great Zeus, whose courage fills us with the will to carry on."

Darkness had fallen upon the deep-water bay where Apollo and his Company had first met the King and his court, as they now gathered for their final evening together. But on that night the waters were not dark, for at the command of the King, hundreds of Hourglass Dolphins swam with wild abandon around the perimeter of the gathering; stirring up billions of tiny phosphorescent microorganisms and filling the waters with their soft green glow. Had any aircraft been flying overhead, it might have looked to the passengers and crew as if the stars of heaven had fallen into the sea and were zipping and zapping through the water in a frenzied attempt to regain the night sky.

After the group of friends had feasted and laughed and sang the same songs of praise that were sung at Godlight, they gathered together in a tight circle, floating on the surface of the opalescent sea. Guided by Lady Selene, the talk turned to the more serious matter of the threat to their world that loomed over the far horizon. And it was then, in her firm but gentle way that the Lady brought the discussion around to the subject that was on all their minds; that of the journey that had brought them there and the one yet to be taken north and east into the unknown.

"My good and gentle friends," the Lady began, "these past several weeks have been a blessing upon our souls. We have grown close to each other and have rejoiced in that togetherness. But even as we revel in its comforting embrace, we know that the hour of our parting draws near. The King and I must return to our home in the south for we have much to do to prepare our Kingdom for what lies ahead."

She looked around the circle, pausing for a moment when her eyes met Apollo's. Then she began again, this time speaking more softly to make them listen harder, for she had learned long ago that a soft-spoken word reaches deeper into a beings' heart and mind than does a shout. "At morning's first light, your Company of the Light will depart, but tonight I must ask each of you a question." As the King had asked her to, she was about to gauge the depth of the their conviction. "Are you certain beyond all doubt that you wish to carry on with the crusade that you began nearly eight months ago? It is a noble mission that has its origins at the dawn of time, when the Ancients swam through seas untainted by man; a mission for which the valiant Zeus has already given his life." She paused to let the memory of Zeus float gently upon their souls. "But it is also a dangerous, and some would say futile, mission." She paused again and then offered an alternative, one that was sure to evoke a positive response were there one to be given. "Or would you like to come home with me, to the relative safety of our homewaters far from the sea lanes of man? And there to wait out this time of darkness."

The question caught the Company by surprise, except Apollo of course, and none answered right away. To assist them in their deliberation, Apollo said, "Lady Selene. The King has told me of your power to gaze into the future. Can you do this now and tell us what you see? Perhaps this will help us decide." He did not want to give away his role in the matter and he was sincere in his request

Lady Selene had been reluctant to do this when the King first asked her but he had insisted. And now as she prepared to do it, the light behind her eyes grew dim and her mind drifted away from the circle. As the others listened in expectant silence, she began to speak: her voice seemed strange, distant and yet compelling.

"I see a pale moon rising through gaps in dark and angry clouds; forked lightning fills the sky but there is no thunder to break the silence or give measure to the passage of time. Beneath the sky, a black sea rages, with mountainous waves lacking pattern or direction smashing into each other in blind fury. The roar of the wind is deafening and constant; so loud that even the voice of God himself might not be heard over it. Stretching from horizon to horizon, I see two vast armies impatient for battle, facing each other above an abyssal plain from which jagged seamounts thrust upward, eagerly awaiting the dead. I see eyes probing for weaknesses, teeth hungering for flesh, hearts beating in savage harmony. I see fear mixed with courage, hesitation with conviction, blind rage railing against a sense of duty. And I see one being come forward to face death alone...

She did not finish. Visibly upset, she broke away from her vision and it took a few moments for her to regain her composure. She glanced at Apollo but quickly looked away. Bearing down on Pan and the two brothers with her piercing gaze, she began again, this time in her normal voice. "Listen to me my precious friends, there is no shame in stopping your journey here and now; no disgrace in turning away from danger, for the Ancients are long dead and their voices grow fainter with each passing generation. Even if you listen to their cry and carry on with your journey, your efforts may be in vain or worse, you may pay the ultimate price for your valor."

A deafening silence fell upon the group, as each member looked deep within himself, including Apollo, for even though he knew that the Lady would put this question to them, he found himself pondering the answer. But then, the memory of Zeus' death flashed before his mind's eye and he knew what he had to do. He looked first at Lady Selene, then the King, and finally the Company and spoke with a power and poise given to few.

"Lady Selene, I cannot in good conscience ask my companions to continue on if their hearts and minds tell them they should not." He glanced at Pan and the brothers. "And I will bear them no ill will if they do not; for they have seen me this far, and more I cannot ask." He looked back at the King and his Lady. "But I know that I must continue on my journey—whatever the outcome may be."

Ares was the first to speak after Apollo finished. "My brother and I are with you, Apollo. To the end." Aegyptus nodded firmly.

"We are too," Pan added without hesitation but there was a deep and abiding sadness behind his eyes. Watching the way Apollo had acted ever since Zeus' death, Pan could tell that something had changed within him, and he sensed it was not for the good. Silently he prayed that Apollo would return to his former self even as he sensed that things were going to get darker before the light shone again—if it ever did.

Lady Selene nodded solemnly, then turned to the King's men and asked them the same question. Boreus replied first, "With the King's permission, and if Apollo will have me, I will join the crusade." Before either the King or Apollo could reply, Hector said he also wanted to join the Company and then, to the surprise of all, Chiron asked whether they would have him too. The King beamed with pride and granted them all their release from his service.

Apollo was thrilled. With a glad heart, he accepted their offers. A new and stronger Company of the Light had been formed and come the dawn they would head north across the Indian Ocean, seven brave and noble beings upon whose sturdy backs rested the future of whalekind.

It was then that the King nodded at his mate and said, "Lady Selene."

She looked questioningly at him. "Now?"

"Yes, now." He turned to the others and said, "Not three weeks ago we lost Zeus, who was dear to us all. Only God knows who else will die in the months ahead. Death is a constant companion in the ocean of life but never more so in times such as these. In the history of mankind that is measured in the tens of thousands of years, there has never been a time without war, but in the history of whalekind that is measured in the tens of millions of years, the opposite is true. Now, all that has changed and with it, our world has changed forever. It is a time of siege and sadness in the Seven Seas, and evil swims among us. The light of hope foretold by our Ancestors, and carried down through countless generations; a light of peace and harmony, now flickers before the gathering storm clouds of war.

"Eight months ago, on our holiest day, Godlight, at the Kingdom of the Ancients, what started as a imprudent protest against the misdeeds of man, has now brought Planet Ocean full in the face of war—a war that our brothers in the Pacific Ocean intend to wage against man, and in what is too terrible to even ponder, a war that man will wage upon us in retaliation. Our last best hope to avoid this evil rests upon the shoulders of you seven brave beings. I pray that God will bless you and keep you, and add his mighty power to your purpose; but, as I told Apollo this afternoon, if your mission to bring reason to Poseidon and his Federation should fail, know this, I and my army will be there with you in the war against evil that must surely follow. For if Poseidon will not listen to reason, then he and all those who follow him must be put to death.

"These are sad thoughts and it pains me to speak of them but I must. Soon, I fear that the seas will be awash in blood and tears—those of whales and man alike. And so, as we now part company, each to face the future as best we can, I can think of no better time for Lady Selene to recite a poem she learned as a child; a poem her mother told to her on the night she died." With that, he turned and looked back at his mate.

It was a poignant moment. The seas grew still and the light of the billions of tiny phosphorescent microorganisms faded as the Hourglass Dolphins ceased their circling. And then, as would be remembered by all who were there that night, the moon appeared from behind clouds in the heavens, and its gentle blue light cascaded down upon the waters, casting an ethereal glow upon them, and creating a halo about Lady Selene. It was an auspicious moment because among beings, the moon has a special place in their folklore and legend. While the sun is the source of all the energy from which life is derived on Planet Ocean, it is the moon whose gravity commands the tides and whose pale light rests gently upon their souls.

And then, in a voice pure and clear Lady Selene recited the words she had learned long ago:

> *Far from here past misty shores,*
> *an ocean calls to which I am bound;*
> *It is a journey I must make alone*
> *but there is freedom to be found.*

Freedom from pain and fear and hate
in a timeless sea, eternal beauty awaits;
Through the Good Light, guided by God,
above the stars, past Heaven's gate.

Life is but a brief neap tide
in the endless ebb and flow of time;
Someday you will all follow me,
but for now the course is mine.

An angel comes to carry me
on wide white wings, I feel no pain;
He will take me to that golden sea
where one day we will meet again.

When Lady Selene finished, no one spoke, no one moved. The seas were silent, expectant. Finally, the King looked upon the beings who were gathered there and said, "Let us all remember that even though we part at dawn and may not see each other again in this life, we will one day be joined together, and in that joining we will know once more the glory that has been ours during these brief days we have spent together, here on the edge of tomorrow.—God be praised."

"God bring us the Light," Apollo replied. *Believe* Zeus had said to him. *Believe* he now said to himself. He had found the will to say it again but even as he did, he wondered whether God was listening.

CHAPTER SEVENTEEN

Betrayal

The great whales who travel through the Seven Seas do so along precise routes and it was along one of these that the new Company of the Light traveled as they made their way northward across the Indian Ocean. Often these routes follow the courses of undersea mountain ranges, which serve two functions; first, the cold waters that surge up from the deeps toward their peaks provide a food source rich in both plant and animal plankton, about half of which is krill upon which the baleen whales feast. These tiny organisms also nourish the fish and squid upon whom the toothed whales feed. And the second use of these submerged mountain ranges is to serve as navigational aids for these open ocean travelers.

It was to just such a use that the Company was putting the Ninety East Ridge, an extensive mid-ocean ridge that, as the name implies, follows the line of longitude designated by man as ninety degrees east. The Company had joined the ridge where it met the West Australian Ridge, northeast of the Kerguélen Islands, and they were now following it toward the home waters of Queen Demeter near the Andaman Islands in the Bay of Bengal, nearly four thousand miles to the north northeast of the fjord where they had rested. They needed every bit of their renewed strength because during the first three weeks of their journey, the waters of the southern Indian Ocean had been stormy and unyielding, and the weak north-flowing West Australian current had been of little help. Over the subsequent two weeks, the weather had moderated and by the time, they reached a point six hundred miles from their final destination, and nearly five weeks after leaving King Hermes and Lady Selene, the sun finally came out. It was the seventh day of March, two weeks before the equinox that would turn winter into spring north of the equator, and summer into fall to the south, and everyone was glad to have left the Roaring Forties far behind.

As they had done on their journey south from the Kingdom of the Ancients to the Cape of Good Hope, the Company had traveled for nine or ten hours each day and rested on Sundays. This seemed to annoy Chiron, who in stark contrast to his slow pace when he guided them up the fjord, now appeared anxious to get to the northern seas. No one paid him much mind, as they were preoccupied with staying the course of the long journey. For his part, Apollo was troubled by what King Hermes had told him about Queen Demeter. The King said that she was an avowed pacifist who was unlikely to join the Loyalist cause. To prepare his case, Apollo discussed his strategy with Pan as they plowed through the swells together, with Pan playing the role of devil's advocate. It was all for naught: Apollo would never get the chance to plead his case.

The night their journey through the Indian Ocean would end, began like any other. At sunset Ares assigned watch duties, which on that night would be the responsibility of Boreus, Chiron and Aegyptus, with Boreus taking the first watch. At the prearranged time, as measured by the movement of the moon and stars overhead, Boreus had turned the watch over to Chiron and retired. For the next several hours all was calm and quiet, but then disaster struck: the Company was attacked from all sides by a large group of Long-finned Pilot Whales, Offshore Killer Whales, and a few Risso's Dolphins; a particularly nasty breed of beings.

In the fight that followed, the Guardians killed some of the attackers and drove off the rest but the Company had become separated. Apollo, Pan, and Chiron were missing; and Aegyptus had suffered a severe injury to his side. In the aftermath of the fight, Boreus and Hector searched the surrounding waters for their absent comrades but to no avail.

"Who were they?" asked Ares when Boreus and Hector returned.

"I do not know. They may have been pirates. There have been reports of them in these waters," replied Boreus.

"We assume that they have taken Apollo, Pan and Chiron prisoner," said Hector.

Aegyptus wanted to go after them right away but, given the extent of his injury, Ares said no. He was unsure whether Aegyptus was going to survive let alone chase the attackers. For the next several hours, Boreus, Hector and Ares, swam alongside Aegyptus, comforting him with their touch and reassuring him with their words. When the first pink and yellow rays of dawn crept over the eastern horizon, Aegyptus was stable but only just and Ares knew his brother needed help. He decided that the best plan would be for him to take his brother north to Queen Demeter's home waters where he could receive medical assistance. Even though six hundred miles lay between their present location and the Andaman Islands, he knew it was his brother's only chance. He asked Boreus and Hector to follow the attackers and try to rescue their three colleagues. They agreed without hesitation.

And so, as the morning sun rose over the equator, the remaining members of the Company of the Light separated, Ares and his wounded brother continuing north, with Boreus and Hector heading due east. It was a brave effort on all their parts because their chances of survival would have been enhanced by staying together. Even if Boreus and Hector caught up with the raiders, it was questionable whether they would be able to rescue their colleagues, assuming of course that they were with them; and Aegyptus' injury would make their journey through those shark-infested waters extremely dangerous. However, none was willing to give up on the possibility that they could still save the mission, if not Apollo himself.

Meanwhile, seventy miles to the south and east, Apollo and Pan were swimming through a warm and sunlit sea but their spirits were anything but. Surrounded on all sides and below, they were being pushed hard by their kidnappers, led by an Offshore Killer Whale whom Pan had seen many months before at the Kingdom of the Ancients. His name was

Paris, one of the Guardians who had left the Gathering with Poseidon, and by his side, acting in every way the smug traitor that he had turned out to be was Chiron.

"We knew we did not like Chiron from the very first day we met," muttered Pan, as he listened to Chiron joking loudly with Paris about how he had fooled King Hermes. His act of treachery would break the King's heart when he learned of it several days later, but by then Chiron and his evil band were too far away for the King to do anything about it.

"Be patient, little one. Our time will come," said Apollo. "They will pay the ultimate price for their deeds." The harshness of his words surprised Pan. Whereas Apollo had once admonished Pan for even talking about killing other beings, now the white dolphin seemed quite willing to do so himself. This only served to underscore the growing darkness that loomed over both their souls.

"Apollo, are you all right?" asked Pan.

"Quiet," barked one of the Long-fins. He gave Pan a harsh thump with his flukes.

This brought a quick response from Apollo who rammed his beak into the side of the Long-fin just behind his left flipper. It is a sensitive pressure point in all beings and the severity of Apollo's attack caused the whale to grunt in pain and fall out of formation. Apollo's act and the Long-finned Pilot Whale's reaction to it brought the entire procession to a halt. Paris and Chiron swam back and as they approached, the Long-fin made a feeble gesture toward Apollo. A sharp command from Paris stopped him. Paris swam over to Apollo, stopping only a few yards from his face. Beings have a personal space about their bodies into which other beings never intrude unless they are welcome, which Paris clearly was not. That he did so was an indication of the dominant position he held over his captives.

"I have orders to bring you back alive but do something like that again and I will have you executed," growled Paris.

Apollo was not intimidated. He closed the distance separating them to a few feet. "Orders from whom?" As he spoke, he arched his back slightly in a threatening posture and for a moment, Pan thought that Apollo was going to attack Paris, which would have been suicidal. But he did not.

Paris too was taken aback by the aggressiveness of Apollo's response. It caused him pull away. But he quickly recovered and sneered, "You will see soon enough." Then he turned to the Long-fin and said, "If you provoke Apollo again you will die with him." With that, Paris returned to the head of the group.

Chiron sneered at Apollo. "Prince of Light. Hah! Soon your light will be extinguished."

Pan started to say something but Apollo beat him to it. "Whatever my fate, I promise you this, Chiron, you will not live to see it."

Chiron did not know how to respond. He laughed a nervous little laugh and then with forced bravado proffered, "Exactly who do you think will stop me?"

"Ares and Aegyptus," snapped Pan. "They will come after us and when they do, they will bite you in half and feed you to the kraken."

Chiron sneered. "You stupid little fool. Ares and Aegyptus are dead." His words sliced through the water as sharply as a shark's dorsal fin.

The comment momentarily stunned Apollo and Pan. Finally, Apollo said, "You lie."

Chiron smiled an evil smile. "Do I? Then where are they?" he taunted. Chiron did not know for certain that the brothers were dead but in the darkness and the confusion of the attack, he saw several large black bodies slipping toward the deeps and this, combined with the absence of any sign of the Guardians, led him to that conclusion. Without further comment, Chiron returned to Paris' side and the group began its journey once more.

Neither Apollo nor Pan could answer the question posed by their captor. Indeed, where were the brothers and their two new companions? The possibility that they might be dead only served to deepen the shadows that had already darkened Apollo's soul. Pan refused to accept it and he whispered words to that effect to Apollo but the white dolphin took no notice of them. His mind was far away, in the Southern Seas, watching Zeus being pulled under the surface by the sinking catcher ship.

For three days and nights, Boreus and Hector continued swimming south and east, stopping infrequently to rest and feed, never picking up any sign of the raiding party or its captives. They had nothing to rely upon other than their instinct to tell them they were on the right course, but instinct is a particular strength among beings, far more developed than it is among humans. And so they continued on, using their earsight only in a passive mode for fear that the raiders would detect their presence if they actively scanned the seas ahead of them. Finally, on the morning of the fourth day, they found evidence that they were on the right course—hard evidence indeed—as they came upon the body of one of the raiders, a Long-finned Pilot Whale. It was being fed upon by Blue Sharks, who fled into the powdery blue depths at the sight of Boreus.

"He has not been dead long," said Boreus scanning the carcass.

"Sometime during the night I think," replied Hector also giving a quick scan of the body with his earsight, and then directing it into a wide arc through the surrounding waters to make sure there were no other hostile beings, alive or dead. There were none.

"Look, here," said Boreus as he examined the left side of the body.

Hector joined him and saw two bruises on the Long-fin's body, a small one behind his flipper and a large one on the side of his head. "Those marks were not made by sharks," said Hector. "Perhaps one of your kind, Boreus?"

"The smaller one was not but the larger one most likely was made by an Orca. And I can tell that it was intended to be a mortal blow."

"What do you think happened?"

Boreus did not get an opportunity to reply as the first wave of pings from a large group of beings bounced off them. Instinctively, Boreus assumed a defensive posture and ordered Hector to get behind him, which he did. Together they hung there, feeling the hundreds of sound probes of a large group of beings who were drawing nearer by the second. Then, from behind the gauzy curtain of blue at the fringes of their primary vision, the first of the oncoming beings appeared. It was a Goosebeaked Whale, twenty-three feet in length, with a robust body, pale brown on top and sides, with cream-colored blotches along his underside. He had a small, goose-beak shaped head and short, up-turned mouth line and he lurched through the waters toward them in an aggressive and unrestrained manner. He was followed closely by near ninety of his kind, most of whom were brown and tan but a few were reddish black. None were smiling and for a second Boreus and Hector prepared for a fight. But it was not to be.

"Who are you," asked the first Goosebeak, who by his manner and words was clearly the leader. The rest of his group spread out around Boreus and Hector, forming an unbroken circle.

"I am Boreus, Guardian of Lord Hermes, King of the Southern Ocean, and this is Hector one of my King's Rangers." He said it in a controlled manner giving no sign of fear or distress. "Who are you to ask?" he countered, showing a hard-edged distrust of all strangers. There had been no Goosebeaks among the raiders the night before but that did not lessen Boreus' guarded demeanor.

The Goosebeak studied the Orca and said "I am Zephyrus, Guardian of Queen Demeter, in whose domain you are trespassing."

"We are not trespassers," snapped Hector. "We are members of a King's court and deserve to be treated as such."

Zephyrus studied the Pygmy Sperm Whale for a moment then looked back at Boreus and said, "You are far from your home waters. What brings you and this sharkface to mine?"

Hector took immediate offense. "I will show you what I do to sharks," he snarled and moved toward the Goosebeak leader, which prompted several of his marines to bear the teeth at the tip of their jaws and start forward. But Zephyrus pulled them back with a barked command. He glanced approvingly at Hector and said, "You are brave for someone facing death. I do not know what the rules are in your Kingdom but here we kill spies without a trial."

"We are not spies, Guardian Zephyrus," replied Boreus seeking to diffuse the tension. He used the more proper manner of addressing the other being. "We are part of a company of seven beings, led by the white dolphin, Apollo. Up until three days ago we were on a mission to meet with your Queen, to seek her help in the coming war with the Federation."

At the mention of Apollo's name, the attitude of Zephyrus and his marines changed visibly. A murmur spread among the Goosebeaks. "We are aware of the Legend of the Ancients and the mission of the white dolphin. But we were told that Apollo was traveling with a company of five, including the mighty Humpback Whale, Zeus, and a Harbor Porpoise by the name of Pan. I see none of them before me."

Boreus nodded with regret. "The Company of the Light who left the Kingdom of the Ancients was five in number, including Apollo, Zeus, Pan, and two of Queen Hera's Guardians, brothers named Ares and Aegyptus. But sadly, Zeus is dead, killed by whalers in the Southern Ocean. Hector and I, along with a Southern Beaked Whale named Chiron, joined the Company when they met with King Hermes five weeks ago." At the mention of Chiron's name, Zephyrus glanced at one of his men but said nothing. Boreus did not notice and continued, "Three nights ago we were attacked by pirates, and we believe they have kidnapped Apollo, Pan, and Chiron. Aegyptus was badly injured and as we speak he and his brother are traveling north to seek help in your Queen's court, while Hector and I pursue the raiders to try to rescue Apollo and Pan." Boreus glanced over at the carcass floating nearby. "It would appear that one of our attackers has already met the fate that we intend to bestow upon the others."

Zephyrus glanced at the dead whale, then looked back at Boreus and with a sympathetic nod he said, "The beings who attacked you were not pirates. They were marines in service to King Poseidon. Word of Apollo's crusade has spread far and wide in the Seven Seas and King Poseidon has sent out many killers to look for Apollo and bring him back alive."

"You said they 'were' marines," probed Boreus.

"Yes. We killed them, not a half a day's journey from here."

"You killed them all?" asked Hector.

"No. A few escaped. And you can thank us because if you had found them before we did, you too would likely now be dead. They outnumbered you ten to one."

Hector's expression indicated he did not agree with the Goosebeak's assessment of their chances but a glance from Boreus stopped him from making a comment.

Zephyrus continued, "This particular group of marines was a raiding party sent from a much larger force from the Federation. We have been monitoring them since they passed through the Torres Strait many weeks ago. They are presently in the Java Sea on our eastern boundary and since those waters are part of the South Pacific Kingdom of Queen Eris, we cannot be certain of their intent. I suspect they mean us harm but we can do nothing about it if they stay outside our territory.

However, the raiding party intruded into our waters and we dealt with them accordingly."

"What of their captives?" asked Hector.

"We saw no captives," replied Zephyrus. "There was a Southern Beaked Whale among the raiders, named Chiron but he was not a captive. He escaped with their leader, an Offshore Orca, named Paris."

"Chiron?" asked Boreus coldly. "Are you sure?"

"Yes. I am sure."

"This is most distressing news," replied Boreus.

"What do you think happened to Apollo and Pan?" asked Hector who was not as troubled by the news of Chiron's defection as was Boreus. There had never been any love lost between Hector and Chiron before and it was certain there would never be now.

"Could they have escaped?" speculated Boreus.

"Possibly" said Zephyrus. "But they might also be dead. Whatever their fate, my marines and I cannot join you in searching for them. We must return to the Andaman Islands to report to the Queen on the status of the enemy army on our eastern border. You are welcome to come with us but if you continue on into Queen Eris' domain and the Federation forces find you, they will show no mercy."

"Thank you for your offer but we must try to find Apollo and Pan," said Boreus. Hector nodded his agreement.

"Perhaps they were never captured to begin with. Maybe they are heading north to see my Queen," said Zephyrus.

"Perhaps, in which case you will likely catch up with them," said Boreus. "But in case they are not, my companion and I will continue heading southeast."

Zephyrus nodded solemnly. "The threat of war saddens the heart of my Queen but she does not wish to be drawn into any global conflict and our orders are to fight only to defend our Kingdom, nothing more."

"Whether she wants to go to war or not, it would appear that war is about to come to her," said Boreus. Like Ares, there was no room in Boreus' world for pacifists. To him they were either weak or stupid, and it was only because of warriors like him, who were willing to fight and die, that pacifists could live in peace.

In an attempt to be more polite, Hector added, "We respect your Queen and her beliefs, Guardian Zephyrus, and it is our fervent hope that war can be averted."

Zephyrus agreed and added, "I apologize for my ill-mannered remark earlier."

"Apology accepted." Pygmy Sperm Whales, like most beings, were quick to anger and equally quick to forgive and forget.

"I pray, Hector, that Apollo still lives, and that he will succeed in his objective, although I do not see how one being can stop a war."

"The Legend of the Light gives us hope, and with a just cause, hope dies last," replied Hector stoically.

"Perhaps you are right," said Zephyrus. "God be praised."

"God bring us the Light," replied Boreus.

With that, the two groups parted; one headed north, the other southeast. One day soon, they would meet again and when they did, all their questions would be answered.

CHAPTER EIGHTEEN

Here Be Dragons

"Master, what is that?" asked Pan as he peered back across the broad sandy flats over which they had just come. It had been three days since they escaped from Poseidon's marines and fearing that Ares and Aegyptus, like Zeus, were dead, Apollo had decided to abandon the journey north to meet with Queen Demeter. Instead, he decided to head toward the Pacific Ocean. Pan had disagreed but Apollo refused to discuss the matter. His mood was foul and his willingness to listen to other viewpoints seemed to have died with Zeus. The shallow sea was calm but the sky was overcast, which made it difficult to see with their first vision, and for fear that the raiders might be following them Apollo had forbidden Pan to use active earsight. Then it began to rain.

"Do not call me that," snapped Apollo as he continued swimming. "And stop looking behind us. There is nothing there. Now hurry up and follow me." Apollo was obsessed with continuing their journey. It was as if he felt that he alone could stop Poseidon, or die trying and either outcome mattered not. At least not anymore. Boreus had told them that the island nation of Sumatra lay to the east and that the passageway into the Pacific Ocean was south of Sumatra. However, without Boreus and Hector acting as their guides, Apollo and Pan were going to have great difficulty finding their way through those shallow seas, filled with danger. Apollo knew this, but he refused to acknowledge it, even to himself.

Ignoring Apollo's command, which was something he had not done before on their journey together; Pan stopped and stared behind them, but saw nothing. "We were sure that we felt something was behind us," he muttered. With a shake of his head, Pan moved off again, following the angry white dolphin. The rain was now coming down harder. What had started as a light pitter-patter on the liquid ceiling above them, little more than a gentle drumming, almost calming in its effect, was now an incessant roaring, ripping sound that only added to Pan's feelings of impending doom.

Their journey had taken them across the gaping underwater wound in the earth's crust known as the Java Trench, a sixty-mile wide and twenty-four thousand feet deep canyon in the ocean floor, and now as they drew nearer to the coast of Sumatra they encountered a small island near the northern end of a chain of islands called Mentawai. It sat in shallow seas so clear and pure that before the rain began it had appeared to Pan and Apollo as if they were flying through air, suspended between the powdery white sand below and a liquid silver ceiling above. But now everything was growing gray and gloomy.

They continued on in silence for another few minutes as the bottom rose up toward them. Despite the gathering gloom, Pan imagined that he was a seabird coming into land on a strip of sand. He had always wanted to fly ever since he was little and he would often spyhop to watch the seabirds riding the wind currents over the water. Suddenly Apollo stopped, and Pan, lost in his dream, floating on gossamer wings getting ready for a landing, crashed headlong into Apollo's flukes. But Apollo took no notice. Instead, he spyhopped and Pan, relieved that he was not going to be chastised, did the same. The torrential downpour made it hard to see anything at all.

"What is it, Master...I mean, Apollo?" Pan tried to see what lay ahead but he could only make out the tops of some dead palm trees through the driving rain. He did not have the body strength to rise up out of the water as high as Apollo could.

With a thrust of his powerful flukes, Apollo rose up even higher, almost to his full body length, and held himself there for a few moments as he surveyed what lay ahead of them. Then he slipped back down under the surface and plowed forward once again.

Pan too slid under the water but before he followed Apollo, something made him turn and stare back across the sand flats in the direction from which they had come. There, in the murky distance at the fringes of his vision, he thought he saw a shape, barely more than an indistinct blur. Forgetting Apollo's orders, he switched to active earsight and probed the waters and what he found sent a chill knifing though his heart. There *was* something there, a gigantic hard-bodied creature with a scaly surface and tapered head with a bulbous nose, and fearsome jaws lined with protruding teeth. Pan had never seen anything like it before, nor could he have, because the killer that was tracking them was only found in the East Asian Seas. Your kind calls it a Salt Water Crocodile, and it was a big one, twenty-one feet in length, weighing over two thousand pounds; but true to its nature as an ambush predator, the beast was not closing on them. Instead it was slithering along through the water, keeping its distance, waiting for the right moment to strike.

"Apollo! Apollo!" shouted Pan as he rocketed after the white dolphin. "A kraken is following us. A *giant* one." He soon caught up with Apollo, who by that point was swimming through water that was barely six feet deep and getting shallower by the minute. "Apollo!" Pan screamed again.

This time, Apollo stopped and turned. "What is it?"

It took a second for Pan to compose himself. He glanced back once, expecting to see the kraken closing upon them with jaws agape. But there was nothing there. Pan looked at Apollo and said, in a calmer voice but only slightly so, "There is a gigantic kraken following us. Unlike any we have ever seen before. We think it is a dragon." Beings knew all about the fire-breathing monsters of ancient human lore, and many believed that dragons did once roam the earth, but no one believed they existed in modern times. No one except Pan, who now was convinced that he had just seen one.

"Do not be ridiculous. There are no..." Apollo caught himself.

Pan turned and there it was, not fifty yards away, hovering in the rain-swept sea, "You see! There it is. *A dragon!*"

Apollo's expression tightened. He nodded deliberately. "I see it. But it is not a dragon. It is a reptile that humans call a crocodile. There were some like it at Oceania. They were kept in another part of the oceanarium. However, from what I remember the crocodiles were not that large."

Pan drew nearer to Apollo. "Do these crocothings eat beings?"

Apollo studied the kraken carefully and replied, "I do not know."

"Oh dear. We hope not. We do not want to be eaten."

"I doubt that he is following us because he wants to make friends. Reptiles do not possess sufficient intelligence for that."

"If you are trying to comfort us, it is not working." Then to Pan's consternation, Apollo headed in the direction of the beast. "What are you doing?" Apollo did not answer. "Oh dear, oh dear," Pan murmured and then with a frightened sigh, he followed.

By the time Pan caught up with Apollo, the white dolphin had stopped within ten yards of the giant crocodile. Other than rising up to the surface to breathe and then sinking partway again, it had not moved. It was an eerie scene; a dark and scaly reptile and a sleek white dolphin, staring into each other's eyes; neither one moving or making any gestures, aggressive or otherwise, toward the other. Pan was not sure who would make the first move, and more to the point what he would do about it. Finally, after an excruciatingly long moment, the reptile looked away and Apollo turned to Pan and said, "He will not harm us." And with that Apollo swam back in the direction they had been heading.

"What! We do not understand?" said the puzzled little porpoise. "Wait," but Apollo ignored him. Pan looked back in the direction of the crocodile but it was gone. He struggled to grasp what had just happened. One minute, the dragon had been there, as big and bad as could be; a giant kraken hovering in the shallows, and now, in an instant, it was gone. For a moment, Pan stayed there staring into the pale blue nothingness across the sandy flats. And then, with a shake of his little head, he swam off after Apollo. *"We guess that dragons do not eat beings after all,"* he muttered. *"And it is a good thing."* But dragons do eat beings, as Pan would soon discover.

At the same time that Pan and Apollo were encountering the crocodile, Hector and Boreus were approaching another island in the same archipelago, one hundred miles further south. During the three days since they met the Goosebeaks, they had headed in a southeasterly direction, taking a diagonal path toward the straits between Sumatra and Java called the Selat Sunda. Boreus' instinct had told him Apollo would be heading toward the Pacific Ocean but he believed Apollo would first continue east until he reached the coast of Sumatra before turning south since the white dolphin was unfamiliar with these waters. If he was correct, Boreus felt that he and Hector could beat them to the Sunda Straits, which was a narrow body of water, twelve miles wide, where they would have a better chance of reuniting with their lost companions.

It was a good plan and one that might have worked were it not for one thing, and it was the one thing that he had worried about ever since he met the Goosebeaks, namely the location of the Federation's forces. Zephyrus had warned them about a large body of Poseidon's marines gathering in the Java Sea. Boreus was uncertain of what route they would take if it was their intent to attack Queen Demeter. They could move either through the Sunda Straits and up the west coast of Sumatra through the Indian Ocean, or travel up the east coast, between Sumatra and Malaysia, through the Straits of Malacca, which was the official boundary between the Indian and Pacific Oceans.

Boreus and Hector had been swimming fast and hard, and they decided now to rest in the shallow waters around one of the smaller islands off Sumatra's western coast. They had not rested long when they heard the unmistakable sound of a large group of beings moving through the water. By their active pinging, Boreus could tell the oncoming beings were not worried about being discovered and by their lack of chatter; he could also tell that they were not a social group. He knew that it must be Poseidon's marines but because he and Hector had been tucked safely on the lee side of the small island, Boreus knew that they had not yet been detected. Staying close to its shore and using the island to shield them from the oncoming marines, he and Hector positioned themselves to see what was happening.

Within a few minutes, a group of over three hundred beings appeared, formed in a long line ten abreast, and moving slowly and steadily up the coast in a northerly direction. The group was made up of dolphins, mostly Rough-toothed and Spotted; toothed whales, including Pilot Whales both Long and Short-finned; and ominously, there were also some Transient Orcas. At the head of the army was Chiron, the betrayer, as well as an Offshore Killer Whale who Boreus correctly assumed was Paris; the leader of the raiders who had attacked them a week earlier.

"Poseidon's army, just like Zephyrus said," whispered Hector.

"Yes, but Zephyrus said they were only gathered at the border. This group has invaded the Queen Demeter's waters and they must be heading north to attack her."

"I agree, but why are they moving so slowly?" It was taking a long time for the band of beings to pass Boreus and Hector's hiding place. Finally, the reason became apparent when Paris and Chiron suddenly reappeared. They were swimming back down the line of marines to where one being, a Roughie, in the last echelon was struggling to keep up. He was injured and because of his slower pace, he was obviously slowing down those around him. As Boreus and Hector watched and listened they saw Paris single out the injured Roughie.

"You must keep up!" barked Paris.

"I am trying," said the Roughie. It was evident that he was in great pain.

"He has not yet healed from his injury from our attack on the white dolphin's company last week," said another Roughie beside him. His interference received a harsh look from Paris that shut him up. Paris turned back to the injured whale and, in a deceptively gentle voice asked, "Perhaps you would like to stop and rest for a while?"

Misreading the Killer Whale, the Roughie replied, "Oh yes, sir. Just for a minute or…"

He never finished his sentence. Without warning, Paris tore into him and ripped off half his flukes. The Roughie screamed in pain and those around him recoiled in horror. "Now you will be able to rest as much as you want. Until the kraken find you that is." Paris ordered everyone to move out, which they quickly did, leaving the grievously wounded whale alone in the sea with blood spilling out of his torn tailstock.

Boreus and Hector waited until the marines had moved on and then swam out to the dying whale. Beings like all mammals are terrified of drowning and the Roughie was struggling to stay afloat. Boreus and Hector propped him up so he could breathe and tried to comfort him. He thanked them for their kindness. Despite their words of encouragement all three knew the Roughie did not have long to live. Boreus explained who they were and in his last moments of life, the Roughie apologized for the part he had played in the ambush a week earlier.

"What happened to the white dolphin and his little companion?" asked Hector.

"They escaped from us when we were attacked by a group of Guardians from Queen Demeter's forces," he answered. "We have not seen them since but Paris believes they are still alive."

Hector smiled and said, "God be praised."

Then the Roughie told them everything they wanted to know about where the advance party of the Federation's forces was headed. He said that his group was only a diversionary force whose mission was to attack Queen Demeter's forces from the southwest to fool the Queen into deploying her army in that direction. Then the main Federal force, numbering nearly four thousand marines, which at that moment was moving up the inside passage, would attack her flank. He also told them this larger force was under the command of Queen Eris.

The Roughie grew weaker and the blood trail in the water brought in the first of the sharks but seeing Boreus and Hector, they kept their distance, forming a circle of death around the three beings. When it was clear that the Roughie could not last much longer, he looked pleadingly at the Orca and asked, "Please, Guardian Boreus give me a GoodDeath."

Boreus hesitated. Offshore Killer Whales were trained to kill but mercy killing was not one of their preferred duties. Finally he nodded. "Very well." With that, Hector turned away and made a false charge at one of the sharks, a large Tiger Shark, who fled as did the others. Hector knew they would be back but before they returned the deed was done. With a sharp and twisting bite behind the Roughie's blowhole, Boreus broke the being's neck. Then he turned to Hector and said, "Come, we must go north to warn the Queen."

"What about Apollo and Pan?"

Boreus shook his head. "They will have to fend for themselves. Warning the Queen must take priority. If her army is destroyed then the Loyalists will not have sufficient might to overcome the Federation.

I believe it is what Apollo would want us to do. Hurry. We must leave now."

"What if we encounter Paris and his marines?" asked Hector.

"They are traveling north along the windward side of the Mentawai Islands. We will stay on the leeward side and since we are only two in number we can beat them to the Andamans."

It was clear that Hector was torn between conscience and duty. It was not an uncommon dilemma for a warrior to face. In the end he went with duty. With a sigh he nodded and said, "Perhaps we will find Apollo and Pan along the way."

"Perhaps," replied Boreus but he did not really believe it. He sensed that Apollo and Pan were heading south and east like he had believed all along. Now they would just have to fend for themselves. And with that he and Hector changed course and headed north at a fast pace.

"What happened to this place?" asked Pan as he and Apollo swam slowly between the guano-covered, rotting buildings and dead palm trees of the deserted village that lay under two feet of water. Everywhere they looked there were signs of the humans who had once lived there; including fire pits, now empty black holes with seaweed-covered stones; broken pots and cooking implements half-buried in the sand; torn clothing caught on pieces of driftwood swaying to and fro in the current; and children's toys sitting forlornly inside the flooded houses.

Apollo replied, "The sea level has risen and driven the humans who once lived here from their homes, leaving it to the wind and waves, and the seabirds and crabs. They will never be able to return and many more will suffer this same fate. I remember the scientists at Point Reyes talking about the rising sea levels but this is the first time I have ever seen its effect upon humans. It is a sorry sight."

"Why are the seas rising?"

"Because of the actions of man. The scientists said it is because of what they call greenhouse gases, which are causing the polar icecaps to melt. One day, before the next century, the rising oceans will render the worlds great sea level cities uninhabitable and endanger the lives of hundreds of millions of human beings who live in coastal zones worldwide."

Pan's eyes widened. "It is bad for man but good for us is it not?" They rounded a corner on what had once been a narrow street but was now a channel between two buildings.

"No. It is bad for all of us, because the seas are also warming, which will kill off many species of fish upon which we feed, and increase the frequency and intensity of hurricanes and typhoons."

"Oh dear. We do not like hurricanes and those...typh-things. (Pan, having lived all his life in or near the Atlantic Ocean had never heard the term typhoon, which man uses to refer to hurricanes in the Pacific Ocean). What can we do?"

"*We* can do nothing. The crisis has been created by humans, only they can solve it. However, it may already be too late because many humans refuse to believe there is a problem, and Poseidon starting a war with them is not going to help them see the light."

"That is why we must stop him."

"Yes—but now that we have lost Zeus I am not sure we can."

"We can and we must. We will carry on with our mission to save the world from destruction," said Pan with the conviction of a child who had not yet been tainted with conventional wisdom.

Apollo nodded but without conviction. He sighed, "I grow weary of this place of sadness. Let us leave here."

For the rest of that day and well into the gathering twilight, Apollo and Pan swam south, leaving the drowned village far behind. They covered over fifty miles by the time the sun sank behind sooty clouds that scudded across a black and moonless sky. After a fitful night spent in the lee shore of a large island, where they managed to avoid the worst of the wind and rain of the last of the winter storms, they headed out early the next day at dawn. They had not gone far when they felt the pinging of an approaching group of beings, which they knew must be the Federation's forces of which Paris had spoken. Apollo debated whether or not they should attempt to head toward the mainland where they could hide in one of the bays but it was too late, for the outswimmers of the army were soon upon them. Within a matter of minutes, they were surrounded by marines. From the chomping of their jaws and the bloodlust in their eyes, it was clear what they had in mind.

"Kill them. Kill them," the crowd of marines chanted.

"Wait," one of them shouted. "Paris wants to do that himself."

"I am sorry, Pan," said Apollo as the circle closed around them.

Pan was calm. "It has been our privilege to know you, Apollo."

"Very touching," said Paris as he entered the circle. With him was Chiron. Paris swam up close to Apollo as he had done several days earlier. "Well, well, well. Here we are together again, Apollo, the Prince of Light, savior of whalekind, blah, blah, blah. A savior who cannot even save himself." A roar of laughter spread across the crowd. "But this time there will be no escape. Queen Eris told me to execute you if we found you again. And here we are."

As Paris spoke, the marines formed a circle in the sea. Each warrior wanting to watch the white dolphin die. "Kill him. Kill him," they chanted, growing louder and louder. "KILL HIM. KILL HIM."

Paris looked around the circle and shouted, "Shut up!" They did. Then he turned back to Apollo and asked, "Do you have any last words?"

"Like, Please do not kill me," taunted Chiron to the delight of the crowd.

Apollo ignored Chiron and stared at Paris. "Do as you wish to me but let Pan live. He represents no threat to you or your Queen."

Paris snorted a laugh. "You are right. He is a sea louse on the flukes of a dead whale; just like the lice that are feeding on Zeus right now as he lies rotting at the bottom of the Southern Ocean." Apollo controlled his emotions but Pan grew furious. Paris ignored him. "Threat or not, the little one dies too, but if you like I will kill him after you so that you are spared seeing his death."

Apollo looked at Pan and as he did, he saw something out of the corner of his eye, in the azure waters beyond the circle. He realized at once what it was. He looked back at Paris and said, "May I approach Pan so that we may say good bye to each other?"

Paris scrunched his toothy mouth. "Go ahead. Be quick about it."

Apollo swam over to Pan and whispered into his ear. "Watch me and do what I do." He pulled back and said loudly, "Good bye, Pan. God be praised."

Pan, unsure of what was happening but with complete trust in Apollo, replied "God bring us the Light."

Apollo turned back toward Paris and then with a sly smile said, "Good bye, Paris."

In that fleeting last second of his life, Paris sensed something was awry. He turned and saw the onrushing Salt Water Crocodile but before he could react, the giant kraken burst into the circle, brushing the other beings aside like clam shells in the surf. In a blur, it grabbed Paris by his head and went into a death spiral that snapped the neck of the hapless Killer Whale. With Paris' limp body clenched firmly in its teeth, the reptile swam away, its enormous tail sweeping slowly from side to side as the other beings watched in horror. No one moved. No one spoke. No one even dared to rise up to the surface to breathe. Instead, the crowd of beings just hung there silently, in awe of the white dolphin. Chiron was aghast. The horror of Paris's death was still upon him but the reality of what was happening, or rather what was not happening, shook him out of his stupor.

"What are you doing!" he shouted at the marines. "He is *not* a god. He is *just* a dolphin. That kraken killed Paris. These waters are full of them. Now kill Apollo!"

But the beings ignored Chiron and began to press closer to the white dolphin, trying to be near him, to touch him. Then one of the Guardians who had defected with Poseidon, said, "Master, will you forgive me?" Apollo did not reply. Then another said it, and another, and soon the entire army was his to do with as he pleased, whether he wanted them or not.

Master? He does not like to be called that thought Pan. He looked at Apollo expecting him to reject their adulation but he did not.

A Rough-toothed whale asked Apollo, "Shall we kill Chiron, Master?"

But instead of Apollo saying no, he said nothing. Instead he just stared at Chiron, the betrayer. There was no mistaking what was on his mind and it was not forgiveness.

As is common with bullies among your kind, Chiron displayed the cowardice that lay just beneath the surface. He pleaded for his life. "Please, Apollo. Please do not let them kill me. Let me rejoin your Company of the Light."

Apollo sneered, "The Company of the Light is no more."

Pan saw the bloodlust in Apollo's eyes and realized what was about to happen. "Oh no! No, Apollo. Remember what you did for Python," cried Pan trying to evoke the memory of the mercy Apollo had shown at the Tongue of the Ocean. But that was many months and many miles ago, and it was not the same Apollo who now sat in judgment of an enemy.

Apollo nodded at the Roughie. Instantly, he and the others set upon the betrayer and in a few moments, it was all over, Chiron's lifeless body sank slowly into the depths. When they were finished, one of the Roughies turned to Apollo and asked, "Where to now, Master?"

"Lead me to the Pacific Ocean; to the home waters of King Poseidon." His stare was distant and detached.

A murmur swept through the ranks of the army. They were out for a monarch's blood; first Queen Demeter had been their target; now it would be King Poseidon; and exactly which royal head rolled mattered not. "Very good, Master. We will take you there and then we will kill the King."

"NO MORE KINGS, NO MORE KINGS," the other marines began to chant.

"Shut up," snapped the Roughie. "Apollo will be our new king."

"APOLLO IS KING, APOLLO IS KING," the others shouted.

The Roughie roared, "Would you *please* shut up?"

Apollo did not reject the idea, which sent a chill through Pan's body. "Apollo," he cried out. But Apollo did not answer. Instead, he and his new army swam away, heading toward the Sunda Straits. For a second, Pan lingered but the memory of the dragon was still fresh in his mind and after a minute he swam off after the army. But he did so with a heavy heart. Even though the white dolphin was alive and their journey continued, Pan feared that their dream of saving whalekind had been lost somewhere along the way.

CHAPTER NINETEEN

To Dwell In Shadows

Seven hundred miles to the north of Apollo and Pan, and Apollo's new army, Ares and Aegyptus moved slowly northward with the dream of saving whalekind still alive in their hearts and minds, but just barely. Because of Aegyptus' injury, it had taken them two weeks to reach the home waters of Queen Demeter near the Andaman Islands; a chain of five chief islands spread across one hundred and fifty miles of ocean on the eastern edge of the Bay of Bengal. On that warm and sunny first day of spring, as they swam slowly through crystal clear, turquoise waters over resplendent coral reefs, past white sand beaches, Ares' dark demeanor seemed out of place surrounded by such pristine beauty. He was growing concerned about his brother's deteriorating physical condition, and their mission to save whalekind had now taken a second place to the mission to save his brother.

"Do you think Apollo and Pan are still alive?" whispered Aegyptus in a feeble voice. The pain in his side was less than it had been on the morning after the attack but the wound was now infected and despite his brave front, he was not doing well. Without help, he would soon die and both he and Ares knew it.

"I do not know, but we have other matters to attend to at this moment my little brother." The anxiety in his tone and manner was palpable.

"Do not worry, Ares, I will be fine," replied Aegyptus wistfully. But the cloudiness behind his normally bright eyes said otherwise, and the fever that raged within him was making him delirious.

"I am sure you will," Ares lied, "but I will still feel better after we find the Queen and have one of her healers treat you. Now please be quiet and reserve your strength."

Aegyptus nodded. He was too smart not to realize that the fatigue and chills he was feeling were a sign of the infection within him. The two Orcas continued on for several more hours, traveling slowly up the west coast of South Andaman Island until they came to the place where Boreus had said they would find Queen Demeter. It was near two small islands called the Sentinels, which along with the Western and Dalrymple Banks that rise to within a few yards of the surface, form the tops of a line of submarine hills parallel to the Andamans. There in the clear, still waters on the leeward side of the islands, Ares and Aegyptus at last came upon Queen Demeter, Ruler of the Indian Ocean; a proud and defiant Gray Whale with a narrow bowed head, mottled skin, and knuckled finless hump, well past her prime but still firmly in control of her court and kingdom.

"Greetings, Queen Demeter," said Ares showing the level of respect required for such a royal encounter, but only just. Both the Orcas and the Queen's retinue had detected each other's presence long before they came face to face but unlike King Hermes in the Southern Ocean, the Queen had not sent out an emissary to greet them. This was bad mannered at best, and it bothered Ares. He chose not to comment on it but there was no mistaking his behavior, which was long on business and short on charm. "We have come…"

"I know why you have come, Guardian Ares," interrupted the Queen. "News of your journey has preceded you. And I regret to tell you that your efforts have been for nothing. I have no intention of joining the Loyalist cause."

Ares restrained himself. "Queen Demeter, I hope that I can change your mind, but for now, what is most important to me is to secure the help of a healer to attend to the wound that festers on the side of my brother."

The Queen ignored his comment about changing her mind, but she showed compassion for the wounded warrior, and instructed several of her Guardians to attend do him. Ares was reluctant to leave his brother's side but after Aegyptus reassured him that he would be all right Ares let him go. The Guardians gently led Aegyptus away. Then the Queen turned back to Ares and said, "My healers are among the best in all of Planet Ocean and I am certain that your brother will be well taken care of."

"Thank you," said Ares. He was grateful for her concern and it gave him hope that he could reason with her. He was wrong.

The Queen continued, "I am sorry for the loss of Zeus. He was a friend of the Sovereign Council and I shall miss him. I also regret the attack on your Company by the raiding party of Poseidon's marines during which you became separated from Apollo and Pan."

"Poseidon's marines!" said an incredulous Ares.

"Yes. They were led by one of your former Guardians named Paris."—Ares flinched as the traitor's image flashed through his mind.—"You were betrayed by Chiron, who conspired with Paris to kidnap Apollo."

"Is Apollo alive?"

Her expression darkened. "We do not know."

Ares studied the Queen closely, slipping a few feet slowly back and forth in the warm water, using his broad flippers to steady himself. Then he asked, "How do you know all this?"

"I make it my business to know," she said abruptly. It was apparent that the reputation Gray Whales have for poor manners and surliness was well deserved. (As I described to you earlier, Gray Whales are the ugliest of all the great whales, with blotchy skin encrusted in barnacles and infested with whale lice, particularly about the head. In the case of the Queen, she had less of these external afflictions than was the rule but her odious personality more than made up for her physical tolerability.)

"Does not the fact that these attacks were carried out by Poseidon's marines serve to prove his intent to destroy us all?" pleaded Ares.

"No," she snapped. "The attack was an unfortunate but isolated act of violence. The marines were simply a raiding party sent to kidnap Apollo, *nothing* more. I do not believe that Poseidon truly wants war and I certainly do not believe that Queen Eris would even consider invading my kingdom. As such I will not allow the presence of a small group of renegades in our home waters to provoke me into joining a global war."

"With all due…"

She cut him off again. "I am sorry, Guardian Ares, but I cannot help you." As she spoke, she drifted slightly upward in the water, enabling her to look down on Ares, shadowing his thirty-foot long body with hers that was longer by half and much stouter. It was a not too subtle metaphor for her position relative to his, and it did not go unnoticed by Ares. Then, almost as a throwaway line, she added, "However, you and your brother are welcome to rest here as long as you wish."

Ares could deal with tyrants and traitors but he had no time for fools. He was disgusted with the foolhardiness of her position but he was still curious about how she knew all of this. It had only been two short weeks since the attack, and he and his brother had not encountered any whales on their journey north who could have given advance notice to the Queen via whalesound. Ratcheting back his aggressive manner, he said, "With all due respect, Queen Demeter, you have still not answered my question about how you learned all this."

Queen Demeter did not answer the question directly. Instead, she slipped back down to the same depth as Ares and pulled slightly away from him. "Allow me to introduce Guardian Zephyrus," she said motioning toward a large male Goosebeak Whale who appeared from out of the group of beings assembled behind her. Ares acknowledged him with a curt nod. She continued, "Zephyrus and his marines have just returned from a scouting mission to the south. After he intercepted the raiding party that attacked you, and dealt with it, Zephyrus met two members of your Company of the Light, Boreus and Hector, who told him where you and your brother were heading, and what he and Hector were trying to do."

Taking his cue from the Queen, Zephyrus took over the story. "One of the raiders confessed that with Chiron's help, they had kidnapped the white dolphin and the Harbor Porpoise, but he said that during our attack, their prisoners had escaped."

"What else did he say?"

"Nothing. He succumbed to his injuries before we could interrogate him further."

"How unfortunate," said Ares, unsure as to whether or not he believed Zephyrus.

"Later, when we encountered Boreus and Hector, we reconstructed the entire sad story."

Ares glanced around the gathering. "Are Boreus and Hector here?" he asked hopefully.

"No. We asked them to accompany us but they said they wanted to go to the Sunda Strait."

"Why?"

"Boreus reasoned that if Apollo and Pan were heading north we would find them, which obviously, we did not. However, if Apollo believed that you two were dead, he might have decided to head to the Pacific Ocean instead of coming here. And if so, Boreus believed that he and Hector would be better off trying to intercept Apollo and Pan at the narrow Sunda Strait."

Ares was puzzled. More to himself than to the others he said, "I do not think Apollo would have abandoned his mission to enlist the Queen's forces." The idea troubled him and he fell silent, drifting back and forth in the clear water, using only the slightest flick of his flippers to keep him in place. No Hector and Boreus. No Apollo and Pan. And yet with convenient explanations from the Queen and Zephyrus for their absence. For a moment, he considered the possibility that he was not among friends; that Queen Demeter had joined the Federation, and that all his friends were dead. But then again, the kind help she had offered to his brother countered these doubts. Regardless, he could see that there was little to be gained by pursuing the Loyalist discussion any further with the Queen.

Zephyrus sensed Ares' frustration and he offered to take him to see his brother, which Ares readily accepted. After excusing themselves from the Queen's presence, they swam to a sheltered cove on North Sentinel Island where Aegyptus had been taken. When they arrived, Zephyrus introduced Ares to his brother's healers. They were Irrawaddy

Dolphins, the strangest looking beings Ares had ever seen: one third of his brother's length, they had large melons, blunt heads with indistinct beaks, pale gray bodies, small stubby fins and large, spatulate flippers. They seemed to move in slow motion but they also appeared to know what they were doing, so Ares greeted them politely and then kept quiet. As he watched, the healers were about to treat the source of the infection. They had already given Aegyptus a mixture of seaweed and minerals to restore his strength. Then several of the healers' assistants, Short-finned Pilot Whales, held Aegyptus while Box Jellyfish were brought in contact with the raw wound on Aegyptus' side. Unlike normal jellyfish, these creatures had eyes located on cup-like structures that hung from their cube-shaped bodies, and as a result of this ability to see, the Box Jellyfish directed their tentacles toward the open wound, like the repellent insect larvae, you call maggots do on land. The pain of their touch was excruciating, which is why the other beings had to hold Aegyptus, but the healers knew that the venom would serve as an antiseptic to clean the wound, and it would also act as an antibiotic to kill the bacteria circulating in Aegyptus' body—that is, if it did not kill him outright. The healers had warned Aegyptus of that possibility beforehand but they had also said that if they did not treat him he would surely die. Given this choice, Aegyptus agreed to the treatment and endured the pain without crying out, which greatly impressed Zephyrus. It did not surprise Ares but he flinched as he watched his brother suffer.

After it was over, Aegyptus rested, while Ares and Zephyrus swam off together. It was evident that despite Ares' earlier doubts and suspicions, a bond was forming between the two Guardians, which transcended their differences. Trying to bridge these, Zephyrus said, "Do not be angry with my Queen, Ares. She truly does not believe that we are on the verge of war."

"Then why did she send you to your eastern waters?"

"Several weeks ago, one of our Rangers reported that a large force of the Federation's marines was gathering in the Timor Sea. The Queen did not then, and does not now, believe they are any threat to us since those waters are technically part of the South Pacific Ocean, which is the Kingdom of Queen Eris, whom she knows and respects."

Ares' eyes narrowed. "Such respect is misplaced." Ares recounted what had happened between the late King Dionysus and Queen Eris."

The news gave Zephyrus pause but he was not convinced. "Queen Eris' behavior is troubling but that still does not prove any evil intent on her part toward our kingdom."

"But surely the Federation's forces are not gathered on your border for peaceful purposes?"

Zephyrus hesitated because he knew there was no good explanation. He thought about it and finally admitted, "I share your concern, Ares, but my Queen is a stubborn lady. She refuses to believe that Queen Eris would betray their friendship and invade our kingdom. And I must follow her commands. You *know* this to be true."

Ares shook his head slowly in reluctant agreement. "What is it going to take to make her understand that evil lurks in the hearts and minds of Poseidon and all his followers?"

"Even if she did acknowledge this, my Queen does not see herself as her brother's or sister's keeper. She wants no part of regime change in others kingdoms. She does not believe that such an action would be what the Ancients wanted of us and she is adamant that we will only attack those who attack us."

"What do you believe?"

The Goosebeak did not answer, which in itself was an answer. Ares stopped swimming. Zephyrus did the same. They were on the windward side of a bright yellow and pink strip of coral over which heavy surf was breaking in giant, sweeping curls of turquoise and aquamarine. It was a moment of great beauty and wonder in a world gone mad. For a little while, they hung there silently, sensing the rhythm of the sea, feeling the sun's rays streaming down on their backs, and watching a group of young Common Dolphins surfing the crashing waves. How innocent they seemed, thought Ares. How carefree. He could not help but contemplate how sad it would be to watch them fight and die in the coming war. He remembered what his father had taught him about humans and their countless wars; that it was old men who started them and young men who fought in them. Now that same curse had come to their world.

Overwhelmed by the senselessness of it all, he turned to his companion, and speaking with a passion that rose from deep inside, he said, "With all due respect, Zephyrus, your Queen is wrong. And soon she may be dead wrong. We live in a time of absolutes—absolute right and absolute wrong. You must join either with the forces of good or those of evil. There is *nothing* in between. By not choosing is to make a choice; one that will lead to pain and suffering, and eventually the death of all that is right and good about our world." He paused, and then added, "The death of those young dolphins over there, and tens of thousands just like them, because of Poseidon's madness and your Queen's unwillingness to stop it, will forever scar the hearts and souls of all whalekind, if we survive at all."

For a long moment, Zephyrus did not reply. The dissonance that Ares' eloquence had provoked within his mind caused him to remain quiet; lost in the silence that sometimes is forced to dwell between truth and duty. He looked at Ares seeking understanding, if not approval, for his Queen's position but finding none. Finally, with a sigh he answered, "You are right. But I am powerless to change things. To join with you would be an act of mutiny and I have taken an oath of loyalty to my Queen; one that I can not and will not break."

Ares stared his companion in the eyes and replied icily, "Blind loyalty has been the cause of war among mankind since time began."

Zephyrus did not respond. But no response would be needed for at that moment, fate took control of the future of these two noble Guardians, one of whom would live and the other who would die, in a war that had now come to both.

"Zephyrus, come quickly," said one of his marines who approached them in a great hurry.

"What is it?"

The Goosebeak glanced at Ares and then back at his superior. "It is Boreus and Hector. They have just arrived and are with the Queen. They bring news of an imminent attack by the Federation's forces."

Zephyrus gave a knowing look at Ares, and said, "Evil rises."

Ares nodded grimly and replied, "It always does."

Without further adieu, the three beings swam toward the royal court and the news that would change everything.

The sun was setting over the Bay of Bengal as Ares and Zephyrus rejoined the others. The burning orange orb suspended in a brown and pink sky, above the copper sea created an eerie scene that was vaguely unsettling to Ares. But the reception he received from the Queen helped push the feeling aside. She was relieved to see them and whereas before she had had an air of aloofness and intolerance, now he found warmth and receptivity. Ares felt a twinge of disdain for the hypocrisy in this sudden change of attitude but he accepted it nevertheless. What did it matter what the motivation was behind her sudden willingness to mobilize her forces, as long as she entered the battle on the side of the Loyalists? But any unpleasantness he felt for the Queen was pushed aside at the sight of his lost companions.

"Boreus. Hector!" he shouted. He swam up to them and came close to rubbing Boreus with his nose but stopped short.

They were equally delighted to see him but their reaction was tempered by the absence of Aegyptus. "Where is your brother?" asked Boreus with trepidation.

"He is fine," replied Ares. He gave a look of appreciation to the Queen, and then turned back to his companions. "Thanks to Queen Demeter and the care of her healers." Then he added with a chuckle, "I am quite certain that Aegyptus will not want to undergo that treatment ever again but he will survive."

"God be praised," said Boreus.

"God bring us the Light," replied Zephyrus with a sly smile toward Ares.

The Queen joined the conversation. "Ares, your companions have done us an invaluable service. They have traveled here at great risk to warn us of the imminent attack by Queen Eris." She shook her head slowly, then regained her composure and continued, "Although it grieves me to acknowledge it, Eris and her army of four thousand marines have moved from the Timor Sea into the Java Sea, and according to your companions it is her intention to travel up the inside passage and attack us. She has also sent a diversionary force up the west coast of Sumatra, numbering three hundred marines, led by a traitorous former fellow Guardian of yours, named Paris."

Ares acknowledged the name with a scowl.

Queen Demeter continued, "The raiding party who attacked you and your Company were a part of the diversionary force and we are fortunate that Hector and Boreus secretly observed them in the

Mentawai Islands. Their objective is to attack from the southwest and hit the right side of my forces to distract us, which will allow their main force to hit our unprotected flank on the left. The plan might have succeeded were it not for your companions who risked being detected by Paris' marines on the way here. Now we must make haste for their assault is to begin upon the new moon, ten days hence." She turned to Zephyrus and asked him for his advice as to what they should do.

Zephyrus glanced at Ares with a respectful smile. "I would like to ask my fellow Guardian for his recommendation for he has given the coming war far greater thought than have I."

Ares nodded and asked, "How big an army can you muster on such short notice?"

"We have a standing army of five thousand marines, one half of which is stationed here in the Andaman Sea. The rest of the army is too far away to help us now."

Five thousand Ares said to himself. *Even the much smaller kingdoms of the Arctic and Southern Oceans had armies larger than that.* "So few?" he asked. It was a rhetorical question and before the Queen was forced to explain Ares politely cut her off to save her any further humiliation. "Never mind. It will have to do. Based on this information, I propose that the best defense will be to take the attack to Queen Eris rather than letting her choose the time and place of the battle."

Zephyrus added his support, "I agree."

Ares continued. "Given our smaller numbers we must marshal our forces as best we can. First, we must look to the safety of mothers with young, sub-adults, and the elderly. Five hundred of your marines should lead this group north into the far reaches of the Bay of Bengal where they will be safe. I recommend that we take the remaining two thousand marines south, and attack the main Federation force before they reach here. They will not be expecting it and we will be better off fighting them in more confined waters where they will lose the benefit of their superior numbers."

Zephyrus interjected, "I know just the place—the Straits of Malacca."

"But what about the other force? The one led by Paris?" asked the Queen.

"By the time they arrive here in the Andamans and find us gone we will have already taken the attack to Eris' army in the south, and by the grace of God, we will have won a decisive victory. Then we can easily turn and face the smaller force led by Paris."

"But what if we have not prevailed against the main body of her army?" asked the Queen. "Will not the other forces attack us from the rear and catch us in a pincer movement like a giant crab?"

Ares' expression grew cold. "With all due respect, your Grace, if we lose the battle at Malacca, then it will not matter, for we will all be dead."

The group fell silent. The Queen thought about what she had heard and then pronounced, "So be it. Tomorrow we will leave for the Straits of Malacca and may God be with us." But even as she invoked the name of the Lord, the Queen could not help but wonder if Poseidon was doing the same thing. It was a disturbing thought and one that would haunt her in the days to come.

After their deadly encounter with Paris and Chiron, Apollo and Pan had journeyed south and east through the coastal waters of the Indian Ocean past the last of the Mentawai Islands and crossed through the Sunda Straits. This was exactly what Boreus had surmised, but obviously, he and Hector were not there to intercept them, and now the white dolphin and his stalwart little companion were on their own; at the head of an army whose allegiance was questionable and whose bloodlust was barely contained, in a foreign and unfriendly sea. It had taken them a week to get there and at that moment Apollo and Pan were preparing to spend the night just offshore from the marshy southeastern coast of Sumatra.

As they made ready to sleep near one of the oil drilling platforms fifty miles northeast of the coast of Java, Pan thought he saw a large shadow under the platform in the flickering light created by the gases being burned off above. "What is that?" asked Pan.

"What?" replied the preoccupied white dolphin.

"We think the dragon is back!" exclaimed Pan.

Apollo was in a sullen mood and Pan's alarm annoyed him even further. He made a cursory investigation of the area and found nothing, but in deference to his worried little companion, and despite the grumbling of the army, Apollo agreed to move farther offshore, which they did. When they reached a spot where Pan could no longer see the oil platform, or the shadow under it, they stopped.

"Will this do?" grumbled Apollo.

"Yes," pouted Pan.

Apollo could tell that something was still bothering Pan. "What is it now?"

"We are no expert in the ways of war but should we not have guards posted to keep watch over us during the night?"

With a sigh, Apollo turned to one of the Roughies and ordered him to post a guard. The Roughie left to do just that and with the shadow under the oil rig now only a memory, Pan said good night to Apollo and went to sleep. After an hour of mental turmoil, filled with self-doubt and infirmity of purpose, Apollo followed suit and fell into a troubled semi-slumber.

Several hours later, Apollo, still half-asleep, thought he heard someone calling his name. "Apollo," said the disembodied voice that echoed through the blackness surrounding him. "Apollo," came the voice again, this time louder and more demanding. "Wake up!" But he did not.

"Apollo! I *command* you to wake-up!" This time the voice boomed through the water so loudly that the sound waves penetrated Apollo's chest and gave him a sharp, short burst of pain. The pain was accompanied by a flash of white light that hit his open eye and brought him to full consciousness. The light was so intense, so overpowering, that Apollo could not see anything except a blinding curtain of pure white. It encircled him and blossomed throughout the surrounding waters, with glimmering fringes and fingers of intense visual energy radiating down and away, until they disappeared in the deeps.

"Who are you?" Apollo cried out without knowing from where the voice was coming. He could still not see anything other than the light and he averted his eyes for his vision was beginning to blur. He started to feel weak and it occurred to him that he might be dying.

"You *know* who I am and why I am here," was the strident reply.

"Your voice is familiar to me," admitted the still dazed white dolphin. "But I cannot see you." With his head canted at an angle away from the center of the light, Apollo tried catch a glimpse of the body behind the voice. Gradually, a shape began to appear; a very large shape that bore some familiarity but was still not fully identifiable.

"Look, Apollo! Here before you," the voice thundered. "Do you not see me, or has your soul become so blackened by hatred, and anger, and self-pity that it blinds your vision and numbs your memory?"

"I do not understand what…"

The resounding voice cut off Apollo's reply. "Look and be afraid! For the hour of your redemption is upon you."

Apollo was now fully awake and equally terrified. As he stared at the looming shape before him, he felt himself sinking deeper in the water and for an instant, he thought he was already dead, and the specter in the light was the Angel of Death come for him. (Beings believe that there is such an angel and that he appears moments before the time of their passing. Beings also know that certain land mammals, particularly dogs, can also see this angel when he comes to take their human masters to their final reward, but that is a whole other story.)

"I bring you not the darkness of death but the light of salvation, Apollo. I have come to save you not to destroy you."

"You…you can read my thoughts," Apollo stammered. "Who are you and why do you torment me so?"

Slowly, the shape took form from within the center of the light, growing, bigger, longer, wider, until at last, it became clear. There was no mistaking what or who it was; for there before him, now backlit by the blinding white light was a mighty Humpback Whale, *the* Humpback Whale.

"Zeus!" Apollo cried out. "You are alive!" Without realizing that he was below the surface Apollo took a breath. Water rushed into his blowhole, momentarily choking him. Reversing his breathing, he quickly exhaled, giving off a hissing sound like a sea serpent in the darkness. Still sputtering, he said, "It is you…" It was more of a question than a statement of fact.

The enormous bulk of the great whale was floating perpendicular in the water with his back arched away from Apollo, his flukes pointed down toward the deeps, and his flippers spread open wide like the wings of an angel. His body was surrounded by an aura, the radiance of which turned the sea at the fringes of the light from jet-black to shades of emerald green and jade. Gradually the light moved out from behind the great whale, to a position overhead, and it shone all about them, bathing both beings and the water surrounding them, in its ethereal glow.

Apollo was now quite certain it was Zeus but there was a difference—a big difference. "You are white. All white!" he exclaimed.

"I am all that I appear to be," replied the whale. Whereas before Zeus' body had been black on top from head to flukes, with only a white underside and flippers, now he was white all over; as white and pure as snow falling on a polar sea, and his skin glowed in the light as if it was covered with a thousand tiny diamonds.

"I thought you were dead: gone from me forever."

"How quickly you forget the words I spoke to you when first we met." The whale's tone and manner had now softened somewhat. They were soothing to Apollo's troubled soul.

Apollo acknowledged his forgetfulness with an embarrassed nod and replied, "You said that you would always be there when I needed you." As he spoke, he unconsciously allowed his body to slip into a perpendicular position, with flippers spread wide, like that of Zeus, such that it now appeared the two beings, one much larger than the other, were hanging on unseen crosses in the sea.

"I did. And here I am."

"Yes I see that but...."

"Why do you doubt what you see before you?"

"Because I saw you die; the harpoon, the catcher ship, the blood..." His voice trailed away. Even in the face of Zeus reborn, the memory of that day was painful to Apollo.

"But as you can see, I live. Do you not believe your eyes?"

"I do not know what to believe." Oily tears appeared in his sorrowful eyes, and formed shimmering bubbles that drifted away on the current. It was all too much for the white dolphin to comprehend. He stared at the giant apparition before him and asked pleadingly, "Tell me, are you God?"

"No. I am only his humble servant. But he is with you now, as he was in the beginning, and will be until the end of time. You need only to believe in him for him to believe in you."

Apollo began to tremble uncontrollably. "Oh, Zeus. I have failed you. I have failed God. I have forsaken my faith and lost my way."

"Yes, Apollo, you have. That is why I am here. To return you to God's ways."

Apollo's body sagged and his heart grew heavy. In a half sob, he begged, "Tell me what to do."

Zeus' body slowly shifted into a horizontal position. He moved closer to Apollo, reached out with his enormous flipper, and gently caressed Apollo's side. "First you must have faith in yourself for if you do not, then you cannot have faith in anyone, including God."

"I do. I will." Apollo's body too now leveled off. He bowed his head and prayed, "Oh God please hear my prayer. Thank you for all that you have given me and forgiven me. And if it is your will to let me return to the paths of righteousness, I promise that I will never stray again. I ask this in the presence of your servant, Zeus, and in the memory of the Ancients who taught us the Legend of the Light. Amen."

Zeus added, "Amen."

Apollo looked up from his prayer and said, "Zeus, there is something that I do not understand. Something that has troubled me for a long while. I believe it is the main reason that I sank into despair and turned away from God."

"What is it?"

"How can I believe in God and at the same time be a part of killing my fellow beings? How can I in good conscience go to war against the Federation and yet still be a child of God? All my life I have believed that the wars man wages upon his own kind are evil. How can there be such a thing as a good war?" When he was finished unleashing this torrent of questions Apollo fell silent, exhausted, and afraid.

Zeus smiled a sad smile and said softly, "In the world of man, there is no such thing as a good war, Apollo. There are only necessary wars. And that is now true in our world. Stopping Poseidon is the only way we will save whalekind from total destruction, and if the few must die so that the many may live, then it must be so."

Apollo pondered the concept and finally nodded his agreement.

"Now, Apollo, the time has come for you to return to the task that you were given by Queen Hera. At dawn, you will take your marines and head north, following an enemy army that has already passed through these waters. You will travel to a place called the Straits of Malacca and there you will help the forces of good destroy the forces of evil. After you are victorious, you will resume your journey to the Pacific Ocean where you will fulfill your destiny, which is to save whalekind."

Apollo nodded. His trembling had stopped and his sense of duty had returned. "Who are these forces of good with whom we are to join?"

"They are part of Queen Demeter's army of the Indian Ocean and they are being led by two who share your destiny, Guardians Ares and Aegyptus."

Apollo closed his eyes and said softly to himself. "They are alive. Thank you God. Thank you." He reopened them and started to ask, "Zeus, will you be there with…" but the blinding white light was suddenly gone and with it Zeus. The waters around him were dark and empty once more, lit only by the first few rays of the sun rising on the eastern horizon. His heart sank and for a moment, he hovered there alone and afraid as the Java Sea held him in its warm embrace. Then shaking off his feelings of despair, he looked around and uttered, "It was all a dream. Yes, that was it. God sent Zeus to me in a dream to help me regain my sense of purpose. And I will." He gathered himself, now free from the feelings of anger and self-pity that had overtaken him. They would not come again. Hurriedly, he searched the waters nearby until he located Pan, whom he awoke with great excitement in his voice. "Pan! Pan! Wake up. I have wondrous news."

"What is it?" asked the sleepy eyed little porpoise.

"I had a dream. A magnificent dream!" he said loudly.

"A dream?"

"Yes. An incredible, glorious dream in which Zeus appeared to me. He told me…" Apollo stopped because he saw Pan was not listening. "What is the matter with you, Pan?" He misinterpreted the porpoise's inattention to be doubt for what he was saying, which made him talk even louder. "Listen to me. I *saw* Zeus. He is an angel. A giant white angel. God must have sent him. Do you understand?"

But Pan did not reply. Instead, he drifted there stone-faced in the water.

"Pan, do you not hear what I am saying?" He saw that Pan was staring into the distance behind him and he seemed to be listening to something. Apollo stopped talking and then he heard it too, it was the sound of whalesong. And not just any whalesong, it was the hymn called

Godsong that beings sing at the Gathering. "Oh my," gasped Apollo. "Can it be?" He turned and listened, and there it was, the words and melody that could calm both stormy sea and savaged soul.

I lift mine eyes unto the skies
from whence my God shall save me.

He feels my pain and once again
he calms the seas around me.

I will not fear the Tempest's Roar
or the kraken's ragged bite.

For I know he will comfort me
through the long and darkening night.

And with the dawn will come the sun
to drive away the darkness.

Mine enemies shall all be dead
my victory will be ageless.

And when at last my days are done,
freed from the ocean's soft embrace.

I will lift mine eyes unto the skies
and dwell with God in paradise.

Apollo now saw what Pan had already seen. And he was overcome with joy and exultation. For there, swimming slowly toward them, just below the surface, and looking every bit as big and bold, and black and white as he had ever been, was Zeus. He reached them and stopped with a big grin on his gentle face and said, "Good morning, Apollo. Good morning, Pan."

For a second, both smaller beings were speechless. Then all at once, Pan shouted, "Zeus!" He launched himself toward the great whale, and nuzzled up to him. He started to bombard Zeus with questions about how he had escaped the whalers and where he had been. But Zeus would have none of that for the moment at least.

"There will be time for explanations later but first we must wake Apollo's new army and instruct them on their mission. As we speak, the Federation's forces under the leadership of Queen Eris, are moving north with the intention of launching a surprise attack upon Queen Demeter's kingdom."

"Why?" asked Pan.

"King Poseidon knows that Apollo was successful in convincing King Hermes to join the Loyalists. Even now King Hermes' forces are approaching Johnston Island in the North Pacific Ocean and Poseidon does not intend to allow this to happen with Queen Demeter even though her army is small and he doubts that they will add much to the cause."

"But the Queen was neutral. What or who convinced her to be otherwise?" asked Pan

All the while that the Harbor Porpoise was questioning Zeus, Apollo remained silent. He just floated there in the clear waters, staring at Zeus, trying to determine the line between dream and reality. Zeus the angel had been all white, and the Zeus the Humpback Whale was his normal coloring. Which one was he? And how could it be that he survived? Apollo bit his tongue to make sure that he was awake. The bite hurt.

Zeus interrupted what he was saying to Pan. He looked at Apollo and said, "I am real, Apollo. You are awake and your eyes do not deceive you." Then Zeus looked back at Pan and continued, "The imminent attack by Queen Eris' forces convinced Queen Demeter that she was wrong. That was the what. However, the who was Ares, whose passion had an impact upon her, even though he could not see it."

"Ares is alive?" asked Pan excitedly.

"Yes, and Aegyptus. As are Boreus and Hector."

"Oh goody, goody," said Pan. "But how do you know all this?"

Zeus winked at Apollo. "It was through whalesound."

"Whalesound?" Pan was not sure he believed the answer but what did it matter? Whether or not Zeus was back in the flesh or he was an angel who had appeared to Apollo in a dream, they were together again. And his little heart was full of joy. "Yes, of course, that was it, whalesound."

"We must go wake your army," said Zeus and with that, he turned and swam slowly toward where the marines were sleeping. As he did both Apollo and Pan saw something that sent a chill through their bodies. There on Zeus back and flukes was the wound from the harpoon and the scars from the steel cable that had pulled him into the deeps.

Pan looked at Apollo with wide eyes, started to say something but Apollo shook his head, and simply whispered, "Believe." And with that, he headed after Zeus with Pan close behind.

The three members of the once and future Company of the Light then woke up the army. Zeus spoke to them with poise, and power, and a sense of purpose that was spellbinding. He asked them to join the Loyalist cause and he warned them that those who did not risked dying in a war with mankind. He said that such a war would lead to the end of all life on Planet Ocean, as they knew it.

It was a compelling argument. The one fundamental truth about life for all of God's creatures is that we will die. Every single one of us. You, me, and all the beings in my story. It is an inescapable reality, and like you, beings seek to delay this inevitability for as long as possible. And there is nothing like the thought of one's own imminent death to focus the mind upon a life-saving mission. And so it was that on the same morning that Ares and Aegyptus were heading south, leading the army of the Indian Ocean, Apollo, Pan and Zeus were heading north at the head of an army of born-again Loyalists. And in between them, the forces of Queen Eris swam on oblivious to what lay in store for them.

CHAPTER TWENTY

The Battle Of Malacca

The Straits of Malacca connect the Andaman Sea of the Indian Ocean with the South China Sea of the North Pacific Ocean. It is a five hundred mile long, funnel-shaped waterway between the Malay Peninsula and the island nation of Sumatra. At its widest point in the north, it is nearly two hundred miles across, but in the south, where the Riau Archipelago crowds the passageway, it is as narrow as twelve miles. Coastal swamps are found along both sides of the straits and its average depth is less than one hundred feet, with many treacherous shoals and reefs; the most famous of which is called the One Fathom Bank. Over this bank sits an unmanned lighthouse with a red and white striped tower and a domed base that looks like a spacecraft from a distant galaxy stuck in the mud of Mother Earth. On average, two hundred ocean going cargo ships ply the waters of the Straits each day along with four hundred other vessels; including naval ships, passenger liners, pleasure craft, and small fishing boats. It was from one such small boat that rifle shots were fired in the overture to a ballet of death that was about to take place in those congested waters polluted by man.

The battle began innocently enough on the morning of the last day in March, seven days after Ares and the now fully healed Aegyptus had begun their journey south into harm's way, not knowing that far to the south, Apollo, Pan, and Zeus were heading north to meet them. As the sun burned through the fog over the milky morning seas, the captain of a decrepit wooden fishing boat operating near the One Fathom Bank lighthouse, discovered a Dugong, or Sea Cow, an endangered member of the class of marine mammals your kind calls Sirenians, trapped in his net. Seeing that the animal, a young female, was in danger of drowning, he jumped into the water to save her, while his crew looked on. And then this act of compassion was repaid with cruelty as a large male Spotted Dolphin, the leader of a group of twenty marines from Queen Eris' army, saw the man swimming in the water, and immediately attacked him. Some among your kind might have thought the dolphin was trying save the Dugong from its attacker, but the dolphin cared little about the marine mammal; he simply saw an opportunity to kill a human and took it.

The crewman watched in horror as the dolphin rammed the captain and drove him under the water. A few seconds later, he popped back up to the surface, with his arms flailing; spitting blood as he gasped for air, but the dolphin hit him again. Hard. As this was going on, the frantic Dugong became even more entangled in the net. The noise of the attack, including the screams of the captain, the cries of the Dugong, and the excited clicks of the other dolphins who were enjoying the spectacle, filled the water for miles around. The killer persisted and soon it was obvious that the man was doomed. Before his body disappeared for good, one of his crewmen retrieved a rifle from below and fired three rounds into the dolphin's head, putting an immediate end to his evil rage. But it was too late to save the captain, or the Dugong. Both died in a senseless act of evil on the part of the dolphin, brought on by the hatred that Poseidon had planted in his psyche: hatred that soon would spread a bloodstain across the Straits and around the globe.

Seeing their leader's head explode shocked and angered the other dolphins and they attacked the fishing boat with a vengeance, smashing holes in its hull and sinking it. Then as the crew swam away from the floundering craft, the beings turned their fury upon the humans and brought their lives of meager existence to a swift and brutal end. If there was any good to come out of the tragedy, it was that this distracted the dolphins and before they knew what hit them, Ares and his brother and the lead units of Queen Demeter's marines swept them away like avenging angels.

Shortly thereafter, the front line of the main force, with Boreus and Hector in the lead arrived at One Fathom Bank. They were rejoined by Ares and Aegyptus. Tipped off now to the nearness of the main force of Queen Eris' army, they divided their own forces into two groups and formed a giant, lazy, upside down L. The smaller of the two groups made up the top of the L, which stretched out into the Strait, while the long arm extended southward at a ninety degree angle, pointing in the direction from which the enemy would come.

Ares was concerned that in a direct frontal assault, Eris would have the advantage because her forces outnumbered Demeter's two to one. To offset this, his plan was to allow the enemy to collide with the top of the L, and once they were so engaged, the strong, long arm would swing into their flank, hopefully catching them by surprise. It was a good plan, risky but no less so than the alternatives and it possessed the element of surprise, which has often swayed the outcome in battles among your kind. The plan would place the beings lined up across the strait in the greatest danger and true to their nature, Ares and his brother, Aegyptus, took command of the forces so deployed; positioning themselves at the center of the line, in front of the One Fathom Bank and directly in harm's way.

Ares then placed Queen Demeter and a group of her Guardians led by Zephyrus to the north of the Bank, in relative safety behind the lines. She objected but he was insistent. Zephyrus was similarly displeased to be positioned away from the front lines but he knew his duty and accepted his assignment. The final two elements of Ares' plan were to have Hector command the beings at the right angle where the arms of the L met, while Boreus would lead the beings placed at the far lower end of the L. As such Boreus would lead the charge into the enemy's flank in a great swinging movement. He was honored to be assigned so important a mission; one that would be key to their victory, if indeed victory was to be theirs at all.

Once the plan was finalized, the army moved into position. This was done in silence after Ares had given the warriors their orders, which was to engage the enemy and stop them at all costs, for such was the importance of what they were doing. Ares further instructed the army that none of the invaders were to be allowed to escape lest they warn Poseidon. They were either to surrender and revoke their allegiance to the Federation's cause or suffer the consequences; and Ares left no doubt in anyone's mind what that meant. He told them that the time for negotiation was over. Once Queen Eris and her army had entered the waters of the Indian Ocean, they had forsaken all their rights, including the right to life itself. It was a dire and harsh order of engagement but one wholly appropriate to the moment, and all of Queen Demeter's forces were fully prepared to carry it out. After satisfying himself that all was ready, Ares took his place beside his brother and prepared for whatever fate had in store for them.

"How long?" whispered Aegyptus.

"Quiet," snapped Ares as they waited in the shadows of the One Fathom Bank light, at the center of the top arm of the L. "Soon," he added, his tone softening a little. "Soon enough."

But it was not to be soon and as morning turned to afternoon, Ares began to worry that one of the pickets who had attacked the fishing boat must have escaped and warned Queen Eris. When twilight came, it was apparent that the battle would not take place that day. Accordingly, Ares assigned Aegyptus to swim west along the shorter portion of the L to give the army its new orders, which were to post the guards for the long night ahead, while he did the same by traveling to the east to meet with Hector at the angle, and then south where he would reconnoiter with Boreus. The brothers agreed to meet back at the center of the line, in front of the One Fathom Bank, to await the dawn. As they parted, the sun slipped slowly below the tree line silhouetted against a copper-colored sky on the western shore. The smoldering red orb seemed to grow larger and angrier as it sank, as if it knew what would happen when it returned, and then, with a flash of green—Angel's Breath—it was gone, leaving the wary and weary marines waiting for the dawn; a dawn that for many would be their last.

As Ares swam slowly eastward, in the gathering darkness along the line of beings he stopped occasionally to chat with the young whales and dolphins whose lives now depended on him. None knew anything about his background or qualifications to lead them into battle; a battle unlike any they had ever known. A few were seasoned marines who had done their share of killing kraken, such as Tiger and Great White

Sharks, Giant Squid or Octopuses, and the like, but most had never killed anything larger than the fish they fed upon, and although that technically was killing, it was a far cry from what they were about to do. Taking the life of another being did not sit well with any of them, as it would violate a law that they had held sacrosanct throughout their lives. But while Ares was a stranger to them, they knew what it meant to be a Guardian, and as he met with them, they jockeyed with each other to give him their views on life and death and everything in between. He listened patiently and tried to give them the reassurance they needed to hear. They spoke of faith and fear and the coming fight. He spoke of duty and honor, God and Queen, the code that had been drilled into him when he first became a Guardian. They could only think about returning home to their friends and family: he could only think about broken bodies slowly sinking into the deeps. It was a painful thought and such thoughts are a heavy burden to all those generals and admirals among your kind who send young soldiers into danger.

Eventually Ares reached the southern tip of the L where he met with Boreus. They spent a few moments together, talking about their shared ancestors one last time, and then Ares retraced his path northward. When he reached the halfway point of the long arm of the L, he saw a young Hump-backed Dolphin, light brown in color. But it was not this skin color that caught Ares attention for it is common for their species. Instead it was the strange way the dolphin was acting. He was drifting all alone above a patch of sea grass and he seemed dazed or worse.

"Is there something wrong, marine?" Ares asked as he approached the motionless dolphin, who was lying on his side at the surface and had not seen him approach.

The dolphin snapped upright, "Oh no, Guardian Ares. No. I was just…staring at the moon."

"Staring at the moon?" queried Ares, flashing an upward glance at the clear night sky and the pale moon rising.

There was something about the way the young dolphin looked and acted that made the battle-hardened Offshore Killer Whale feel a sudden sense of sadness, although he did not know why. "What is your name, son?" In the soft glow of the moonlight, Ares noticed that one of the dolphin's flippers was small and misshapen.

"My name is Hesperus, sir."

"Where are you from, Hesperus?"

"From the Maldives, sir."

"You have never been in battle before have you?"

"No. Never."

"Well, there is a first time for all of us. Is there anything that you would like to ask me? About the coming fight or anything else for that matter?"

"That is very kind of you, Guardian Ares, but you must have more important things to do."

"I have nothing more important to do," replied Ares and he meant it.

The dolphin nodded his head appreciatively, then summoning his courage he asked, "Well sir, I am not afraid of dying, but what I am afraid of is dying alone."

Ares was taken aback by the statement. The image of the young being facing death was not pleasant to the veteran Guardian, but to die alone was a thought unkind. In a fatherly tone, Ares replied, "I would be a liar if I said that none among us will die tomorrow. But believe me, Hesperus; none of us will be alone as we go into battle."

"With all due respect, sir, I will be."

Ares looked around. "Where are the other members of your tribe? And your chieftain?" Beings, who serve in a monarch's army, always do so in groups chosen from their own tribe and led by one of their own. It is the way of beings, as they believe that no one from any given tribe should ever be asked to serve in a company of strangers.

Hesperus sighed. "They are over there..." he answered, pointing with his head off to the right toward the shoreline, "by that sand bar fifty yards from here." The dolphin added softly, "They do not want me around. With my physical handicap they are afraid that I will place them in jeopardy."

The young dolphin's answer pained Ares. He thought about it then said, "Wait here." After awhile, he returned with the other members of Hesperus' tribe following meekly behind him. One in particular, who had been the chieftain, looked terrified. Ares swam over to Hesperus and said, "You are hereby promoted to be the chieftain of this tribe and you are hereby placed in command of this section of the line. Your fellow tribe members are to take orders from you and only you. If they disobey your orders, you are to bring them to my attention and they will be dealt with as traitors." He glared at the others and growled, "I have told them what we do to traitors. Right?" They all nodded obediently. Their newfound allegiance to Hesperus was obviously based on the ice-cold fear that Ares had instilled in them, but sometimes the rule of reason is not enough and rule of fear is the only motivator. Used properly, it can be a great motivator indeed. And soon enough it would be replaced by respect but not until after the first blood flowed. "Good," he snapped, and turned back to Hesperus. "Chieftain Hesperus, I trust you will do your part in the coming battle. This section of the line and your flanking movement will be integral to our victory."

The dolphin's expression brightened as if a light had been switched on behind his eyes. "I will not let you down, Guardian Ares."

Ares smiled a knowing smile. "That thought never entered my mind." Ares knew that a great force of arms will fall before a greater force of the heart, and there was no mistaking the strength of heart that beat in this young being's chest.

As Ares started to leave, Hesperus called out to him, "God be praised."

Ares stopped short, turned back, and replied with a subdued smile, "God bring us the Light." With that the mighty warrior swam off leaving the young dolphin with the deformed flipper in charge of a group who, come the dawn, would fight with an intensity unmatched by the enemy they would face in battle. And they would do so under the sure and steady leadership of one who had not sought greatness but had had greatness thrust upon him. Such is often the way of heroes in their world just as it is in yours.

The Battle of Malacca, which would prove to be the biggest, bloodiest and most brutal fight between beings in the history of Planet Ocean, began like an opus for the apocalypse shortly before dawn on April 1st, a day that would live forever in the hearts and minds of those who survived, or etched upon the eternal souls of those who did not. The conductor was the devil himself, who had swum silently out of the boiling cauldron of hell and had taken his place in the still-dark waters of the Straits, directly between the combatants. The first downward stroke of his flipper unleashed a terrible swift collision between the leading edge of Queen Eris' army and Queen Demeter's marines positioned in the center of the upper arm of the L, as body slammed into body, teeth met teeth, and flukes crashed down upon flukes. It quickly built into an unrelenting crescendo of death and destruction that filled the shallow seas with an unbroken series of frantic clicks, shrill bursts of high pitched sound, and sickening concussions of flesh upon flesh, all of which could be felt for ten miles and heard for fifty.

Then as abruptly as it had begun, it stopped. The two groups of those still living separated to reconnoiter and regroup. The seas became deathly quiet, as the curtain of silence fell upon the submerged theater of war. There was no wind, no waves, no movement, nor any other sign of life, and no line of demarcation between the forces of good or evil. It was as if the Straits of Malacca, along its entire length, was holding its breath, waiting for the beginning of the end.

And so it came. Softly, with a deceptive innocence about it that belied its inexorable purpose, a faint rumbling, gurgling sound penetrated the stillness, muted at first, but gradually growing louder and louder, until it became so powerful, so profoundly visceral, that it might have been the storm surge of God crashing upon the beaches of heaven. Simultaneously, the seafloor began to shake, sending pebbles dancing across hard-packed sand, and tiny sea creatures scurrying for safe haven, while fronds of sea grass swayed in timid harmony. Above the water, the veil of night released its grip upon the world, and a pastel wash of crimson and yellow crept slowly over the horizon, like watercolors seeping up a celestial blotter. And then, when the devil and his orchestral minions were set, he brought his giant red flukes crashing down in one final stroke and the last act of the Battle of Malacca began.

At the exact moment that Eris' main force began its final, frontal attack against the upper arm of the Loyalist L, the long line of Loyalist beings positioned on the lower arm of the L began their westward advance. With an unshakable sense of purpose, they sliced through the blood-soaked seas; their dorsal fins silhouetted against the thin, red dawn, gathering speed as they went. In a deadly sweeping arc, they raced through the unguarded waters on the enemy's right flank, in a symphony of fluid shock and awe until at last, in the horrifying collision of an unstoppable force meeting an immovable object, Queen Demeter's forces crashed headlong into the flank of Queen Eris' army and hundreds upon hundreds of beings began to die, while high overhead, angels wept.

War, in all its bitter glory, with its shocking yet seductive ways, had now left the land behind and flooded into the Seven Seas, and unless wiser heads prevailed, it would take root in the deeps from where its evil would rise up again and again, as it had in the world of man, until it poisoned the hearts and souls of whalekind forever.

By the time Apollo, Pan and Zeus reached the scene of the battle, it was all over and their army of converts were not needed other than to convince by show of force those among the enemy who might have believed otherwise, that all was now lost. It was readily apparent to Apollo and his colleagues that the Loyalist forces had won, and because of their appearance along the southern edge of battle, none of the enemy was able to flee to the Pacific Ocean where King Poseidon waited for news of a victory that would never come. But even in victory, it was a sorrowful sight that greeted Apollo and the others as they swam slowly among the dead and dying of both sides.

Four thousand beings had invaded the waters of the Kingdom of the Indian Ocean several weeks earlier, and attacked the army of Queen Demeter at dawn that day. When the battle ended, only half remained alive and of that group, only half again had surrendered and begged for mercy, which was given upon receiving their oaths of allegiance. Those who refused to surrender turned to flee but found their way blocked by the oncoming forces of Apollo. In panic, they headed west, but in their terror, they beached themselves along the shores of the Strait, there to die a slow and agonizing death, beyond the reach of Queen Demeter's marines who could not help them even if they had wanted to. And for their part, the price of glory for Queen Demeter's army had been a bitter one indeed, for barely more than half had lived to see another day. In all, over five thousand beings had died in or beside those blood-soaked waters, which for generations to come would never see another whale or dolphin pass through what had become, in a few short hours, the Straits of Hell.

"Oh dear. Oh dear," said Pan as he surveyed the grisly scene.

Apollo said nothing as he scanned the waters, desperately seeking the two beings whose lives meant most to him, not that the death of any being was less meaningful than that of another. And then, finally, he saw them, bloodied but unbowed, Ares and Aegyptus, moving slowly among the dead and wounded, ministering to those who were not beyond help.

When Aegyptus spied their long lost companions, he was overjoyed and he rushed to greet them. "Apollo! Apollo! You are alive," he gushed.

Ares followed and once they were all together, they formed a tight circle. With Pan and Apollo at its center, and Ares, Aegyptus and Zeus at its outer edge, the reunited Company of the Light hovered there without speaking, for the somber silence that surrounded them said more than any words ever could.

Finally, Pan broke the silence. "They told us you were dead," he said to the two Guardians. "We are so happy that you are not."

Aegyptus smiled a sad smile. "We were afraid that *you* were dead."

Ares looked at Zeus and added, "I saw *you* die, with my own eyes."

Zeus detected the hint of coldness in Ares voice but chose not to acknowledge it. "Your eyes deceived you then but they do not now, my friend." Zeus' smile faded as he surveyed the scene about them and said, "We are alive but sadly many beings are not. God was with you in your fight but his heart must be broken that it took place at all."

"If God's heart is broken then why did he not prevent this in the first place?" Ares' question pierced the water like a shard of ice. "This was but the first battle of a war that may destroy our kind. What then? What will God think when we are all dead?"

Zeus's eyes narrowed. He could sense the pain in Ares' words and the profound anger behind them. He moved closer to the Guardian and said softly. "Ares, the Ancients taught us that God is all powerful and all knowing but that he will not interfere in the choices we make. Poseidon has chosen one course of action that will lead to destruction. We have chosen another that will lead to salvation. It is within our power, and ours alone, to affect the eventual outcome. And we must do so with courage and conviction." He paused and reached out to Ares with his large flipper, touching the Orca on his side. "I share your anger and your heartache for those who have died here this day, but my brave and noble warrior friend, it will serve no purpose for us to debate what

God should or should not do. He will not save us from ourselves. Only we can do that."

Ares heard Zeus' words but he did not listen to them, for there is a difference. Instead, he fell back into a troubled silence.

However, Aegyptus did hear, and did listen, and added softly, "Amen."

"Amen," echoed Pan and the others.

"What of Boreus and Hector?" asked Apollo.

A cheerless shake of Aegyptus' head told him they were not to be found among the living. "They died bravely and we owe our victory in large measure to them."

The news hit Pan the hardest. His little body sagged and he whispered, "We pray that they are swimming through those golden seas where one day we will all meet again." His reciting of a line from the poem that Lady Selene had taught them, cast another note of sadness upon the solemn gathering.

"God rest their souls," whispered Apollo.

Zeus added, "And all those who died with them, regardless of their allegiance, for the sin here was not among the beings who brought war to these waters but it rests with the King who waits in far distant seas; seas to which we must now turn our attention."

"What happened to Queen Eris?" asked Apollo.

"We do not know. We have not found her either among the living or the dead," replied Aegyptus.

"And you will not," came the reply from behind them. It was the voice of Zephyrus.

All turned to see Guardian Zephyrus and Queen Demeter who now approached them. Greetings were exchanged and the Queen thanked Ares for the victory that he had orchestrated. Then Zephyrus explained, "One of the prisoners told us that the Queen abandoned her army when she saw that defeat was all but certain. She is headed back to the Pacific."

"She will get a fine reception, returning without her army," said Aegyptus with scorn.

"If she gets back at all," interjected Ares. It was more of a wish than an expression of doubt.

Zephyrus clarified what had happened. "She was not alone. Several beings accompanied her, led by a black Bottlenose Dolphin."

"A black dolphin?" asked Ares, his interest level now piqued. A nod from Zephyrus confirmed it.

Apollo's expression darkened. "What was the dolphin's name?"

"Python," replied Zephyrus.

"Oh my!" gasped Pan.

"Do you know him?"

"Yes," said Apollo. He did not elaborate, which Zephyrus took as a hint not to pursue the matter.

Aegyptus flashed a glance at Apollo whose eyes were locked upon Zephyrus. Apollo shook his head in anger and disbelief. "I do not understand how they could have gotten by us?"

"Queen Eris is adept at hiding by laying low in the sea grass beds," replied Queen Demeter. "It is a trick she taught me to avoid Transient Orcas when we were friends once, long ago…" Her voice trailed away as bittersweet memories flashed before her eyes.

"It does not matter how, only that she did," replied Zeus. "Right now she and her companions are likely racing through the waters of the Java Sea to join King Poseidon. And with or without her army, Poseidon will still welcome Eris back. She is a cunning warrior and the marines she abandoned here were only a small part of their total force. Poseidon needs all the help he can get because even as we speak Loyalist armies are advancing steadily toward Johnston Island. Among them are the armies of Queen Hera, and Kings Pluto and Triton coming around Cape Horn, and Queen Selene traveling past Point Leuwin at the bottom of Australia."

"*Queen* Selene!" said Ares and Aegyptus in unison.

Zeus tipped his mighty head once. "As I told Apollo and Pan on our journey here, the good and kind King Hermes is dead. A group of traitors, loyal to Poseidon, murdered the King shortly after you left the Kerguélen Islands. The traitors were soon captured and put to death and Lady Selene was appointed Queen."

When Zeus had first given Apollo the news, he had remembered the look in King Hermes' eyes and the sadness behind his words when they spoke of the coming war. Now as he heard the words again, it suddenly made sense to him. The King must have had a premonition of his own death but in a last unselfish act he did not share it with Apollo for fear that it would cast a further shadow upon his Company's mission.

For a moment no one spoke, as each in their own way honored the memory of King Hermes, the first of the Loyalist monarchs to die in the struggle to save whalekind. Finally, Queen Demeter broke the silence. "Who are the forces who have followed you here, Zeus?" she asked pointing with her head to the marines gathered in the near distance. They seemed hesitant to break ranks and move among the dead, many of whom only short days ago had been their comrades. And more than just a few shuddered at what their own fate might have been were it not for the death of Paris.

"I will let Apollo answer for he is their leader, not I."

"They were once a Federation raiding party led by a Guardian named Paris," replied Apollo. "Among their number was the traitor, Chiron. Paris was killed by a kraken…"

"It was a dragon!" interjected Pan with wide eyes.

Apollo looked kindly at his little companion. "Actually it was a Salt Water Crocodile. Upon Paris' death, his marines believed that I was responsible for the attack, and that somehow I controlled the kraken, which I did not"—by Pan's expression it was clear he knew better—"but they switched their allegiance to me anyway."

"They executed Chiron," added Pan.

"I see," said Queen Demeter eyeing the white dolphin with guarded admiration. "Well it certainly served our purposes here today and I thank you for coming to our aid."

"No your Grace. Thank Zeus for it was he who saved me from the darkness that had overtaken my soul."

"He has a reputation for doing that," replied the Queen.

Ares and Aegyptus exchanged a knowing look. Over the months that they had spent with Zeus, they had come to suspect that there was more to the mysterious Humpback Whale with white flippers and wily ways than met the eye, and his survival when the catcher ship sank only served to reinforce this. Regardless of who or what he was, they were glad to have him back again. Very glad.

"A reputation for that and a lot more," added Apollo with a wry smile.

Uncomfortable with the direction the conversation was heading, Zeus interjected, "Be that as it may, Queen Demeter, now that Paris is dead and we have defeated all those who invaded your Kingdom with him, we must turn our attention to the Pacific Ocean and the mission with which the Company of the Light was charged in the first place, many months, many miles—and many lives ago."

"You are right, Zeus. She turned to the white dolphin. "Apollo, please tell us what you would have us do?" By asking this, it was now clear to all that the white dolphin had become the leader they all had hoped he would be. And more.

A bittersweet smile spread across Apollo's face He paused before replying and then said, "Let us leave this place of sadness, and head south and east to the darkening seas where evil dwells."

But Ares was not quite ready to depart. "Before we do, Apollo, there is someone whose fate I must know." Even as he said it, there was a lingering reluctance in his voice to learn the answer.

"There is no need to look for him, Ares," replied Zephyrus, "for I believe I know of whom you speak. It is a Hump-backed Dolphin with a misshapen flipper is it not?"

"Yes," Ares answered with trepidation "Has heaven this day received an angel with a broken wing?"

A warm smile spread across Zephyrus' face. "God has welcomed many beings into heaven this day, Ares, but an angel with a broken wing was not among them." He signaled to the crowd behind the Queen, and there, drifting gently on the swells, was Chieftain Hesperus who swam over to join them.

"Hello, Guardian Ares," Hesperus said with a smile on his face that injected at least a tiny bit of happiness into the sorrow of the moment. He turned and nodded his head to his Queen.

Zephyrus said to the others, "Permit me to introduce you to one of the heroes of this battle. He is a being who led his marines with great courage; and who played a key role in the success of the flanking movement that saved the day. I give you, Chieftain Hesperus."

"Hello, everyone," said the embarrassed dolphin. Then, he turned back to face Ares and with a nod said, "I said I would not let you down, sir."

For a moment the tough Killer Whale was speechless. All he could do was swim over and nudge the dolphin gently with his nose. Seeing such emotion from so strong a warrior touched the hearts of everyone and for a brief moment, amidst all the worry and woe, there was just the hint of brighter days ahead; for all could sense that if this living angel with a broken wing could survive such a brutal fight in which so many, much bigger and stronger than he, had perished then surely God's Good Light would prevail.

And that was that. The Battle of Malacca was over. Soon the northerly currents would wash away the blood, and gravity would usher the dead to the bottom of the Straits where they would be returned to clay. Meanwhile, the living would rest and regroup in the waters that at first would be hated by those who fought there, but later would be hallowed by all those who had not. Soon the reunited Company of the Light and the Queen would be joined by the rest of her army who had been summoned from all over her Kingdom, and two weeks after the battle, the rested and reinforced Army of the Indian Ocean would leave their home waters and head east toward the Pacific where the greater part of evil awaited them.

Even as they did, word of the mass killing of whales and dolphins that had occurred in the Straits of Malacca would spread throughout the world of man, feeding the frenzy of the highly-charged political debate that found their world divided into three factions, each of which could be categorized according to their position along a continuum: first, there were those at one extreme who said the deaths were proof that man was destroying the oceans. Their shrill cries and prophesies of doom, punctuated by acts of civil disobedience or worse, helped no one, least of all the beings. These Eco-zealots stood in stark contrast to those at the other end of the continuum, the Intelligentsia, both those who actually were and those who only pretended to be. They took a more reasoned but still self-serving view. They said that the deaths were likely the result of a massive bloom of poisonous algae, over which man had no control, and which was simply nature's way of controlling the overpopulation of the seas.

And finally, positioned ponderously in the middle of the continuum, was the third group, much larger than the other two; more sensible than the first and more sensitive than the second, but lost in their own self-servitude. They were the Inertials, who paid no attention whatsoever to the deaths of thousands of dolphins in that narrow stretch of water on the other side of the world, and through their ignorance and apathy, they brought the entire planet one step closer to disappearing into the black hole of history.

CHAPTER TWENTY-ONE

Great And Restless Sea

The first thousand miles of the last and longest leg of the Company of the Light's journey from the Kingdom of the Ancients to the home waters of King Poseidon took Apollo and his companions over three weeks. It should have taken them a third less time but their battle wounds were a drag upon their bodies, and the memories of the friends and fellow marines they had left behind were a heavy burden upon their souls. Their labored trip had taken them south from the Straits of Malacca through the Java Sea, past the east coast of Borneo and finally across the Celebes Sea. This passage through the littoral waters of Indonesia was an uneventful prelude to what was to come. On the last day of the first week of May, they stopped for the night near some small islands off the southern coast of Mindanao. Ahead lay over four thousand miles of open ocean, but after what they had been through during the previous seven months; the weariness and wonder; the tragedy and triumph; the separation and coming together; Apollo and his Company of the Light faced the vast confluence of wind, water and sky that lay before them with a grim determination that neither fear nor fatigue could conquer.

"Why do humans call this ocean the Pacific?" asked Pan as they drifted on the gentle swells that rolled past the island in whose lee they had taken shelter for the night. The rest of the Company were close by, while Queen Demeter and her army were resting a longer distance off.

Even though it was the ocean in which Apollo's global odyssey had begun, and in which it would end, he did not know the answer but Zeus did. "The name was given to it by a human explorer named Magellan who found the ocean very peaceful when he sailed westward from the Straits named after him at Cape Horn all the way to these waters where we are now. Pacifique means peaceful in the French language."

"Are these seas peaceful?" asked Pan.

"Hardly," interjected Ares. "La Mer Sauvage, or Savage Sea, would have been a better name, and it is a name that Magellan might have given it had he seen its true nature." (As I told you when my tale began, beings learn the languages of the humans who live on the margins of their watery world, and in the Guardians' case, they had come in contact with a French adventurer who spent his entire life trying to save the oceans of the world. It now appeared that the Frenchman's dream might have died with him but that did not make it any less worthy to the beings who had known and loved him.)

"Sometimes it is savage but sometimes not," said Aegyptus, always one to add a touch of moderation to his brother's penchant for melodrama.

Zeus nodded. "Aegyptus is right. To use one adjective to describe the enormity of this vast body of water is akin to trying to take the measure of all whalekind, or mankind for that matter, by virtue of the actions of only a few."

"Like King Poseidon has done?" asked Pan.

"Exactly," replied Zeus. "Very good, little one."

Pan was delighted by Zeus' praise and it did not bother him at all that Zeus called him little because at that moment he felt as big as a Blue Whale, in spirit if not bulk He wiggled his body from side to side and tilted his head to see if the others were paying attention. They were and it made Pan's heart swell. In his entire life before he had left the safety of the Gulf of Mexico and headed out across the Atlantic Ocean in search of the Kingdom of the Ancients, he had never felt that he belonged anywhere; that he was part of something greater than himself. But at that moment, he truly began to believe that he could accomplish anything. It was a feeling that would serve him well in the days to come.

Zeus continued, "It is often better not to judge any than to judge all as one."

"We hope that we do not see the Pacific's savage side," added Pan.

The great whale did not answer. His stare drifted away from the Company, past the land and waters that surrounded them, out toward the mighty ocean upon whose fringes they now rested and he began to speak in soft and dulcet tones:

> *Hear us oh great and restless sea,*
> *oh wondrous ocean deep and wide.*
> *Your boundaries all beings keep,*
> *your storms and tempests we abide.*
> *Pray let us pass in the days to come,*
> *free from thy wrath, safe on thy tides.*
> *That we may cross thy mighty plains,*
> *and suffer not like those who died.*
> *And in the end, with our journey done,*
> *may we to thee simple sojourners be.*
> *Once here in time and place, then gone,*
> *from thee oh great and restless sea.*

As Zeus spoke his last few words, the others in the Company drifted off into a half-sleep; all but Ares that is, who took the first watch, and Zeus, of course, who never slept. Zeus told Ares he would be back at dawn and disappeared into the shadows. Meanwhile, Ares, fortified by Zeus' prayer and confident in his own muscular body, powerful jaws with their deadly rows of teeth, and war-hardened spirit, began to prowl the waters of the night. In the Battle of Malacca, Ares had killed many of his enemies and he was prepared to kill many more. Indeed, he had grown to like killing. Some would say too much.

Contrary to what many among your kind might believe, the open oceans thousands of miles from the nearest land are sterile marine deserts; vast featureless bodies of water deep and wide, with their surface layers all but devoid of flora and fauna. This is particularly true for the Pacific Ocean. In both longitude and latitude, it is the largest body of water on earth, stretching over eight thousand miles from the Bering Sea in the north to the Ross Sea in the south, and nearly eleven thousand miles from the coast of Columbia in the east to the Straits of Malacca in the west. It also contains the lowest point on earth and the deepest part of any ocean known as the Mariana Trench, an area that reaches depths of over thirty-five thousand feet and into which Mount Everest could be placed with over a mile of water above it.

However, there are two exceptions to the barrenness of the Pacific Ocean; the first are the places where its two main gyres and the complex system of equatorial currents and counter currents that divide them, meet to form invisible barriers that catch and hold the plankton that rise up from the deeps. There, billions of tiny organisms form great, snaking masses of living food chains that drift just below the surface and attract great schools of fish such as sardines or mackerel, which in turn bring in the large ocean predators, like marlin, sailfish, sharks and, of course, whales and dolphins.

The second exception to the desolateness of the Pacific Ocean are the parallel chains of volcanic islands and their extensions in the form of submerged seamounts that represent one of the most striking features of the world's largest body of water. And it was toward one of these chains that Apollo and his Company of the Light, and Queen Demeter and her army, headed at dawn the next morning. Their objective was the Johnston Atoll seven hundred and fifty miles west of the Hawaiian Islands, and four thousand miles east northeast of where they had spent the night. Their journey would first take them through the Federated States of Micronesia and then past the Marshall Islands, tiny pinpoints of land in the middle of the ocean, until at last they reached the Johnston Atoll, one of the most isolated atolls in the world. It is comprised of four islands, the largest of which is called Johnston Island.

The American military used the atoll as a nuclear weapon test site after World War II, and later as a storage and disposal site for chemical and radioactive materials. The islands were subsequently turned over to the Fish and Wildlife Service of the U.S. Department of the Interior. Despite their reassignment as a wildlife refuge, their history as part of man's open-air testing and storage of weapons of mass destruction was the reason that King Poseidon had chosen the site as the gathering point for the armies of the Federation as they prepared for war with man. It was not a part of his kingdom where he or other beings often ventured but now it suited his purposes perfectly and therefore, it was also the locus of the five converging Loyalists armies who were coming to stop him.

On that bright and clear morning in early May, as Apollo and his Company left the protected waters off Mindanao behind them, thoughts of what lay ahead, in terms of both the long distance they still had to cover, and the deadly confrontation that was waiting for them, pushed the memory of the Battle of Malacca out of their minds. Instead, their heads were filled with a collective ennui that made just the simple act of swimming through the unusually calm seas an almost Herculean task. Within one hundred miles of their starting point the bottom fell away, dropping from several hundred feet deep where they had spent the night to the twenty thousand foot depths of the Philippines' Trench. This rendered the active pinging of their earsight quickly unusable, even for Zeus.

"We do not like the deeps," said Pan as they reached the western edge of the trench that was twenty-five miles wide at the point where they would cross it. The water through which they were swimming was so clear, so pristine, that it lacked form and substance. It was as if they were hanging suspended in a vast empty space bounded only by distant walls of royal blue that receded before them; while overhead, the shimmering surface of silver made it appear that the entire world had been turned upside down, with sky below and sea above. It was a topsy-turvy world that fooled the senses and made Pan all the more uncomfortable and disoriented. He glanced down into the hazy blueness far below and asked, "Are there dragons down there?"

"No," replied Apollo with a chuckle. "But there are real kraken, so keep moving, my friend, keep moving."

"Never look down! Never look back," whispered the little Harbor Porpoise to himself, and as he said it, the memories of his own journey alone to the Kingdom of the Ancients flashed across his mind. That trip had turned out to be a safe one, thanks in large part to the two brave Orcas who now flanked him on this journey, and their late brother. The shadows of their large black bodies slicing through the waters beside him gave him a measure of confidence that he might just survive this journey as well. Whether or not the same would hold true for what lay at the end of the journey was an entirely different matter. But best not dwell on that now he thought.

Once the Company crossed the invisible line that separated the littoral seas from the open ocean, they seemed to draw strength from the very waters through which they passed, as if in some unexplained way, the mighty Pacific Ocean had listened to Zeus' prayer and conferred on them its support for their noble cause. As a result, their passage through Micronesia and the Marshall Islands, although almost double the first leg in distance, took the same amount of time. Each night whenever possible they rested above one of the seamounts of the volcanic archipelagoes through which they were traveling, or in the lee shelter of an up-thrusting island covered in lush green vegetation: the later being the relatively younger cousin of the former. Once a volcano became extinct, the winds and the waves began the inexorable process of grinding the island down from pointed peak with fringing reef, to rounded hump with barrier reef, to coral atoll with flatland strips of silver sand, until at last all vestiges of land and reef were gone, slipped beneath the hungry sea.

With the forbearance of the sea, whose dangers they had escaped so far, their journey had been uneventful until early one day in late May as they passed an uninhabited atoll in the Ratak Chain of the Marshall Islands. It was the last such archipelago they would encounter before crossing a two-thousand mile wide featureless stretch of bluewater that lay between them and the Johnston Atoll, and it was there that they came upon a heartbreaking scene. Their earsight had announced it long before they neared the atoll and when they drew close everyone except Zeus spyhopped and what they saw chilled their souls more deeply than the tropical seas could ever warm their bodies. Clutching tightly to the wreckage of a large sailboat that was aground upon a coral reef, they saw two children, a boy, and a girl, neither one yet ten years old. The children were obviously terrified and the blisters on their faces told Apollo and the others that they had been there at least a day or two, but no longer or they would not have been there at all.

"Oh dear, oh dear," said Pan. "What happened to them? Where are their parents?"

"I think what happened is obvious," said Apollo. "Through either storm or navigation error they were shipwrecked upon the reef and whatever adults there were are now lost to the sea."

"It was neither storm nor poor navigation that placed them there," said Ares in a low, guttural growl. "Look at those marks on the side of the hull. Those were made by collisions with beings not rocks. And there are teeth marks of an Orca on the broken rudder."

Zeus now spyhopped as well but he was careful not to rise up too high out of the water lest his massive bulk frighten the children more than they already were and send them to their deaths. Once he slipped back under the surface he told the others, "Ares is right. That boat was sunk by beings, likely members of the Guardians who are traveling with Eris back to join Poseidon."

"What do we do?" asked Pan.

"There is nothing we can do," said Ares, "other than kill their killers."

"In due course," said Apollo, "but for now we must save the children."

"With all due respect, Apollo," said Ares, "to try to reach them would risk stranding ourselves on the reef, and even if we could, what would we do when we got to them?"

Apollo was undeterred by Ares' challenge. He looked at Zeus. "We passed a break in this reef a half a mile back. If you swim back there and come up on the inside of the lagoon, and breach near the reef, the wave from your body might be enough to free the wreckage."

"And then what?" asked Ares. It was obvious that the Guardian was becoming vexed with Apollo. Ever since he and his brother were reunited with Apollo and Pan, the relationship between Ares and Apollo had been strained. Apollo sensed that there was something behind it but he had not yet chosen to raise the matter.

"When it washes off the reef, we will rescue the children and take them to that inhabited island we passed earlier," said Apollo.

Ares disagreed. "Even if Zeus can dislodge the boat, how will the children know our intentions? The very sight of me or my brother swimming toward them with our dorsal fins towering above them would be enough to frighten them to death before we could save them."

"You are right, Ares. Pan and I will save the children."

Pan piped up. "*Yes!* We will save the children." Then he gave Apollo a puzzled look and asked, "How will we save them? How will they know what to do unless…" He caught himself. "Unless you do a mindlink with them."

"Exactly."

"And break the Tenth Commandment?" asked Ares in disbelief.

"Yes. It is the right thing to do," stated Aegyptus.

Zeus nodded. "I agree. We must hurry for the children will not last much longer. When I am in position I will sound my call." He moved his massive bulk swiftly away from them toward the gap in the reef.

Apollo turned to Ares and locked eyes with the Guardian, probing beyond their glassy surface into his soul and said softly, "Ares, my friend and protector, I have already broken the Tenth Commandment once, and in a more selfish and less worthy cause than this. If in saving these children and breaking the law of our ancestors again, I am dooming myself to spend eternity in hell, then so be it. There are some causes that transcend the laws of our ancestors." Apollo paused and then said softly, "Trust me, Ares, for I know what I am doing."

Ares nodded. There was no hostility in it but neither was their warmth. Apollo knew that he would soon have to address the growing gap between them but this was neither the time nor place. Apollo added, "I want you to go tell the Queen what we are doing, but do not mention the mindlink. Tell her to continue on her way and that we will catch up with them later."

Ares swam off and Apollo turned back to Pan and asked, "Are you ready?"

"Yes, Master," came the reply. "We are ready."

Apollo pretended to be annoyed. "I wish you would stop calling me that." However, the truth was he did not mind it when Pan called him Master because he sensed that it made Pan feel more secure when he did it. With others, however, it was a different matter.

"We cannot, for you are all that the term implies, and more."

Apollo looked at Aegyptus. "Watch out for kraken. If any come near kill them."

With a wry smile, the Guardian replied, "It will be my pleasure."

Apollo and Pan got ready and within a few minutes, the booming sound of the great whale rumbled through the seas on both sides of the reef and soon a wave of monstrous proportions pushed the wrecked boat off the reef, out over the dark blue waters beyond, where Apollo and Pan were waiting. Before it sank, Apollo drew up close to the overturned hull and spoke with the children, sending his words directly into their minds in a way they had never heard before or ever would again, but with such power, balanced with tenderness that they did what they were bid; they released their grip on the wreckage and grabbed onto the dorsal fins of the beings, the little boy to Apollo and his sister to Pan. Soon they were off, heading along the surface on the watery path that separated the deserted atoll from the heavily populated island several miles away.

Once there, Apollo and Pan took the children to the pristine shallows of the lagoon where several women waded out to take the orphans into their loving embrace; while out past the reef, the dorsal fins of two Killer Whales and the broad back of a Humpback Whale swam in a lazy circle in the waters of a great and, on this day at least, tranquil sea. The islanders were not surprised by what was happening, for it was not the first time that they had seen dolphins saving humans. Leaving their charges in the care of the women Apollo and Pan tipped their heads and then swam away.

"Do you think the children will tell?" asked Pan as they swam out of the lagoon.

"It does not matter because no one will believe them," replied Apollo.

"Pity. If human adults listened more to children, the world would be a better place."

Later when the children were reunited with their grandparents in America, they told them that the white dolphin and the little porpoise were angels sent by their parents from heaven to save them. And that these angels had spoken to them. As Apollo predicted, no one believed them. One day perhaps they would.

It was a powerful and poignant experience for the Company of the Light and as they headed out across the deep blue sea that lay before them, their hearts were filled with the joy that comes from giving selflessly to others, and their spirits were lifted above the very waves through which their streamlined bodies were now swimming. It was a grand and glorious moment and even though each member of the Company knew it would not last, that did not dull its immensity.

"We did well today, Apollo, did we not?" said Pan as he skimmed along the waves beside him.

"Yes, you did," replied Apollo with a smile.

"We *both* did," added Pan. For a while, they swam in silence until Pan broke it once more. "Apollo," he said, not yet ready to fall into the quiet mode of travel.

"Yes, Pan?"

"We love you."

Apollo was taken aback by Pan's words. He drifted over closer to his stalwart little companion who had come so far and done so much. Apollo reached out with his right flipper and touched Pan's left one and with deep conviction said, "I love you too, little one."

It was an appellation of affection that Pan had come to treasure but given his penchant for mischief, he could not resist replying, "We are glad. But we must remind you that we are not little. We are quite large for our size."

They both laughed in the way of beings and Pan did a quick little barrel roll around Apollo as they swam together. It would be the last time that they smiled in a very long time.

CHAPTER TWENTY-TWO

The Right Of Challenge

When Apollo and the Company arrived at Johnston Atoll, the scene that greeted them was dire. A state of siege and sadness had overtaken that desolate strip of sand and coral in the center of the Pacific Ocean. Overhead, the turbulent skies of an on-rushing typhoon had smothered the sun and unleashed a deluge of rain that roared across the waves, ripping off their tops and sending the surging seas into a state of chaos, while below the surface, a storm of equal proportions was brewing in the tormented minds of the thousands of beings gathered there. To Apollo, the tempestuous scene formed a fitting backdrop for what was about to happen as the forces of good and evil were poised on the edge of the abyss, both literally and figuratively. For millennia, the world of whales and dolphins had been free from the bitter potion of war, which had served as a heady elixir to the armies of mankind throughout history. But now, as the Company drew near to the atoll, the gray and angry seas were thick with fear and foreboding. Everywhere the Company looked, the sights and sounds of the imminent battle filled the ocean, and the overpowering presence of what was about to happen, near that flat and isolated atoll paralyzed their minds, pained their hearts and pummeled their souls.

Below the tumult of the surface, whales and dolphins of all sizes and shapes struggled to hold their positions on opposite sides of an imaginary line that ran in a diagonal direction, southwest to northeast, along the length of the six-mile reef with the atoll located at its center. Seven armies, one drawn from each of the Seven Seas, faced each other across the line, with two armies of the Federation to the north of it, and five Loyalist armies to the south. But these numbers were deceiving because the Federation's forces outnumbered their Loyalist adversaries three to two. And now, as these two great, living and breathing, killing machines faced each other across that sickening stretch of savage waters, the weather deteriorated even further as the full fury of the typhoon fell upon them.

It was the 20th of June, the eve of Godlight, but what a godforsaken Godlight this would be; for at dawn everything good that had ever been, or might have been, in the world of beings would vanish forever. Along with the thousands of lives that would soon be lost would come the loss of the one thing that their world could never regain; innocence: something that the world of man had lost so very long ago. What had started one year earlier as an angry protest by the rebel King Poseidon at the Gathering half a world away, had now brought whalekind full in the face of war. And as night fell on the ocean, no one knew how to escape the maelstrom of evil that swirled about then, threatening to suck them into the deeps; but everyone knew the time for talking was done. Nothing remained now but to fight and die.

Ironically, Poseidon had not wanted war with his own kind. That had never been his purpose. Driven by hatred for the arrogant two-legged beings with whom whalekind shared Planet Ocean, the King had intended that the Federation would begin its attack on humans on Godlight, nothing more; but the Loyalists armies spread out before him intended to put an end to what they saw as his madness nothing less. As that long day journeyed into an even longer night, the renegade King and his mistress Queen, Eris, met with their war council in the somewhat sheltered waters inside the reef, where they planned their strategy for the coming battle.

Meanwhile, to the southeast, what was left of the Sovereign Council formed a council of war. Among them were three queens, Hera, Demeter and Selene, and two kings, Pluto and Triton. Unlike their opponents, they were not so fortunate to have protected waters in which to meet. They were congregated beneath the roiling waves three miles from the front line while their five armies lay like a giant sea snake alongside the line, waiting to be sprung into battle.

In all, it was the largest gathering of beings ever to assemble on Planet Ocean in one place, at one time, and were it not for its deadly purpose; it would have been magnificent in its magnitude. Despite its geographical isolation, the congregation of thousands upon thousands of beings might have been witnessed by sailors passing by or the pilots of aircraft high overhead. As it was the typhoon had ensured that there were no human eyes within a hundred miles of what was about to be a self-inflicted slaughter of whales on a scale that no human whaler could ever have imagined in his wildest dreams. Fifty thousand whales and dolphins waited impatiently along both sides of the seven mile reef. They waited for the dawn that they hoped would bring an end to the storm and calm the angry seas. They waited for the dawn that would bring the orders to send them into battle; a battle from which many knew they would not return. But mostly they waited simply for the waiting to end, as the prolonged prospect of death was worse than death itself.

As this horrible drama was about to unfold, the rest of whalekind hovered in a sad and lonely silence throughout the Seven Seas as their world prepared to tear itself apart. It was almost more than their hearts and minds could bear for theirs had always been a race apart; each individual being a reflection of the bright and shining stars that rose each night over the oceans far from the land where mankind lived lives of lesser existence. While humans engaged in an endless succession of wars, beings had remained at peace, not allowing hatred to dim their stars; and for millennia, neither friend nor foe had been able to extinguish them. Any and all disputes had been settled without collective bloodshed. While death by their own kind was not unknown to beings, it had never found them in rows and ranks as those seven armies were now. And so it was, that a once great race of beings under God was no longer pure, and the evils of man had finally spread its contagion to the last race of innocent beings on the planet.

With the ruins of a shattered sensibility spread across the troubled seas, the last best hope to avoid death and self-destruction upon the waves lay with a white dolphin, named Apollo. With that crushing burden resting upon him, Apollo entered the battle zone accompanied by the Company of the Light; four beings who had journeyed with him half way around the globe; Pan, a brave little Harbor Porpoise, Ares and Aegyptus, two battle-hardened Killer Whales and Zeus, a mysterious and mighty Humpback Whale. There were no cheering crowds to greet them, no fanfare, or great expectations. Instead, they slipped silently through the ranks of the Loyalist armies and joined the Sovereign Council in their hour of deepest despair and greatest need.

After subdued greetings, Apollo briefed the Council on the tragedy that had unfolded in the Straits of Malacca. When he was finished, a silence fell upon the Council; one that even the normally loquacious Pan chose not to break. Finally, Queen Hera spoke. "We are honored to have you and your army join us, Queen Demeter, and we thank you for the sacrifice that your forces made in that first battle of this war. I know I speak for Kings Pluto and Triton, when I say how grateful we are to have you and Queen Selene part of the Loyalist cause," she glanced approvingly at Apollo and the Company, "thanks to Apollo and his Company of the Light." Apollo acknowledged her with a polite nod but there was no joy in it. Hera continued, "However, it grieves me to say that even with your help, I fear tomorrow holds no victory for our cause. Our armies are tired from their long journeys around the three capes, while those of Poseidon and Eris are rested and ready for battle; and their commanders know these waters far better than do ours."

The others accepted what the Queen was saying without debate but it was left to the newest royal among them, Queen Selene, to raise the question that lay heavily upon all their minds. She looked nervously around the ring of monarchs, honored guests, and said, "If you will indulge me, Queen Hera, even as I have led my army here in honor of my fallen King and mate, I have struggled with how it could have come to this? How is it that we are gathered here on the eve of a battle that will decide the fate of whalekind, and quite possibly that of the entire planet as well, when for generations stretching back to the time of the Ancients, beings have avoided the plague of war. Have we now become what we have so long detested in humans, arrogant, intolerant and stupid? Have the ravages of pollution, plundering, and global warming that he has inflicted upon the seas, poisoned our hearts and minds even as they are destroying our bodies?" She paused and shook her head in frustration.

To your kind, a Southern Right Whale is not the most sleek or graceful of all the great whales but as she spoke, there was an elegance about her that transcended her physical form and seemed to grow in proportion to her passion. She began again, "While these are the latest and perhaps the most terrible of man's evils, surely there have been other evils perpetrated upon us by mankind down through the millennia; trials and tribulations that we have somehow been able to withstand without it coming to this. How is it that we are brought to this terrible turning point at this time and place? Is Poseidon the devil?—or are we all devils in a choir of death and he is but our conductor?"

For a long moment, no one spoke as furtive glances flashed through the darkening waters, forcing each being to use earsight to gauge the reactions of the other. Queen Hera was the first to reply. "Queen Selene, you have raised telling questions, which I possess neither the wisdom nor insight to answer. I can only remind us all that this is what the Ancients foretold to us in the Legend of the Light." Without pausing, she recited the lines that everyone knew well:

> *And it shall come to pass in the day that*
> *the Lord shall make his Light to shine*
> *upon the mighty waters under Heaven.*
> *The spirit of the Lord shall come upon you,*
> *and he will drive darkness from the face of the*
> *deep and deliver the great whales from evil.*

After which, all but one recited;

> *God be praised.*
> *God bring us the Light.*

The being who did not respond was Apollo, for his heart was heavy as he wrestled with the self-doubt and fear that he had failed them. Was he not the Chosen One, the Prince of Light, whom God had appointed to save whalekind from destruction? And yet what had he done, what solutions had he brought to them to deliver them from this evil? And even as he asked this of himself, he was certain that the others around him were thinking the same thought but were too polite to say it. Apollo looked at Pan, hoping he would find a clue to the answer in the little one's eyes but he found none there. *And now even you, my talkative little friend, are given to silence,* Apollo thought. *Oh God. Why have you brought me here if not to be your Light?*

No one else chose to address Queen Selene's comments and the gathering fell silent once more. Finally, the mighty Zeus spoke up and just as he did, the eye of the typhoon reached the Johnston Atoll: the seas became calm and the winds above them died, as if even the angels in heaven wanted to hear him speak. "Your Majesties, and my fellow sojourners, I believe I have the answer to the central question that Queen Selene has so eloquently placed before this august body. There is a reason why beings have not gone to war in recent millennia but lest you think it is because we are so superior to man that war is beyond our will, or that we are without evil ways; it is not and we are not. While it is true that for over two hundred generations even the thought of war, let alone the reality of it, has not crossed our minds. During the past five millennia, we have been living in an era of enlightenment, while man has dwelt in darkness.

"But back before this five thousand year reign of peace in Planet Ocean, there were many times when the kings of that day—and only kings for there were no queens then—sought to fight each other in wars that would have been the equal of that which now faces us. There were many more kings and kingdoms than there are now, and angry disputes between neighboring kingdoms were not unknown. However, mass bloodshed was avoided by an ancient right that these kings invoked and by which they lived. It was called the Right of Challenge and under it, a monarch who had a grievance against another king, or who aspired to take over another king's domain, could invoke this right and the one who was challenged could not refuse it. Each king would select a champion who would fight to the death. No mercy was asked or ever given, and the winner took all. There were only three rules governing this combat; first, the challenge fight had to be among the same species for obvious reasons; second, the king being challenged had the right to pick his champion first, and third, there was no appeal of the outcome."

Zeus paused as his words sunk in. Then he added, "For countless millennia back to the beginning of time, the ancient Right of Challenge ruled the Seven Seas, and it prevented war between the kingdoms; but then gradually the need for it began to fade away, as our kind became more civilized. Finally, at some point in our history, as jealousy and greed dissipated, the Right faded into the deeps of history, forgotten to all but a few." Finished with his explanation, Zeus looked at Queen Selene. "Your Grace, that is why whalekind does not know war. It is not that its evil was unknown to our kind, simply that we dealt with it in a different manner."

Queen Selene nodded. She was as impressed with the concept of the ancient right as she was by the fact that Zeus seemed to be the only one who knew about it. But before she could make any comment, King Triton asked, "Can the king represent himself?" It was a leading question, and its hidden meaning was not lost on any of them, for Triton was a big and powerful Sperm Whale and they knew that he would gladly fight Poseidon for the future of whalekind, even unto death.

But Zeus quashed the notion. "No. A king may not be his own champion," He added, "And by the same token, nor can a queen."

"How did the victor know that the vanquished would honor the outcome?" asked Ares.

"He did not but in the history of whalekind no monarch ever reneged."

"How do you know all this, Zeus?" asked King Pluto.

"I learned it from my father." He did not elaborate.

The King was not satisfied. "Who was your...?"

Queen Hera interrupted Pluto. "Does it matter?" Her question was rhetorical and it was obvious that Queen Hera did not like where the conversation was heading. She turned to Zeus and demanded, "Are you suggesting we invoke this ancient right now?"

Zeus ignored the confrontational tone of her question. "I am not suggesting anything, your Grace. I was simply explaining how it was that our kind had never fought in any wars. It is up to the Sovereign Council to decide if this is worthy of consideration. I am simply the messenger not the message," he added with a knowing smile.

"With all due respect, Zeus," Hera began with more than a hint of sarcasm in her voice, "We are not going to risk the future of our world upon the abilities of one being, regardless of how willing and able he, or she, may be." She said it with an air of finality that only she was ready to accept. "We will proceed with…"

"Excuse me, Queen Hera," interrupted King Triton, "but you contradict yourself. Only moments ago you were opining as to the likelihood of our defeat tomorrow and now, you seem willing to go blindly into battle without considering an intriguing alternative; one that I believe deserves consideration."

His tone was respectful but only barely so and Pan noticed a distinct change in the tenor of the Council's interactions with each other compared to when he had first appeared before it.

"I do not wish to discuss this further," Hera replied raising her voice and growing visibly agitated. And the agitation of a Blue Whale was not something to be taken lightly especially by beings of much smaller physical size such as Apollo and Pan. However, neither made any move to distance themselves from her, as she arched her back slightly in the threatening pose characteristic of a great whale.

"Queen Hera, I think it would be wise to hear your peers out," said Zeus. His voice was deep and strong, and the look in his eyes had a calming influence upon her. Zeus knew that she meant well but she had chosen the wrong time and the wrong place to try to impose her views on the others, and her adversarial manner created a problem for Ares and Aegyptus, whose primary responsibility was to protect her. They looked to Zeus for direction and with a simple nod of his head and a calming look in his eyes; he reassured them that everything would be all right.

However, Triton was neither calmed by Zeus nor intimidated by Hera. In his new role of King of the South Atlantic Ocean, after having replaced the traitorous King Dionysus, he was the youngest and most outspoken of the monarchs and he carried himself with a self-confidence bordering on brashness typical of Sperm Whales. "Queen Hera, this is *not* the Gathering, and you are *no longer* our Moderator. I for one think we should invoke the ancient Right of Challenge with King Poseidon. I submit that it may be our only hope." His words were strong but there was still a measure of respect in the way he uttered them. (For obvious reasons, there would be no Gathering on this Godlight, and therefore no Moderator. Ironically, had there been one, it was scheduled to occur in the North Pacific and King Poseidon would have filled that role.)

"Very well," said Hera with a hint of displeasure still in her voice, but her stiff posture relaxed slightly, which was a sign that the confrontation had passed. Then she looked at the other monarchs and asked, "What would you suggest that we do?"

King Pluto spoke next. "I agree with King Triton. We should invoke the Right of Challenge. Poseidon may refuse in which case we have lost nothing and if he accepts, I think we know who he will choose as his champion."

"Who?" asked Queen Selene.

"The Guardian, Orion," said Pluto.

"Yes," said Aegyptus. "Orion is the half-brother of Paris but stronger and more cunning than his sibling was."

"And crueler of heart," added Aegyptus.

With a steely look in his cold eyes, Ares said, "I can take him. Let me go speak with Poseidon. I will get him to accept the challenge and then I will fight Orion. And I will kill him."

Lady Selene was impressed by the Guardian's intensity. "I believe you could, Ares." She turned to Queen Hera. "I agree with Triton and Pluto."

Queen Hera glanced at Queen Demeter who reluctantly shook her head yes. And that was that. Hera looked around the Council and said, "So let it be done." She turned to Zeus and asked, "How should we proceed? Shall I go to see King Poseidon or should we let Ares?"

"Neither," replied Zeus. "Send Apollo." Ares was surprised and disappointed but he knew better than to challenge Zeus.

"Why Apollo?" asked Hera.

"Because Apollo is the only one among us whom Poseidon fears." Zeus said it with a matter-of-factness that forestalled debate. "You all know that during the time that Apollo and his Company of the Light journeyed here, word that he was the Chosen One spread far and wide across the Seven Seas. And it is precisely this perception that Poseidon fears more than the reality of whether or not Apollo is in fact the embodiment of the Legend of the Ancients."

"I do not understand," said Queen Selene.

"It is not Apollo himself but what he has come to represent, which poses the greatest threat to Poseidon's power; because it gives our Loyalist forces the one thing that can sway the coming battle in our favor, which is hope: hope for victory over the Federation, hope for a brighter future than that which Poseidon has forecast, and most of all, hope that God has not turned his back on whalekind as Poseidon believes he has done to man. The truth is that even among his own forces, Poseidon knows that Apollo has become larger than life, and whether he is, or is not the Chosen One no longer matters. Even more than you realize, Apollo's perceived power holds great sway over Poseidon's actual power, and as such if any among us can convince him to accept the Right of Challenge, it is Apollo."

When Zeus finished speaking, there was no further debate. They all agreed that Apollo would leave at once and with him would go their hopes of a way to avoid war.

An hour later, after Apollo had crossed the deserted zone between the two armies, he found himself face-to-face with Poseidon and Eris who floated like two giant shadows above the large Table Coral that covered the lagoon off the northeast shore of Johnston Island. With them were several of their Guardians but Python was nowhere to be seen.

The eye of the typhoon was still upon them and a nervous moon shone down from between the circling clouds, casting a ghostly glow upon the ocean. Pan had refused to stay behind, and now hovered close beside Apollo. As he had from the moment they went over the edge in what seemed an eternity ago, Pan insisted upon sharing Apollo's fate whatever that might be, and this, perhaps the last and greatest moment of Apollo's odyssey, was no exception.

It was a strange scene with the two great whales facing a dolphin and a porpoise in the calm waters of the lagoon; it would be long remembered by those among the Federation's forces, who witnessed it. When word reached King Poseidon that Apollo wanted to talk, he had agreed at once, which had infuriated Eris. And now after hearing what Apollo had to say, she became even angrier. "Please tell me, King that you do not intend to accept this preposterous challenge?" Eris demanded.

Poseidon ignored her question and instead focused his attention on Apollo, whose white skin radiated an ethereal glow. For a long while the King remained silent, then just when Pan was convinced, they would both be put to death; Poseidon began to speak in a strange, soft tone as his mind drifted away to a kinder, gentler time and place. "Once when I was very young, I remember the elders among my tribe talking about this ancient ritual." He stared off into the dark waters beyond the edge of the reef, where the bottom fell away toward the deeps. "I remember how they admired both the victors and the vanquished. It was a time of honor and duty, of great kings and a greater glory, a time for all times, before man spoiled everything…" For a moment, he fell silent, and then suddenly, he returned to the present. He looked back at Apollo and without further discussion, said, "I accept." With a wry smile he added, "Although I suppose, if we are to follow the ways of the ancient kings, I really had no choice but to accept the challenge, did I?"

Apollo's expression was flat and cold, "No. You did not." Pan said nothing. This had been a condition of him being allowed to accompany Apollo. Moreover, he was intimidated by Eris who kept eying him as if he were a school of herring that at any moment she would suck into her enormous mouth. Apollo stared at the Sperm Whale and added, "Now you must choose your champion."

Pan glanced at Orion, who seemed all to eager to fight…

"So I must." Poseidon's eyes were locked on Apollo's and for a long moment, they seemed oblivious to those gathered around them. Slowly, an evil smile spread along the full length of the Sperm Whale's narrow mouth. Then, lowering his voice to a deep rumble, he answered, "I choose…Python."

"Python!" blurted Pan unable to remain silent upon hearing the name.

"Yes—Python," replied Poseidon without taking his eyes off the white dolphin.

The look on Apollo's face was one of quiet satisfaction. This did not go unnoticed by Pan. For an instant, the little Harbor Porpoise was puzzled but then it hit him. "Oh my," he muttered to himself. "Oh my." He realized then that it had not been Poseidon's choice at all because destiny had made the choice for him, just as it had driven every choice that each of them had made ever since Poseidon abandoned the

Gathering. And in that realization, Pan lost any fear that he had had regarding the future. All would end well. It had to. It just had to.

"Ah yes. Our black dolphin with the heart to match," said, Queen Eris. "Good choice," she murmured. "Very good."

"So be it!" said Apollo.

"Who will be the champion for your side?" asked Poseidon. It was a rhetorical question. He knew there could only be one answer.

Without equivocation Apollo replied, "I will."

Pan acknowledged the answer with a simple nod. He sensed it was coming and he accepted it. But he also knew that Queen Hera and the Council would not be pleased. They were certain that King Poseidon would choose Orion, and had instructed Apollo to announce Ares as their champion. The Council had not considered any other outcome, but now that Apollo had given his reply, the Council was honor bound, regardless of the consequences, and what monumental consequences they would be.

"Done!" said an ebullient Poseidon. "Tomorrow, you and Python will fight to the death" He paused then added with the self-satisfaction of a tyrant who believed his side has already won, "Winner takes all. If you win, the war with mankind will be abandoned. But if Python wins, the war will begin with the full force and fury of every being in the seven armies from the Seven Seas. Agreed?"

Apollo answered, "Agreed."

Without further discussion, Apollo started to swim away with Pan following behind but as they did Poseidon called out after them. "Wait!" They stopped and turned back. Poseidon rolled slightly on his side and stared at Apollo with one wicked eye.

"What is it?" asked Apollo.

"There is something you should know, Apollo." Savoring the moment, Poseidon hung there, black on black, a dark shape looming in the darkness that surrounded them, as if trying to prolong the psychological climax that he was experiencing. Then, when he could hold back his pleasure no longer, he said, "Python is your father." The words slithered off his tongue like squid fat.

Apollo was stunned. Pan was crushed. Eris was startled but her surprise quickly turned to joy. No one moved. No one said anything. The eyes of Apollo and Poseidon were locked again upon each other in an icy stare. With an evil grin that melted the ice, Poseidon added,

"A pity is it not, that to save the lives of all those who believe in you, you must kill the very being who gave you life?—How ironic.—How delicious.—How perfect!"

For a moment, Apollo did not move or respond. Then, with narrowed eyes and an expression that could freeze brine, he said, "Python did not give me life. God did. And only God can take it away." With that, Apollo turned and, accompanied by Pan, he swam away.

The journey back to the Loyalist lines was not a pleasant one for either of them. The brief intermission in the storm had come to an abrupt end and with crashing thunder and unremitting flashes of lightening, the typhoon returned with a vengeance. As they left the confines of the lagoon and headed out across open water, the deepening tempest of sea and sky only served to accentuate the crisis that had enveloped their world.

"Apollo?" shouted Pan as he struggled to keep up through the frenzied swells as sea below and sky above fused into one. Except for their necessary rises to breathe, the two beings stayed beneath the surface lest they be blown off course and get lost in the seamless liquid universe that had engulfed them.

"Yes, Pan," replied the brooding white dolphin as he plowed ahead, seemingly oblivious to the storm.

"Are you really going to fight your father?"

"I have no choice."

Pan thought about it for a long moment and then with the innocence of a child, Pan asked, "But if you kill him, how will you ever be able to come home with us to our nostos? How could you face your mother and the tribe?"

Apollo stopped dead in the dark water as did Pan. He faced his little companion and spoke words that cut into Pan more sharply than any kraken's bite ever could. "I *will* kill him because I *must*. But it does not matter that I do. What I told you that night in the Southern Ocean was a lie. I will not return to our nostos with you."

Pan began to tremble. He tried not to cry as anger was mixed with sadness inside him. "Will you ever return?"

"I do not know." It was the truth. Apollo did not know, but then he added, "And I do not care." It was an unkind cut to someone who had loved him and followed him half way around the world.

Pan said nothing more. His heart was broken.

When they reached the Sovereign Council, Pan barely listened as Apollo briefed Queen Hera and the others about what had happened. It did not surprise Pan when the Council expressed their shock and dismay at the outcome of the discussion, or when Queen Hera tried to convince the others that they should rescind their challenge. The Council adamantly rejected her proposal.

Apollo was angered that she would doubt him and left the Council to be alone. Pan did not follow him. He was disgusted with the entire matter, and wished he could be anywhere but there. *Apollo had lied to him. Lied,* he thought. *And he did not care. What did it matter now whether Apollo lived or died? Even if he did win, they would not be together in nostos. And what if there was no God, what if this was all there was to life, an endless struggle through a life of quiet desperation followed by eternal darkness? What if...what if?* It was too much for the little one to deal with. Perhaps if he could just get some sleep; perhaps everything would be better in the morning. Perhaps. Or perhaps not.

But sleep would not come easily to Pan that night. As the winds of the typhoon stirred the seas into a cauldron, it became increasingly difficult for the little being to get his breath at the surface while fully awake, let alone in the semi-consciousness of sleep. Aegyptus noticed that Pan was in distress, both physical and emotional and after leaving Ares to guard Queen Hera, Aegyptus took Pan back across the line separating the two armies. There, in the lee shore of Hikina Island, the most easterly of the atoll, they found some relief from the waves and, while Aegyptus guarded Pan, he was finally able to drift off to sleep.

Several hours later, while Pan slept protected by Aegyptus, Apollo and Zeus swam slowly together through the dark waters far beneath the frantic waves. Above the surface, the winds howled and the rain came in horizontal sheets that slashed off the tops of the waves, sending froth tumbling down into the troughs like the decapitated heads of helpless sea creatures but deep below, all was quiet, calm, almost peaceful.

"Tell me, Zeus," said Apollo, "Have I done the right thing?"

Zeus gazed at Apollo with deep affection but for the moment, said nothing, allowing Apollo to give full vent to his mental torment.

Apollo continued, "Am I right in believing that I will win? Or do you think Hera was right? Should we abandon the Challenge and go into battle against the Federation?"

Zeus came to a stop, then in a voice powerful in both its sound and the message it carried, he replied, "No, Apollo. We should not abandon the Right of Challenge. You have done the right thing, the *only* thing that you could have done. You must go forward—it is your destiny."

"My destiny or the will of God?"

"They are one and the same," replied Zeus solemnly. It has always been so, since time began.

Apollo shook his head and in an anguished tone asked, "Why me?—Why here?—Why now?"

At first, Zeus did not answer. Instead he began to shift his great body and it seemed to Apollo that it grew even greater as he did. In slow motion, Zeus arched his back, pulling his head up and extending his flukes downward toward the deeps. Then he spread his white flippers wide apart like the wings of an angel, and as he did, a strange thing began to happen above them. The storm abated, and the surface of the seas grew silent and still. The moon reappeared and shone so brightly that its reflection became a giant pool of liquid light radiating in all directions upon the sea. It cast an intense glow that probed the depths down and around Zeus just like the light had done in the dream Apollo had had in the waters of the Java Sea. And then when all was settled and serene, Zeus began to recite a poem, slowly in a rhythmic cadence that was more whalesong than whalespeak; the words of which came from somewhere deep within his soul:

> *Through the deep bluewaters of our existence*
> *most see nothing more than what lies ahead.*
> *They spend their lives taking in what is given,*
> *giving back only what they do not want or need.*
>
> *But from a chosen few, more is expected,*
> *than to spend their lives in endless ebb and flow.*
> *God breathes in them a tiny breath of greatness,*
> *that becomes a tempest to set where they must go.*
>
> *In these beings there sounds a special calling,*
> *from deep within, it swells with unbound pride.*
> *Until its voice echoes across the oceans,*
> *to drown out evil and cast the devil's pawns aside.*

Like the pale and silent moon whose gentle face,
reflects God's Good Light upon the mighty ocean.
They go forth alone into that dark night,
protected by the glow of heavenly consecration.

For the course of destiny is lonely and unyielding,
a journey on dark currents and fearsome tides.
With enemies in legions rising up against them,
they face this challenge alone and unafraid.

At journey's end with battles won and foes defeated,
they turn away from cheering crowds and victory.
To pause in proudful silence before their God,
then head out again across the great and restless sea.

When Zeus was finished, Apollo remained quiet for a long while. Finally, he asked, "So I am not the first to have been chosen for greatness, or the first to reflect God's Good Light?"

Zeus peered into the white dolphin's eyes. "No. And you will not be the last. But at this moment in our history, you are the one upon who all hope rests."

Apollo nodded slowly, the way beings do when they are deep in thought. "Does that mean there will always be evil in the world?"

Zeus paused before answering. And when he did, it was not what Apollo was hoping to hear. "The battle between good and evil has existed since the beginning of time, on land and in the sea. It will always exist as long as sin dwells in the hearts and minds of man and whale."

"But I thought that we were above that, that this was the first time evil had come to our world?"

Zeus shook his head sadly. "No, Apollo. This is the first time war has come to our world but not evil. Had there been no evil among whalekind there would not have been a need for the Right of Challenge."

Apollo nodded and said nothing more. There was nothing more to say. He knew what he must do and he knew why. And as he had said to Poseidon, the rest was up to God.

CHAPTER TWENTY-THREE

A Thousand Points Of Light

The day that would change the world of whalekind forever dawned over a sea that was itself in a state of change. During the night, a massive cold front had rolled down from the Bering Sea in a sweeping, flanking movement from the north northwest. Born in the frigid canopy that blankets the subpolar gyre, which is comprised of the deeply anchored Alaska and Aleutian Currents in the east and the Oyashio Current in the west, the cold air mass muscled its way into the warm, wet wall of the typhoon and pushed it off to the east. The wind lost its will to wage war upon the waves, and soon the seas that only hours earlier had been heaving mountains of blue-gray liquid concrete, awash in dirty white foam, dissolved into placid swells of aquamarine rolling quietly in regimented rows toward the horizon.

A pale yellow sun rose slowly behind a gauzy curtain of clouds set against a pastel blue sky but even as the weather abated few among the seven great armies who now faced each other expected the rift that had torn their world apart would ever, or could ever, be mended. The unthinkable had now happened; a society of sentient beings, who had lived in peace since the beginning of time, now had come face to face with the one thing they all shared—mortality. Regardless of their beliefs about the justness of their cause, none could deny that whoever won, nothing in their world would ever be the same again. For the wicked ways of war had come to the Seven Seas and would likely never leave.

So it was that in a matter of hours an ending would come to the saga that had gathered them there, and for the first time in the history of Planet Ocean, beings would go into battle against their fellow beings—whale against whale, dolphin against dolphin, and all pairings in between. But before the blood-letting began, beings along both sides of the battle lines, believers and disbelievers alike, floating in the emerald green waters of the far off Pacific Ocean, whispered to themselves, *Please, God, have mercy upon my soul.*

By the time, the sun took its rightful place at the pinnacle of the heavens, the armies were prepared for the battle that most believed would soon commence. They were drawn in more tightly than they had been the night before and were now positioned in several large, three-dimensional formations located in the uppermost layers of the sea. Here and there along the front lines there had been minor skirmishes but no blood had been drawn and no advantage gained. The sea was devoid of any other signs of life for not a single finned creature could be seen anywhere. It was as if the fish knew what was about to happen and had left for parts unknown.

In total, there were roughly twenty thousand beings on the Loyalist side, and one and a half times as many on the Federation side, separated by a chasm in the crystal clear water a mile long, five hundred yards wide and twenty-five thousand feet deep. While the alignment varied somewhat within each of the seven armies, generally beings of the same species were grouped together facing like combatants across the chasm, although there was no rule against inter-species combat. In fact, there were no rules at all since war was new to every one of them, and the killing of other beings was unfamiliar to all but the Transient Orcas among them.

This latter group could only be found on the Federation's side. On orders of King Poseidon no Transients had killed, much less eaten, any beings since the start of his campaign. His strict orders had forced this cannibalistic group to switch their menu to sharks and large pelagic fish. While Poseidon's dictum had been followed on pain of death, there was no doubt in the other beings' minds that just beneath their slick black skin, these Transient Orcas viewed both friend and foe alike as a prospective meal. They were the pariahs of the world of beings and despite Poseidon's orders even their fellow fighters eschewed their company. But the Transients did not care and the only thing that kept them in line was their fear of Poseidon, who had warned them that if they did not obey his orders, every Sperm Whale in every ocean would seek out and destroy their kind. Of course, this presumed that Poseidon would win the war, an outcome that the Transients believed was all but certain.

Located at the center of the Federation's forces were King Poseidon and Queen Eris, along with their war council and army commanders, while directly across from them were Queens Hera, Demeter, and Selene; and Kings, Pluto and Triton; and their respective army groups. The center of the Loyalist side also included Ares and Aegyptus and in between them, Pan, but noticeable by their absence were Zeus and Apollo. Neither of them had been seen by anyone in the Loyalist camp since the night before, causing a few cynics to speculate that Zeus had helped Apollo to flee; however, the vast majority refused to believe that he had.

"There he is," proclaimed Queen Hera with relief in her voice. Everyone turned to look and there, swimming slowly down the topmost layer of the liquid chasm were Apollo and Zeus.

"I knew he would come," said Aegyptus in a whale whisper.

"Of course he would," said Ares. He added with an admiring gaze, "He is made of sterner stuff than any King or Guardian ever was. Look at him, how brave, strong, and true. Was there ever such a being? Will there ever be again?"

On the night before the battle, when Apollo had returned to tell the Council what had happened between him and Poseidon, and how he had selected himself to fight Python, any doubts that Ares had had about Apollo's rightful position as the Chosen One vanished. He was ashamed that he had ever had such doubts. He was also ashamed that he had let his feelings be known to others. In fact, three times during the hours that Apollo was away, Ares had openly questioned the Council's decision to let Apollo represent them. He had done this in front of not only Aegyptus but others as well. But all that was in the past, and now he hoped and prayed for two things; first, that Apollo would win, and second, that Apollo would forgive him.

Aegyptus watched Apollo approach with admiration mixed with apprehension. Like his big brother, he would gladly have taken Apollo's place in the challenge, but it was too late for that now. Much too late.

With the eyes of seven great armies fixed upon him, Apollo moved between the living walls of the chasm with poise and an easy grace that belied his fateful purpose. As he passed each successive echelon of warriors, there was something about him, something everyone could see and feel; something indefinable and yet overpowering; it was an air of dignity and self-assurance tinged with loneliness. A quantum of hearts began to beat as one, and no one surfaced to breathe lest they miss a single second of the spectacle unfolding before them. It was a spellbinding moment as the white Bottlenose Dolphin, and the black and white Humpback Whale moved majestically through the sparkling blue-green waters. And among all those watching Apollo, even the armies aligned against him, there was a palpable sense of excitement and wonder, as all knew that they were all about to witness history.

Finally, when Apollo and Zeus reached the center point of the opposing forces, the seven monarchs swam out into the chasm to join them, as did Python. Pan wanted to go too but Ares told him it would not be appropriate. This troubled Pan for he had not seen Apollo since the previous evening and he wanted to talk with him and wish him well. Deep inside he was torn with guilt over the thoughts he had had after they returned from the meeting with Poseidon, careless and selfish thoughts. Since they left the Kingdom of the Ancients nine months earlier, they had been inseparable, but now as Pan watched Apollo from a distance he feared that they would never be together again. He stared intently at Apollo hoping to catch his eye and share one last moment of closeness despite their physical separation. In desperation, he was about to signal with his earsight. He knew everyone would hear it and respond by turning to look at him but he did not care. But before he could, Apollo broke away from the others and swam over to the little Harbor Porpoise, who was nestled between the two Guardians, and spoke to him, softly from the heart.

"Forgive me, Pan, for lying to you. I only did it to spare your feelings. Deep inside I knew that we would not go home together and I could not bring myself to break your heart."

Tears welled up in Pan's eyes. "Are you telling us that you are going to die?" he asked with a trembling voice, tucking his little flippers tightly against his side.

With a tender smile Apollo replied, "I do not know."

"But you said you were certain that we would be victorious?" pleaded Pan, desperately trying to hold onto hope.

Apollo stared deeply into the little one's eyes and in a calm voice said, "I am certain that I will kill my father and that our cause will prevail. But..." He caught himself.

"But what? Please tell us."

Apollo did not reply. Just then, King Poseidon called out for Apollo to rejoin them. He acknowledged the King and then moved closer to Pan. He rubbed his beak against the little porpoise who he loved more than life itself, and whispered, "Good bye, my precious little one. Be brave. And know that I will always love you." Then Apollo turned and looked at Ares who was hovering beside Pan.

Ares started to apologize. "Master, please forgive me for I am not worthy. I have..."

Apollo hushed him. "Ares, without you, we would not have made it here to this defining moment in our history. We all owe our lives to you. It was you who protected us time and again, you who saved your brother's life, you who won the Battle of Malacca, where defeat would have meant the end of our journey. You are *my* hero and you owe me no apology." Apollo then looked at Aegyptus who was on the other side of Pan, protecting him as he had done ever since they first met in what seemed a lifetime ago. "And you, Aegyptus, you are the kindest and most thoughtful protector that has ever graced God's oceans. Like your brother, you have been a trusted and noble companion and it has been an honor to know you." Aegyptus nodded sadly. Then Apollo drifted back a little so that he could see all three beings who had shared his odyssey from the very beginning. Gathering his emotions, he said, "No matter what happens here this day, you must all be strong, for me and for all those who believe in me. And if it is God's will that I leave you now, I will take the memories of the days we have shared together with me into paradise." Then he tipped his head once in tribute and thanks, turned, and swam away.

When Apollo reached Poseidon, Hera, Zeus, and the others in the center of the gaping chasm between the two great forces, he took his place face-to-face with the black dolphin. "Have you changed your mind, Apollo?" asked Poseidon. Even as he asked, it was impossible not to notice an air of admiration and respect on the part of the rebel King; respect for an enemy who had come so far, who had endured so much, and who was now willing to lay down his life for his cause. However, his admiration was not shared by Queen Eris, as reflected in the scornful expression upon her face.

Apollo answered with an unequivocal, "No."

Poseidon looked at the Loyalist monarchs, "And you, Queen Hera, and your fellow members of the Sovereign Council. Do you agree to the binding nature of this challenge?" Unlike his tone with Apollo, Poseidon showed no respect to them, and in turn, none was given."

"Yes," Hera replied with icy hostility, as cold as the arctic air that lay heavily above the shimmering surface overhead.

"Good," replied Poseidon.

In a shrill tone, Queen Eris interjected, "There can be no turning back, you know. The Right of Challenge allows for no appeal. When Python kills Apollo, you will have to obey my…that is, our commands."

It was a breach of protocol for Eris to enter the discussion as only the heads of the two sides were supposed to speak. Poseidon was not pleased that she had done so but Queen Hera replied calmly, "We understand that full well." Hera paused and then added with an undercurrent of scorn that was as strong as the strongest riptide, "Do you?"

Before Eris could say anything Poseidon replied, "*I* understand and that is sufficient." His comment angered Eris and in a fit of pique, she powered her massive bulk away with a sharp downstroke of her flukes that created a mini vortex in the water. It rocked Python and Apollo slightly but had no effect on the others. Poseidon ignored her and looked at Zeus. No words passed between them, just a look, a simple acknowledgement of what was and what would be. Later, much later, when the events of that momentous day were told and retold, some who were there would recall that look and swear that it was then, at that moment, when a change had come over Poseidon. Few realized it at the time, but they were right; something had passed between them that would affect all the events that followed in the days and years to come.

They had been witnesses to a defining moment when good looked evil in the eye, and evil blinked.

Finally, Poseidon turned away from Zeus, looked at Apollo and Python, and said, "Let us get on with this. There are no rules. No time limits. No mercy is to be asked or given. The fight is to the death. Is that understood?" They acknowledged Poseidon's instructions. "So be it. At my command, you will begin."

With that Poseidon, Hera and the others returned to opposite sides of the battle line, leaving the two Bottlenose Dolphins; one black, one white; father and son; now combatants to the death, alone in the center of the yawning chasm of silent and still bluewater. It was now apparent to the marines in the opposing armies that something other than an all-out attack was about to take place. Neither side had been told that the monarchs had decided to invoke the ancient Right of Challenge, and few among them would have known that such a right even existed. But as word of what was about to happen spread through the ranks, all were filled with a mixture of joy and apprehension. Suddenly it was clear that one being and only one would die that day, and the overwhelming majority on both sides of the battle line believed it would be Apollo.

Queen Hera took her place beside the other four Loyalist monarchs and before the fight began, she looked pleadingly at Zeus who had returned with her, and asked, "Pray tell me, Zeus, will Apollo live?"

With his head canted slightly upward in the characteristic way of all great whales, Zeus eyed the Queen and replied, "Our cause is just. We will prevail." It was not a direct answer but she took it to mean that he would. Then Zeus excused himself and swam away to watch the challenge with Pan. After he left, Hera called out to Ares and Aegyptus to come to her. Leaving Pan in the company of Zeus, they did and when they got there, she said, "I pray that Apollo will win but regardless of the outcome, promise me that there will be no further killing." She expected them to object but they did not and, despite her great intelligence, she was too upset to figure out why.

Ares replied coldly for both of them, "Yes, your Grace." But as they returned to join Pan and Zeus, Ares said quietly to his brother, "If Apollo dies; the next two to die will be Poseidon and Eris."

Aegyptus nodded and said in a whale whisper, "And then Python too—for Danaus."

"Yes. For Danaus."

When all were back in position, Poseidon shouted the order to begin. Apollo and Python now found themselves alone in a vast empty canyon of water, bounded laterally at the edges of their vision by row upon row of silent spectators. Above them lay the shimmering liquid silver surface, a mirror reflecting their images back at them, while far below, where the color of the water turned to Indigo and black, the deeps lay waiting patiently to embrace the loser.

For a moment neither one spoke. It was high noon, the exact moment of Godlight, and one year since the madness began. As they hung there facing each other barely ten yards apart, the vertical fingers of sunlight streaming down upon them had a dappled effect upon the darker body of Python while they cast Apollo's white body in almost ghostly glow. At thirteen feet in length and twelve hundred pounds, Python was the bigger of the two by nearly a foot in length and two hundred pounds in bulk. And more to the point, Python was by far the more proficient fighter with countless kills to his credit compared to only one for Apollo, and that was by way of administering GoodDeath to Morpheus, which was not the same thing. But Apollo was twenty years younger with the nimbleness and stamina to go with it.

Finally, Python broke the lingering silence. "So it has come to this, my son. After all the years and all the miles, one of us must now kill the other."

"I am your son in blood only," replied Apollo without emotion.

"What other ways are there?" asked Python with a sly smile. There was a faint echo of regret in his voice and a flicker of pain behind his eyes.

"That you have to ask that question proves my point."

The smile faded from the black dolphin's mouth. "Do not confuse me with riddles. This is neither the time nor the place for mind games." He began to swim in a slow circle to his right. If there had been any desire to reach out to his son to try to bridge the emotional gap between them, Apollo's rebuff had put an end to it.

Apollo followed suit and began to swim to his right, keeping a constant distance between them, as each eyed the other looking for an opportunity to strike. "I agree. This is ..."

With a ferocity that caught Apollo off-guard, Python broke out of his circular course and zoomed directly at him, aiming his beak at Apollo's left side just behind his flipper. It was a vulnerable area where a blow of sufficient power would be deadly. At the last second, Apollo snapped his body down and to the right, preventing a mortal wound but not in time to avoid the attack completely. As Python zipped by, he opened his mouth and his teeth sliced across Apollo's tailstock, releasing a tiny spurt of blood into the sea. Apollo flinched but recovered quickly. As the momentum of Python's attack carried him deeper, Apollo drove himself sharply up and over in an inside, back loop that brought him around in time to hit Python in his right side. The sharp blow made Python grunt, which brought a cheer from the Loyalist side.

Before the black dolphin could retaliate, Apollo shot upward toward the surface, driven by powerful thrusts of his flukes. Breaking through its glimmering sheen, he leapt up in a high arc and then plunged down head first just as Python was coming up for air. To avoid a punishing blow from the plummeting white dolphin, Python had to adjust his course. Quickly slanting to his right, he broke the surface just as Apollo sliced down into the water beside him. Using gravity to his advantage, Apollo struck Python's side. It was only a glancing blow but it prevented Python from getting the complete breath that his already taxed muscles required. This forced Python to stay on the surface in an attempt to give himself time to catch his breath.

As he did, Apollo pulled out of his deep dive and rocketed back up toward Python's now exposed underbelly. This time, the collision was solid, with Apollo's beak catching the black dolphin in his chest near his diaphragm. This produced a loud grunt from Python, as air was forced out of his lungs, exacerbating his already compromised oxygen supply. Stunned by the force of the blow, and startled by the adeptness of his young opponent, Python struggled to pull himself away from Apollo. He swam rapidly in a wide, sweeping curve, taking a full breath of air as he went and throwing up a rooster tail of spray.

But instead of pursuing his winded opponent, which is what a trained killer would have done, Apollo circled away in the opposite direction, giving Python time to regroup. This brought a groan from the Loyalist side, and even from some among the Federation forces, but it also evoked a shriek of delight from Eris, so loud and hideous that it caused Apollo to lose focus. It was a serious mistake on the white dolphin's part and all could sense that he was about to pay dearly for it.

They were right. Python, who by now had shaken off the shock of Apollo's blow, and seizing the moment, made a sudden sharp turn and sped across the distance that separated them. Apollo's loss of concentration was only momentary but that was all Python needed. As the Loyalists watched in horror, Python hurtled across the ten yards separating them, aiming for Apollo's neck. At the last second, Apollo felt the shock wave of his onrushing attacker and began a twisting dive down and away. But it was too late to avoid a blow.

Python's beak caught Apollo's thick tailstock two feet behind his dorsal fin with a punishing strike that knocked Apollo into a sideways somersault. The pain was excruciating but the blow did not break Apollo's spine as it would have done had he not made the last-second move. However, Apollo had been seriously hurt, and as he tried to swim away, he was unable to get any power from his flukes. Instead of the forceful downstroke characteristic of his species, he was only able to manage a few feeble thrusts, none of which moved him very far. Apollo now began to sink.

Watching his opponent struggle, Python made a wide circle, getting ready for his final attack; this time putting enough distance between him and his son to generate the velocity he required for a killing blow. When he reached the far side of the circle, he turned and headed toward Apollo, gathering speed as he went: but this time it was not Apollo's body that was the target; instead, he was aiming for a spot just behind and above Apollo's left eye, directly at the star-shaped birthmark. The significance of what was about to happen was not lost on anyone. Some among the Federation's army shouted support for their champion but not all, while every being in the Loyalist army prepared for the worst.

"Frightens us," gasped Pan. "Frightens us." He looked away, unwilling to see the outcome.

"Come on, Apollo. Come on," exhorted Ares as he moved forward, ready to kill Python the moment that Apollo died.

"Look out, Apollo," shouted Aegyptus.

Queen Hera looked away as did the other Loyalist monarchs. On the other side, Poseidon's expression darkened while Eris was ecstatic with anticipation.

It seemed to all that the end was near. Certain death for Apollo. Certain victory for Python. But then something happened that changed everything: something totally unexpected, and something that I can only attribute to the will of God. I know there are some among you who do not believe in him, and who will never accept that there is a supreme force for good in the universe: a force that cannot be seen or touched; but which touches us and our lives in ways we will never know. But for those of you who do believe, or who are willing to suspend your disbelief, I will now describe what happened when that force reached out and touched the heart of Python.

At the last possible instant, just as Python reached full speed, and zeroed in upon his struggling son; when he was literally within nanoseconds of killing Apollo, he suddenly swerved, and missed his target completely. A crescendo of cheers arose from the Loyalists mixed with jeers from some on the other side. After he harmlessly passed by Apollo, Python went into a slow, sinking turn, as if he was suddenly laden down by a heavy weight. By this time, Apollo had shaken off his pain and confusion, and had regained his full range of motion. To the amazement of most and the consternation of some, the tide had turned: it was now the father who was exposed and vulnerable.

Without giving thought to what had just happened and why, Apollo gathered speed for his counterattack, aiming for a killing blow as his father had done. As Apollo zeroed in for the kill, some swore they saw a look of desperation on Python's face but many more claimed that it was a look of acceptance and even satisfaction that filled the father's eyes.

Then, with a sickening thud, Apollo's beak hit Python with deadly force just behind his left flipper, collapsing his rib cage, puncturing his lung, and sending a tiny shard of broken rib into his heart. Even the mighty Guardians flinched at the sight and sound of the deadly blow. Apollo's momentum carried him and his mortally wounded father forward a few more yards in a T-shaped death lock. Then they came to a halt and Apollo pulled back. For a moment neither the victor nor the vanquished moved. Slowly, blood began to stream out of Python's blowhole filling the water with a crimson hue. There had been an instinctive, initial burst of cheers from among some Loyalists, and groans among their opponents, but they were all soon silenced as Apollo swam over to his dying father and gently pushed him up to the surface. It was an act of mercy that mesmerized everyone along both sides of the battle lines.

Hovering there under the pale blue sky, and surrounded by a thousand points of light that danced across the surface like tiny diamonds in the noon day sun, Python looked at his son through glazed eyes and said, softly, "The victory is yours, my son."

Hundreds upon hundreds of beings, both Loyalists and Federalists, large and small, rose up to the surface and formed a vast circle with father and son at its center. The sea was filled with a cacophony of earsight pings as every being tried to see what was happening.

Apollo did not notice anyone except his father. He was lost in a sea change of emotions. He did not know what to say but he could tell that the time to say it was quickly running out. Finally, he asked, "Why have you hated me so from the moment I was born?"

Coughing up more blood, and racked with pain, Python whispered, "Because I was afraid."

"Afraid of what?"

"Of you," came the labored reply. "When your mother told me about her dream…about how the angel spoke of the coming of the white dolphin, I was jealous and afraid." He coughed and struggled to continue. "I was afraid that you would grow up to be everything that I wanted to be, but never could." He gasped and the death rattle began. His lungs were now rapidly filling with blood. He coughed again, spewing more blood into the sea. "I could not bear to let my son outshine me…I could not…"

Apollo knew the end was near. It pained him to see Python this way: as an enemy, he had been a powerful and intimidating presence in the sea, to be respected if not admired; but that enemy was gone. Now all that lay before him was his dying father, facing a godless end to an unforgiving life. Apollo was overcome with conflicting emotions: anger and fear, hate and love all rolled into one. "Then why did you not kill me just now when you had the chance?"

Through glassy eyes of fading light, Python looked at his son and said, "Because I love you. And even though I could not admit it to myself, I realized that I always have."

It was more than Apollo could bear to hear. "Oh, Father, my Father. We could have been so much more together than we have been apart."

Python slowly rolled onto his side and with his last breath whispered, "Good bye, my son. Please forgive…" His voice drifted up and away on the last, lonely tiny, little bubble.

"I do. I forgive you. And I love you too," cried Apollo but it was too late. Python was gone.

Apollo's heart was broken. He closed his eyes, lowered his head, and began to weep uncontrollably. Sobs wracked his body. All about him, the marines who had risen to the surface hung there in a stunned and caring silence. For a long, lonely moment Apollo stayed at the surface, holding up the body of his dead father. Then, Zeus surfaced beside him. More than any of those watching, the mighty Humpback Whale with the broad black back and great white wings felt the pain of both father and son; two beings who had spent their lives trying to find what neither could alone; peace—peace with each other and peace with himself. And now sadly, they had both finally found that peace, each in their own way. With a gentle touch, he told Apollo it was time to let his father go, which Apollo did. Then together, Zeus and Apollo slipped beneath the waves and watched as Python's body drifted down past the kings and queens, past their armies, past Pan and Ares and Aegyptus. Past them all into eternity.

A great stillness had fallen upon all the armies along both sides of the battle line. Although it was clear that Apollo had won, it was not yet clear that the armies of the Federation were ready to accept the victory. And had the day ended on that note, the situation might not have been resolved in a positive manner for the Loyalists. But fate now took a hand in the outcome and what happened next shocked everyone, Loyalist and Federalist alike, and the somber silence of the scene was about to be broken by an act of hatred that would seal the destiny of one and all.

From out of the gathering, there arose a high pitched scream, emanating from Queen Eris. She shrieked at Poseidon. "Do something!

Kill him! Kill the white dolphin!" She repeated it over and over and over again. When Poseidon did not respond, she turned to face their army and screamed at them, "Attack them! Kill them all!" But no one moved. No one obeyed. All were too startled to act. Even those among her own army, the Army of the South Pacific did nothing. Later some would say it was because the cowardly Queen had abandoned her marines at the Battle of Malacca. Others would say it was because her followers finally saw her for what she was, the devil's mistress. In the end, it did not matter for the outcome was the same.

Incensed at what was happening she turned back to Poseidon and butted him harshly in his side with her long, sinister head; once, and then again. He did not react except to pull away from her. Her actions and his reaction sent a signal to all watching, both friend and foe alike, and threw her into a blind rage. In a demonic voice, she berated him, calling him weak and afraid. But Poseidon did not respond to her. Instead, he looked at Queen Hera and said, "You have won. There will be no war between us. No war with mankind."

Queen Hera nodded and turned to thank Apollo, their champion, but before she could, Eris launched herself toward Apollo with a fury born in hell. To the horror of everyone, she opened her enormous mouth and grabbed the white dolphin by his flukes, and while still holding tightly onto him, plunged down toward the deeps and disappeared into darkness.

"No!" screamed Pan. "No..."

"Oh my God," exclaimed Queen Hera.

Ares and Aegyptus immediately dove after Eris and so too did Poseidon. However, the two Guardians lost sight of Eris for the Sei Whale is the fastest being in the ocean, and she had plummeted straight into the deeps taking the white dolphin with her. Short of air, the brothers were forced to turn back but Poseidon kept going and he soon disappeared into the abyssal darkness below. The brothers reluctantly returned to the surface and reported that they had been unsuccessful in their rescue attempt.

In the horror and confusion of the moment, no one noticed that Zeus was gone except Pan who assumed that Zeus had also dived into the deeps after Apollo. An hour later when Poseidon finally returned to the surface, he said he had not seen either Apollo or Zeus. Everyone then assumed that Zeus had died trying to save Apollo and a crushing darkness fell upon the beings gathered there. The war had been averted but at what cost? What terrible cost?

If there had been any doubt in anyone's mind among the Federation that they should ignore the death of Python, and seize the moment to defeat the Loyalist army, the insanity of the attack by Eris had put an end to it. The stunning reversal of fortune that had now taken the white dolphin, in his moment of greatest glory to his death in the deeps, along with the puzzling disappearance of his mentor, the mighty Zeus, sealed the alliance of peace and put an end to the threat of war.

No one seemed to know what to do or what to say. Instead, the five Loyalist monarchs huddled close together despite their enormous bulk, each needing to touch and be touched. Finally, Poseidon who hung all alone over the spot where Apollo had disappeared, joined them and asked Queen Hera if he might address her armies along with his. She readily agreed and with her blessing, he looked out upon the legions and began to speak slowly and with great passion:

"My fellow warriors, one year ago today our journey into darkness began with a rebellion led by me. During these past twelve months, a great evil has enveloped the Seven Seas, turning us against each other in a war of words and actions that culminated several weeks ago in a bloody battle in the Straits of Malacca. And today, were it not for the sacrifice of Apollo, all whalekind might have disappeared into the abyss of eternal darkness."

Poseidon swallowed hard; oily tears glistened in his big black eyes. His emotional pain was mirrored on the faces of the thousands upon thousands of beings floating silently in the sea before him. Even the Loyalist marines, who over the past year had come to fear and hate Poseidon, now only felt compassion for him.

"Regardless of whether you believe that Apollo was the Prince of Light of whom the Ancients spoke, or just a simple being with a selfless heart, he died today trying to save us and his voice of reason and hope has now been stilled forever—I fear that we shall never see his likes again."

The Sperm Whale's voice began to crack. He struggled to continue. Hovering in the front row before him, Pan's heart skipped a beat, and alongside him even the brave and noble Guardians, had to struggle to keep from losing control of their emotions. But strengthened by their nearness to each other, the Harbor Porpoise and Orcas alike reached down deep inside and forced themselves to be strong, as Apollo had asked them to be.

"It remains now for me and those who followed me here in my misguided desire to fight with man, and all those who came to stop me, to make a choice. We can turn away from the abyss. We can turn our backs on war. We can listen to each other, not with our heads, but with our hearts, and in so doing, reject the intolerance of yesterday and embrace the promise of tomorrow. Or we can choose to stay the course, which I wrongly set and watch more of our kind die and with them, Planet Ocean. Lest there be any among you who doubt it, know that this path, once taken leads to an abysmal darkness from which there is no return."

The King paused again, and for a fleeting moment that would last forever in the memories of all who watched, he looked up to the heavens for strength, and guidance, and comfort from God; and in that one small act for a great whale, he reached out and touched the souls of all whalekind. Steeling himself, he stared out across the beings hovering in the sunlit waters before him and began to speak again, with an authority granted to him by a force more mighty than all the kings and queens who had ever ruled.

"To my fellow kings and queens, I hereby pledge my allegiance to the cause of peace, to the cause of love, to the cause of life itself. I do not know how we can stem the forces that are carrying our planet toward destruction. It is not for me to decide whether we should, or even if we can, reach out to the human beings with whom we share this precious planet, and seek their help in saving it. All I can say is that I will work with the Sovereign Council to do what is right for our kind whatever that course may be. For we must save life by living for our cause not by dying for it.—I did not know that then but I do now."

With that, Poseidon fell silent. He looked at Queen Hera through cheerless eyes and then turned and swam away, passing through the blue curtain that hung at the back of beyond in that vast and mighty ocean. All eyes watched him go until there was nothing left but the enormous presence of his absence, combined with a vague feeling of unease. His few words of contrition echoed through all their minds, drowning out the memories of a year's worth of polemics. For a lingering moment, no one moved, seven mighty armies rising and falling on the swells of the once savage sea, until finally Queen Hera looked across the somber scene and said, "Go home everyone. Go home. It is over."

Then slowly, one by one or in groups, beings from all the Seven Seas did just that. And as they headed away from that place of great sadness, it was left to Pan, the brave little Harbor Porpoise, to close this tragic chapter in the Legend of the Light, when he said, "God be praised. God brought us the Light."

CHAPTER TWENTY-FOUR

Never Look Back

The journey from Johnston Atoll to the Gulf of Mexico took Pan and the two Guardians nine months, which was three months longer than it might have normally taken them, moving at the speed of one hundred miles a day, six days a week, to which Pan had become accustomed during his journey with Apollo. The most direct route down to Cape Horn and up the east coast of South America comprised a distance of twelve thousand miles, but had they gone that way, they would have reached the Cape in September when the Southern Ocean was still subject to fierce late-winter storms, and Ares worried that the passage would have been too hard on Pan. Pan disagreed but his broken heart had dimmed his penchant for debate. Therefore, the three beings had headed due east from the Atoll and spent the rest of the northern hemisphere's summer and early autumn in the warm, equatorial waters of the Galapagos Islands.

Pan knew it was the place where Apollo had rested briefly as he began his odyssey nearly nine years earlier, and just the fact that the white dolphin had passed through those waters rested gently on Pan's soul. This added two thousand miles to the journey but by waiting until summer began in the Southern Hemisphere, their trip through the Straits of Magellan and up the coast of South America had been uneventful. And except for the stinging emptiness left inside by the loss of Apollo and Zeus, the little Harbor Porpoise did quite well on the last leg of his twenty-two month journey around the world.

On the first day of spring in the Northern Hemisphere, Pan and his two companions, who were all that remained of the Company of the Light that had gone over the edge a year and a half earlier, reached the Straits of Florida where their long journey together would finally come to an end.

"Are you sure you will be all right, little one?" asked Ares on that bright morning as the three of them hovered in the calm and pleasant waters off Marathon in the Florida Keys.

"Yes, we will be fine, Ares. And we would like to point out…"

"Yes. Yes. That we are quite big for our size," interrupted Aegyptus with a chuckle.

For a moment, Pan feigned annoyance but he could not keep a straight face and finally he broke into a belly laugh that quickly spread to the two Killer Whales, and soon the waters about them echoed with the sounds of laughter. But it was bittersweet laughter tempered by the memory of their long lost companions, Danaus, Apollo and Zeus.

"What about you two?" asked Pan. "Do you think you can make it the rest of the way back to the Kingdom of the Ancients by yourselves, or should we accompany you?" He smiled and then added, "Just in case a kraken attacks you?"

"Without your fat little belly to tempt them, I doubt that we will see any kraken," said Ares with a subdued sparkle in his eye.

For a moment no one said anything. Then, Aegyptus said wistfully, "It has been very good to know you, Pan."

"More than that," added Ares, "it has been an honor. You are the bravest, smartest, and funniest *big* Harbor Porpoise I have ever known. I shall miss you very much."

"Then stay with us here," pleaded Pan, already knowing the answer. "We would love to have you join our tribe. We are certain that our mother, Leto, will feel the same way."

By now, news of what had happened in the North Pacific Ocean had traveled around the world on whalesound, and every being throughout the Seven Seas knew of the outcome of the fight between the father and son. There were very few who did not mourn the loss of the white dolphin even as they rejoiced in the knowledge that through his sacrifice, whalekind had avoided war. Similarly, the Company already knew that Leto was now the chieftain of what had been Python's tribe. She had sent a message via whalesound to Pan that she and the tribe eagerly awaited his return.

Ares shook his head. "No. But thank you. Our duty calls us back to Queen Hera's court." The winter storms in the Southern Ocean had been no deterrent for the Blue Whale and she had returned to the Kingdom of the Ancients several months earlier.

"Besides, Pan, it is your tribe not ours," added Aegyptus. "It is your nostos—where you belong."

"Yes. It is our nostos. Where we belong," echoed Pan but there was something in his eyes and in the way he said it that lacked conviction.

The Orcas took it to be the sadness of the loss of his friend but it was deeper than that and far more profound. Time would heal or at least soften the first, but what lay behind Pan's melancholy would not and could not be lessened by the turning of the tides, or the rotation of the planet on its axis. The truth was that Pan had come back to a place that was no longer his home, for he had lost his nostos, and once lost, it can never be found again.

This is often true among your kind as some discover when they return to the place of their childhood after a long absence and everything suddenly looks smaller and less important than it once did. They are left with a longing in their hearts for the way it once was, but can never be again. And when the reality does not match the memory then there is nothing to do but move on, because to stay would spoil it; then they would have neither the memory nor the reality. In his journey around the world with the white dolphin, this is what had happened to Pan. He just did not realize it yet.

Aegyptus moved close and gently stroked Pan with his flipper. "Do not be sad, Pan, perhaps someday we will travel together again."

Big tears welled up in Pan's little eyes, "Yes. Perhaps here or in that golden sea," he replied recalling once again that line from the poem that Queen Selene had recited for them in the Southern Ocean, "where Apollo and Zeus and Danaus await us."

"Where the Company of the Light will be reunited forever and after," added Aegyptus.

"Yes. In the company of angels," added Ares.

"A company of angels. We like that," said Pan barely above a whisper.

For a moment, no one spoke. Then, shaking off the unhappiness of the moment, Pan's expression brightened. "Enough of this sadness, lest we grow too fond of it." With forced but not insincere conviction, he continued, "We think it is time for us to go find Leto and tell her that her wayward child has come home."

"Yes. He has come home," said Aegyptus.

Pan looked around them at the smooth white sand and the clear azure waters and said proudly, "*Some* home!"

To which Ares added, "*Some* child!"

And that was that. The time for parting had finally come. Pan had already asked them not to say good-bye and so instead, the two Orcas gave him one last rub with their noses then turned and swam away. Throughout all they had been through, the death of their brother Danaus, the dangers they had faced together, and the losses of Apollo and Zeus, twice in the case of the Humpback, neither Orca had shed any tears, because Guardians are not supposed to cry. But now as they swam away from Pan, the two battle hardened Killer Whales began to weep openly. They felt no shame in it but they did not want to make their parting any harder on Pan than it already was, so they kept their eyes fixed firmly on the sea ahead.

For just a fraction of an instant, Ares thought about turning back but he knew if he suggested the possibility, Aegyptus would have readily agreed, so he did not. In truth, they could not. For such is the way of Guardians, where duty must take priority over matters of the heart. It had always been so and would always be as long as there were enemies of whalekind above and below the waves. And somewhere in the deepest recesses of his mind, Ares feared that evil would rise again.

Pan watched them go all the way, until their big black shapes disappeared in the filmy distance and then he turned and swam north, toward the place he had left behind in what seemed a lifetime ago.

"Welcome home, my darling little one," cried Leto as she swam out to greet him. He had covered the distance between the Keys and Shark River Island in a few hours, twice as fast as he had when he left home all those months ago. His muscles had grown strong in his journey around the world and his heart and lungs were now those of a porpoise half his age. It was the place where Leto had told him they were to meet, when she sent word to him through whalesound. The significance of it was not lost upon him, for it was near the estuary known as Little Shark River, where Apollo had been born twenty two years earlier, and not far from the place where Pan had entered the world five years before that.

"Thank you, Mother," Pan replied, choosing not to make any comment about her use of the word he had hated for so long. It just did not seem to matter any more. Leto was obviously delighted to see him as were the other members of the tribe who all gathered around him. "We are so glad to see you." He looked around. "Where is Aurora?"

The smile faded from Leto's face. "She is gone. I know not where. She left soon after we learned of Python's death."

"We understand." And he did. Aurora had been Python's lover, even while he was Leto's mate. Thinking he was changing the subject, Pan added with a sad sigh, "We are sorry for your loss."

She shook her head. "Do not be. I loved Python once, but that was a long time ago. I got over him; I suppose my sister never did."

It was Pan's turn to shake his head. "No, Mother. We were referring to Apollo."

For a moment, she hesitated. A look of puzzlement spread across her face. "What do you mean?" And then she realized what he was saying. "Oh my. You do not know! Do you?"

"Know what?"

"Of course you do not know," she said to herself. "How thoughtless of me. No one outside our tribe knows. We did not tell anyone because he asked us not to."

"Who asked you not to? And tell us what?"

With a glowing smile that flooded the seas about them with its radiance, Leto announced, "Apollo is alive!"

Her words hit Pan with the force of a wave breaking on hard-packed sand. For a moment, he hung there suspended in time and space, unable to move or speak, his mind filled with a thousand thoughts all caught on the windspray of happiness. His stout little body began to shake with joy and he said, "Did you just say what we thought you said? That Apollo lives!" As he asked it there was fear in his voice; fear that he may have misunderstood. The pain of such a misunderstanding would have been monumental.

"Yes. Yes!" she beamed. "Apollo is alive and well."

"Oh my. Oh my. Is he here?" asked Pan glancing around the sparkling waters about them.

"No. But do not worry, I know where he is."

The horrible images from that day flashed through Pan's mind. "We do not understand. How did he survive? How did he get back here?"

"Wait, Pan. Wait. I will tell you the whole story. Exactly as he told it to me. But first, you must rest and eat. Doing so will not dull the story nor change its outcome."

"No," Pan replied firmly. "Please, Mother. We must know now." There was an urgency in his voice driven by the sudden release of sadness that had been pent up inside him since he left Johnston Atoll.

She smiled with the patience of a mother looking at her impetuous child. Even though Pan was not her own flesh and blood, in every other way he was her child and would always be, ever since she had found him alone and hurt on the day a shark killed his real mother. Leto had nursed him back to health and protected him from those who wanted to abandon him, including Python. But it was Python who was now dead and Pan who was alive, just like her biological son, Apollo, and the joy she felt at that moment was enough to fill the ocean. "Very well. Come, swim with me."

Together mother and adopted son, meandered slowly through the clear waters of his childhood and she began to recount the events of that dark day nine long and lonely months ago; a day that had been lost in darkness but would now shine forever more.

"According to Apollo, this is the way it happened. As Queen Eris dragged him down into the deeps, he struggled to escape but this only made her tighten her bite even more. With each passing strata he knew the end was near and so he closed his eyes and prayed. And then, just when his breath was about to give out, he felt her shudder, as if something had hit her with great force. He opened his eyes and saw that the sea all about them was lit with a strange light, one unlike any he had ever seen before.

"Then he saw what the source of the light was; fifteen perhaps twenty giant kraken had set upon the Queen. And on the long tentacles of each giant squid, between each sucker there were lights that shone like tiny pink and purple stars in the blackness of the deeps. The kraken grabbed her head and body, and with their wicked beaks, they began to tear at her flesh. But they did not touch Apollo. In her agony she let Apollo go but he did not have the strength to return to the surface. Then suddenly out of the darkness Zeus appeared."

"Zeus! We *knew* he did not die," exclaimed Pan.

"Apollo saw at once that it was Zeus except that his entire body was white and he seemed to fly through the deeps on great white wings."

"Just like in his dream," whispered Pan remembering their experience in the Java Sea.

"So he said. Still uncertain of whether or not he was dreaming again, his breath ran out: he closed his eyes and surrendered to his fate. When he awoke, he found himself back at the surface, where he drew a life giving breath into his burning lungs, but when he looked around, he was completely alone; there were no armies or monarchs, no Pan and no Zeus. He was floating under the bright afternoon sun, in the middle of an empty ocean. Bruised and bloodied from his battle with Python, his heart still pounding from his encounter with Eris, he was weak but alive."

"The deep ocean currents must have carried him away from us," said Pan as he absorbed what Leto was saying.

"Perhaps," replied Leto. "Apollo said he drifted for a long time but then a Striped Dolphin appeared. Apollo said he was overjoyed to see that it was his long-lost friend, Ganymede. And soon they were joined by several more dolphins, three of whom had been with Apollo in his journey to Cape Horn. Ganymede told him that they were part of a large group of dolphins from a research institute in Hawaii operated by the U.S. Navy, and they guided Apollo back to their nearby research ship. And there, leaning over the railing, Apollo saw a human friend with whom he had lost contact many long years before."

"Captain Jackson," said Pan excitedly.

"Yes. Captain Stanley Jackson, who recognized Apollo at once. He quickly had him lifted onto the vessel, which then took him back to the institute and there over the next several months he was nursed back to health. And it was during that time that Apollo broke our code of silence and spoke with Captain Jackson and told him everything."

"It was not the first time that Apollo had spoken with a human," said Pan.

"I know," said Leto. "I know. But Apollo believed in his heart that it was the right thing to do. He said refusing to talk with our enemies does not make them our friends. And that it is only through this link that together, humans and whales will find a way to stop the slow but steady destruction of Planet Ocean."

Pan was overwhelmed by the story. "Goody, goody. It is just too wonderful," exclaimed Pan. He closed his eyes and whispered, "Thank you, God. Thank you." Then he opened them again and asked, "But how did Apollo get back here?"

"After Apollo had fully recovered, Captain Jackson told him that he was leaving the Navy and that he was going to take a job at a research institute on an island in the Caribbean Sea. He said he planned to work on finding ways to use the vast knowledge we possess for peaceful purposes not those of war. The island is near a place called the Tongue of the Ocean."

"Sinclair Cay," interrupted Pan. "We know it well."

Leto smiled. "Apollo said you would. And the best part of the story is that Captain Jackson obtained approval from the Navy to take Apollo with him to Sinclair Cay. They traveled there by plane, which Apollo said he had done once before." Leto paused then added, "Then Apollo came to see me and said to tell you when you came home that he would be waiting for you there."

It was the most wonderful news that Pan could have received. Literally shaking with excitement, he said, "I must go to him."

"What! Now?"

"Yes, now." Then he realized the significance of what he was saying. "We are sorry, Mother. We love you but we must go. We hope you will understand."

She sighed. "Of course. I understand," she said with the same exquisite pain that a mother always feels when a child leaves home. In this case for the second time. But she knew he must. And she knew she would see him again. He hesitated and then she whispered lovingly to him, "It is all right, Pan. Go to him."

The light that had gone out behind his eyes in the far off Pacific Ocean suddenly switched back on. "We love you, Mother. We love God. We love everyone!"

She laughed. "I love you too, Son. Now go and find your brother."

"Yes, our *brother*!" exclaimed Pan. Throughout the long and arduous journey that they had taken together, through the happiness and sadness that they had experienced in each other's company, Pan had never really given that much thought. But now, hearing his adopted mother say the word, it suddenly dawned on him that the white dolphin whom he loved with all his heart was indeed, in all ways except blood, his brother. And the thought filled him with pure and absolute joy. "Yes, we shall go find our brother."

And that is exactly what he did. He swam south and east, across the azure waters of Florida Bay, literally flying through the warm shallow seas. When he reached the edge of the Florida reefs, he paused momentarily, and looked down into the deep waters that lay below him in seven shades of blue, from azure to cerulean and cobalt, to denim and navy, then sapphire and finally midnight blue. Then, taking a deep breath, he plunged over the reefs, heading toward the Tongue of the Ocean and as he did, he smiled and said to himself, "Never look down! Never look back."

He never would again.

AFTERWORD

And so here we are at the end of my tale but it is also the beginning of the rest of the story. The war among whalekind has been averted but the war against those among your kind who would destroy our planet has not yet begun. And if it happens, it will be *the* war to end all wars, because there will be no winners, for it will lead to the destruction of the planet itself; an ignominious ending to what was once the glory of God, brought about by the arrogance, intolerance and stupidity of humankind. But it is *not* too late. If you have understood the moral of my tale of the whales and dolphins who rule the Seven Seas, then you know that that day has not yet come. The greatest joy about waking up each morning is that God has given us all another chance to correct the wrongs of the past. Take it. Use it. Please—for all our sakes.

As I promised you in the beginning, there are two questions to be answered now; Who am I? And more to the point, What am I? The astute among you already know the answers, but for the rest I shall answer the last question first: I am human, like you; like some of you that is, but not like all of you and therein lies the problem. I am a friend and ally to those among you who seek to preserve the beauty and splendor of our planet; and I am an enemy to those who do not. That is the what, and now for the who; my name is Caitlin Quinn or Trainer Quinn, as you have known me. I am a soul mate of Apollo's as he is to me. I am someone who loves him as I hope you have now come to do.

As I have already told you that is not his real name. Only beings know his name but in many ways you know him better than you think you do. He is that feeling of profound joy that rises up within you each time you see the glistening backs of dolphins breaking the surface of the sea, or watch the mighty flukes of a great whale slip beneath it. He is the spirit of all that is good that dwells within you. He is your conscience, your heart and your soul. He is the will to do what is right and the way to make it so. He is your past, your present and your future.

He is not a man and yet in a sense he is every man. For as you have read this story, his story, as he told it to me, he has lived for you, and through you. Without you he would be just an idea on the written page, and the sleek but fleeting image of a dorsal fin slicing through the waves far out upon the bluewater. With you, he will come alive and even though, like you and me, one day he too will die, if you believe in him, the dreams you have shared together will live forever.

Mine was the voice that has been speaking to you from the beginning of our journey together through the Seven Seas, but the thoughts and ideas were those of the white dolphin, as was the message they carried. And if you have listened to that message, if you have taken its meaning into your heart and soul, you will do what is right. And so, while this is the end of my tale it is also the beginning of the rest of the story of man and whale. Together we are joined in the endless circle of life, and death, and renewal on this once-lovely blue marble drifting silently through the eternity of space; this place of terrible beauty and incredible potential that you and I call Earth but beings know as Planet Ocean.

Oh and what about Pan and Apollo you ask? Good question. Perhaps the best way to end this story and explain what happened to them is to tell you what I am going to do next. After I finish typing this page on my laptop, I am going to sit back and stare at these, the final words of my story. And then I am going to reach over and hit the SAVE key, and shut down my computer as I have done every day since I began to write Apollo's tale. Then I will stand up and walk across my bright and airy room, with its pastel colored walls and gossamer curtains blowing on the gentle breezes coming in through the wide open windows overlooking the sea. I will go into my husband's book-filled study and give him a kiss for he is the love of my life whom I met because of Apollo. My husband's name is Dr. Stanley Jackson, or Captain Jackson, USN (Retired) as you know him. Like Apollo, he is a child of the universe who is working with those who care to save our planet.

And then I will walk out of our white stucco house with the red tile roof and green shutters that is built high on a narrow strip of land on the eastern side of the island known as Sinclair Cay. I will stroll down the bluff through the slender, waving sea grass, under the tall coconut palms and out across the smooth white sand beach, stripping off my skirt and blouse as I go, revealing a bright red one-piece bathing suit underneath that Apollo loves so well. When I reach the water's edge, I will run through the shallows with my long blond hair trailing behind me and dive into the gentle surf, feeling the welcoming warmth of Mother Sea against my tanned body.

I will swim strongly, unhesitatingly away from the shore, through the crystal clear waters, across a rippled, sandy bottom until it drops away leaving only a deep blue nothingness below me. But I will not be afraid, for soon two shadows will rise up from the deeps to greet me. One is a white Bottlenose Dolphin with a purple star birthmark on the side of his head and the other is a Harbor Porpoise with a crescent-shaped scar on his flukes. You know them as Apollo and Pan, two wayfarers of the open waves joined together again now and always.

Without moving their mouths they will speak to me, like they do every day, sending their thoughts directly into my mind and in return reading my thoughts, as only beings can. But unlike all the other days since we were reunited, today will be different. For today, Apollo will ask me, Did you finish it? And I will tell him, Yes. It is done. Then he will ask, Do you think they will listen? And I will say what he already knows in his heart, that the answer lies not with me but with you, the readers of this tale. His tale. And the best way you can answer him is not through words but actions. Let your conscience guide you as mine has done. Speak up on his behalf. Tell all those who will listen, and do not give up on those who will not, that we must act before it is too late. We must save our oceans and the whales and dolphins that live in them. We must save our planet. Please hear Apollo's cry. If you do not. Who will?

And then, as we have done every day, and I pray that we can continue to do until my days here are through, Apollo and Pan and I will swim together through the clear blue waters and as we do, in the distance we will hear the lilting voice of a Humpback Whale, that will fill our minds and hearts with the unbounded joy of whalesong; it is Zeus' song. And perhaps one day, if you are lucky, you may hear it too.

Printed in the United States
218538BV00002B/1/P

9 781438 965604